CHARLES O'MALLEY
The Irish Dragoon

BY CHARLES LEVER.

IN TWO VOLUMES.

Volume I.

TO THE   MOST NOBLE THE MARQUESS OF DOURO, M.P., D.C.L., ETC., ETC.   MY DEAR LORD,—   The imperfect attempt to picture forth some scenes of the most brilliant period of my country's history might naturally suggest their   dedication to the son of him who gave that era its glory. I feel,   however, in the weakness of the effort, the presumption of such a   thought, and would simply ask of you to accept these volumes as a   souvenir of many delightful hours passed long since in your society, and a testimony of the deep pride with which I regard the honor of your   friendship.   Believe me, my dear Lord, with every respect and esteem,   Yours, most sincerely,   THE AUTHOR.   BRUSSELS, November, 1841.

A WORD OF EXPLANATION.

KIND PUBLIC,—

Having so lately taken my leave of the stage, in a farewell benefit, it is but fitting that I should explain the circumstances which once more bring me before you,—that I may not appear intrusive, where I have met with but too much indulgence.

A blushing *debutant—entre nous*, the most impudent Irishman that ever swaggered down Sackville Street—has requested me to present him to your acquaintance. He has every ambition to be a favorite with you; but says—God forgive him—he is too bashful for the foot-lights.

He has remarked—as, doubtless, many others have done—upon what very slight grounds, and with what slender pretension, *my* Confessions have met with favor at the hands of the press and the public; and the idea has occurred to him to indite his *own*. Had his determination ended here, I should have nothing to object to; but unfortunately, he expects me to become his editor, and in some sort responsible for the faults of his production. I have wasted much eloquence and more breath in assuring him that I was no tried favorite of the public, who dared take liberties with them; that the small rag of reputation I enjoyed, was a very scanty covering for my own nakedness; that the plank which swam with one, would most inevitably sink with two; and lastly, that the indulgence so often bestowed upon a first effort is as frequently converted into censure on the older offender. My arguments have, however, totally failed, and he remains obdurate and unmoved. Under these circumstances I have yielded; and as, happily for me, the short and pithy direction to the river Thames, in the Critic, "to keep between its banks," has been imitated by my friend, I find all that is required of me is to write my name upon the title and go in peace. Such, he informs me, is modern editorship.

In conclusion, I would beg, that if the debt he now incurs at your hands remain unpaid, you would kindly bear in mind that your remedy lies against the drawer of the bill and not against its mere humble indorser,

HARRY LORREQUER
BRUSSELS, March, 1840.

PREFACE

The success of Harry Lorrequer was the reason for writing Charles O'Malley. That I myself was in no wise prepared for the favor the public bestowed on, my first attempt is easily enough understood. The ease with which I strung my stories together,—and in reality the Confessions of Harry Lorrequer are little other than a note-book of absurd and laughable incidents,—led me to believe that I could draw on this vein of composition without any limit whatever. I felt, or thought I felt, an inexhaustible store of fun and buoyancy within me, and I began to have a misty, half-confused impression that Englishmen generally labored under a sad-colored temperament, took depressing views of life, and were proportionately grateful to any one who would rally them even passingly out of their despondency, and give them a laugh without much trouble for going in search of it.

When I set to work to write Charles O'Malley I was, as I have ever been, very low with fortune, and the success of a new venture was pretty much as eventful to me as the turn of the right color at *rouge-et-noir*. At the same time I had then an amount of spring in my temperament, and a power of enjoying life which I can honestly say I never found surpassed. The world had for me all the interest of an admirable comedy, in which the part allotted myself, if not a high or a foreground one, was eminently suited to my taste, and brought me, besides, sufficiently often on the stage to enable me to follow all the fortunes of the piece. Brussels, where I was then living, was adorned at the period by a most agreeable English society. Some leaders of the fashionable world of London had come there to refit and recruit, both in body and estate. There were several pleasant and a great number of pretty people among them; and so far as I could judge, the fashionable dramas of Belgrave Square and its vicinity were being performed in the Rue Royale and the Boulevard de Waterloo with very considerable success. There were dinners, balls, déjeûners, and picnics in the Bois de Cambre, excursions to Waterloo, and select little parties to Bois-fort,—a charming little resort in the forest whose intense cockneyism became perfectly inoffensive as being in a foreign land, and remote from the invasion of home-bred vulgarity. I mention all these things to show the adjuncts by which I was aided, and the rattle of gayety by which I was, as it were, "accompanied," when I next tried my voice.

The soldier element tinctured strongly our society, and I will say most agreeably. Among those whom I remember best were several old Peninsulars. Lord Combermere was of this number, and another of our set was an officer who accompanied, if indeed he did not command, the first boat party who crossed the Douro. It is needless to say how I cultivated a society so full of all the storied details I was eager to obtain, and how generously disposed were they to give me all the information I needed. On topography especially were they valuable to me, and with such good result that I have been more than once complimented on the accuracy of my descriptions of places which I have never seen and whose features I have derived entirely from the narratives of my friends.

When, therefore, my publishers asked me could I write a story in the Lorrequer vein, in which active service and military adventure could figure more prominently than mere civilian life, and where the achievements of a British army might form the staple of the narrative,—when this question was propounded me, I was ready to reply: Not one, but fifty. Do not mistake me, and suppose that any overweening confidence in my literary powers would have emboldened me to make this reply; my whole strength lay in the fact that I could not recognize anything like literary effort in the matter. If the world would only condescend to read that which I wrote precisely as I was in the habit of talking, nothing could be easier than for me to occupy them. Not alone was it very easy to me, but it was intensely interesting and amusing to myself, to be so engaged.

The success of Harry Lorrequer had been freely wafted across the German ocean, but even in its mildest accents it was very intoxicating incense to me; and I set to work on my second book with a thrill of hope as regards the world's favor which—and it is no small thing to say it—I can yet recall.

I can recall, too, and I am afraid more vividly still, some of the difficulties of my task when I endeavored to form anything like an accurate or precise idea of some campaigning incident or some passage of arms from the narratives of two distinct and separate "eye-witnesses." What mistrust I conceived for all eye-witnesses from my own brief experience of their testimonies! What an impulse did it lend me to study the nature and the temperament of narrator, as indicative of the peculiar coloring he might lend his narrative; and how it taught me to know the force of the French epigram that has declared how it was entirely the alternating popularity of Marshal Soult that decided whether he won or lost the battle of Toulouse.

While, however, I was sifting these evidences, and separating, as well as I might, the wheat from the chaff, I was in a measure training myself for what, without my then knowing it, was to become my career in life. This was not therefore altogether without a certain degree of labor, but so light and pleasant withal, so full of picturesque peeps at character and humorous views of human nature, that it would be the very rankest ingratitude of me if I did not own that I gained all my earlier experiences of the world in very pleasant company,—highly enjoyable at the time, and with matter for charming souvenirs long after.

That certain traits of my acquaintances found themselves embodied in some of the characters of this story I do not to deny. The principal of natural selection adapts itself to novels as to Nature, and it would have demanded an effort above my strength to have disabused myself at the desk of all the impressions of the dinner-table, and to have forgotten features which interested or amused me.

One of the personages of my tale I drew, however, with very little aid from fancy. I would go so far as to say that I took him from the life, if my memory did not confront me with the lamentable inferiority of my picture to the great original it was meant to portray.

With the exception of the quality of courage, I never met a man who contained within himself so many of the traits of Falstaff as the individual who furnished me with Major Monsoon. But the major—I must call him so, though that rank was far beneath his own—was a man of unquestionable bravery. His powers as a story-teller were to my thinking unrivalled; the peculiar reflections on life which he would passingly introduce, the wise apothegms, were after a morality essentially of his own invention. Then he would indulge in the unsparing exhibition of himself in situations such as other men would never have confessed to, all blended up with a racy enjoyment of life, dashed occasionally with sorrow that our tenure of it was short of patriarchal. All these, accompanied by a face redolent of intense humor, and a voice whose modulations were managed with the skill of a consummate artist,—all these, I say, were above me to convey; nor indeed as I re-read any of the adventures in which he figures, am I other than ashamed at the weakness of my drawing and the poverty of my coloring.

That I had a better claim to personify him than is always the lot of a novelist; that I possessed, so to say, a vested interest in his life and adventures,—I will relate a little incident in proof; and my accuracy, if necessary, can be attested by another actor in the scene, who yet survives.

I was living a bachelor life at Brussels, my family being at Ostende for the bathing, during the summer of 1840. The city was comparatively empty,—all the so-called society being absent at the various spas or baths of Germany. One member of the British legation, who remained at his post to represent the mission, and myself, making common cause of our desolation and ennui, spent much of our time together, and dined *tête-à-tête* every day.

It chanced that one evening, as we were hastening through the park on our way to dinner, we espied the major—for as major I must speak of him—lounging along with that half-careless, half-observant air we had both of us remarked as indicating a desire to be somebody's, anybody's guest, rather than surrender himself to the homeliness of domestic fare.

"There's that confounded old Monsoon," cried my diplomatic friend. "It's all up if he sees us, and I can't endure him."

Now, I must remark that my friend, though very far from insensible to the humoristic side of the major's character, was not always in the vein to enjoy it; and when so indisposed he could invest the object of his dislike with something little short of antipathy. "Promise me," said he, as Monsoon came towards us,—"promise me, you'll not ask him to dinner." Before I could make any reply, the major was shaking a hand of either of us, and rapturously expatiating over his good luck at meeting us. "Mrs. M.," said he, "has got a dreary party of old ladies to dine with her, and I have come out here to find some pleasant fellow to join me, and take our mutton-chop together."

"We're behind our time, Major," said my friend, "sorry to leave you so abruptly, but must push on. Eh, Lorrequer," added he, to evoke corroboration on my part.

"Harry says nothing of the kind," replied Monsoon, "he says, or he's going to say, 'Major, I have a nice bit of dinner waiting for me at home, enough for two, will feed three, or if there be a short-coming, nothing easier than to eke out the deficiency by another bottle of Moulton; come along with us then, Monsoon, and we shall be all the merrier for your company.'"

Repeating his last words, "Come along, Monsoon," etc., I passed my arm within his, and away we went. For a moment my friend tried to get free and leave me, but I held him fast and carried him along in spite of himself. He was, however, so chagrined and provoked that till the moment we reached my door he never uttered a word, nor paid the slightest attention to Monsoon, who talked away in a vein that occasionally made gravity all but impossible.

Our dinner proceeded drearily enough, the diplomatist's stiffness never relaxed for a moment, and my own awkwardness damped all my attempts at conversation. Not so, however, Monsoon, he ate heartily, approved of everything, and pronounced my wine to be exquisite. He gave us a perfect discourse on sherry and Spanish wines in general, told us the secret of the Amontillado flavor, and explained that process of browning by boiling down wine which some are so fond of in England. At last, seeing perhaps that the protection had little charm for us, with his accustomed tact, he diverged into anecdote. "I was once fortunate enough," said he, "to fall upon some of that choice sherry from the St. Lucas Luentas which is always reserved for royalty. It was a pale wine, delicious in the drinking, and leaving no more flavor in the mouth than a faint dryness that seemed to say, another glass. Shall I tell you how I came by it?" And scarcely pausing for reply, he told the story of having robbed his own convoy, and stolen the wine he was in charge of for safe conveyance.

I wish I could give any, even the weakest idea of how he narrated that incident,—the struggle that he portrayed between duty and temptation, and the apologetic tone of his voice in which he explained that the frame of mind that succeeds to any yielding to seductive influences, is often, in the main, more profitable to a man than is the vain-glorious sense of having resisted a temptation. "Meekness is the mother of all the virtues," said he, "and there is no being meek without frailty." The story, told as he told it, was too much for the diplomatist's gravity, he resisted all signs of attention as long as he was able, and at last fairly roared out with laughter.

As soon as I myself recovered from the effects of his drollery, I said, "Major, I have a proposition to make you. Let me tell the story in print, and I'll give you five naps."

"Are you serious, Harry?" asked he. "Is this on honor?"

"On honor, assuredly," I replied.

"Let me have the money down, on the nail, and I'll give you leave to have me and my whole life, every adventure that ever befell me, ay, and if you like, every moral reflection that my experiences have suggested."

3

"Done!" cried I, "I agree."

"Not so fast," cried the diplomatist, "we must make a protocol of this; the high contracting parties must know what they give and what they receive, I'll draw out the treaty."

He did so at full length on a sheet of that solemn blue-tinted paper, so dedicated to despatch purposes; he duly set fourth the concession and the consideration. We each signed the document; he witnessed and sealed it; and Monsoon pocketed my five napoleons, filling a bumper to any success the bargain might bring me, and of which I have never had reason to express deep disappointment.

This document, along with my university degree, my commission in a militia regiment, and a vast amount of letters very interesting to me, was seized by the Austrian authorities on the way from Como to Florence, in the August of 1847, being deemed part of a treasonable correspondence,—probably purposely allegorical in form,—and never restored to me. I fairly own that I'd give all the rest willingly to repossess myself of the Monsoon treaty, not a little for the sake of that quaint old autograph, faintly shaken by the quiet laugh with which he wrote it.

That I did not entirely fail in giving my major some faint resemblance to the great original from whom I copied him, I may mention that he was speedily recognized in print by the Marquis of Londonderry, the well-known Sir Charles Stuart of the Peninsular campaign. "I know that fellow well," said he, "he once sent me a challenge, and I had to make him a very humble apology. The occasion was this: I had been out with a single aide-de-camp to make a reconnaissance in front of Victor's division; and to avoid attracting any notice, we covered over our uniform with two common gray overcoats which reached to the feet, and effectually concealed our rank as officers. Scarcely, however, had we topped a hill which commanded the view of the French, than a shower of shells flew over and around us. Amazed to think how we could have been so quickly noticed, I looked around me, and discovered, quite close in my rear, your friend Monsoon with what he called his staff,—a popinjay set of rascals dressed out in green and gold, and with more plumes and feathers than the general staff ever boasted. Carried away by momentary passion at the failure of my reconnaissance, I burst out with some insolent allusion to the harlequin assembly which had drawn the French fire upon us. Monsoon saluted me respectfully, and retired without a word; but I had scarcely reached my quarters when a 'friend' of his waited on me with a message, a very categorical message it was, too, 'it must be a meeting or an ample apology.' I made the apology, a most full one, for the major was right, and I had not a fraction of reason to sustain me in my conduct, and we have been the best of friends ever since."

I myself had heard the incident before this from Monsoon, but told among other adventures whose exact veracity I was rather disposed to question, and did not therefore accord it all the faith that was its due; and I admit that the accidental corroboration of this one event very often served to puzzle me afterwards, when I listened to stories in which the major seemed a second Munchausen, but might, like in this of the duel, have been among the truest and most matter-of-fact of historians. May the reader be not less embarrassed than myself, is my sincere, if not very courteous, prayer.

I have no doubt myself, that often in recounting some strange incident,—a personal experience it always was,—he was himself more amused by the credulity of the hearers, and the amount of interest he could excite in them, than were they by the story. He possessed the true narrative gusto, and there was a marvellous instinct in the way in which he would vary a tale to suit the tastes of an audience; while his moralizings were almost certain to take the tone of a humoristic quiz on the company.

Though fully aware that I was availing myself of the contract that delivered him into my hands, and dining with me two or three days a week, he never lapsed into any allusion to his appearance in print; and the story had been already some weeks published before he asked me to lend him "that last thing—he forgot the name of it—I was writing."

Of Frank Webber I have said, in a former notice, that he was one of my earliest friends, my chum in college, and in the very chambers where I have located Charles O'Malley, in Old Trinity. He was a man of the highest order of abilities, and with a memory that never forgot, but ruined and run to seed by the idleness that came of a discursive, uncertain temperament. Capable of anything, he spent his youth in follies and eccentricities; every one of which, however, gave indications of a mind inexhaustible in resources, and abounding in devices and contrivances that none other but himself would have thought of. Poor fellow, he died young; and perhaps it is better it should have been so. Had he lived to a later day, he would most probably have been found a foremost leader of Fenianism; and from what I knew of him, I can say he would have been a more dangerous enemy to English rule than any of those dealers in the petty larceny of rebellion we have lately seen among us.

I have said that of Mickey Free I had not one but one thousand types. Indeed, I am not quite sure that in my last visit to Dublin, I did not chance on a living specimen of the "Free" family, much readier in repartée, quicker with an apropos, and droller in illustration than my own Mickey. This fellow was "boots" at a great hotel in Sackville Street; and I owe him more amusement and some heartier laughs than it has been always my fortune to enjoy in a party of wits. His criticisms on my sketches of Irish character were about the shrewdest and the best I ever listened to; and that I am not bribed to this by any flattery, I may remark that they were more often severe than complimentary, and that he hit every blunder of image, every mistake in figure, of my peasant characters, with an acuteness and correctness which made me very grateful to know that his daily occupations were limited to blacking boots, and not polishing off authors.

I believe I have now done with my confessions, except I should like to own that this story was the means of according me a more heartfelt glow of satisfaction, a more gratifying sense of pride, than anything I ever have or ever shall write, and in this wise. My brother, at that time the rector of an Irish parish, once forwarded to me a letter from a lady unknown to him, but who had heard he was the brother of "Harry Lorrequer," and who addressed him not knowing where a letter might be directed to myself. The letter was the grateful expression of a mother, who said, "I am the widow of a field officer, and with an only son, for whom I obtained a presentation to Woolwich; but seeing in my boy's nature certain traits of nervousness and timidity which induced me to hesitate on embarking him in the career of a soldier, I became very unhappy and uncertain which course to decide on.

"While in this state of uncertainty, I chanced to make him a birthday present of 'Charles O'Malley,' the reading of which seemed to act like a charm on his whole character, inspiring him with a passion for movement and adventure, and spiriting him to an eager desire for a military life. Seeing that this was no passing enthusiasm, but a decided and determined bent, I accepted the cadetship for him; and his career has been not alone distinguished as a student, but one which has marked him out for an almost hare-brained courage, and for a dash and heroism that give high promise for his future.

"Thank your brother for me," wrote she, "a mother's thanks for the welfare of an only son; and say how I wish that my best wishes for him and his could recompense him for what I owe him."

I humbly hope that it may not be imputed to me as unpardonable vanity,—the recording of this incident. It gave me an intense pleasure when I heard it; and now, as I look back on it, it invests this story for myself with an interest which nothing else that I have written can afford me.

I have now but to repeat what I have declared in former editions, my sincere gratitude for the favor the public still continues to bestow on me,—a favor which probably associates the memory of this book with whatever I have since done successfully, and compels me to remember that to the popularity of "Charles O'Malley" I am indebted for a great share of that kindliness in criticism, and that geniality in judgment, which—for more than a quarter of a century—my countrymen have graciously bestowed on their faithful friend and servant,
CHARLES LEVER. TRIESTE, 1872.

CHARLES O'MALLEY.
THE IRISH DRAGOON.

CHAPTER I.

DALY'S CLUB-HOUSE.

The rain was dashing in torrents against the window-panes, and the wind sweeping in heavy and fitful gusts along the dreary and deserted streets, as a party of three persons sat over their wine, in that stately old pile which once formed the resort of the Irish Members, in College Green, Dublin, and went by the name of Daly's Club-House. The clatter of falling tiles and chimney-pots, the jarring of the window-frames, and howling of the storm without seemed little to affect the spirits of those within as they drew closer to a blazing fire before which stood a small table covered with the remains of a dessert, and an abundant supply of bottles, whose characteristic length of neck indicated the rarest wines of France and Germany; while the portly magnum of claret—the wine *par excellence* of every Irish gentleman of the day—passed rapidly from hand to hand, the conversation did not languish, and many a deep and hearty laugh followed the stories which every now and then were told, as some reminiscence of early days was recalled, or some trait of a former companion remembered.

One of the party, however, was apparently engrossed by other thoughts than those of the mirth and merriment around; for in the midst of all he would turn suddenly from the others, and devote himself to a number of scattered sheets of paper, upon which he had written some lines, but whose crossed and blotted sentences attested how little success had waited upon his literary labors. This individual was a short, plethoric-looking, white-haired man of about fifty, with a deep, round voice, and a chuckling, smothering laugh, which, whenever he indulged not only shook his own ample person, but generally created a petty earthquake on every side of him. For the present, I shall not stop to particularize him more closely; but when I add that the person in question was a well-known member of the Irish House of Commons, whose acute understanding and practical good sense were veiled under an affected and well-dissembled habit of blundering that did far more for his party than the most violent and pointed attacks of his more accurate associates, some of my readers may anticipate me in pronouncing him to be Sir Harry Boyle. Upon his left sat a figure the most unlike him possible. He was a tall, thin, bony man, with a bolt-upright air and a most saturnine expression; his eyes were covered by a deep green shade, which fell far over his face, but failed to conceal a blue scar that crossing his cheek ended in the angle of his mouth, and imparted to that feature, when he spoke, an apparently abortive attempt to extend towards his eyebrow; his upper lip was covered with a grizzly and ill-trimmed mustache, which added much to the ferocity of his look, while a thin and pointed beard on his chin gave an apparent length to the whole face that completed its rueful character. His dress was a single-breasted, tightly buttoned frock, in one button-hole of which a yellow ribbon was fastened, the decoration of a foreign service, which conferred upon its wearer the title of count; and though Billy Considine, as he was familiarly called by his friends, was a thorough Irishman in all his feelings and affections, yet he had no objection to the designation he had gained in the Austrian army. The Count was certainly no beauty, but somehow, very few men of his day had a fancy for telling him so. A deadlier hand and a steadier eye never covered his man in the Phoenix; and though he never had a seat in the House, he was always regarded as one of the government party, who more than once had damped the ardor of an opposition member by the very significant threat of "setting Billy at him." The third figure of the group was a large, powerfully built, and handsome man, older than either of the others, but not betraying in his voice or carriage any touch of time. He was attired in the green coat and buff vest which formed the livery of the club; and in his tall, ample forehead, clear, well-set eye, and still handsome mouth, bore evidence that no great flattery was necessary at the time which called Godfrey O'Malley the handsomest man in Ireland.

"Upon my conscience," said Sir Harry, throwing down his pen with an air of ill-temper, "I can make nothing of it! I have got into such an infernal habit of making bulls, that I can't write sense when I want it!"

"Come, come," said O'Malley, "try again, my dear fellow. If you can't succeed, I'm sure Billy and I have no chance."

"What have you written? Let us see," said Considine, drawing the paper towards him, and holding it to the light. "Why, what the devil is all this? You have made him 'drop down dead after dinner of a lingering illness brought on by the debate of yesterday.'"

"Oh, impossible!"

"Well, read it yourself; there it is. And, as if to make the thing less credible, you talk of his 'Bill for the Better Recovery of Small Debts.' I'm sure, O'Malley, your last moments were not employed in that manner."

"Come, now," said Sir Harry, "I'll set all to rights with a postscript. 'Any one who questions the above statement is politely requested to call on Mr. Considine, 16 Kildare Street, who will feel happy to afford him every satisfaction upon Mr. O'Malley's decease, or upon miscellaneous matters.'"

"Worse and worse," said O'Malley. "Killing another man will never persuade the world that I'm dead."

"But we'll wake you, and have a glorious funeral."

"And if any man doubt the statement, I'll call him out," said the Count.

"Or, better still," said Sir Harry, "O'Malley has his action at law for defamation."

"I see I'll never get down to Galway at this rate," said O'Malley; "and as the new election takes place on Tuesday week, time presses. There are more writs flying after me this instant than for all the government boroughs."

"And there will be fewer returns, I fear," said Sir Harry.

"Who is the chief creditor?" asked the Count.

"Old Stapleton, the attorney in Fleet Street, has most of the mortgages."

"Nothing to be done with him in this way?" said Considine, balancing the corkscrew like a hair trigger.

"No chance of it."

"May be," said Sir Harry, "he might come to terms if I were to call and say, 'You are anxious to close accounts, as your death has just taken place.' You know what I mean."

"I fear so should he, were you to say so. No, no, Boyle, just try a plain, straightforward paragraph about my death; we'll have it in Falkner's paper to-morrow. On Friday the funeral can take place, and, with the blessing o' God, I'll come to life on Saturday at Athlone, in time to canvass the market."

"I think it wouldn't be bad if your ghost were to appear to old Timins the tanner, in Naas, on your way down. You know he arrested you once before."

"I prefer a night's sleep," said O'Malley. "But come, finish the squib for the paper."

"Stay a little," said Sir Harry, musing; "it just strikes me that if ever the matter gets out I may be in some confounded scrape. Who knows if it is not a breach of privilege to report the death of a member? And to tell you truth, I dread the Sergeant and the Speaker's warrant with a very lively fear."

"Why, when did you make his acquaintance?" said the Count.

"Is it possible you never heard of Boyle's committal?" said O'Malley. "You surely must have been abroad at the time. But it's not too late to tell it yet."

"Well, it's about two years since old Townsend brought in his Enlistment Bill, and the whole country was scoured for all our voters, who were scattered here and there, never anticipating another call of the House, and supposing that the session was just over. Among others, up came our friend Harry, here, and the night he arrived they made him a 'Monk of the Screw,' and very soon made him forget his senatorial dignities. On the evening after his reaching town, the bill was brought in, and at two in the morning the division took place,—a vote was of too much consequence not to look after it closely,—and a Castle messenger was in waiting in Exchequer Street, who, when the debate was closing, put Harry, with three others, into a coach, and brought them down to the House. Unfortunately, however, they mistook their friends, voted against the bill, and amidst the loudest cheering of the opposition, the government party were defeated. The rage of the ministers knew no bounds, and looks of defiance and even threats were exchanged between the ministers and the deserters. Amidst all this poor Harry fell fast asleep and dreamed that he was once more in Exchequer Street, presiding among the monks, and mixing another tumbler. At length he awoke and looked about him. The clerk was just at the instant reading out, in his usual routine manner, a clause of the new bill, and the remainder of the House was in dead silence. Harry looked again around on every side, wondering where was the hot water, and what had become of the whiskey bottle, and above all, why the company were so extremely dull and ungenial. At length, with a half-shake, he roused up a little, and giving a look of unequivocal contempt on every side, called out, 'Upon my soul, you're pleasant companions; but I'll give you a chant to enliven you!' So saying, he cleared his throat with a couple of short coughs, and struck up, with the voice of a Stentor, the following verse of a popular ballad:—

'And they nibbled away, both night and day,   Like mice in a round of Glo'ster;   Great rogues they were all, both great and small,   From Flood to Leslie Foster.   Great rogues all.

Chorus, boys!' If he was not joined by the voices of his friends in the song, it was probably because such a roar of laughing never was heard since the walls were roofed over. The whole House rose in a mass, and my friend Harry was hurried over the benches by the sergeant-at-arms, and left for three weeks in Newgate to practise his melody."

"All true," said Sir Harry; "and worse luck to them for not liking music. But come, now, will this do? 'It is our melancholy duty to announce the death of Godfrey O'Malley, Esq., late member for the county of Galway, which took place on Friday evening, at Daly's Club-House. This esteemed gentleman's family—one of the oldest in Ireland, and among whom it was hereditary not to have any children—'"

Here a burst of laughter from Considine and O'Malley interrupted the reader, who with the greatest difficulty could be persuaded that he was again bulling it.

"The devil fly away with it," said he; "I'll never succeed."

"Never mind," said O'Malley, "the first part will do admirably; and let us now turn our attention to other matters."

A fresh magnum was called for, and over its inspiring contents all the details of the funeral were planned; and as the clock struck four the party separated for the *night*, well satisfied with the result of their labors.

CHAPTER II.

THE ESCAPE.

When the dissolution of Parliament was announced the following morning in Dublin, its interest in certain circles was manifestly increased by the fact that Godfrey O'Malley was at last open to arrest; for as in olden times certain gifted individuals possessed some happy immunity against death by fire or sword, so the worthy O'Malley seemed to enjoy a no less valuable privilege, and for many a year had passed among the myrmidons of the law as writ-proof. Now, however, the charm seemed to have yielded; and pretty much with the same feeling as a storming party may be supposed to experience on the day that a breach is reported as practicable, did the honest attorneys retained in the various suits against him rally round each other that morning in the Four Courts.

Bonds, mortgages, post-obits, promissory notes—in fact, every imaginable species of invention for raising the O'Malley exchequer for the preceding thirty years—were handed about on all sides, suggesting to the mind of an uninterested observer the notion that had the aforesaid O'Malley been an independent and absolute monarch, instead of merely being the member for Galway, the kingdom over whose destinies he had been called to preside would have suffered not a little from a depreciated currency and an extravagant issue of paper. Be that as it might, one thing was clear,—the whole estates of the family could not possibly pay one fourth of the debt; and the only question was one which occasionally arises at a scanty dinner on a mail-coach road,—who was to be the lucky individual to carve the joint, where so many were sure to go off hungry?

It was now a trial of address between these various and highly gifted gentlemen who should first pounce upon the victim; and when the skill of their caste is taken into consideration, who will doubt that every feasible expedient for securing him was resorted to? While writs were struck against him in Dublin, emissaries were despatched to the various surrounding counties to procure others in the event of his escape. *Ne exeats* were sworn, and water-bailiffs engaged to follow him on the high seas; and as the great Nassau balloon did not exist in those days, no imaginable mode of escape appeared possible, and bets were offered at long odds that within twenty-four hours the late member would be enjoying his *otium cum dignitate* in his Majesty's jail of Newgate.

Expectation was at the highest, confidence hourly increasing, success all but certain, when in the midst of all this high-bounding hope the dreadful rumor spread that O'Malley was no more. One had seen it just five minutes before in the evening edition of Falkner's paper; another heard it in the courts; a third overheard the Chief-Justice stating it to the Master of the Rolls; and lastly, a breathless witness arrived from College Green with the news that Daly's Club-House was shut up, and the shutters closed. To describe the consternation the intelligence caused on every side is impossible; nothing in history equals it,—except, perhaps, the entrance of the French army into Moscow, deserted and forsaken by its former inhabitants. While terror and dismay, therefore, spread amidst that wide and respectable body who formed O'Malley's creditors, the preparations for his funeral were going on with every rapidity. Relays of horses were ordered at every stage of the journey, and it was announced that, in testimony of his worth, a large party of his friends were to accompany his remains to Portumna Abbey,—a test much more indicative of resistance in the event of any attempt to arrest the body, than of anything like reverence for their departed friend.

Such was the state of matters in Dublin when a letter reached me one morning at O'Malley Castle, whose contents will at once explain the writer's intention, and also serve to introduce my unworthy self to my reader. It ran thus:—

DALY'S, *about eight in the evening.* Dear Charley,—*Your uncle Godfrey, whose debts (God pardon him!) are more numerous than the hairs of his wig, was obliged to die here last night. We did the thing for him completely; and all doubts as to the reality of the event are silenced by the circumstantial detail of the newspaper, "that he was confined six weeks to his bed from a cold he caught, ten days ago, while on guard." Repeat this; for it is better we had all the same story till he comes to life again, which, may be, will not take place before Tuesday or Wednesday. At the same time, canvass the county for him, and say he'll be with his friends next week, and up in Woodford and the Scariff barony. Say he died a true Catholic; it will serve him on the hustings. Meet us in Athlone on Saturday, and bring your uncle's mare with you. He says he'd rather ride home. And tell Father Mac Shane, to have a bit of dinner ready about four o'clock, for the corpse can get nothing after he leaves Mountmellick. No more now, from Yours ever,* HARRY BOYLE To CHARLES O'MALLEY, *Esq., O'Malley Castle, Galway.*

When this not over-clear document reached me I was the sole inhabitant of O'Malley Castle,—a very ruinous pile of incongruous masonry, that stood in a wild and dreary part of the county of Galway, bordering on the Shannon. On every side stretched the property of my uncle, or at least what had once been so; and indeed, so numerous were its present claimants that he would have been a subtle lawyer who could have pronounced upon the rightful owner. The demesne around the castle contained some well-grown and handsome timber, and as the soil was undulating and fertile, presented many features of beauty; beyond it, all was sterile, bleak, and barren. Long tracts of brown heath-clad mountain or not less unprofitable valleys of tall and waving fern were all that the eye could discern, except where the broad Shannon, expanding into a tranquil and glassy lake, lay still and motionless beneath the dark mountains, a few islands, with some ruined churches and a round tower, alone breaking the dreary waste of water.

Here it was that I passed my infancy and my youth; and here I now stood, at the age of seventeen, quite unconscious that the world contained aught fairer and brighter than that gloomy valley with its rugged frame of mountains.

When a mere child, I was left an orphan to the care of my worthy uncle. My father, whose extravagance had well sustained the family reputation, had squandered a large and handsome property in contesting elections for his native county, and in keeping up that system of unlimited hospitality for which Ireland in general, and Galway more especially, was renowned. The result was, as might be expected, ruin and beggary. He died, leaving every one of his estates encumbered with heavy debts, and the only legacy he left to his brother was a boy four years of age, entreating him with his last breath, "Be anything you like to him, Godfrey, but a father, or at least such a one as I have proved."

Godfrey O'Malley some short time previous had lost his wife, and when this new trust was committed to him he resolved never to remarry, but to rear me up as his own child and the inheritor of his estates. How weighty and onerous an obligation this latter might prove, the reader can form some idea. The intention was, however, a kind one; and to do my uncle justice, he loved me with all the affection of a warm and open heart.

From my earliest years his whole anxiety was to fit me for the part of a country gentleman, as he regarded that character,—namely, I rode boldly with fox-hounds; I was about the best shot within twenty miles of us; I could swim the Shannon at Holy Island; I drove four-in-hand better than the coachman himself; and from finding a hare to hooking a salmon, my equal could not be found from Killaloe to Banagher. These were the staple of my endowments. Besides which, the parish priest had taught me a little Latin, a little French, a little geometry, and a great deal of the life and opinions of Saint Jago, who presided over a holy well in the neighborhood, and was held in very considerable repute.

When I add to this portraiture of my accomplishments that I was nearly six feet high, with more than a common share of activity and strength for my years, and no inconsiderable portion of good looks, I have finished my sketch, and stand before my reader.

It is now time I should return to Sir Harry's letter, which so completely bewildered me that, but for the assistance of Father Roach, I should have been totally unable to make out the writer's intentions. By his advice, I immediately set out for Athlone, where, when I arrived, I found my uncle addressing the mob from the top of the hearse, and recounting his miraculous escapes as a new claim upon their gratitude.

"There was nothing else for it, boys; the Dublin people insisted on my being their member, and besieged the club-house. I refused; they threatened. I grew obstinate; they furious. 'I'll die first,' said I. 'Galway or nothing!'"

"Hurrah!" from the mob. "O'Malley forever!"

"And ye see, I kept my word, boys,—I did die; I died that evening at a quarter past eight. There, read it for yourselves; there's the paper. Was waked and carried out, and here I am after all, ready to die in earnest for you, but never to desert you."

The cheers here were deafening, and my uncle was carried through the market down to the mayor's house, who, being a friend of the opposite party, was complimented with three groans; then up the Mall to the chapel, beside which father Mac Shane resided. He was then suffered to touch the earth once more; when, having shaken hands with all of his constituency within reach, he entered the house, to partake of the kindest welcome and best reception the good priest could afford him.

My uncle's progress homeward was a triumph. The real secret of his escape had somehow come out, and his popularity rose to a white heat. "An' it's little O'Malley cares for the law,—bad luck to it; it's himself can laugh at judge and jury. Arrest him? Nabocklish! Catch a weasel asleep!" etc. Such were the encomiums that greeted him as he passed on towards home; while shouts of joy and blazing bonfires attested that his success was regarded as a national triumph.

The west has certainly its strong features of identity. Had my uncle possessed the claims of the immortal Howard; had he united in his person all the attributes which confer a lasting and an ennobling fame upon humanity,—he might have passed on unnoticed and unobserved; but for the man that had duped a judge and escaped the sheriff, nothing was sufficiently flattering to mark their approbation. The success of the exploit was twofold; the news spread far and near, and the very story canvassed the county better than Billy Davern himself, the Athlone attorney.

This was the prospect now before us; and however little my readers may sympathize with my taste, I must honestly avow that I looked forward to it with a most delighted feeling. O'Malley Castle was to be the centre of operations, and filled with my uncle's supporters; while I, a mere stripling, and usually treated as a boy, was to be intrusted with an important mission, and sent off to canvass a distant relation, with whom my uncle was not upon terms, and who might possibly be approachable by a younger branch of the family, with whom he had never any collision.

CHAPTER III.
MR. BLAKE.

Nothing but the exigency of the case could ever have persuaded my uncle to stoop to the humiliation of canvassing the individual to whom I was now about to proceed as envoy-extraordinary, with full powers to make any or every *amende*, provided only his interest and that of his followers should be thereby secured to the O'Malley cause. The evening before I set out was devoted to giving me all the necessary instructions how I was to proceed, and what difficulties I was to avoid.

"Say your uncle's in high feather with the government party," said Sir Harry, "and that he only votes against them as a *ruse de guerre*, as the French call it."

"Insist upon it that I am sure of the election without him; but that for family reasons he should not stand aloof from me; that people are talking of it in the country."

"And drop a hint," said Considine, "that O'Malley is greatly improved in his shooting."

"And don't get drunk too early in the evening, for Phil Blake has beautiful claret," said another.

"And be sure you don't make love to the red-headed girls," added a third; "he has four of them, each more sinfully ugly than the other."

"You'll be playing whist, too," said Boyle; "and never mind losing a few pounds. Mrs. B., long life to her, has a playful way of turning the king."

"Charley will do it all well," said my uncle; "leave him alone. And now let us have in the supper."

It was only on the following morning, as the tandem came round to the door, that I began to feel the importance of my mission, and certain misgivings came over me as to my ability to fulfil it. Mr. Blake and his family, though estranged from my uncle for several years past, had been always most kind and good-natured to me; and although I could not, with propriety, have cultivated any close intimacy with them, I had every reason to suppose that they entertained towards me nothing but sentiments of good-will. The head of the family was a Galway squire of the oldest and most genuine stock, a great sportsman, a negligent farmer, and most careless father; he looked upon a fox as an infinitely more precious part of the creation than a French governess, and thought that riding well with hounds was a far better gift than all the learning of a Parson. His daughters were after his own heart,—the best-tempered, least-educated, most high-spirited, gay, dashing, ugly girls in the county, ready to ride over a four-foot paling without a saddle, and to dance the "Wind that shakes the barley" for four consecutive hours, against all the officers that their hard fate, and the Horse Guards, ever condemned to Galway.

The mamma was only remarkable for her liking for whist, and her invariable good fortune thereat,—a circumstance the world were agreed in ascribing less to the blind goddess than her own natural endowments.

Lastly, the heir of the house was a stripling of about my own age, whose accomplishments were limited to selling spavined and broken-winded horses to the infantry officers, playing a safe game at billiards, and acting as jackal-general to his sisters at balls, providing them with a sufficiency of partners, and making a strong fight for a place at the supper-table for his mother. These fraternal and filial traits, more honored at home than abroad, had made Mr. Matthew Blake a rather well-known individual in the neighborhood where he lived.

Though Mr. Blake's property was ample, and strange to say for his county, unencumbered, the whole air and appearance of his house and grounds betrayed anything rather than a sufficiency of means. The gate lodge was a miserable mud-hovel with a thatched and falling roof; the gate itself, a wooden contrivance, one half of which was boarded and the other railed; the avenue was covered with weeds, and deep with ruts; and the clumps of young plantation, which had been planted and fenced with care, were now open to the cattle, and either totally uprooted or denuded of their bark and dying. The lawn, a handsome one of some forty acres, had been devoted to an exercise-ground for training horses, and was cut up by their feet beyond all semblance of its original destination; and the house itself, a large and venerable structure of above a century old, displayed every variety of contrivance, as well as the usual one of glass, to exclude the weather. The hall-door hung by a single hinge, and required three persons each morning and evening to open and shut it; the remainder of the day it lay pensively open; the steps which led to it were broken and falling; and the whole aspect of things without was ruinous in the extreme. Within, matters were somewhat better, for though the furniture was old, and none of it clean, yet an appearance of comfort was evident; and the large grate, blazing with its pile of red-hot turf, the deep-cushioned chairs, the old black mahogany dinner-table, and the soft carpet, albeit deep with dust, were not to be despised on a winter's evening, after a hard day's run with the "Blazers." Here it was, however, that Mr. Philip Blake had dispensed his hospitalities for above fifty years, and his father before him; and here, with a retinue of servants as *gauches* and ill-ordered as all about them, was he accustomed to invite all that the county possessed of rank and wealth, among which the officers quartered in his neighborhood were never neglected, the Miss Blakes having as decided a taste for the army as any young ladies of the west of Ireland; and while the Galway squire, with his cords and tops, was detailing the latest news from Ballinasloe in one corner, the dandy from St. James's Street might be seen displaying more arts of seductive flattery in another than his most accurate *insouciane* would permit him to practise in the elegant salons of London or Paris, and the same man who would have "cut his brother," for a solecism of dress or equipage, in Bond Street, was now to be seen quietly domesticated, eating family dinners, rolling silk for the young ladies, going down the middle in a country dance, and even descending to the indignity of long whist at "tenpenny" points, with only the miserable consolation that the company were not honest.

It was upon a clear frosty morning, when a bright blue sky and a sharp but bracing air seem to exercise upon the feelings a sense no less pleasurable than the balmiest breeze and warmest sun of summer, that I whipped my leader short round, and entered the precincts of "Gurt-na-Morra." As I proceeded along the avenue, I was struck by the slight traces of repairs here and there evident,—a gate or two that formerly had been parallel to the horizon had been raised to the perpendicular; some ineffectual efforts at paint were also perceptible upon the palings; and, in short, everything seemed to have undergone a kind of attempt at improvement.

When I reached the door, instead of being surrounded, as of old, by a tribe of menials frieze-coated, bare-headed, and bare-legged, my presence was announced by a tremendous ringing of bells from the hands of an old functionary in a very formidable livery, who peeped at me through the hall-window, and whom, with the greatest difficulty, I recognized as my quondam acquaintance, the butler. His wig alone would have graced a king's counsel; and the high collar of his coat, and the stiff pillory of his cravat denoted an eternal adieu to so humble a vocation as drawing a cork. Before I had time for any conjecture as to the altered circumstances about, the activity of my friend at the bell had surrounded me with "four others worse than himself," at least they were exactly similarly attired; and probably from the novelty of their costume, and the restraints of so unusual a thing as dress, were as perfectly unable to assist themselves or others as the Court of Aldermen would be were they to rig out in plate armor of the fourteenth century. How much longer I might have gone on conjecturing the reasons for the masquerade around, I cannot say; but my servant, an Irish disciple of my uncle's, whispered in my ear, "It's a red-breeches day, Master Charles,—they'll have the hoith of company in the house." From the phrase, it needed little explanation to inform me that it was one of those occasions on which Mr. Blake attired all the hangers-on of his house in livery, and that great preparations were in progress for a more than usually splendid reception.

In the next moment I was ushered into the breakfast-room, where a party of above a dozen persons were most gayly enjoying all the good cheer for which the house had a well-deserved repute. After the usual shaking of hands and hearty greetings were over, I was introduced in all form to Sir George Dashwood, a tall and singularly handsome man of about fifty, with an undress military frock and ribbon. His reception of me was somewhat strange; for as they mentioned my relationship to Godfrey O'Malley, he smiled slightly, and whispered something to Mr. Blake, who replied, "Oh, no, no; not the least. A mere boy; and besides—" What he added I lost, for at that moment Nora Blake was presenting me to Miss Dashwood.

If the sweetest blue eyes that ever beamed beneath a forehead of snowy whiteness, over which dark brown and waving hair fell less in curls than masses of locky richness, could only have known what wild work they were making of my poor heart, Miss Dashwood, I trust, would have looked at her teacup or her muffin rather than at me, as she actually did on that fatal morning. If I were to judge from her costume, she had only just arrived, and the morning air had left upon her cheek a bloom that contributed greatly to the effect of her lovely countenance. Although very young, her form had all the roundness of womanhood; while her gay and sprightly manner indicated all the *sans gêne* which only very young girls possess, and which, when tempered with perfect good taste, and accompanied by beauty and no small share of talent, forms an irresistible power of attraction.

Beside her sat a tall, handsome man of about five-and-thirty or perhaps forty years of age, with a most soldierly air, who as I was presented to him scarcely turned his head, and gave me a half-nod of very unequivocal coldness. There are moments in life in which the heart is, as it were, laid bare to any chance or casual impression with a wondrous sensibility of pleasure or its opposite. This to me was one of those; and as I turned from the lovely girl, who had received me with a marked courtesy, to the cold air and repelling *hauteur* of the dark-browed captain, the blood rushed throbbing to my forehead; and as I walked to my place at the table, I eagerly sought his eye, to return him a look of defiance and disdain, proud and contemptuous as his own. Captain Hammersley, however, never took further notice of me, but continued to recount, for the amusement of those about him, several excellent stories of his military career, which, I confess, were heard with every test of delight by all save me. One thing galled me particularly,— and how easy is it, when you have begun by disliking a person, to supply food for your antipathy,—all his allusions to his military life were coupled with half-hinted and ill-concealed sneers at civilians of every kind, as though every man not a soldier were absolutely unfit for common intercourse with the world, still more for any favorable reception in ladies' society.

The young ladies of the family were a well-chosen auditory, for their admiration of the army extended from the Life Guards to the Veteran Battalion, the Sappers and Miners included; and as Miss Dashwood was the daughter of a soldier, she of course coincided in many of, if not all, his opinions. I turned towards my neighbor, a Clare gentleman, and tried to engage him in conversation, but he was breathlessly attending to the captain. On my left sat Matthew Blake, whose eyes were firmly riveted upon the same person, and who heard his marvels with an interest scarcely inferior to that of his sisters. Annoyed and in ill-temper, I ate my breakfast in silence, and resolved that the first moment I could obtain a hearing from Mr. Blake I would open my negotiation, and take my leave at once of Gurt-na-Morra.

We all assembled in a large room, called by courtesy the library, when breakfast was over; and then it was that Mr. Blake, taking me aside, whispered, "Charley, it's right I should inform you that Sir George Dashwood there is the Commander of the Forces, and is come down here at this moment to—" What for, or how it should concern me, I was not to learn; for at that critical instant my informant's attention was called off by Captain Hammersley asking if the hounds were to hunt that day.

"My friend Charley here is the best authority upon that matter," said Mr. Blake, turning towards me.

"They are to try the Priest's meadows," said I, with an air of some importance; "but if your guests desire a day's sport, I'll send word over to Brackely to bring the dogs over here, and we are sure to find a fox in your cover."

"Oh, then, by all means," said the captain, turning towards Mr. Blake, and addressing himself to him,—"by all means; and Miss Dashwood, I'm sure, would like to see the hounds throw off."

Whatever chagrin the first part of his speech caused me, the latter set my heart a-throbbing; and I hastened from the room to despatch a messenger to the huntsman to come over to Gurt-na-Morra, and also another to O'Malley Castle to bring my best horse and my riding equipments as quickly as possible.

"Matthew, who is this captain?" said I, as young Blake met me in the hall.

"Oh, he is the aide-de-camp of General Dashwood. A nice fellow, isn't he?"

"I don't know what you may think," said I, "but I take him for the most impertinent, impudent, supercilious—"

The rest of my civil speech was cut short by the appearance of the very individual in question, who, with his hands in his pockets and a cigar in his mouth, sauntered forth down the steps, taking no more notice of Matthew Blake and myself than the two fox-terriers that followed at his heels.

However anxious I might be to open negotiations on the subject of my mission, for the present the thing was impossible; for I found that Sir George Dashwood was closeted closely with Mr. Blake, and resolved to wait till evening, when chance might afford me the opportunity I desired.

As the ladies had retired to dress for the hunt, and as I felt no peculiar desire to ally myself with the unsocial captain, I accompanied Matthew to the stable to look after the cattle, and make preparations for the coming sport.

"There's Captain Hammersley's mare," said Matthew, as he pointed out a highly bred but powerful English hunter. "She came last night; for as he expected some sport, he sent his horses from Dublin on purpose. The others will be here to-day."

"What is his regiment?" said I, with an appearance of carelessness, but in reality feeling curious to know if the captain was a cavalry or infantry officer.

"The —th Light Dragoons,"

"You never saw him ride?" said I.

"Never; but his groom there says he leads the way in his own country."

"And where may that be?"

"In Leicestershire, no less," said Matthew.

"Does he know Galway?"

"Never was in it before. It's only this minute he asked Moses Daly if the ox-fences were high here."

"Ox-fences! Then he does not know what a wall is?"

"Devil a bit; but we'll teach him."

"That we will," said I, with as bitter a resolution to impart the instruction as ever schoolmaster did to whip Latin grammar into one of the great unbreeched.

"But I had better send the horses down to the Mill," said Matthew; "we'll draw that cover first."

So saying, he turned towards the stable, while I sauntered alone towards the road by which I expected the huntsman. I had not walked half a mile before I heard the yelping of the dogs, and a little farther on I saw old Brackely coming along at a brisk trot, cutting the hounds on each side, and calling after the stragglers.

"Did you see my horse on the road, Brackely?" said I.

"I did, Misther Charles; and troth, I'm sorry to see him. Sure yerself knows better than to take out the Badger, the best steeple-chaser in Ireland, in such a country as this,—nothing but awkward stone-fences, and not a foot of sure ground in the whole of it."

"I know it well, Brackely; but I have my reasons for it."

"Well, may be you have; what cover will your honor try first?"

"They talk of the Mill," said I; "but I'd much rather try Morran-a-Gowl."

"Morran-a-Gowl! Do you want to break your neck entirely?"

"No, Brackely, not mine."

"Whose, then, alannah?"

"An English captain's, the devil fly away with him! He's come down here to-day, and from all I can see is a most impudent fellow; so, Brackely—"

"I understand. Well, leave it to me; and though I don't like the only deer-park wall on the hill, we'll try it this morning with the blessing. I'll take him down by Woodford, over the Devil's Mouth,—it's eighteen foot wide this minute with the late rains,—into the four callows; then over the stone-walls, down to Dangan; then take a short cast up the hill, blow him a bit, and give him the park wall at the top. You must come in then fresh, and give him the whole run home over Sleibhmich. The Badger knows it all, and takes the road always in a fly,—a mighty distressing thing for the horse that follows, more particularly if he does not understand a stony country. Well, if he lives through this, give him the sunk fence and the stone wall at Mr. Blake's clover-field, for the hounds will run into the fox about there; and though we never ride that leap since Mr. Malone broke his neck at it, last October, yet upon an occasion like this, and for the honor of Galway—"

"To be sure, Brackely; and here's a guinea for you, and now trot on towards the house. They must not see us together, or they might suspect something. But, Brackely," said I, calling out after him, "if he rides at all fair, what's to be done?"

"Troth, then, myself doesn't know. There is nothing so bad west of Athlone. Have ye a great spite again him?"

"I have," said I, fiercely.

"Could ye coax a fight out of him?"

"That's true," said I; "and now ride on as fast as you can."

Brackely's last words imparted a lightness to my heart and my step, and I strode along a very different man from what I had left the house half an hour previously.

CHAPTER IV.

THE HUNT.

Although we had not the advantages of a southerly wind and cloudy sky, the day towards noon became strongly over-cast, and promised to afford us good scenting weather; and as we assembled at the meet, mutual congratulations were exchanged upon the improved appearance of the day. Young Blake had provided Miss Dashwood with a quiet and well-trained horse, and his sisters were all mounted as usual upon their own animals, giving to our turnout quite a gay and lively aspect. I myself came to cover upon a hackney, having sent Badger with a groom, and longed ardently for the moment when, casting the skin of my great-coat and overalls, I should appear before the world in my well-appointed "cords and tops." Captain Hammersley had not as yet made his appearance, and many conjectures were afloat as to whether "he might have missed the road, or changed his mind," or "forgot all about it," as Miss Dashwood hinted.

"Who, pray, pitched upon this cover?" said Caroline Blake, as she looked with a practised eye over the country on either side.

"There is no chance of a fox late in the day at the Mill," said the huntsman, inventing a lie for the occasion.

"Then of course you never intend us to see much of the sport; for after you break cover, you are entirely lost to us."

"I thought you always followed the hounds," said Miss Dashwood, timidly.

"Oh, to be sure we do, in any common country, but here it is out of the question; the fences are too large for any one, and if I am not mistaken, these gentlemen will not ride far over this. There, look yonder, where the river is rushing down the hill: that stream, widening as it advances, crosses the cover nearly midway,—well, they must clear that; and then you may see these walls of large loose stones nearly five feet in height. That is the usual course the fox takes, unless he heads towards the hills and goes towards Dangan, and then there's an end of it; for the deer-park wall is usually a pull up to every one except, perhaps, to our friend Charley yonder, who has tried his fortune against drowning more than once there."

"Look, here he comes," said Matthew Blake, "and looking splendidly too,—a little too much in flesh perhaps, if anything."

"Captain Hammersley!" said the four Miss Blakes, in a breath. "Where is he?"

"No; it's the Badger I'm speaking of," said Matthew, laughing, and pointing with his finger towards a corner of the field where my servant was leisurely throwing down a wall about two feet high to let him pass.

"Oh, how handsome! What a charger for a dragoon!" said Miss Dashwood.

Any other mode of praising my steed would have been much more acceptable. The word "dragoon" was a thorn in my tenderest part that rankled and lacerated at every stir. In a moment I was in the saddle, and scarcely seated when at once all the *mauvais honte* of boyhood left me, and I felt every inch a man. I often look back to that moment of my life, and comparing it with similar ones, cannot help acknowledging how purely is the self-possession which so often wins success the result of some slight and trivial association. My confidence in my horsemanship suggested moral courage of a very different kind; and I felt that Charles O'Malley curvetting upon a thorough-bred, and the same man ambling upon a shelty, were two and very dissimilar individuals.

"No chance of the captain," said Matthew, who had returned from a *reconnaissance* upon the road; "and after all it's a pity, for the day is getting quite favorable."

While the young ladies formed pickets to look out for the gallant *militaire*, I seized the opportunity of prosecuting my acquaintance with Miss Dashwood, and even in the few and passing observations that fell from her, learned how very different an order of being she was from all I had hitherto seen of country belles. A mixture of courtesy with *naïveté*; a wish to please, with a certain feminine gentleness, that always flatters a man, and still more a boy that fain would be one,—gained momentarily more and more upon me, and put me also on my mettle to prove to my fair companion that I was not altogether a mere uncultivated and unthinking creature, like the remainder of those about me.

"Here he is at last," said Helen Blake, as she cantered across a field waving her handkerchief as a signal to the captain, who was now seen approaching at a brisk trot.

As he came along, a small fence intervened; he pressed his horse a little, and as he kissed hands to the fair Helen, cleared it in a bound, and was in an instant in the midst of us.

"He sits his horse like a man, Misther Charles," said the old huntsman; "troth, we must give him the worst bit of it."

Captain Hammersley was, despite all the critical acumen with which I canvassed him, the very beau-ideal of a gentleman rider; indeed, although a very heavy man, his powerful English thorough-bred, showing not less bone than blood, took away all semblance of overweight; his saddle was well fitting and well placed, as also was his large and broad-reined snaffle; his own costume of black coat, leathers, and tops was in perfect keeping, and even to his heavy-handled hunting-whip I could find nothing to cavil at. As he rode up he paid his respects to the ladies in his usual free and easy manner, expressed some surprise, but no regret, at hearing that he was late, and never deigning any notice of Matthew or myself, took his place beside Miss Dashwood, with whom he conversed in a low undertone.

"There they go!" said Matthew, as five or six dogs, with their heads up, ran yelping along a furrow, then stopped, howled again, and once more set off together. In an instant all was commotion in the little valley below us. The huntsman, with his hand to his mouth, was calling off the stragglers, and the whipper-in followed up the leading dogs with the rest of the pack. "They've found! They're away!" said Matthew; and as he spoke a yell burst from the valley, and in an instant the whole pack were off at full speed. Rather more intent that moment upon showing off my horsemanship than anything else, I dashed spurs into Badger's sides, and turned him towards a rasping ditch before me; over we went, hurling down behind us a rotten bank of clay and small stones, showing how little safety there had been in topping instead of clearing it at a bound. Before I was well-seated again the captain was beside me. "Now for it, then," said I; and away we went. What might be the nature of his feelings I cannot pretend to state, but my own were a strange *mélange* of wild, boyish enthusiasm, revenge, and recklessness. For my own neck I cared little,—nothing; and as I led the way by half a length, I muttered to myself, "Let him follow me fairly this day, and I ask no more."

The dogs had got somewhat the start of us; and as they were in full cry, and going fast, we were a little behind. A thought therefore struck me that, by appearing to take a short cut upon the hounds, I should come down upon the river where its breadth was greatest, and thus, at one coup, might try my friend's mettle and his horse's performance at the same time. On we went, our speed increasing, till the roar of the river we were now approaching was plainly audible. I looked half around, and now perceived the captain was standing in his stirrups, as if to obtain a view of what was before him; otherwise his countenance was calm and unmoved, and not a muscle betrayed that he was not cantering on a parade. I fixed myself firmly in my seat, shook my horse a little together, and with a shout whose import every Galway hunter well knows rushed him at the river. I saw the water dashing among the large stones; I heard it splash; I felt a bound like the *ricochet* of a shot; and we were over, but so narrowly that the bank had yielded beneath his hind legs, and it needed a bold effort of the noble animal to regain his footing. Scarcely was he once more firm, when Hammersley flew by me, taking the lead, and sitting quietly in his saddle, as if racing. I know of little in my after-life like the agony of that moment; for although I was far, very far, from wishing real ill to him, yet I would gladly have broken my leg or my arm if he could not have been able to follow me. And now, there he was, actually a length and a half in advance! and worse than all, Miss Dashwood must have witnessed the whole, and doubtless his leap over the river was better and bolder than mine. One consolation yet remained, and while I whispered it to myself I felt comforted again. "His is an English mare. They understand these leaps; but what can he make of a Galway wall?" The question was soon to be solved. Before us, about three fields, were the hounds still in full cry; a large stone-wall lay between, and to it we both directed our course together. "Ha!" thought I, "he is floored at last," as I perceived that the captain held his course rather more in hand, and suffered me to lead. "Now, then, for it!" So saying, I rode at the largest part I could find, well knowing that Badger's powers were here in their element. One spring, one plunge, and away we were, galloping along at the other side. Not so the captain; his horse had refused the fence, and he was now taking a circuit of the field for another trial of it.

"Pounded, by Jove!" said I, as I turned round in my saddle to observe him. Once more she came at it, and once more balked, rearing up, at the same time, almost so as to fall backward.

My triumph was complete; and I again was about to follow the hounds, when, throwing a look back, I saw Hammersley clearing the wall in a most splendid manner, and taking a stretch of at least thirteen feet beyond it. Once more he was on my flanks, and the contest renewed. Whatever might be the sentiments of the riders (mine I confess to), between the horses it now became a tremendous struggle. The English mare, though evidently superior in stride and strength, was slightly overweighted, and had not, besides, that cat-like activity an Irish horse possesses; so that the advantages and disadvantages on either side were about equalized. For about half an hour now the pace was awful. We rode side by side, taking our leaps at exactly the same instant, and not four feet apart. The hounds were still considerably in advance, and were heading towards the Shannon, when suddenly the fox doubled, took the hillside, and made for Dangan. "Now, then, comes the trial of strength," I said, half aloud, as I threw my eye up a steep and rugged mountain, covered with wild furze and tall heath, around the crest of which ran, in a zigzag direction, a broken and dilapidated wall, once the enclosure of a deer park. This wall, which varied from four to six feet in height, was of solid masonry, and would, in the most favorable ground, have been a bold leap. Here, at the summit of a mountain, with not a yard of footing, it was absolutely desperation.

By the time that we reached the foot of the hill, the fox, followed closely by the hounds, had passed through a breach in the wall; while Matthew Blake, with the huntsmen and whipper-in, was riding along in search of a gap to lead the horses through. Before I put spurs to Badger to face the hill, I turned one look towards Hammersley. There was a slight curl, half-smile, half-sneer, upon his lip that actually maddened me, and had a precipice yawned beneath my feet, I should have dashed at it after that. The ascent was so steep that I was obliged to take the hill in a slanting direction; and even thus, the loose footing rendered it dangerous in the extreme.

At length I reached the crest, where the wall, more than five feet in height, stood frowning above and seeming to defy me. I turned my horse full round, so that his very chest almost touched the stones, and with a bold cut of the whip and a loud halloo, the gallant animal rose, as if rearing, pawed for an instant to regain his balance, and then, with a frightful struggle, fell backwards, and rolled from top to bottom of the hill, carrying me along with him; the last object that crossed my sight, as I lay bruised and motionless, being the captain as he took the wall in a flying leap, and disappeared at the other side. After a few scrambling efforts to rise, Badger regained his legs and stood beside me; but such was the shock and concussion of my fall that all the objects around seemed wavering and floating before me, while showers of bright sparks fell in myriads before my eyes. I tried to rise, but fell back helpless. Cold perspiration broke over my forehead, and I fainted. From that moment I can remember nothing, till I felt myself galloping along at full speed upon a level table-land, with the hounds about three fields in advance, Hammersley riding foremost, and taking all his leaps coolly as ever. As I swayed to either side upon my saddle, from weakness, I was lost to all thought or recollection, save a flickering memory of some plan of vengeance, which still urged me forward. The chase had now lasted above an hour, and both hounds and horses began to feel the pace at which they were going. As for me, I rode mechanically; I neither knew nor cared for the dangers before me. My eye rested on but one object; my whole being was concentrated upon one vague and undefined sense of revenge. At this instant the huntsman came alongside of me.

"Are you hurted, Misther Charles? Did you fall? Your cheek is all blood, and your coat is torn in two; and, Mother o' God! his boot is ground to powder; he does not hear me! Oh, pull up! pull up, for the love of the Virgin! There's the clover-field and the sunk fence before you, and you'll be killed on the spot!"

"Where?" cried I, with the cry of a madman. "Where's the clover-field; where's the sunk fence? Ha! I see it; I see it now."

So saying, I dashed the rowels into my horse's flanks, and in an instant was beyond the reach of the poor fellow's remonstances. Another moment I was beside the captain. He turned round as I came up; the same smile was upon his mouth; I could have struck him. About three hundred yards before us lay the sunk fence; its breadth was about twenty feet, and a wall of close brickwork formed its face. Over this the hounds were now clambering; some succeeded in crossing, but by far the greater number fell back, howling, into the ditch.

I turned towards Hammersley. He was standing high in his stirrups, and as he looked towards the yawning fence, down which the dogs were tumbling in masses, I thought (perhaps it was but a thought) that his cheek was paler. I looked again; he was pulling at his horse. Ha! it was true then; he would not face it. I turned round in my saddle, looked him full in the face, and as I pointed with my whip to the leap, called out in a voice hoarse with passion, "Come on!" I saw no more. All objects were lost to me from that moment. When next my senses cleared, I was standing amidst the dogs, where they had just killed. Badger stood blown and trembling beside me, his head drooping and his flanks gored with spur-marks. I looked about, but all consciousness of the past had fled; the concussion of my fall had shaken my intellect, and I was like one but half-awake. One glimpse, short and fleeting, of what was taking place shot through my brain, as old Brackely whispered to me, "By my soul, ye did for the captain there." I turned a vague look upon him, and my eyes fell upon the figure of a man that lay stretched and bleeding upon a door before me. His pale face was crossed with a purple stream of blood that trickled from a wound beside his eyebrow; his arms lay motionless and heavily at either side. I knew him not. A loud report of a pistol aroused me from my stupor; I looked back. I saw a crowd that broke suddenly asunder and fled right and left. I heard a heavy crash upon the ground; I pointed with my finger, for I could not utter a word.

"It is the English mare, yer honor; she was a beauty this morning, but she's broke her shoulder-bone and both her legs, and it was best to put her out of pain."

CHAPTER V.

THE DRAWING-ROOM.

On the fourth day following the adventure detailed in the last chapter, I made my appearance in the drawing-room, my cheek well blanched by copious bleeding, and my step tottering and uncertain. On entering the room, I looked about in vain for some one who might give me an insight into the occurrences of the four preceding days; but no one was to be met with. The ladies, I learned, were out riding; Matthew was buying a new setter, Mr. Blake was canvassing, and Captain Hammersley was in bed. Where was Miss Dashwood?—in her room; and Sir George?—he was with Mr. Blake.

"What! Canvassing, too?"

"Troth, that same was possible," was the intelligent reply of the old butler, at which I could not help smiling. I sat down, therefore, in the easiest chair I could find, and unfolding the county paper, resolved upon learning how matters were going on in the political world. But somehow, whether the editor was not brilliant or the fire was hot or that my own dreams were pleasanter to indulge in than his fancies, I fell sound asleep.

How differently is the mind attuned to the active, busy world of thought and action when awakened from sleep by any sudden and rude summons to arise and be stirring, and when called into existence by the sweet and silvery notes of softest music stealing over the senses, and while they impart awakening thoughts of bliss and beauty, scarcely dissipating the dreamy influence of slumber! Such was my first thought, as, with closed lids, the thrilling chords of a harp broke upon my sleep and aroused me to a feeling of unutterable pleasure. I turned gently round in my chair and beheld Miss Dashwood. She was seated in a recess of an old-fashioned window; the pale yellow glow of a wintry sun at evening fell upon her beautiful hair, and tinged it with such a light as I have often since then seen in Rembrandt's pictures; her head leaned upon the harp, and as she struck its chords at random, I saw that her mind was far away from all around her. As I looked, she suddenly started from her leaning attitude, and parting back her curls from her brow, she preluded a few chords, and then sighed forth, rather than sang, that most beautiful of Moore's melodies,—

"She is far from the land where her young hero sleeps."

Never before had such pathos, such deep utterance of feeling, met my astonished sense; I listened breathlessly as the tears fell one by one down my cheek; my bosom heaved and fell; and when she ceased, I hid my head between my hands and sobbed aloud. In an instant, she was beside me, and placing her hand upon my shoulder, said,—

"Poor dear boy, I never suspected you of being there, or I should not have sung that mournful air."

I started and looked up; and from what I know not, but she suddenly crimsoned to her very forehead, while she added in a less assured tone,—

"I hope, Mr. O'Malley, that you are much better; and I trust there is no imprudence in your being here."

"For the latter, I shall not answer," said I, with a sickly smile; "but already I feel your music has done me service."

"Then let me sing more for you."

"If I am to have a choice, I should say, Sit down, and let me hear you talk to me. My illness and the doctor together have made wild work of my poor brain; but if you will talk to me—"

"Well, then, what shall it be about? Shall I tell you a fairy tale?"

"I need it not; I feel I am in one this instant."

"Well, then, what say you to a legend; for I am rich in my stores of them?"

"The O'Malleys have their chronicles, wild and barbarous enough without the aid of Thor and Woden."

"Then, shall we chat of every-day matters? Should you like to hear how the election and the canvass go on?"

"Yes; of all things."

"Well, then, most favorably. Two baronies, with most unspeakable names, have declared for us, and confidence is rapidly increasing among our party. This I learned, by chance, yesterday; for papa never permits us to know anything of these matters,—not even the names of the candidates."

"Well, that was the very point I was coming to; for the government were about to send down some one just as I left home, and I am most anxious to learn who it is."

"Then am I utterly valueless; for I really can't say what party the government espouses, and only know of our own."

"Quite enough for me that you wish it success," said I, gallantly. "Perhaps you can tell me if my uncle has heard of my accident?"

"Oh, yes; but somehow he has not been here himself, but sent a friend,—a Mr. Considine, I think; a very strange person he seemed. He demanded to see papa, and it seems, asked him if your misfortune had been a thing of his contrivance, and whether he was ready to explain his conduct about it; and, in fact, I believe he is mad."

"Heaven confound him!" I muttered between my teeth.

"And then he wished to have an interview with Captain Hammersley. However, he is too ill; but as the doctor hoped he might be down-stairs in a week, Mr. Considine kindly hinted that he should wait."

"Oh, then, do tell me how is the captain."

"Very much bruised, very much disfigured, they say," said she, half smiling; "but not so much hurt in body as in mind."

"As how, may I ask?" said I, with an appearance of innocence.

"I don't exactly understand it; but it would appear that there was something like rivalry among you gentlemen *chasseurs* on that luckless morning, and that while you paid the penalty of a broken head, he was destined to lose his horse and break his arm."

"I certainly am sorry,—most sincerely sorry for any share I might have had in the catastrophe; and my greatest regret, I confess, arises from the fact that I should cause *you* unhappiness."

"*Me*? Pray explain."

"Why, as Captain Hammersley—"

"Mr. O'Malley, you are too young now to make me suspect you have an intention to offend; but I caution you, never repeat this."

I saw that I had transgressed, but how, I most honestly confess, I could not guess; for though I certainly was the senior of my fair companion in years, I was most lamentably her junior in tact and discretion.

The gray dusk of evening had long fallen as we continued to chat together beside the blazing wood embers,—she evidently amusing herself with the original notions of an untutored, unlettered boy, and I drinking deep those draughts of love that nerved my heart through many a breach and battlefield.

Our colloquy was at length interrupted by the entrance of Sir George, who shook me most cordially by the hand, and made the kindest inquiries about my health.

"They tell me you are to be a lawyer. Mr. O'Malley," said he; "and if so, I must advise you to take better care of your headpiece."

"A lawyer, Papa; oh dear me! I should never have thought of his being anything so stupid."

"Why, silly girl, what would you have a man be?"

"A dragoon, to be sure, Papa," said the fond girl, as she pressed her arm around his manly figure, and looked up in his face with an expression of mingled pride and affection.

That word sealed my destiny.

CHAPTER VI.

THE DINNER.

When I retired to my room to dress for dinner, I found my servant waiting with a note from my uncle, to which, he informed me, the messenger expected an answer.

I broke the seal and read:—

DEAR CHARLEY,—Do not lose a moment in securing old Blake,—if you have not already done so,—as information has just reached me that the government party has promised a cornetcy to young Matthew if he can bring over his father. And these are the people I have been voting with—a few private cases excepted—for thirty odd years! I am very sorry for your accident. Considine informs me that it will need explanation at a later period. He has been in Athlone since Tuesday, in hopes to catch the new candidate on his way down, and get him into a little private quarrel before the day; if he succeeds, it will save the county much expense, and conduce greatly to the peace and happiness of all parties. But "these things," as Father Roach says, "are in the hands of Providence." You must also persuade old Blake to write a few lines to Simon Mallock, about the Coolnamuck mortgage. We can give him no satisfaction at present, at least such as he looks for; and don't be philandering any longer where you are, when your health permits a change of quarters. Your affectionate uncle, GODFREY O'MALLEY. P.S. I have just heard from Considine. He was out this morning and shot a fellow in the knee; but finds that after all he was not the candidate, but a tourist that was writing a book about Connemara. P.S. No. 2. Bear the mortgage in mind, for old Mallock is a spiteful fellow, and has a grudge against me, since I horsewhipped his son in Banagher. Oh, the world, the world! G. O'M.

Until I read this very clear epistle to the end, I had no very precise conception how completely I had forgotten all my uncle's interests, and neglected all his injunctions. Already five days had elapsed, and I had not as much as mooted the question to Mr. Blake, and probably all this time my uncle was calculating on the thing as concluded; but, with one hole in my head and some half-dozen in my heart, my memory was none of the best.

18

Snatching up the letter, therefore, I resolved to lose no more time, and proceeded at once to Mr. Blake's room, expecting that I should, as the event proved, find him engaged in the very laborious duty of making his toilet.

"Come in, Charley," said he, as I tapped gently at the door. "It's only Charley, my darling. Mrs. B. won't mind you."

"Not the least in life," responded Mrs. B., disposing at the same time a pair of her husband's corduroys tippet fashion across her ample shoulders, which before were displayed in the plenitude and breadth of coloring we find in a Rubens. "Sit down, Charley, and tell us what's the matter."

As until this moment I was in perfect ignorance of the Adam-and-Eve-like simplicity in which the private economy of Mr. Blake's household was conducted, I would have gladly retired from what I found to be a mutual territory of dressing-room had not Mr. Blake's injunctions been issued somewhat like an order to remain.

"It's only a letter, sir," said I, stuttering, "from my uncle about the election. He says that as his majority is now certain, he should feel better pleased in going to the poll with all the family, you know, sir, along with him. He wishes me just to sound your intentions,—to make out how you feel disposed towards him; and—and, faith, as I am but a poor diplomatist, I thought the best way was to come straight to the point and tell you so."

"I perceive," said Mr. Blake, giving his chin at the moment an awful gash with the razor,—"I perceive; go on."

"Well, sir, I have little more to say. My uncle knows what influence you have in Scariff, and expects you'll do what you can there."

"Anything more?" said Blake, with a very dry and quizzical expression I didn't half like,—"anything more?"

"Oh, yes; you are to write a line to old Mallock."

"I understand; about Coolnamuck, isn't it?"

"Exactly; I believe that's all."

"Well, now, Charley, you may go down-stairs, and we'll talk it over after dinner."

"Yes, Charley dear, go down, for I'm going to draw on my stockings," said the fair Mrs. Blake, with a look of very modest consciousness.

When I had left the room I couldn't help muttering a "Thank God!" for the success of a mission I more than once feared for, and hastened to despatch a note to my uncle, assuring him of the Blake interest, and adding that for propriety's sake I should defer my departure for a day or two longer.

This done, with a heart lightened of its load and in high spirits at my cleverness, I descended to the drawing-room. Here a very large party were already assembled, and at every opening of the door a new relay of Blakes, Burkes, and Bodkins was introduced. In the absence of the host, Sir George Dashwood was "making the agreeable" to the guests, and shook hands with every new arrival with all the warmth and cordiality of old friendship. While thus he inquired for various absent individuals, and asked most affectionately for sundry aunts and uncles not forthcoming, a slight incident occurred which by its ludicrous turn served to shorten the long half-hour before dinner. An individual of the party, a Mr. Blake, had, from certain peculiarities of face, obtained in his boyhood the sobriquet of "Shave-the-wind." This hatchet-like conformation had grown with his growth, and perpetuated upon him a nickname by which alone was he ever spoken of among his friends and acquaintances; the only difference being that as he came to man's estate, brevity, that soul of wit, had curtailed the epithet to mere "Shave." Now, Sir George had been hearing frequent reference made to him always by this name, heard him ever so addressed, and perceived him to reply to it; so that when he was himself asked by some one what sport he had found that day among the woodcocks, he answered at once, with a bow of very grateful acknowledgment, "Excellent, indeed; but entirely owing to where I was placed in the copse. Had it not been for Mr. Shave there—"

I need not say that the remainder of his speech, being heard on all sides, became one universal shout of laughter, in which, to do him justice, the excellent Shave himself heartily joined. Scarcely were the sounds of mirth lulled into an apparent calm, when the door opened and the host and hostess appeared. Mrs. Blake advanced in all the plenitude of her charms, arrayed in crimson satin, sorely injured in its freshness by a patch of grease upon the front about the same size and shape as the continent of Europe in Arrowsmith's Atlas. A swan's-down tippet covered her shoulders; massive bracelets ornamented her wrists; while from her ears descended two Irish diamond ear-rings, rivalling in magnitude and value the glass pendants of a lustre. Her reception of her guests made ample amends, in warmth and cordiality, for any deficiency of elegance; and as she disposed her ample proportions upon the sofa, and looked around upon the company, she appeared the very impersonation of hospitality.

After several openings and shuttings of the drawing-room door, accompanied by the appearance of old Simon the butler, who counted the party at least five times before he was certain that the score was correct, dinner was at length announced. Now came a moment of difficulty, and one which, as testing Mr. Blake's tact, he would gladly have seen devolve upon some other shoulders; for he well knew that the marshalling a room full of mandarins, blue, green, and yellow, was "cakes and gingerbread" to ushering a Galway party in to dinner.

First, then, was Mr. Miles Bodkin, whose grandfather would have been a lord if Cromwell had not hanged him one fine morning. Then Mrs. Mosey Blake's first husband was promised the title of Kilmacud if it was ever restored; whereas Mrs. French of Knocktunmor's mother was then at law for a title. And lastly, Mrs. Joe Burke was fourth cousin to Lord Clanricarde, as is or will be every Burke from this to the day of judgment. Now, luckily for her prospects, the lord was alive; and Mr. Blake, remembering a very sage adage about "dead lions," etc., solved the difficulty at once by gracefully tucking the lady under his arm and leading the way. The others soon followed, the priest of Portumna and my unworthy self bringing up the rear.

When, many a year afterwards, the hard ground of a mountain bivouac, with its pitiful portion of pickled cork-tree yclept mess-beef, and that pyroligneous aquafortis they call corn-brandy have been my hard fare, I often looked back to that day's dinner with a most heart-yearning sensation,—a turbot as big as the Waterloo shield, a sirloin that seemed cut from the sides of a rhinoceros, a sauce-boat that contained an oyster-bed. There was a turkey, which singly would have formed the main army of a French dinner, doing mere outpost duty, flanked by a picket of ham and a detached squadron of chickens carefully ambushed in a forest of greens; potatoes, not disguised *à la maître d'hôtel* and tortured to resemble bad macaroni, but piled like shot in an ordnance-yard, were posted at different quarters; while massive decanters of port and sherry stood proudly up like standard bearers amidst the goodly array. This was none of your austere "great dinners," where a cold and chilling *plateau* of artificial nonsense cuts off one-half of the table from intercourse with the other; when whispered sentences constitute the conversation, and all the friendly recognition of wine-drinking, which renews acquaintance and cements an intimacy, is replaced by the ceremonious filling of your glass by a lackey; where smiles go current in lieu of kind speeches, and epigram and smartness form the substitute for the broad jest and merry story. Far from it. Here the company ate, drank, talked, laughed,—did all but sing, and certainly enjoyed themselves heartily. As for me, I was little more than a listener; and such was the crash of plates, the jingle of glasses, and the clatter of voices, that fragments only of what was passing around reached me, giving to the conversation of the party a character occasionally somewhat incongruous. Thus such sentences as the following ran foul of each other every instant:—

"No better land in Galway"—"where could you find such facilities"—"for shooting Mr. Jones on his way home"—"the truth, the whole truth, and nothing but the truth"—"kiss"—"Miss Blake, she's the girl with a foot and ankle"—"Daly has never had wool on his sheep"—"how could he"—"what does he pay for the mountain"—"four and tenpence a yard"—"not a penny less"—"all the cabbage-stalks and potato-skins"—"with some bog stuff through it"—"that's the thing to"—"make soup, with a red herring in it instead of salt"—"and when he proposed for my niece, ma'am, says he"—"mix a strong tumbler, and I'll make a shake-down for you on the floor"—"and may the Lord have mercy on your soul"—"and now, down the middle and up again"—"Captain Magan, my dear, he is the man"—"to shave a pig properly"—"it's not money I'm looking for, says he, the girl of my heart"—"if she had not a wind-gall and two spavins"—"I'd have given her the rights of the church, of coorse," said Father Roach, bringing up the rear of this ill-assorted jargon.

Such were the scattered links of conversation I was condemned to listen to, till a general rise on the part of the ladies left us alone to discuss our wine and enter in good earnest upon the more serious duties of the evening.

Scarcely was the door closed when one of the company, seizing the bell-rope, said, "With your leave, Blake, we'll have the 'dew' now."

"Good claret,—no better," said another; "but it sits mighty cold on the stomach."

"There's nothing like the groceries, after all,—eh, Sir George?" said an old Galway squire to the English general, who acceded to the fact, which he understood in a very different sense.

"Oh, punch, you are my darlin'," hummed another, as a large, square, half-gallon decanter of whiskey was placed on the table, the various decanters of wine being now ignominiously sent down to the end of the board without any evidence of regret on any face save Sir George Dashwood's, who mixed his tumbler with a very rebellious conscience.

Whatever were the noise and clamor of the company before, they were nothing to what now ensued. As one party were discussing the approaching contest, another was planning a steeple-chase, while two individuals, unhappily removed from each other the entire length of the table, were what is called "challenging each other's effects" in a very remarkable manner,—the process so styled being an exchange of property, when each party, setting an imaginary value upon some article, barters it for another, the amount of boot paid and received being determined by a third person, who is the umpire. Thus a gold breast-pin was swopped, as the phrase is, against a horse; then a pair of boots, then a Kerry bull, etc.,—every imaginable species of property coming into the market. Sometimes, as matters of very dubious value turned up, great laughter was the result. In this very national pastime, a Mr. Miles Bodkin, a noted fire-eater of the west, was a great proficient; and it is said he once so completely succeeded in despoiling an uninitiated hand, that after winning in succession his horse, gig, harness, etc., he proceeded *seriatim* to his watch, ring, clothes, and portmanteau, and actually concluded by winning all he possessed, and kindly lent him a card-cloth to cover him on his way to the hotel. His success on the present occasion was considerable, and his spirits proportionate. The decanter had thrice been replenished, and the flushed faces and thickened utterance of the guests evinced that from the cold properties of the claret there was but little to dread. As for Mr. Bodkin, his manner was incapable of any higher flight, when under the influence of whiskey, than what it evinced on common occasions; and as he sat at the end of the table fronting Mr. Blake, he assumed all the dignity of the ruler of the feast, with an energy no one seemed disposed to question. In answer to some observations of Sir George, he was led into something like an oration upon the peculiar excellences of his native country, which ended in a declaration that there was nothing like Galway.

"Why don't you give us a song, Miles? And may be the general would learn more from it than all your speech-making."

"To be sure," cried the several voices together,—"to be sure; let us hear the 'Man for Galway'!"

Sir George having joined most warmly in the request, Mr. Bodkin filled up his glass to the brim, bespoke a chorus to his chant, and clearing his voice with a deep hem, began the following ditty, to the air which Moore has since rendered immortal by the beautiful song, "Wreath the Bowl," etc. And, although the words are well known in the west, for the information of less-favored regions, I here transcribe—

THE MAN FOR GALWAY. To drink a toast, A proctor roast, Or bailiff as the case is; To kiss your wife, Or take your life At ten or fifteen paces; To keep game-cocks, to hunt the fox, To drink in punch the Solway, With debts galore, but fun far more,— Oh, that's "the man for Galway." CHORUS: With debts, etc. The King of Oude Is mighty proud, And so were onst the Caysars; But ould Giles Eyre Would make them stare, Av he had them with the Blazers. To the devil I fling—ould Runjeet Sing, He's only a prince in a small way, And knows nothing at all of a six-foot wall; Oh, he'd never "do for Galway." CHORUS: With debts, etc. Ye think the Blakes Are no "great shakes;" They're all his blood relations. And the Bodkins sneeze At the grim Chinese, For they come from the Phenaycians. So fill the brim, and here's to him Who'd drink in punch the Solway, With debts galore, but fun far more,— Oh, that's "the man for Galway." CHORUS: With debts, etc.

I much fear that the reception of this very classic ode would not be as favorable in general companies as it was on the occasion I first heard it; for certainly the applause was almost deafening, and even Sir George, the defects of whose English education left some of the allusions out of his reach, was highly amused, and laughed heartily.

The conversation once more reverted to the election; and although I was too far from those who seemed best informed on the matter to hear much, I could catch enough to discover that the feeling was a confident one. This was gratifying to me, as I had some scruples about my so long neglecting my uncle's cause.

"We have Scariff to a man," said Bodkin.

"And Mosey's tenantry," said another. "I swear, though there's not a freehold registered on the estate, that they'll vote, every mother's son of them, or devil a stone of the court-house they'll leave standing on another."

"And may the Lord look to the returning officer!" said a third, throwing up his eyes.

"Mosey's tenantry are droll boys; and like their landlord, more by token, they never pay any rent."

"And what for shouldn't they vote?" said a dry-looking little old fellow in a red waistcoat; "when I was the dead agent—"

"The dead agent!" interrupted Sir George, with a start.

"Just so," said the old fellow, pulling down his spectacles from his forehead, and casting a half-angry look at Sir George, for what he had suspected to be a doubt of his veracity.

"The general does not know, may be, what that is," said some one.

"You have just anticipated me," said Sir George; "I really am in most profound ignorance."

"It is the dead agent," says Mr. Blake, "who always provides substitutes for any voters that may have died since the last election. A very important fact in statistics may thus be gathered from the poll-books of this county, which proves it to be the healthiest part of Europe,—a freeholder has not died in it for the last fifty years."

"The 'Kiltopher boys' won't come this time; they say there's no use trying to vote when so many were transported last assizes for perjury."

"They're poor-spirited creatures," said another.

"Not they,—they are as decent boys as any we have; they're willing to wreck the town for fifty shillings' worth of spirits. Besides, if they don't vote for the county, they will for the borough."

This declaration seemed to restore these interesting individuals to favor; and now all attention was turned towards Bodkin, who was detailing the plan of a grand attack upon the polling-booths, to be headed by himself. By this time, all the prudence and guardedness of the party had given way; whiskey was in the ascendant, and every bold stroke of election policy, every cunning artifice, every ingenious device, was detailed and applauded in a manner which proved that self-respect was not the inevitable gift of "mountain dew."

The mirth and fun grew momentarily more boisterous, and Miles Bodkin, who had twice before been prevented proposing some toast by a telegraphic signal from the other end of the table, now swore that nothing should prevent him any longer, and rising with a smoking tumbler in his hand, delivered himself as follows:—

"No, no, Phil Blake, ye needn't be winkin' at me that way; it's little I care for the spawn of the ould serpent. [Here great cheers greeted the speaker, in which, without well knowing why, I heartily joined.] I'm going to give a toast, boys,—a real good toast, none of your sentimental things about wall-flowers or the vernal equinox, or that kind of thing, but a sensible, patriotic, manly, intrepid toast,—toast you must drink in the most universal, laborious, and awful manner: do ye see now? [Loud cheers.] If any man of you here present doesn't drain this toast to the bottom [here the speaker looked fixedly at me, as did the rest of the company]—then, by the great-gun of Athlone, I'll make him eat the decanter, glass-stopper and all, for the good of his digestion: d'ye see now?"

The cheering at this mild determination prevented my hearing what followed; but the peroration consisted in a very glowing eulogy upon some person unknown, and a speedy return to him as member for Galway. Amidst all the noise and tumult at this critical moment, nearly every eye at the table was turned upon me; and as I concluded that they had been drinking my uncle's health, I thundered away at the mahogany with all my energy. At length the hip-hipping over, and comparative quiet restored, I rose from my seat to return thanks; but, strange enough, Sir George Dashwood did so likewise. And there we both stood, amidst an uproar that might well have shaken the courage of more practised orators; while from every side came cries of "Hear, hear!"—"Go on, Sir George!"—"Speak out, General!"—"Sit down, Charley!"—"Confound the boy!"—"Knock the legs from under him!" etc. Not understanding why Sir George should interfere with what I regarded as my peculiar duty, I resolved not to give way, and avowed this determination in no very equivocal terms. "In that case," said the general, "I am to suppose that the young gentleman moves an amendment to your proposition; and as the etiquette is in his favor, I yield." Here he resumed his place amidst a most terrific scene of noise and tumult, while several humane proposals as to my treatment were made around me, and a kind suggestion thrown out to break my neck by a near neighbor. Mr. Blake at length prevailed upon the party to hear what I had to say,—for he was certain I should not detain them above a minute. The commotion having in some measure subsided, I began: "Gentlemen, as the adopted son of the worthy man whose health you have just drunk—" Heaven knows how I should have continued; but here my eloquence was met by such a roar of laughing as I never before listened to. From one end of the board to the other it was one continued shout, and went on, too, as if all the spare lungs of the party had been kept in reserve for the occasion. I turned from one to the other; I tried to smile, and seemed to participate in the joke, but failed; I frowned; I looked savagely about where I could see enough to turn my wrath thitherward,—and, as it chanced, not in vain; for Mr. Miles Bodkin, with an intuitive perception of my wishes, most suddenly ceased his mirth, and assuming a look of frowning defiance that had done him good service upon many former occasions, rose and said:—

"Well, sir, I hope you're proud of yourself. You've made a nice beginning of it, and a pretty story you'll have for your uncle. But if you'd like to break the news by a letter the general will have great pleasure in franking it for you; for, by the rock of Cashel, we'll carry him in against all the O'Malley's that ever cheated the sheriff."

Scarcely were the words uttered, when I seized my wineglass, and hurled it with all my force at his head; so sudden was the act, and so true the aim, that Mr. Bodkin measured his length upon the floor ere his friends could appreciate his late eloquent effusion. The scene now became terrific; for though the redoubted Miles was *hors-de-combat*, his friends made a tremendous rush at, and would infallibly have succeeded in capturing me, had not Blake and four or five others interposed. Amidst a desperate struggle, which lasted for some minutes, I was torn from the spot, carried bodily up-stairs, and pitched headlong into my own room; where, having doubly locked the door on the outside, they left me to my own cool and not over-agreeable reflections.

CHAPTER VII.
THE FLIGHT FROM GURT-NA-MORRA.

It was by one of those sudden and inexplicable revulsions which occasionally restore to sense and intellect the maniac of years standing, that I was no sooner left alone in my chamber than I became perfectly sober. The fumes of the wine—and I had drunk deeply—were dissipated at once; my head, which but a moment before was half wild with excitement, was now cool, calm, and collected; and stranger than all, I, who had only an hour since entered the dining-room with all the unsuspecting freshness of boyhood, became, by a mighty bound, a man,—a man in all my feelings of responsibility, a man who, repelling an insult by an outrage, had resolved to stake his life upon the chance. In an instant a new era in life had opened before me; the light-headed gayety which fearlessness and youth impart was replaced by one absorbing thought,—one all-engrossing, all-pervading impression, that if I did not follow up my quarrel with Bodkin, I was dishonored and disgraced, my little knowledge of such matters not being sufficient to assure me that I was now the aggressor, and that any further steps in the affair should come from his side.

So thoroughly did my own griefs occupy me, that I had no thought for the disappointment my poor uncle was destined to meet with in hearing that the Blake interest was lost to him, and the former breach between the families irreparably widened by the events of the evening. Escape was my first thought; but how to accomplish it? The door, a solid one of Irish oak, doubly locked and bolted, defied all my efforts to break it open; the window was at least five-and-twenty feet from the ground, and not a tree near to swing into. I shouted, I called aloud, I opened the sash, and tried if any one outside were within hearing; but in vain. Weary and exhausted, I sat down upon my bed and ruminated over my fortunes. Vengeance—quick, entire, decisive vengeance—I thirsted and panted for; and every moment I lived under the insult inflicted on me seemed an age of torturing and maddening agony. I rose with a leap; a thought had just occurred to me. I drew the bed towards the window, and fastening the sheet to one of the posts with a firm knot, I twisted it into a rope, and let myself down to within about twelve feet of the ground, when I let go my hold, and dropped upon the grass beneath safe and uninjured. A thin, misty rain was falling, and I now perceived, for the first time, that in my haste I had forgotten my hat; this thought, however, gave me little uneasiness, and I took my way towards the stable, resolving, if I could, to saddle my horse and get off before any intimation of my escape reached the family.

When I gained the yard, all was quiet and deserted; the servants were doubtless enjoying themselves below stairs, and I met no one on the way. I entered the stable, threw the saddle upon "Badger," and before five minutes from my descent from the window, was galloping towards O'Malley Castle at a pace that defied pursuit, had any one thought of it.

It was about five o'clock on a dark, wintry morning as I led my horse through the well-known defiles of out-houses and stables which formed the long line of offices to my uncle's house. As yet no one was stirring; and as I wished to have my arrival a secret from the family, after providing for the wants of my gallant gray, I lifted the latch of the kitchen-door—no other fastening being ever thought necessary, even at night—and gently groped my way towards the stairs; all was perfectly still, and the silence now recalled me to reflection as to what course I should pursue. It was all-important that my uncle should know nothing of my quarrel, otherwise he would inevitably make it his own, and by treating me like a boy in the matter, give the whole affair the very turn I most dreaded. Then, as to Sir Harry Boyle, he would most certainly turn the whole thing into ridicule, make a good story, perhaps a song out of it, and laugh at my notions of demanding satisfaction. Considine, I knew, was my man; but then he was at Athlone,—at least so my uncle's letter mentioned. Perhaps he might have returned; if not, to Athlone I should set off at once. So resolving, I stole noiselessly up-stairs, and reached the door of the count's chamber; I opened it gently and entered; and though my step was almost imperceptible to myself, it was quite sufficient to alarm the watchful occupant of the room, who, springing up in his bed, demanded gruffly, "Who's there?"

"Charles, sir," said I, shutting the door carefully, and approaching his bedside. "Charles O'Malley, sir. I'm come to have a bit of your advice; and as the affair won't keep, I have been obliged to disturb you."

"Never mind, Charley," said the count; "sit down, there's a chair somewhere near the bed,—have you found it? There! Well now, what is it? What news of Blake?"

"Very bad; no worse. But it is not exactly *that* I came about; I've got into a scrape, sir."

"Run off with one of the daughters," said Considine. "By jingo, I knew what those artful devils would be after."

"Not so bad as that," said I, laughing. "It's just a row, a kind of squabble; something that must come—"

"Ay, ay," said the count, brightening up; "say you so, Charley? Begad, the young ones will beat us all out of the field. Who is it with,—not old Blake himself; how was it? Tell me all."

I immediately detailed the whole events of the preceding chapter, as well as his frequent interruptions would permit, and concluded by asking what farther step was now to be taken, as I was resolved the matter should be concluded before it came to my uncle's ears.

"There you are all right; quite correct, my boy. But there are many points I should have wished otherwise in the conduct of the affair hitherto."

Conceiving that he was displeased at my petulance and boldness, I was about to commence a kind of defence, when he added,—

"Because, you see," said he, assuming an oracular tone of voice, "throwing a wine-glass, with or without wine, in a man's face is merely, as you may observe, a mark of denial and displeasure at some observation he may have made,—not in any wise intended to injure him, further than in the wound to his honor at being so insulted, for which, of course, he must subsequently call you out. Whereas, Charley, in the present case, the view I take is different; the expression of Mr. Bodkin, as regards your uncle, was insulting to a degree,—gratuitously offensive,—and warranting a blow. Therefore, my boy, you should, under such circumstances, have preferred aiming at him with a decanter: a cut-glass decanter, well aimed and low, I have seen do effective service. However, as you remark it was your first thing of the kind, I am pleased with you—very much pleased with you. Now, then, for the next step." So saying, he arose from his bed, and striking a light with a tinder-box, proceeded to dress himself as leisurely as if for a dinner party, talking all the while.

"I will just take Godfrey's tax-cart and the roan mare on to Meelish, put them up at the little inn,—it is not above a mile from Bodkin's; and I'll go over and settle the thing for you. You must stay quiet till I come back, and not leave the house on any account. I've got a case of old broad barrels there that will answer you beautifully; if you were anything of a shot, I'd give you my own cross handles, but they'd only spoil your shooting."

"I can hit a wine-glass in the stem at fifteen paces," said I, rather nettled at the disparaging tone in which he spoke of my performance.

"I don't care sixpence for that; the wine-glass had no pistol in his hand. Take the old German, then; see now, hold your pistol thus,—no finger on the guard there, these two on the trigger. They are not hair-triggers; drop the muzzle a bit; bend your elbow a trifle more; sight your man outside your arm,—outside, mind,—and take him in the hip, and if anywhere higher, no matter."

By this time the count had completed his toilet, and taking the small mahogany box which contained his peace-makers under his arm, led the way towards the stables. When we reached the yard, the only person stirring there was a kind of half-witted boy, who, being about the house, was employed to run of messages from the servants, walk a stranger's horse, or to do any of the many petty services that regular domestics contrive always to devolve upon some adopted subordinate. He was seated upon a stone step formerly used for mounting, and though the day was scarcely breaking, and the weather severe and piercing, the poor fellow was singing an Irish song, in a low monotonous tone, as he chafed a curb chain between his hands with some sand. As we came near he started up, and as he pulled off his cap to salute us, gave a sharp and piercing glance at the count, then at me, then once more upon my companion, from whom his eyes were turned to the brass-bound box beneath his arm,—when, as if seized with a sudden impulse, he started on his feet, and set off towards the house with the speed of a greyhound, not, however, before Considine's practised eye had anticipated his plan; for throwing down the pistol-case, he dashed after him, and in an instant had seized him by the collar.

"It won't do, Patsey," said the count; "you can't double on me."

"Oh, Count, darlin', Mister Considine avick, don't do it, don't now," said the poor fellow, falling on his knees, and blubbering like an infant.

"Hold your tongue, you villain, or I'll cut it out of your head," said Considine.

"And so I will; but don't do it, don't for the love of—"

"Don't do what, you whimpering scoundrel? What does he think I'll do?"

"Don't I know very well what you're after, what you're always after too? Oh, wirra, wirra!" Here he wrung his hands, and swayed himself backwards and forwards, a true picture of Irish grief.

"I'll stop his blubbering," said Considine, opening the box and taking out a pistol, which he cocked leisurely, and pointed at the poor fellow's head; "another syllable now, and I'll scatter your brains upon that pavement."

"And do, and divil thank you; sure, it's your trade."

The coolness of the reply threw us both off our guard so completely that we burst out into a hearty fit of laughing.

"Come, come," said the count, at last, "this will never do; if he goes on this way, we'll have the whole house about us. Come, then, harness the roan mare; and here's half a crown for you."

"I wouldn't touch the best piece in your purse," said the poor boy; "sure it's blood-money, no less."

The words were scarcely spoken, when Considine seized him by the collar with one hand, and by the wrist with the other, and carried him over the yard to the stable, where, kicking open the door, he threw him on a heap of stones, adding, "If you stir now, I'll break every bone in your body;" a threat that seemed certainly considerably increased in its terrors, from the rough gripe he had already experienced, for the lad rolled himself up like a ball, and sobbed as if his heart were breaking.

Very few minutes sufficed us now to harness the mare in the tax-cart, and when all was ready, Considine seized the whip, and locking the stable-door upon Patsey, was about to get up, when a sudden thought struck him. "Charley," said he, "that fellow will find some means to give the alarm; we must take him with us." So saying, he opened the door, and taking the poor fellow by the collar, flung him at my feet in the tax-cart.

We had already lost some time, and the roan mare was put to her fastest speed to make up for it. Our pace became, accordingly, a sharp one; and as the road was bad, and the tax-cart no "patent inaudible," neither of us spoke. To me this was a great relief. The events of the last few days had given them the semblance of years, and all the reflection I could muster was little enough to make anything out of the chaotic mass,—love, mischief, and misfortune,—in which I had been involved since my leaving O'Malley Castle.

"Here we are, Charley," said Considine, drawing up short at the door of a little country ale-house, or, in Irish parlance, *shebeen*, which stood at the meeting of four bleak roads, in a wild and barren mountain tract beside the Shannon. "Here we are, my boy! Jump out and let us be stirring."

"Here, Patsey, my man," said the count, unravelling the prostrate and doubly knotted figure at our feet; "lend a hand, Patsey." Much to my astonishment, he obeyed the summons with alacrity, and proceeded to unharness the mare with the greatest despatch. My attention was, however, soon turned from him to my own more immediate concerns, and I followed my companion into the house.

"Joe," said the count to the host, "is Mr. Bodkin up at the house this morning?"

"He's just passed this way, sir, with Mr. Malowney of Tillnamuck, in the gig, on their way from Mr. Blake's. They stopped here to order horses to go over to O'Malley Castle, and the gossoon is gone to look for a pair."

"All right," said Considine, and added, in a whisper, "we've done it well, Charley, to be beforehand, or the governor would have found it all out and taken the affair into his own hands. Now all you have to do is to stay quietly here till I come back, which will not be above an hour at farthest. Joe, send me the pony; keep an eye on Patsey, that he doesn't play us a trick. The short way to Mr. Bodkin's is through Scariff. Ay, I know it well; good-by, Charley. By the Lord, we'll pepper him!"

These were the last words of the worthy count as he closed the door behind him, and left me to my own not very agreeable reflections. Independently of my youth and perfect ignorance of the world, which left me unable to form any correct judgment on my conduct, I knew that I had taken a great deal of wine, and was highly excited when my unhappy collision with Mr. Bodkin occurred. Whether, then, I had been betrayed into anything which could fairly have provoked his insulting retort or not, I could not remember; and now my most afflicting thought was, what opinion might be entertained of me by those at Blake's table; and above all, what Miss

Dashwood herself would think, and what narrative of the occurrence would reach her. The great effort of my last few days had been to stand well in her estimation, to appear something better in feeling, something higher in principle, than the rude and unpolished squirearchy about me; and now here was the end of it! What would she, what could she, think, but that I was the same punch-drinking, rowing, quarrelling bumpkin as those whom I had so lately been carefully endeavoring to separate myself from? How I hated myself for the excess to which passion had betrayed me, and how I detested my opponent as the cause of all my present misery. "How very differently," thought I, "her friend the captain would have conducted himself. His quiet and gentlemanly manner would have done fully as much to wipe out any insult on his honor as I could do, and after all, would neither have disturbed the harmony of a dinner-table, nor made himself, as I shuddered to think I had, a subject of rebuke, if not of ridicule." These harassing, torturing reflections continued to press on me, and I paced the room with my hands clasped and the perspiration upon my brow. "One thing is certain,—I can never see her again," thought I; "this disgraceful business must, in some shape or other, become known to her, and all I have been saying these last three days rise up in judgment against this one act, and stamp me an impostor! I that decried—nay, derided—our false notion of honor. Would that Considine were come! What can keep him now?" I walked to the door; a boy belonging to the house was walking the roan before the door. "What had, then, become of Pat?" I inquired; but no one could tell. He had disappeared shortly after our arrival, and had not been seen afterwards. My own thoughts were, however, too engrossing to permit me to think more of this circumstance, and I turned again to enter the house, when I saw Considine advancing up the road at the full speed of his pony.

"Out with the mare, Charley! Be alive, my boy!—all's settled." So saying, he sprang from the pony and proceeded to harness the roan with the greatest haste, informing me in broken sentences, as he went on with all the arrangements.

"We are to cross the bridge of Portumna. They won the ground, and it seems Bodkin likes the spot; he shot Peyton there three years ago. Worse luck now, Charley, you know; by all the rule of chance, he can't expect the same thing twice,—never four by honors in two deals. Didn't say that, though. A sweet meadow, I know it well; small hillocks, like molehills; all over it. Caught him at breakfast; I don't think he expected the message to come from us, but said it was a very polite attention,—and so it was, you know."

So he continued to ramble on as we once more took our seats in the tax-cart and set out for the ground.

"What are you thinking of, Charley?" said the count, as I kept silent for some minutes.

"I'm thinking, sir, if I were to kill him, what I must do after."

"Right, my boy; nothing like that, but I'll settle all for you. Upon my conscience, if it wasn't for the chance of his getting into another quarrel and spoiling the election, I'd go back for Godfrey; he'd like to see you break ground so prettily. And you say you're no shot?"

"Never could do anything with the pistol to speak of, sir," said I, remembering his rebuke of the morning.

"I don't mind that. You've a good eye; never take it off him after you're on the ground,—follow him everywhere. Poor Callaghan, that's gone, shot his man always that way. He had a way of looking without winking that was very fatal at a short distance; a very good thing to learn, Charley, when you have a little spare time."

Half-an-hour's sharp driving brought us to the river side, where a boat had been provided by Considine to ferry us over. It was now about eight o'clock, and a heavy, gloomy morning. Much rain had fallen overnight, and the dark and lowering atmosphere seemed charged with more. The mountains looked twice their real size, and all the shadows were increased to an enormous extent. A very killing kind of light it was, as the count remarked.

CHAPTER VIII.

THE DUEL.

As the boatmen pulled in towards the shore we perceived, a few hundred yards off, a group of persons standing, whom we soon recognized as our opponents. "Charley," said the count, grasping my arm tightly, as I stood up to spring on the land,—"Charley, although you are only a boy, as I may say, I have no fear for your courage; but still more than that is needful here. This Bodkin is a noted duellist, and will try to shake your nerve. Now, mind that you take everything that happens quite with an air of indifference; don't let him think that he has any advantage over you, and you'll see how the tables will be turned in your favor."

"Trust to me, Count" said I; "I'll not disgrace you."

He pressed my hand tightly, and I thought that I discerned something like a slight twitch about the corners of his grim mouth, as if some sudden and painful thought had shot across his mind; but in a moment he was calm, and stern-looking as ever.

"Twenty minutes late, Mr. Considine," said a short, red-faced little man, with a military frock and foraging cap, as he held out his watch in evidence.

"I can only say, Captain Malowney, that we lost no time since we parted. We had some difficulty in finding a boat; but in any case, we are here *now*, and that, I opine, is the important part of the matter."

"Quite right,—very just indeed. Will you present me to your young friend. Very proud to make your acquaintance, sir; your uncle and I met more than once in this kind of way. I was out with him in '92,—was it? no, I think it was '93,—when he shot Harry Burgoyne, who, by-the-bye, was called the crack shot of our mess; but, begad, your uncle knocked his pistol hand to shivers, saying, in his dry way, 'He must try the left hand this morning.' Count, a little this side, if you please."

While Considine and the captain walked a few paces apart from where I stood, I had leisure to observe my antagonist, who stood among a group of his friends, talking and laughing away in great spirits. As the tone they spoke in was not of the lowest, I could catch much of their conversation at the distance I was from them. They were discussing the last occasion that Bodkin had visited this spot, and talking of the fatal event which happened then.

"Poor devil," said Bodkin, "it wasn't his fault; but you see some of the —th had been showing white feathers before that, and he was obliged to go out. In fact, the colonel himself said, 'Fight, or leave the corps.' Well, out he came; it was a cold morning in February, with a frost the night before going off in a thin rain. Well, it seems he had the consumption or something of that sort, with a great cough and spitting of blood, and this weather made him worse; and he was very weak when he came to the ground. Now, the moment I got a glimpse of him, I said to myself, 'He's pluck enough, but as nervous as a lady;' for his eye wandered all about, and his mouth was constantly twitching. 'Take off your great-coat, Ned,' said one of his people, when they were going to put him up; 'take it off, man.' He seemed to hesitate for an instant, when Michael Blake remarked, 'Arrah, let him alone; it's his mother makes him wear it, for the cold he has.' They all began to laugh at this; but I kept my eye upon him, and I saw that his cheek grew quite livid and a kind of gray color, and his eyes filled up. 'I have you now,' said I to myself, and I shot him through the lung."

"And this poor fellow," thought I, "was the only son of a widowed mother." I walked from the spot to avoid hearing further, and felt, as I did so, something like a spirit of vengeance rising within me, for the fate of one so untimely cut off.

"Here we are, all ready," said Malowney, springing over a small fence into the adjoining field. "Take your ground, gentlemen."

Considine took my arm and walked forward. "Charley," said he, "I am to give the signal; I'll drop my glove when you are to fire, but don't look at me at all. I'll manage to catch Bodkin's eye; and do you watch him steadily, and fire when he does."

"I think that the ground we are leaving behind us is rather better," said some one.

"So it is," said Bodkin; "but it might be troublesome to carry the young gentleman down that way,—here all is fair and easy."

The next instant we were placed; and I well remember the first thought that struck me was, that there could be no chance of either of us escaping.

"Now then," said the count, "I'll walk twelve paces, turn and drop this glove; at which signal you fire, and *together* mind. The man who reserves his shot falls by my hand." This very summary denunciation seemed to meet general approbation, and the count strutted forth. Notwithstanding the advice of my friend, I could not help turning my eyes from Bodkin to watch the retiring figure of the count. At length he stopped; a second or two elapsed; he wheeled rapidly round, and let fall the glove. My eye glanced towards my opponent; I raised my pistol and fired. My hat turned half round upon my head, and Bodkin fell motionless to the earth. I saw the people around me rush forward; I caught two or three glances thrown at me with an expression of revengeful passion; I felt some one grasp me round the waist, and hurry me from the spot; and it was at least ten minutes after, as we were skimming the surface of the broad Shannon, before I could well collect my scattered faculties to remember all that was passing, as Considine, pointing to the two bullet-holes in my hat, remarked, "Sharp practice, Charley; it was the overcharge saved you."

"Is he killed, sir?" I asked.

"Not quite, I believe, but as good. You took him just above the hip."

"Can he recover?" said I, with a voice tremulous from agitation, which I vainly endeavored to conceal from my companion.

"Not if the doctor can help it," said Considine; "for the fool keeps poking about for the ball. But now let's think of the next step,—you'll have to leave this, and at once, too."

Little more passed between us. As we rowed towards the shore, Considine was following up his reflections, and I had mine,—alas! too many and too bitter to escape from.

As we neared the land a strange spectacle caught our eye. For a considerable distance along the coast crowds of country people were assembled, who, forming in groups and breaking into parties of two and three, were evidently watching with great anxiety what was taking place at the opposite side. Now, the distance was at least a mile, and therefore any part of the transaction which had been enacting there must have been quite beyond their view. While I was wondering at this, Considine cried out suddenly, "Too infamous, by Jove! We're murdered men!"

"What do you mean?" said I.

"Don't you see that?" said he, pointing to something black which floated from a pole at the opposite side of the river.

"Yes; what is it?"

"It's his coat they've put upon an oar to show the people he's killed,—that's all. Every man here's his tenant; and look—there! They're not giving us much doubt as to their intention."

Here a tremendous yell burst forth from the mass of people along the shore, which rising to a terrific cry sunk gradually down to a low wailing, then rose and fell again several times as the Irish death-cry filled the air and rose to Heaven, as if imploring vengeance on a murderer.

The appalling influence of the *keen*, as it is called, had been familiar to me from my infancy; but it needed the awful situation I was placed in to consummate its horrors. It was at once my accusation and my doom. I knew well—none better—the vengeful character of the Irish peasant of the west, and that my death was certain I had no doubt. The very crime that sat upon my heart quailed its courage and unnerved my arm. As the boatmen looked from us towards the shore and again at our faces, they, as if instinctively, lay upon their oars, and waited for our decision as to what course to pursue.

"Rig the spritsail, my boys," said Considine, "and let her head lie up the river; and be alive, for I see they're bailing a boat below the little reef there, and will be after us in no time."

The poor fellows, who, although strangers to us, sympathizing in what they perceived to be our imminent danger, stepped the light spar which acted as mast, and shook out their scanty rag of canvas in a minute. Considine meanwhile went aft, and steadying her head with an oar, held the small craft up to the wind till she lay completely over, and as she rushed through the water, ran dipping her gun-wale through the white foam.

"Where can we make without tacking, boys?" inquired the count.

"If it blows on as fresh, sir, we'll run you ashore within half a mile of the Castle."

"Put an oar to leeward," said Considine, "and keep her up more to the wind, and I promise you, my lads, you will not go home fresh and fasting if you land us where you say."

"Here they come," said the other boatman, as he pointed back with his finger towards a large yawl which shot suddenly from the shore, with six sturdy fellows pulling at their oars, while three or four others were endeavoring to get up their rigging, which appeared tangled and confused at the bottom of the boat; the white splash of water which fell each moment beside her showing that the process of bailing was still continued.

"Ah, then, may I never—av it isn't the ould 'Dolphin' they have launched for the cruise," said one of our fellows.

"What's the 'Dolphin,' then?"

"An ould boat of the Lord's [Lord Clanricarde's] that didn't see water, except when it rained, these four years, and is sun-cracked from stem to stern."

"She can sail, however," said Considine, who watched with a painful anxiety the rapidity of her course through the water.

"Nabocklish, she was a smuggler's jolly-boat, and well used to it. Look how they're pulling. God pardon them, but they're in no blessed humor this morning."

"Lay out upon your oars, boys; the wind's failing us," cried the count, as the sail flapped lazily against the mast.

"It's no use, yer honor," said the elder. "We'll be only breaking our hearts to no purpose. They're sure to catch us."

"Do as I bade you, at all events. What's that ahead of us there?"

"The Oat Rock, sir. A vessel with grain struck there and went down with all aboard, four years last winter. There's no channel between it and the shore,—all sunk rocks, every inch of it. There's the breeze."

The canvas fell over as he spoke, and the little craft lay down to it till the foaming water bubbled over her lee bow.

"Keep her head up, sir; higher—higher still."

But Considine little heeded the direction, steering straight for the narrow channel the man alluded to.

"Tear and ages, but you're going right for the cloch na quirka!"

"Arrah, an' the devil a taste I'll be drowned for your devarsion!" said the other, springing up.

"Sit down there, and be still," roared Considine, as he drew a pistol from the case at his feet, "if you don't want some leaden ballast to keep you so! Here, Charley, take this, and if that fellow stirs hand or foot—you understand me."

The two men sat sulkily in the bottom of the boat, which now was actually flying through the water. Considine's object was a clear one. He saw that in sailing we were greatly overmatched, and that our only chance lay in reaching the narrow and dangerous channel between Oat Rock and the shore, by which we should distance the pursuit, the long reef of rocks that ran out beyond requiring a wide berth to escape from. Nothing but the danger behind us could warrant so rash a daring. The whole channel was dotted with patches of white and breaking foam,—the sure evidence of the mischief beneath,—while here and there a dash of spurting spray flew up from the dark water, where some cleft rock lay hid below the flood. Escape seemed impossible; but who would not have preferred even so slender a chance with so frightful an alternative behind him? As if to add terror to the scene, Considine had scarcely turned the boat ahead of the channel when a tremendous blackness spread over all around, the thunder pealed forth, and amidst the crashing of the hail and the bright glare of lightning a squall struck us and laid us nearly keel uppermost for several minutes. I well remember we rushed through the dark and blackened water, our little craft more than half filled, the oars floating off to leeward, and we ourselves kneeling on the bottom planks for safety. Roll after roll of loud thunder broke, as it were, just above our heads; while in the swift dashing rain that seemed to hiss around us every object was hidden, and even the other boat was lost to our view. The two poor fellows—I shall never forget their expression. One, a devout Catholic, had placed a little leaden image of a saint before him in the bow, and implored its intercession with a torturing agony of suspense that wrung my very heart. The other, apparently less alive to such consolations as his Church afforded, remained with his hands clasped, his mouth compressed, his brows knitted, and his dark eyes bent upon me with the fierce hatred of a deadly enemy; his eyes were sunken and bloodshot, and all told of some dreadful conflict within. The wild ferocity of his look fascinated my gaze, and amidst all the terrors of the scene I could not look from him. As I gazed, a second and more awful squall struck the boat; the mast went over, and with a loud report like a pistol-shot smashed at the thwart and fell over, trailing the sail along the milky sea behind us. Meanwhile the water rushed clean over us, and the boat seemed settling. At this dreadful moment the sailor's eye was bent upon me, his lips parted, and he muttered, as if to himself, "This it is to go to sea with a murderer." Oh, God! the agony of that moment! the heartfelt and accusing conscience that I was judged and doomed! that the brand of Cain was upon my brow! that my fellow-men had ceased forever to regard me as a brother! that I was an outcast and a wanderer forever! I bent forward till my forehead fell upon my knees, and I wept. Meanwhile the boat flew through the water, and Considine, who alone among us seemed not to lose his presence of mind, cut away the mast and sent it overboard. The storm began now to abate; and as the black mass of cloud broke from around us we beheld the other boat, also dismasted, far behind us, while all on board of her were employed in bailing out the water with which she seemed almost sinking. The curtain of mist that had hidden us from each other no sooner broke than they ceased their labors for a moment, and looking towards us, burst forth into a yell so wild, so savage, so dreadful, my very heart quailed as its cadence fell upon my ear.

"Safe, my boy," said Considine, clapping me on the shoulder, as he steered the boat forth from its narrow path of danger, and once more reached the broad Shannon,—"safe, Charley; though we've had a brush for it." In a minute more we reached the land, and drawing our gallant little craft on shore, set out for O'Malley Castle.

CHAPTER IX.

THE RETURN.

O'Malley Castle lay about four miles from the spot we landed at, and thither accordingly we bent our steps without loss of time. We had not, however, proceeded far, when, before us on the road, we perceived a mixed assemblage of horse and foot, hurrying along at a tremendous rate. The mob, which consisted of some hundred country people, were armed with sticks, scythes, and pitchforks, and although not preserving any very military aspect in their order of march, were still a force quite formidable enough to make us call a halt, and deliberate upon what we were to do.

"They've outflanked us, Charley," said Considine; "however, all is not yet lost. But see, they've got sight of us; here they come."

At these words, the vast mass before us came pouring along, splashing the mud on every side, and huzzaing like so many Indians. In the front ran a bare-legged boy, waving his cap to encourage the rest, who followed him at about fifty yards behind.

"Leave that fellow for me," said the count, coolly examining the lock of his pistol; "I'll pick him out, and load again in time for his friends' arrival. Charley, is that a gentleman I see far back in the crowd? Yes, to be sure it is? He's on a large horse—now he's pressing forward; so let—no—oh—ay, it's Godfrey O'Malley himself, and these are our own people." Scarcely were the words out when a tremendous cheer arose from the multitude, who, recognizing us at the same instant, sprang from their horses and ran forward to welcome us. Among the foremost was the scarecrow leader, whom I at once perceived as poor Patsey, who, escaping in the morning, had returned at full speed to O'Malley Castle, and raised the whole country to my rescue. Before I could address one word to my faithful followers I was in my uncle's arms.

"Safe, my boy, quite safe?"

"Quite safe, sir."

"No scratch anywhere?"

"Nothing but a hat the worse, sir," said I, showing the two bullet-holes in my headpiece.

His lip quivered as he turned and whispered something into Considine's ear, which I heard not; but the count's reply was, "Devil a bit, as cool as you see him this minute."

"And Bodkin, what of him?"

"This day's work's his last," said Considine; "the ball entered here. But come along, Godfrey; Charley's new at this kind of thing, and we had better discuss matters in the house."

Half-an-hour's brisk trot—for we were soon supplied with horses—brought us back to the Castle, much to the disappointment of our cortege, who had been promised a *scrimmage*, and went back in very ill-humor at the breach of contract.

The breakfast-room, as we entered, was filled with my uncle's supporters, all busily engaged over poll-books and booth tallies, in preparation for the eventful day of battle. These, however, were immediately thrown aside to hasten round me and inquire all the details of my duel. Considine, happily for me, however, assumed all the dignity of an historian, and recounted the events of the morning so much to my honor and glory, that I, who only a little before felt crushed and bowed down by the misery of my late duel, began, amidst the warm congratulations and eulogiums about me, to think I was no small hero, and in fact, something very much resembling "the man for Galway." To this feeling a circumstance that followed assisted in contributing. While we were eagerly discussing the various results likely to arise from the meeting, a horse galloped rapidly to the door and a loud voice called out, "I can't get off, but tell him to come here." We rushed out and beheld Captain Malowney, Mr. Bodkin's second, covered with mud from head to foot, and his horse reeking with foam and sweat. "I am hurrying on to Athlone for another doctor; but I've called to tell you that the wound is not supposed to be mortal,—he may recover yet." Without waiting for another word, he dashed spurs into his nag and rattled down the avenue at full gallop. Mr. Bodkin's dearest friend on earth could not have received the intelligence with more delight; and I now began to listen to the congratulations of my friends with a more tranquil spirit. My uncle, too, seemed much relieved by the information, and heard with great good temper my narrative of the few days at Gurt-na-Morra. "So then," said he, as I concluded, "my opponent is at least a gentleman; that is a comfort."

"Sir George Dashwood," said I, "from all I have seen, is a remarkably nice person, and I am certain you will meet with only the fair and legitimate opposition of an opposing candidate in him,—no mean or unmanly subterfuge."

"All right, Charley. Well, now, your affair of this morning must keep you quiet for a few days, come what will; by Monday next, when the election takes place, Bodkin's fate will be pretty clear, one way or the other, and if matters go well, you can come into town; otherwise, I have arranged with Considine to take you over to the Continent for a year or so; but we'll discuss all this in the evening. Now I must start on a canvass. Boyle expects to meet you at dinner to-day; he is coming from Athlone on purpose. Now, good-by!"

When my uncle had gone, I sank into a chair and fell into a musing fit over all the changes a few hours had wrought in me. From a mere boy whose most serious employment was stocking the house with game or inspecting the kennel, I had sprung at once into man's estate, was complimented for my coolness, praised for my prowess, lauded for my discretion, by those who were my seniors by nearly half a century; talked to in a tone of confidential intimacy by my uncle, and, in a word, treated in all respects as an equal,—and such was all the work of a few hours. But so it is; the eras in life are separated by a narrow boundary,—some trifling accident, some casual *rencontre* impels us across the Rubicon, and we pass from infancy to youth, from youth to manhood, from manhood to age, less by the slow and imperceptible step of time than by some one decisive act or passion which, occurring at a critical moment, elicits a long latent feeling, and impresses our existence with a color that tinges us for many a long year. As for me, I had cut the tie which bound me to the careless gayety of boyhood with a rude gash. In three short days I had fallen deeply, desperately in love, and had wounded, if not killed, an antagonist in a duel. As I meditated on these things, I was aroused by the noise of horses' feet in the yard beneath. I opened the window and beheld no less a person than Captain Hammersley. He was handing a card to a servant, which he was accompanying by a verbal message; the impression of something like hostility on the part of the captain had never left my mind, and I hastened downstairs just in time to catch him as he turned from the door.

"Ah, Mr. O'Malley!" said he, in a most courteous tone. "They told me you were not at home."

I apologized for the blunder, and begged of him to alight and come in.

"I thank you very much, but, in fact, my hours are now numbered here. I have just received an order to join my regiment; we have been ordered for service, and Sir George has most kindly permitted my giving up my staff appointment. I could not, however, leave the country without shaking hands with you. I owe you a lesson in horsemanship, and I'm only sorry that we are not to have another day together."

"Then you are going out to the Peninsula?" said I.

"Why, we hope so; the commander-in-chief, they say, is in great want of cavalry, and we scarcely less in want of something to do. I'm sorry you are not coming with us."

"Would to Heaven I were!" said I, with an earnestness that almost made my brain start.

"Then, why not?"

"Unfortunately, I am peculiarly situated. My worthy uncle, who is all to me in this world, would be quite alone if I were to leave him; and although he has never said so, I know he dreads the possibility of my suggesting such a thing to him: so that, between his fears and mine, the matter is never broached by either party, nor do I think ever can be."

"Devilish hard—but I believe you are right; something, however, may turn up yet to alter his mind, and if so, and if you do take to dragooning, don't forget George Hammersley will be always most delighted to meet you; and so good-by, O'Malley, good-by."

He turned his horse's head and was already some paces off, when he returned to my side, and in a lower tone of voice said,—

"I ought to mention to you that there has been much discussion on your affair at Blake's table, and only one opinion on the matter among all parties,—that you acted perfectly right. Sir George Dashwood,—no mean judge of such things,—quite approves of your conduct, and, I believe, wishes you to know as much; and now, once more, good-by."

CHAPTER X.

THE ELECTION.

The important morning at length arrived, and as I looked from my bed-room window at daybreak, the crowd of carriages of all sorts and shapes decorated with banners and placards; the incessant bustle; the hurrying hither and thither; the cheering as each new detachment of voters came up, mounted on jaunting-cars, or on horses whose whole caparison consisted in a straw rope for a bridle, and a saddle of the same frail material,—all informed me that the election day was come. I lost no further time, but proceeded to dress with all possible despatch. When I appeared in the breakfast-room, it was already filled with some seventy or eighty persons of all ranks and ages, mingled confusedly together, and enjoying the hospitable fare of my uncle's house, while they discussed all the details and prospects of the election. In the hall, the library, the large drawing-room, too, similar parties were also assembled, and as newcomers arrived, the servants were busy in preparing tables before the door and up the large terrace that ran the entire length of the building. Nothing could be more amusing than the incongruous mixture of the guests, who, with every variety of eatable that chance or inclination provided, were thus thrown into close contact, having only this in common,—the success of the cause they were engaged in. Here was the old Galway squire, with an ancestry that reached to Noah, sitting side by side with the poor cotter, whose whole earthly possession was what, in Irish phrase, is called a "potato garden,"—meaning the exactly smallest possible patch of ground out of which a very Indian-rubber conscience could presume to vote. Here sat the old simple-minded, farmer-like man, in close conversation with a little white-foreheaded, keen-eyed personage, in a black coat and eye-glass,—a flash attorney from Dublin, learned in flaws of the registry, and deep in the subtleties of election law. There was an Athlone horse-dealer, whose habitual daily practices in imposing the halt, the lame, and the blind upon the unsuspecting, for beasts of blood and mettle, well qualified him for the trickery of a county contest. Then there were scores of squireen gentry, easily recognized on common occasions by a green coat, brass buttons, dirty cords, and dirtier top-boots, a lash-whip, and a half-bred fox-hound; but now, fresh-washed for the day, they presented something the appearance of a swell mob, adjusted to the meridian of Galway. A mass of frieze-coated, brow-faced, bullet-headed peasantry filled up the large spaces, dotted here and there with a sleek, roguish-eyed priest, or some low electioneering agent detailing, for the amusement of the company, some of those cunning practices of former times which if known to the proper authorities would in all likelihood cause the talented narrator to be improving the soil of Sidney, or fishing on the banks of the Swan river; while at the head and foot of each table sat some personal friend of my uncle, whose ready tongue, and still readier pistol, made him a personage of some consequence, not more to his own people than to the enemy. While of such material were the company, the fare before them was no less varied: here some rubicund squire was deep in amalgamating the contents of a venison pasty with some of Sneyd's oldest claret; his neighbor, less ambitious, and less erudite in such matters, was devouring rashers of bacon, with liberal potations of potteen; some pale-cheeked scion of the law, with all the dust of the Four Courts in his throat, was sipping his humble beverage of black tea beside four sturdy cattle-dealers from Ballinasloe, who were discussing hot whiskey punch and *spoleaion* (boiled beef) at the very primitive hour of eight in the morning. Amidst the clank of decanters, the crash of knives and plates, and the jingling of glasses, the laughter and voices of the guests were audibly increasing; and the various modes of "running a buck" (*Anglicé*, substituting a vote), or hunting a badger, were talked over on all sides, while the price of a *veal* (a calf), or a voter, was disputed with all the energy of debate.

Refusing many an offered place, I went through the different rooms in search of Considine, to whom circumstances of late had somehow greatly attached me.

"Here, Charley," cried a voice I was very familiar with,—"here's a place I've been keeping for you."

"Ah, Sir Harry, how do you do? Any of that grouse-pie to spare?"

"Abundance, my boy; but I'm afraid I can't say as much for the liquor. I have been shouting for claret this half-hour in vain,—do get us some nutriment down here, and the Lord will reward you. What a pity it is," he added, in a lower tone, to his neighbor—"what a pity a quart-bottle won't hold a quart; but I'll bring it before the House one of these days." That he kept his word in this respect, a motion on the books of the Honorable House will bear me witness.

"Is this it?" said he, turning towards a farmer-like old man, who had put some question to him across the table; "is it the apple-pie you'll have?"

"Many thanks to your honor,—I'd like it, av it was wholesome."

"And why shouldn't it be wholesome?" said Sir Harry.

"Troth, then, myself does not know; but my father, I heerd tell, died of an apple-plexy, and I'm afeerd of it."

I at length found Considine, and learned that, as a very good account of Bodkin had arrived, there was no reason why I should not proceed to the hustings; but I was secretly charged not to take any prominent part in the day's proceedings. My uncle I only saw for an instant,—he begged me to be careful, avoid all scrapes, and not to quit Considine. It was past ten o'clock when our formidable procession got under way, and headed towards the town of Galway. The road was, for miles, crowded with our followers; banners flying and music playing, we presented something the spectacle of a very ragged army on its march. At every cross-road a mountain-path reinforcement awaited us, and as we wended along, our numbers were momentarily increasing; here and there along the line, some energetic and not over-sober adherent was regaling his auditory with a speech in laudation of the O'Malleys since the days of Moses, and more than one priest was heard threatening the terrors of his Church in aid of a cause to whose success he was pledged and bound. I rode beside the count, who, surrounded by a group of choice spirits, recounted the various happy inventions by which he had, on divers occasions, substituted a personal quarrel for a contest. Boyle also contributed his share of election anecdote, and one incident he related, which, I remember, amused me much at the time.

"Do you remember Billy Calvert, that came down to contest Kilkenny?" inquired Sir Harry.

"What, ever forget him!" said Considine, "with his well-powdered wig and his hessians. There never was his equal for lace ruffles and rings."

"You never heard, may be, how he lost the election?"

"He resigned, I believe, or something of that sort."

"No, no," said another; "he never came forward at all. There's some secret in it; for Tom Butler was elected without a contest."

"Jack, I'll tell you how it happened. I was on my way up from Cork, having finished my own business, and just carried the day, not without a push for it. When we reached,—Lady Mary was with me,—when we reached Kilkenny, the night before the election, I was not ten minutes in town till Butler heard of it, and sent off express to see me; I was at my dinner when the messenger came, and promised to go over when I'd done. But faith, Tom didn't wait, but came rushing up-stairs himself, and dashed into the room in the greatest hurry.

"'Harry,' says he, 'I'm done for; the corporation of free smiths, that were always above bribery, having voted for myself and my father before, for four pounds ten a man, won't come forward under six guineas and whiskey. Calvert has the money; they know it. The devil a farthing we have; and we've been paying all our fellows that can't read in Hennesy's notes, and you know the bank's broke this three weeks.'

"On he went, giving me a most disastrous picture of his cause, and concluded by asking if I could suggest anything under the circumstances.

"'You couldn't get a decent mob and clear the poll?'

"'I am afraid not,' said he, despondingly.

"'Then I don't see what's to be done, if you can't pick a fight with himself. Will he go out?'

"'Lord knows! They say he's so afraid of that, that it has prevented him coming down till the very day. But he is arrived now; he came in the evening, and is stopping at Walsh's in Patrick Street.'

"'Then I'll see what can be done,' said I.

"'Is that Calvert, the little man that blushes when the Lady-Lieutenant speaks to him?' said Lady Mary.

"'The very man.'

"'Would it be of any use to you if he could not come on the hustings to-morrow?' said she, again.

"''Twould gain us the day. Half the voters don't believe he's here at all, and his chief agent cheated all the people on the last election; and if Calvert didn't appear, he wouldn't have ten votes to register. But why do you ask?'

"'Why, that, if you like, I'll bet you a pair of diamond ear-rings he sha'n't show.'

"'Done!' said Butler. 'And I promise a necklace into the bargain, if you win; but I'm afraid you're only quizzing me.'

"'Here's my hand on it,' said she. 'And now let's talk of something else.'"

As Lady Mary never asked my assistance, and as I knew she was very well able to perform whatever she undertook, you may be sure I gave myself very little trouble about the whole affair; and when they came, I went off to breakfast with Tom's committee, not knowing anything that was to be done.

Calvert had given orders that he was to be called at eight o'clock, and so a few minutes before that time a gentle knock came to the door.

'Come in,' said he, thinking it was the waiter, and covering himself up in the clothes; for he was the most bashful creature ever was seen,—'come in.'

The door opened, and what was his horror to find that a lady entered in her dressing-gown, her hair on her shoulders, very much tossed and dishevelled. The moment she came in, she closed the door and locked it, and then sat leisurely down upon a chair.

Billy's teeth chattered, and his limbs trembled; for this was an adventure of a very novel kind for him. At last he took courage to speak.

'I am afraid, madam,' said he, 'that you are under some unhappy mistake, and that you suppose this chamber is—'

'Mr. Calvert's,' said the lady, with a solemn voice, 'is it not?'

'Yes, madam, I am that person.'

'Thank God!' said the lady, with a very impressive tone. 'Here I am safe.'

Billy grew very much puzzled at these words; but hoping that by his silence the lady would proceed to some explanation, he said no more. She, however, seemed to think that nothing further was necessary, and sat still and motionless, with her hands before her and her eyes fixed on Billy.

"'You seem to forget me, sir?' said she, with a faint smile.

"'I do, indeed, madam; the half-light, the novelty of your costume, and the strangeness of the circumstance altogether must plead for me, if I appear rude enough.'

"'I am Lady Mary Boyle,' said she.

"'I do remember you, madam; but may I ask—'

"'Yes, yes; I know what you would ask. You would say, Why are you here? How comes it that you have so far outstepped the propriety of which your whole life is an example, that alone, at such a time, you appear in the chamber of a man whose character for gallantry—'

"'Oh, indeed—indeed, my lady, nothing of the kind!'

"'Ah, alas! poor defenceless women learn, too late, how constantly associated is the retiring modesty which decries, with the pleasing powers which ensure success—'

"Here she sobbed, Billy blushed, and the clock struck nine.

"'May I then beg, madam—'

"'Yes, yes, you shall hear it all; but my poor scattered faculties will not be the clearer by your hurrying me. You know, perhaps,' continued she, 'that my maiden name was Rogers?' He of the blankets bowed, and she resumed, 'It is now eighteen years since, that a young, unsuspecting, fond creature, reared in all the care and fondness of doting parents, tempted her first step in life, and trusted her fate to another's keeping. I am that unhappy person; the other, that monster in human guise that smiled but to betray, that won but to ruin and destroy, is he whom you know as Sir Harry Boyle.'

"Here she sobbed for some minutes, wiped her eyes, and resumed her narrative. Beginning at the period of her marriage, she detailed a number of circumstances in which poor Calvert, in all his anxiety to come *au fond* at matters, could never perceive bore upon the question in any way; but as she recounted them all with great force and precision, entreating him to bear in mind certain circumstances to which she should recur by and by, his attention was kept on the stretch, and it was only when the clock struck ten that he was fully aware how his morning was passing, and what surmises his absence might originate.

"'May I interrupt you for a moment, dear madam? Was it nine or ten o'clock which struck last?'

"'How should I know?' said she, frantically. 'What are hours and minutes to her who has passed long years of misery?'

"'Very true, very true,' replied he, timidly, and rather fearing for the intellect of his fair companion.

"She continued. The narrative, however, so far from becoming clearer, grew gradually more confused and intricate; and as frequent references were made by the lady to some previous statement, Calvert was more than once rebuked for forgetfulness and inattention, where in reality nothing less than short-hand could have borne him through.

"'Was it in '93 I said that Sir Harry left me at Tuam?'

"'Upon my life, madam, I am afraid to aver; but it strikes me—'

"'Gracious powers! and this is he whom I fondly trusted to make the depository of my woes! Cruel, cruel man!'

"Here she sobbed considerably for several minutes, and spoke not. A loud cheer of 'Butler forever!' from the mob without now burst upon their hearing, and recalled poor Calvert at once to the thought that the hours were speeding fast and no prospect of the everlasting tale coming to an end.

"'I am deeply, most deeply grieved, my dear madam,' said the little man, sitting up in a pyramid of blankets; 'but hours, minutes, are most precious to me this morning. I am about to be proposed as member for Kilkenny.'

"At these words the lady straightened her figure out, threw her arms at either side, and burst into a fit of laughter which poor Calvert knew at once to be hysterics. Here was a pretty situation! The bell-rope lay against the opposite wall; and even if it did not, would he be exactly warranted in pulling it?

"'May the devil and all his angels take Sir Harry Boyle and his whole connection to the fifth generation!' was his sincere prayer as he sat like a Chinese juggler under his canopy.

"At length the violence of the paroxysm seemed to subside; the sobs became less frequent, the kicking less forcible, and the lady's eyes closed, and she appeared to have fallen asleep.

"'Now is the moment,' said Billy. 'If I could only get as far as my dressing-gown.' So saying, he worked himself down noiselessly to the foot of his bed, looked fixedly at the fallen lids of the sleeping lady, and essayed one leg from the blanket. 'Now or never,' said he, pushing aside the curtain and preparing for a spring. One more look he cast at his companion, and then leaped forth; but just as he lit upon the floor she again roused herself, screaming with horror. Billy fell upon the bed, and rolling himself in the bedclothes, vowed never to rise again till she was out of the visible horizon.

"'What is all this? What do you mean, sir?' said the lady, reddening with indignation.

"'Nothing, upon my soul, madam; it was only my dressing-gown.'

"'Your dressing-gown!' said she, with an emphasis worthy of Siddons; 'a likely story for Sir Harry to believe, sir! Fie, fie, sir!'

"This last allusion seemed a settler; for the luckless Calvert heaved a profound sigh, and sunk down as if all hope had left him. 'Butler forever!' roared the mob. 'Calvert forever!' cried a boy's voice from without. 'Three groans for the runaway!' answered this announcement; and a very tender inquiry of, 'Where is he?' was raised by some hundred mouths.

"'Madam,' said the almost frantic listener,—'madam, I must get up! I must dress! I beg of you to permit me!'

"'I have nothing to refuse, sir. Alas, disdain has long been my only portion! Get up, if you will.'

"'But,' said the astonished man, who was well-nigh deranged at the coolness of this reply,—'but how am I to do so if you sit there?'

"'Sorry for any inconvenience I may cause you; but in the crowded state of the hotel I hope you see the impropriety of my walking about the passages in this costume?'

"'And, great God! madam, why did you come out in it?'

"A cheer from the mob prevented her reply being audible. One o'clock tolled out from the great bell of the cathedral.

"'There's one o'clock, as I live!'

"'I heard it,' said the lady.

"'The shouts are increasing. What is that I hear? "Butler is in!" Gracious mercy! is the election over?'

"The lady stepped to the window, drew aside the curtain, and said, 'Indeed, it would appear so. The mob are cheering Mr. Butler.' A deafening shout burst from the street. 'Perhaps you'd like to see the fun, so I'll not detain you any longer. So, good-by, Mr. Calvert; and as your breakfast will be cold, in all likelihood, come down to No. 4, for Sir Harry's a late man, and will be glad to see you.'"

CHAPTER XI.

AN ADVENTURE.

As thus we lightened the road with chatting, the increasing concourse of people, and the greater throng of carriages that filled the road, announced that we had nearly reached our destination.

"Considine," said my uncle, riding up to where we were, "I have just got a few lines from Davern. It seems Bodkin's people are afraid to come in; they know what they must expect, and if so, more than half of that barony is lost to our opponent."

"Then he has no chance whatever."

"He never had, in my opinion," said Sir Harry.

"We'll see soon," said my uncle, cheerfully, and rode to the post.

The remainder of the way was occupied in discussing the various possibilities of the election, into which I was rejoiced to find that defeat never entered.

In the goodly days I speak of, a county contest was a very different thing indeed from the tame and insipid farce that now passes under that name: where a briefless barrister, bullied by both sides, sits as assessor; a few drunken voters, a radical O'Connellite grocer, a demagogue priest, a deputy grand-purple-something from the Trinity College lodge, with some half-dozen followers, shouting, "To the Devil with Peel!" or "Down with Dens!" form the whole *corp-de-ballet*. No, no; in the times I refer to the voters were some thousands in number, and the adverse parties took the field, far less dependent for success upon previous pledge or promise made them than upon the actual stratagem of the day. Each went forth, like a general to battle, surrounded by a numerous and well-chosen staff,—one party of friends, acting as commissariat, attended to the victualling of the voters, that they obtained a due, or rather undue allowance of liquor, and came properly drunk to the poll; others, again, broke into skirmishing parties, and scattered over the country, cut off the enemy's supplies, breaking down their post-chaises, upsetting their jaunting-cars, stealing their poll-books, and kidnapping their agents. Then there were secret-service people, bribing the enemy and enticing them to desert; and lastly, there was a species of sapper-and-miner force, who invented false documents, denied the identity of the opposite party's people, and when hard pushed, provided persons who took bribes from the enemy, and gave evidence afterwards on a petition. Amidst all these encounters of wit and ingenuity, the personal friends of the candidate formed a species of rifle brigade, picking out the enemy's officers, and doing sore damage to their tactics by shooting a proposer or wounding a seconder,—a considerable portion of every leading agent's fee being intended as compensation for the duels he might, could, would, should, or ought to fight during the election. Such, in brief, was a contest in the olden time. And when it is taken into consideration that it usually lasted a fortnight or three weeks; that a considerable military force was always engaged (for our Irish law permits this), and which, when nothing pressing was doing, was regularly assailed by both parties; that far more dependence was placed in a bludgeon than a pistol; and that the man who registered a vote without a cracked pate was regarded as a kind of natural phenomenon,—some faint idea may be formed how much such a scene must have contributed to the peace of the county, and the happiness and welfare of all concerned in it.

As we rode along, a loud cheer from a road that ran parallel to the one we were pursuing attracted our attention, and we perceived that the cortége of the opposite party was hastening on to the hustings. I could distinguish the Blake girls on horseback among a crowd of officers in undress, and saw something like a bonnet in the carriage-and-four which headed the procession, and which I judged to be that of Sir George Dashwood. My heart beat strongly as I strained my eyes to see if Miss Dashwood was there; but I could not discern her, and it was with a sense of relief that I reflected on the possibility of our not meeting under circumstances wherein our feelings and interests were so completely opposed. While I was engaged in making this survey, I had accidentally dropped behind my companions; my eyes were firmly fixed upon that carriage, and in the faint hope that it contained the object of all my wishes, I forgot everything else. At length the cortége entered the town, and passing beneath a heavy stone gateway, was lost to my view. I was still lost in revery, when an under-agent of my uncle's rode up.

"Oh, Master Charles!" said he, "what's to be done? They've forgotten Mr. Holmes at Woodford, and we haven't a carriage, chaise, or even a car left to send for him."

"Have you told Mr. Considine?" inquired I.

"And sure you know yourself how little Mr. Considine thinks of a lawyer. It's small comfort he'd give me if I went to tell him. If it was a case of pistols or a bullet mould he'd ride back the whole way himself for them."

"Try Sir Harry Boyle, then."

"He's making a speech this minute before the court-house."

This had sufficed to show me how far behind my companions I had been loitering, when a cheer from the distant road again turned my eyes in that direction; it was the Dashwood carriage returning after leaving Sir George at the hustings. The head of the britska, before thrown open, was now closed, and I could not make out if any one were inside.

"Devil a doubt of it," said the agent, in answer to some question of a farmer who rode beside him; "will you stand to me?"

"Troth, to be sure I will."

"Here goes, then," said he, gathering up his reins and turning his horse towards the fence at the roadside; "follow me now, boys."

The order was well obeyed; for when he had cleared the ditch, a dozen stout country fellows, well mounted, were beside him. Away they went, at a hunting pace, taking every leap before them, and heading towards the road before us.

Without thinking further of the matter, I was laughing at the droll effect the line of frieze coats presented as they rode side by side over the stone-walls, when an observation near me aroused my attention.

"Ah, then, av they know anything of Tim Finucane, they'll give it up peaceably; it's little he'd think of taking the coach from under the judge himself."

"What are they about, boys?" said I.

"Goin' to take the chaise-and-four forninst ye, yer honor," said the man.

I waited not to hear more, but darting spurs into my horse's sides, cleared the fence in one bound. My horse, a strong-knit half-breed, was as fast as a racer for a short distance; so that when the agent and his party had come up with the carriage, I was only a few hundred yards behind. I shouted out with all my might, but they either heard not or heeded not, for scarcely was the first man over the fence into the road when the postilion on the leader was felled to the ground, and his place supplied by his slayer; the boy on the wheeler shared the same fate, and in an instant, so well managed was the attack, the carriage was in possession of the assailants. Four stout fellows had climbed into the box and the rumble, and six others were climbing to the interior, regardless of the aid of steps. By this time the Dashwood party had got the alarm, and returned in full force, not, however, before the other had laid whip to the horses and set out in full gallop; and now commenced the most terrific race I ever witnessed.

The four carriage-horses, which were the property of Sir George, were English thorough-breds of great value, and, totally unaccustomed to the treatment they experienced, dashed forward at a pace that threatened annihilation to the carriage at every bound. The pursuers, though well mounted, were speedily distanced, but followed at a pace that in the end was certain to overtake the carriage. As for myself, I rode on beside the road at the full speed of my horse, shouting, cursing, imploring, execrating, and beseeching at turns, but all in vain; the yells and shouts of the pursuers and pursued drowned all other sounds, except when the thundering crash of the horses' feet rose above all. The road, like most western Irish roads until the present century, lay straight as an arrow for miles, regardless of every opposing barrier, and in the instance in question, crossed a mountain at its very highest point. Towards this pinnacle the pace had been tremendous; but owing to the higher breeding of the cattle, the carriage party had still the advance, and when they reached the top they proclaimed the victory by a cheer of triumph and derision. The carriage disappeared beneath the crest of the mountain, and the pursuers halted as if disposed to relinquish the chase.

"Come on, boys; never give up," cried I, springing over into the road, and heading the party to which by every right I was opposed.

It was no time for deliberation, and they followed me with a hearty cheer that convinced me I was unknown. The next instant we were on the mountain top, and beheld the carriage half way down beneath us, still galloping at full stretch.

"We have them now," said a voice behind me; "they'll never turn Lurra Bridge, if we only press on."

The speaker was right; the road at the mountain foot turned at a perfect right angle, and then crossed a lofty one-arched bridge over a mountain torrent that ran deep and boisterously beneath. On we went, gaining at every stride; for the fellows who rode postilion well knew what was before them, and slackened their pace to secure a safe turning. A yell of victory arose from the pursuers, but was answered by the others with a cheer of defiance. The space was now scarcely two hundred yards between us, when the head of the britska was flung down, and a figure that I at once recognized as the redoubted Tim Finucane, one of the boldest and most reckless fellows in the county, was seen standing on the seat, holding,—gracious Heavens! it was true,—holding in his arms the apparently lifeless figure of Miss Dashwood.

"Hold in!" shouted the ruffian, with a voice that rose high above all the other sounds. "Hold in! or by the Eternal, I'll throw her, body and bones, into the Lurra Gash!" for such was the torrent called that boiled and foamed a few yards before us.

He had by this time got firmly planted on the hind seat, and held the drooping form on one arm with all the ease of a giant's grasp.

"For the love of God!" said I, "pull up. I know him well; he'll do it to a certainty if you press on."

"And we know you, too," said a ruffianly fellow, with a dark whisker meeting beneath his chin, "and have some scores to settle ere we part—"

But I heard no more. With one tremendous effort I dashed my horse forward. The carriage turned an angle of the road, for an instant was out of sight, another moment I was behind it.

"Stop!" I shouted, with a last effort, but in vain. The horses, maddened and infuriated, sprang forward, and heedless of all efforts to turn them the leaders sprang over the low parapet of the bridge, and hanging for a second by the traces, fell with a crash into the swollen torrent beneath. By this time I was beside the carriage. Finucane had now clambered to the box, and regardless of the death and ruin around, bent upon his murderous object, he lifted the light and girlish form above his head, bent backwards as if to give greater impulse to his effort, when, twining my lash around my wrist, I levelled my heavy and loaded hunting-whip at his head. The weighted ball of lead struck him exactly beneath his hat; he staggered, his hands relaxed, and he fell lifeless to the ground; the same instant I was felled to the earth by a blow from behind, and saw no more.

CHAPTER XII.

MICKEY FREE.

Nearly three weeks followed the event I have just narrated ere I again was restored to consciousness. The blow by which I was felled—from what hand coming it was never after discovered—had brought on concussion of the brain, and for several days my life was despaired of. As by slow steps I advanced towards recovery, I learned from Considine that Miss Dashwood, whose life was saved by my interference, had testified, in the warmest manner, her gratitude, and that Sir George had, up to the period of his leaving the country, never omitted a single day to ride over and inquire for me.

"You know, of course," said the count, supposing such news was the most likely to interest me,—"you know we beat them?"

"No. Pray tell me all. They've not let me hear anything hitherto."

"One day finished the whole affair. We polled man for man till past two o'clock, when our fellows lost all patience and beat their tallies out of the town. The police came up, but they beat the police; then they got soldiers, but, begad, they were too strong for them, too. Sir George witnessed it all, and knowing besides how little chance he had of success, deemed it best to give in; so that a little before five o'clock he resigned. I must say no man could behave better. He came across the hustings and shook hands with Godfrey; and as the news of the *scrimmage* with his daughter had just arrived, said that he was sorry his prospect of success had not been greater, that in resigning he might testify how deeply he felt the debt the O'Malleys had laid him under."

"And my uncle, how did he receive his advances?"

"Like his own honest self,—grasped his hand firmly; and upon my soul, I think he was half sorry that he gained the day. Do you know, he took a mighty fancy to that blue-eyed daughter of the old general's. Faith, Charley, if he was some twenty years younger, I would not say but—Come, come, I didn't mean to hurt your feelings; but I have been staying here too long. I'll send up Mickey to sit with you. Mind and don't be talking too much to him."

So saying, the worthy count left the room fully impressed that in hinting at the possibility of my uncle's marrying again, he had said something to ruffle my temper.

For the next two or three weeks my life was one of the most tiresome monotony. Strict injunctions had been given by the doctors to avoid exciting me; and consequently, every one that came in walked on tiptoe, spoke in whispers, and left me in five minutes. Reading was absolutely forbidden; and with a sombre half-light to sit in, and chicken broth to support nature, I dragged out as dreary an existence as any gentleman west of Athlone.

Whenever my uncle or Considine were not in the room, my companion was my own servant, Michael, or as he was better known, "Mickey Free." Now, had Mickey been left to his own free and unrestricted devices, the time would not have hung so heavily; for among Mike's manifold gifts he was possessed of a very great flow of gossiping conversation. He knew all that was doing in the county, and never was barren in his information wherever his imagination could come into play. Mickey was the best hurler in the barony, no mean performer on the violin, could dance the national bolero of "Tatter Jack Walsh" in a way that charmed more than one soft heart beneath a red woolsey bodice, and had, withal, the peculiar free-and-easy devil-may-care kind of off-hand Irish way that never deserted him in the midst of his wiliest and most subtle moments, giving to a very deep and cunning fellow all the apparent frankness and openness of a country lad.

He had attached himself to me as a kind of sporting companion; and growing daily more and more useful, had been gradually admitted to the honors of the kitchen and the prerogatives of cast clothes, without ever having been actually engaged as a servant; and while thus no warrant officer, as, in fact, he discharged all his duties well and punctually, was rated among the ship's company, though no one could say at what precise period he changed his caterpillar existence and became the gay butterfly with cords and tops, a striped vest, and a most knowing jerry hat who stalked about the stable-yard and bullied the helpers. Such was Mike. He had made his fortune, such as it was, and had a most becoming pride in the fact that he made himself indispensable to an establishment which, before he entered it, never knew the want of him. As for me, he was everything to me. Mike informed me what horse was wrong, why the chestnut mare couldn't go out, and why the black horse could. He knew the arrival of a new covey of partridge quicker than the "Morning Post" does of a noble family from the Continent, and could tell their whereabouts twice as accurately. But his talents took a wider range than field sports afford, and he was the faithful chronicler of every wake, station, wedding, or christening for miles round; and as I took no small pleasure in those very national pastimes, the information was of great value to me. To conclude this brief sketch, Mike was a devout Catholic in the same sense that he was enthusiastic about anything,—that is, he believed and obeyed exactly as far as suited his own peculiar notions of comfort and happiness. Beyond *that*, his scepticism stepped in and saved him from inconvenience; and though he might have been somewhat puzzled to reduce his faith to a rubric, still it answered his purpose, and that was all he wanted. Such, in short, was my valet, Mickey Free, and who, had not heavy injunctions been laid on him as to silence and discretion, would well have lightened my weary hours.

"Ah, then, Misther Charles!" said he, with a half-suppressed yawn at the long period of probation his tongue had been undergoing in silence,—"ah, then, but ye were mighty near it!"

"Near what?" said I.

"Faith, then, myself doesn't well know. Some say it's purgathory; but it's hard to tell."

"I thought you were too good a Catholic, Mickey, to show any doubts on the matter?"

"May be I am; may be I ain't," was the cautious reply.

"Wouldn't Father Roach explain any of your difficulties for you, if you went over to him?"

"Faix, it's little I'd mind his explainings."

"And why not?"

"Easy enough. If you ax ould Miles there, without, what does he be doing with all the powther and shot, wouldn't he tell you he's shooting the rooks, and the magpies, and some other varmint? But myself knows he sells it to Widow Casey, at two-and-fourpence a pound; so belikes, Father Roach may be shooting away at the poor souls in purgathory, that all this time are enjoying the hoith of fine living in heaven, ye understand."

"And you think that's the way of it, Mickey?"

"Troth, it's likely. Anyhow, I know its not the place they make it out."

"Why, how do you mean?"

"Well, then, I'll tell you, Misther Charles; but you must not be saying anything about it afther, for I don't like to talk about these kind of things."

Having pledged myself to the requisite silence and secrecy, Mickey began:—

"May be you heard tell of the way my father, rest his soul wherever he is, came to his end. Well, I needn't mind particulars, but, in short, he was murdered in Ballinasloe one night, when he was baitin' the whole town with a blackthorn stick he had; more by token, a piece of a scythe was stuck at the end of it,—a nate weapon, and one he was mighty partial to; but those murdering thieves, the cattle-dealers, that never cared for diversion of any kind, fell on him and broke his skull.

"Well, we had a very agreeable wake, and plenty of the best of everything, and to spare, and I thought it was all over; but somehow, though I paid Father Roach fifteen shillings, and made him mighty drunk, he always gave me a black look wherever I met him, and when I took off my hat, he'd turn away his head displeased like.

"'Murder and ages,' says I, 'what's this for?' But as I've a light heart, I bore up, and didn't think more about it. One day, however, I was coming home from Athlone market, by myself on the road, when Father Roach overtook me. 'Devil a one a me 'ill take any notice of you now,' says I, 'and we'll see what'll come out of it.' So the priest rid up and looked me straight in the face.

"'Mickey,' says he,—'Mickey.'

"'Father,' says I.

"'Is it that way you salute your clargy,' says he, 'with your caubeen on your head?'

"'Faix,' says I, 'it's little ye mind whether it's an or aff; for you never take the trouble to say, "By your leave," or "Damn your soul!" or any other politeness when we meet.'

"'You're an ungrateful creature,' says he; 'and if you only knew, you'd be trembling in your skin before me, this minute.'

"'Devil a tremble,' says I, 'after walking six miles this way.'

"'You're an obstinate, hard-hearted sinner,' says he; 'and it's no use in telling you.'

"'Telling me what?' says I; for I was getting curious to make out what he meant.

"'Mickey,' says he, changing his voice, and putting his head down close to me,—'Mickey, I saw your father last night.'

"'The saints be merciful to us!' said I, 'did ye?'

"'I did,' says he.

"'Tear an ages,' says I, 'did he tell you what he did with the new corduroys he bought in the fair?'

"'Oh, then, you are a could-hearted creature!' says he, 'and I'll not lose time with you.' With that he was going to ride away, when I took hold of the bridle.

"'Father, darling,' says I, 'God pardon me, but them breeches is goin' between me an' my night's rest; but tell me about my father?'

"'Oh, then, he's in a melancholy state!'

"'Whereabouts is he?' says I.

"'In purgathory,' says he; 'but he won't be there long.'

"'Well,' says I, 'that's a comfort, anyhow.'

"'I am glad you think so,' says he; 'but there's more of the other opinion.'

"'What's *that?*' says I.

"'That hell's worse.'

"'Oh, melia-murther!' says I, 'is that it?'

"'Ay, that's it.'

"Well, I was so terrified and frightened, I said nothing for some time, but trotted along beside the priest's horse.

"'Father,' says I, 'how long will it be before they send him where you know?'

"'It will not be long now,' says he, 'for they're tired entirely with him; they've no peace night or day,' says he. 'Mickey, your father is a mighty hard man.'

"'True for you, Father Roach,' says I to myself; 'av he had only the ould stick with the scythe in it, I wish them joy of his company.'

"'Mickey,' says he, 'I see you're grieved, and I don't wonder; sure, it's a great disgrace to a decent family.'

"'Troth, it is,' says I; 'but my father always liked low company. Could nothing be done for him now, Father Roach?' says I, looking up in the priest's face.

"'I'm greatly afraid, Mickey, he was a bad man, a very bad man.'

"'And ye think he'll go there?' says I.

"'Indeed, Mickey, I have my fears.'

"'Upon my conscience,' says I, 'I believe you're right; he was always a restless crayture.'

"'But it doesn't depind on him,' says the priest, crossly.

"'And, then, who then?' says I.

"'Upon yourself, Mickey Free,' says he, 'God pardon you for it, too!'

"'Upon me?' says I.

"'Troth, no less,' says he; 'how many Masses was said for your father's soul; how many Aves; how many Paters? Answer me.'

"'Devil a one of me knows!—may be twenty.'

"'Twenty, twenty!—no, nor one.'

"'And why not?' says I; 'what for wouldn't you be helping a poor crayture out of trouble, when it wouldn't cost you more nor a handful of prayers?'

"'Mickey, I see,' says he, in a solemn tone, 'you're worse nor a haythen; but ye couldn't be other, ye never come to yer duties.'

"'Well, Father,' says I, Looking very penitent, 'how many Masses would get him out?'

"'Now you talk like a sensible man,' says he. 'Now, Mickey, I've hopes for you. Let me see,' here he went countin' upon his fingers, and numberin' to himself for five minutes. 'Mickey,' says he, 'I've a batch coming out on Tuesday week, and if you were to make great exertions, perhaps your father could come with them; that is, av they have made no objections.'

"'And what for would they?' says I; 'he was always the hoith of company, and av singing's allowed in them parts—'

"'God forgive you, Mickey, but yer in a benighted state,' says he, sighing.

"'Well,' says I, 'how'll we get him out on Tuesday week? For that's bringing things to a focus.'

"'Two Masses in the morning, fastin',' says Father Roach, half aloud, 'is two, and two in the afternoon is four, and two at vespers is six,' says he; 'six Masses a day for nine days is close by sixty Masses,—say sixty,' says he; 'and they'll cost you—mind, Mickey, and don't be telling it again, for it's only to yourself I'd make them so cheap—a matter of three pounds.'

"'Three pounds!' says I; 'be-gorra ye might as well ax me to give you the rock of Cashel.'

"'I'm sorry for ye, Mickey,' says he, gatherin' up the reins to ride off,—'I'm sorry for ye; and the time will come when the neglect of your poor father will be a sore stroke agin yourself.'

"'Wait a bit, your reverence,' says I,—'wait a bit. Would forty shillings get him out?'

"'Av course it wouldn't,' says he.

"'May be,' says I, coaxing,—'may be, av you said that his son was a poor boy that lived by his indhustry, and the times was bad—'

"'Not the least use,' says he.

"'Arrah, but it's hard-hearted they are,' thinks I. 'Well, see now, I'll give you the money, but I can't afford it all at onst; but I'll pay five shillings a week. Will that do?'

"'I'll do my endayvors,' says Father Roach; 'and I'll speak to them to treat him peaceably in the meantime.'

"'Long life to yer reverence, and do. Well, here now, here's five hogs to begin with; and, musha, but I never thought I'd be spending my loose change that way.'

"Father Roach put the six tinpinnies in the pocket of his black leather breeches, said something in Latin, bid me good-morning, and rode off.

"Well, to make my story short, I worked late and early to pay the five shillings a week, and I did it for three weeks regular; then I brought four and fourpence; then it came down to one and tenpence halfpenny, then ninepence, and at last I had nothing at all to bring.

"'Mickey Free,' says the priest, 'ye must stir yourself. Your father is mighty displeased at the way you've been doing of late; and av ye kept yer word, he'd be near out by this time.'

"'Troth,' says I, 'it's a very expensive place.'

"'By coorse it is,' says he; 'sure all the quality of the land's there. But, Mickey, my man, with a little exertion, your father's business is done. What are you jingling in your pocket there?'

"'It's ten shillings, your reverence, I have to buy seed potatoes.'

"'Hand it here, my son. Isn't it better your father would be enjoying himself in paradise, than if ye were to have all the potatoes in Ireland?'

"'And how do ye know,' says I, 'he's so near out?'

"'How do I know,—how do I know, is it? Didn't I see him?'

"'See him! Tear an ages, was you down there again?'

"'I was,' says he; 'I was down there for three quarters of an hour yesterday evening, getting out Luke Kennedy's mother. Decent people the Kennedy's; never spared expense.'

"'And ye seen my father?' says I.

"'I did,' says he; 'he had an ould flannel waistcoat on, and a pipe sticking out of the pocket av it.'

"'That's him,' says I. 'Had he a hairy cap?'

"'I didn't mind the cap,' says he; 'but av coorse he wouldn't have it on his head in that place.'

"'Thrue for you,' says I. 'Did he speak to you?'

"'He did,' says Father Roach; 'he spoke very hard about the way he was treated down there; that they was always jibin' and jeerin' him about *drink*, and fightin', and the course he led up here, and that it was a queer thing, for the matter of ten shillings, he was to be kept there so long.'

"'Well,' says I, taking out the ten shillings and counting it with one hand, 'we must do our best, anyhow; and ye think this'll get him out surely?'

"'I know it will,' says he; 'for when Luke's mother was leaving the place, and yer father saw the door open, he made a rush at it, and, be-gorra, before it was shut he got his head and one shoulder outside av it,—so that, ye see, a thrifle more'll do it.'

"'Faix, and yer reverence,' says I, 'you've lightened my heart this morning.' And I put my money back again in my pocket.

"'Why, what do you mean?' says he, growing very red, for he was angry.

"'Just this,' says I, 'that I've saved my money; for av it was my father you seen, and that he got his head and one shoulder outside the door, oh, then, by the powers!' says I, 'the devil a jail or jailer from hell to Connaught id hould him. So, Father Roach, I wish you the top of the morning.' And I went away laughing; and from that day to this I never heard more of purgathory; and ye see, Master Charles, I think I was right."

Scarcely had Mike concluded when my door was suddenly burst open, and Sir Harry Boyle, without assuming any of his usual precautions respecting silence and quiet, rushed into the room, a broad grin upon his honest features, and his eyes twinkling in a way that evidently showed me something had occurred to amuse him.

"By Jove, Charley, I mustn't keep it from you; it's too good a thing not to tell you. Do you remember that very essenced young gentleman who accompanied Sir George Dashwood from Dublin, as a kind of electioneering friend?"

"Do you mean Mr. Prettyman?"

"The very man; he was, you are aware, an under-secretary in some government department. Well, it seems that he had come down among us poor savages as much from motives of learned research and scientific inquiry, as though we had been South Sea Islanders; report had gifted us humble Galwayans with some very peculiar traits, and this gifted individual resolved to record them. Whether the election week might have sufficed his appetite for wonders I know not; but he was peaceably taking his departure from the west on Saturday last, when Phil Macnamara met him, and pressed him to dine that day with a few friends at his house. You know Phil; so that when I tell you Sam Burke, of Greenmount, and Roger Doolan were of the party, I need not say that the English traveller was not left to his own unassisted imagination for his facts. Such anecdotes of our habits and customs as they crammed him with, it would appear, never were heard before; nothing was too hot or too heavy for the luckless cockney, who, when not sipping his claret, was faithfully recording in his tablet the mems. for a very brilliant and very original work on Ireland.

"Fine country, splendid country; glorious people,—gifted, brave, intelligent, but not happy,—alas! Mr. Macnamara, not happy. But we don't know you, gentlemen,—we don't indeed,—at the other side of the Channel. Our notions regarding you are far, very far from just."

"I hope and trust," said old Burke, "you'll help them to a better understanding ere long."

"Such, my dear sir, will be the proudest task of my life. The facts I have heard here this evening have made so profound an impression upon me that I burn for the moment when I can make them known to the world at large. To think—just to think that a portion of this beautiful island should be steeped in poverty; that the people not only live upon the mere potatoes, but are absolutely obliged to wear the skins for raiment, as Mr. Doolan has just mentioned to me!"

"'Which accounts for our cultivation of lumpers,' added Mr. Doolan, 'they being the largest species of the root, and best adapted for wearing apparel.'

"'I should deem myself culpable—indeed I should—did I not inform my countrymen upon the real condition of this great country.'

"'Why, after your great opportunities for judging,' said Phil, 'you ought to speak out. You've seen us in a way, I may fairly affirm, few Englishmen have, and heard more.'

"'That's it,—that's the very thing, Mr. Macnamara. I've looked at you more closely; I've watched you more narrowly; I've witnessed what the French call your *vie intime*.'

"'Begad you have,' said old Burke, with a grin, 'and profited by it to the utmost.'

"'I've been a spectator of your election contests; I've partaken of your hospitality; I've witnessed your popular and national sports; I've been present at your weddings, your fairs, your wakes; but no,—I was forgetting,—I never saw a wake.'

"'Never saw a wake?' repeated each of the company in turn, as though the gentleman was uttering a sentiment of very dubious veracity.

"'Never,' said Mr. Prettyman, rather abashed at this proof of his incapacity to instruct his English friends upon *all* matters of Irish interest.

"'Well, then,' said Macnamara, 'with a blessing, we'll show you one. Lord forbid that we shouldn't do the honors of our poor country to an intelligent foreigner when he's good enough to come among us.'

"'Peter,' said he, turning to the servant behind him, 'who's dead hereabouts?'

"'Sorra one, yer honor. Since the scrimmage at Portumna the place is peaceable.'

"'Who died lately in the neighborhood?'

"'The widow Macbride, yer honor.'

"'Couldn't they take her up again, Peter? My friend here never saw a wake.'

"'I'm afeered not; for it was the boys roasted her, and she wouldn't be a decent corpse for to show a stranger,' said Peter, in a whisper.

"Mr. Prettyman shuddered at these peaceful indications of the neighborhood, and said nothing.

"'Well, then, Peter, tell Jimmy Divine to take the old musket in my bedroom, and go over to the Clunagh bog,—he can't go wrong. There's twelve families there that never pay a halfpenny rent; and *when it's done*, let him give notice to the neighborhood, and we'll have a rousing wake.'

"'You don't mean, Mr. Macnamara,—you don't mean to say—' stammered out the cockney, with a face like a ghost.

"'I only mean to say,' said Phil, laughing, 'that you're keeping the decanter very long at your right hand.'

"Burke contrived to interpose before the Englishman could ask any explanation of what he had just heard,—and for some minutes he could only wait in impatient anxiety,—when a loud report of a gun close beside the house attracted the attention of the guests. The next moment old Peter entered, his face radiant with smiles.

"'Well, what's that?' said Macnamara.

"''T was Jimmy, yer honor. As the evening was rainy, he said he'd take one of the neighbors; and he hadn't to go far, for Andy Moore was going home, and he brought him down at once.'

"'Did he shoot him?' said Mr. Prettyman, while cold perspiration broke over his forehead. 'Did he murder the man?'

"'Sorra murder,' said Peter, disdainfully. 'But why shouldn't he shoot him when the master bid him?'

"I needn't tell you more, Charley; but in ten minutes after, feigning some excuse to leave the room, the terrified cockney took flight, and offering twenty guineas for a horse to convey him to Athlone, he left Galway, fully convinced that they don't yet know us on the other side of the Channel."

CHAPTER XIII.

THE JOURNEY.

The election concluded, the turmoil and excitement of the contest over, all was fast resuming its accustomed routine around us, when one morning my uncle informed me that I was at length to leave my native county and enter upon the great world as a student of Trinity College, Dublin. Although long since in expectation of this eventful change, it was with no slight feeling of emotion I contemplated the step which, removing me at once from all my early friends and associations, was to surround me with new companions and new influences, and place before me very different objects of ambition from those I had hitherto been regarding.

My destiny had been long ago decided. The army had had its share of the family, who brought little more back with them from the wars than a short allowance of members and shattered constitutions; the navy had proved, on more than one occasion, that the fate of the O'Malleys did not incline to hanging; so that, in Irish estimation, but one alternative remained, and that was the bar. Besides, as my uncle remarked, with great truth and foresight, "Charley will be tolerably independent of the public, at all events; for even if they never send him a brief, there's law enough in the family to last *his* time,"—a rather novel reason, by-the-bye, for making a man a lawyer, and which induced Sir Harry, with his usual clearness, to observe to me:—

"Upon my conscience, boy, you are in luck. If there had been a Bible in the house, I firmly believe he'd have made you a parson."

Considine alone, of all my uncle's advisers, did not concur in this determination respecting me. He set forth, with an eloquence that certainly converted *me*, that my head was better calculated for bearing hard knocks than unravelling knotty points, that a shako would become it infinitely better than a wig; and declared, roundly, that a boy who began so well and had such very pretty notions about shooting was positively thrown away in the Four Courts. My uncle, however, was firm, and as old Sir Harry supported him, the day was decided against us, Considine murmuring as he left the room something that did not seem quite a brilliant anticipation of the success awaiting me in my legal career. As for myself, though only a silent spectator of the debate, all my wishes were with the count. From my earliest boyhood a military life had been my strongest desire; the roll of the drum, and the shrill fife that played through the little village, with its ragged troop of recruits following, had charms for me I cannot describe; and had a choice been allowed me, I would infinitely rather have been a sergeant in the dragoons than one of his Majesty's learned in the law. If, then, such had been the cherished feeling of many a year, how much more strongly were my aspirations heightened by the events of the last few days. The tone of superiority I had witnessed in Hammersley, whose conduct to me at parting had placed him high in my esteem; the quiet contempt of civilians implied in a thousand sly ways; the exalted estimate of his own profession,—at once wounded my pride and stimulated my ambition; and lastly, more than all, the avowed preference that Lucy Dashwood evinced for a military life, were stronger allies than my own conviction needed to make me long for the army. So completely did the thought possess me that I felt, if I were not a soldier, I cared not what became of me. Life had no other object of ambition for me than military renown, no other success for which I cared to struggle, or would value when obtained. "*Aut Caesar aut nullus*," thought I; and when my uncle determined I should be a lawyer, I neither murmured nor objected, but hugged myself in the prophecy of Considine that hinted pretty broadly, "the devil a stupider fellow ever opened a brief; but he'd have made a slashing light dragoon."

The preliminaries were not long in arranging. It was settled that I should be immediately despatched to Dublin to the care of Dr. Mooney, then a junior fellow in the University, who would take me into his especial charge; while Sir Harry was to furnish me with a letter to his old friend, Doctor Barret, whose advice and assistance he estimated at a very high price. Provided with such documents I was informed that the gates of knowledge were more than half ajar for me, without an effort upon my part. One only portion of all the arrangements I heard with anything like pleasure; it was decided that my man Mickey was to accompany me to Dublin, and remain with me during my stay.

It was upon a clear, sharp morning in January, of the year 18—, that I took my place upon the box-seat of the old Galway mail and set out on my journey. My heart was depressed, and my spirits were miserably low. I had all that feeling of sadness which leave-taking inspires, and no sustaining prospect to cheer me in the distance. For the first time in my life, I had seen a tear glisten in my poor uncle's eye, and heard his voice falter as he said, "Farewell!" Notwithstanding the difference of age, we had been perfectly companions together; and as I thought now over all the thousand kindnesses and affectionate instances of his love I had received, my heart gave way, and the tears coursed slowly down my cheeks. I turned to give one last look at the tall chimneys and the old woods, my earliest friends; but a turn of the road had shut out the prospect, and thus I took my leave of Galway.

My friend Mickey, who sat behind with the guard, participated but little in my feelings of regret. The potatoes in the metropolis could scarcely be as wet as the lumpers in Scariff; he had heard that whiskey was not dearer, and looked forward to the other delights of the capital with a longing heart. Meanwhile, resolved that no portion of his career should be lost, he was lightening the road by anecdote and song, and held an audience of four people, a very crusty-looking old guard included, in roars of laughter. Mike had contrived, with his usual *savoir faire*, to make himself very agreeable to an extremely pretty-looking country girl, around whose waist he had most lovingly passed his arm under pretence of keeping her from falling, and to whom, in the midst of all his attentions to the party at large, he devoted himself considerably, pressing his suit with all the aid of his native minstrelsy.

"Hould me tight, Miss Matilda, dear."

"My name's Mary Brady, av ye plase."

"Ay, and I do plase.

'Oh, Mary Brady, you are my darlin', You are my looking-glass from night till morning; I'd rayther have ye without one farthen, Nor Shusey Gallagher and her house and garden.'

May I never av I wouldn't then; and ye needn't be laughing."

"Is his honor at home?"

This speech was addressed to a gaping country fellow that leaned on his spade to see the coach pass.

"Is his honor at home? I've something for him from Mr. Davern."

Mickey well knew that few western gentlemen were without constant intercourse with the Athlone attorney. The poor countryman accordingly hastened through the fence and pursued the coach with all speed for above a mile, Mike pretending all the time to be in the greatest anxiety for his overtaking them, until at last, as he stopped in despair, a hearty roar of laughter told him that, in Mickey's *parlance*, he was "sould."

"Taste it, my dear; devil a harm it'll do ye. It never paid the king sixpence."

Here he filled a little horn vessel from a black bottle he carried, accompanying the action with a song, the air to which, if any of my readers feel disposed to sing it, I may observe, bore a resemblance to the well-known, "A Fig for Saint Denis of France."

POTTEEN, GOOD LUCK TO YE, DEAR. Av I was a monarch in state, Like Romulus or Julius Caysar, With the best of fine victuals to eat, And drink like great Nebuchadnezzar, A rasher of bacon I'd have, And potatoes the finest was seen, sir, And for drink, it's no claret I'd crave, But a keg of ould Mullens's potteen, sir, With the smell of the smoke on it still. They talk of the Romans of ould, Whom they say in their own times was frisky; But trust me, to keep out the cowld, The Romans at home here like whiskey. Sure it warms both the head and the heart, It's the soul of all readin' and writin'; It teaches both science and art, And disposes for love or for fightin'. Oh, potteen, good luck to ye, dear.

This very classic production, and the black bottle which accompanied it, completely established the singer's pre-eminence in the company; and I heard sundry sounds resembling drinking, with frequent good wishes to the provider of the feast,—"Long life to ye, Mr. Free," "Your health and inclinations, Mr. Free," etc.; to which Mr. Free responded by drinking those of the company, "av they were vartuous." The amicable relations thus happily established promised a very lasting reign, and would doubtless have enjoyed such, had not a slight incident occurred which for a brief season interrupted them. At the village where we stopped to breakfast, three very venerable figures presented themselves for places in the inside of the coach; they were habited in black coats, breeches, and gaiters, wore hats of a very ecclesiastic breadth in their brim, and had altogether the peculiar air and bearing which distinguishes their calling, being no less than three Roman Catholic prelates on their way to Dublin to attend a convocation. While Mickey and his friends, with the ready tact which every low Irishman possesses, immediately perceived who and what these worshipful individuals were, another traveller who had just assumed his place on the outside participated but little in the feelings of reverence so manifestly displayed, but gave a sneer of a very ominous kind as the skirt of the last black coat disappeared within the coach. This latter individual was a short, thick-set, bandy-legged man of about fifty, with an enormous nose, which, whatever its habitual coloring, on the morning in question was of a brilliant purple. He wore a blue coat with bright buttons, upon which some letters were inscribed; and around his neck was fastened a ribbon of the same color, to which a medal was attached. This he displayed with something of ostentation whenever an opportunity occurred, and seemed altogether a person who possessed a most satisfactory impression of his own importance. In fact, had not this feeling been participated in by others, Mr. Billy Crow would never have been deputed by No. 13,476 to carry their warrant down to the west country, and establish the nucleus of an Orange Lodge in the town of Foxleigh; such being, in brief, the reason why he, a very well known manufacturer of "leather continuations" in Dublin, had ventured upon the perilous journey from which he was now returning. Billy was going on his way to town rejoicing, for he had had most brilliant success: the brethren had feasted and fêted him; he had made several splendid orations, with the usual number of prophecies about the speedy downfall of Romanism, the inevitable return of Protestant ascendancy, the pleasing prospect that with increased effort and improved organization they should soon be able to have everything their own way, and clear the Green Isle of the horrible vermin Saint Patrick forgot when banishing the others; and that if Daniel O'Connell (whom might the Lord confound!) could only be hanged, and Sir Harcourt Lees made Primate of all Ireland, there were still some hopes of peace and prosperity to the country.

Mr. Crow had no sooner assumed his place upon the coach than he saw that he was in the camp of the enemy. Happily for all parties, indeed, in Ireland, political differences have so completely stamped the externals of each party that he must be a man of small penetration who cannot, in the first five minutes he is thrown among strangers, calculate with considerable certainty whether it will be more conducive to his happiness to sing, "Croppies Lie Down," or "The Battle of Ross." As for Billy Crow, long life to him! you might as well attempt to pass a turkey upon M. Audubon for a giraffe, as endeavor to impose a Papist upon him for a true follower of King William. He could have given you more generic distinctions to guide you in the decision than ever did Cuvier to designate an antediluvian mammoth; so that no sooner had he seated himself upon the coach than he buttoned up his great-coat, stuck his hands firmly in his side-pockets, pursed up his lips, and looked altogether like a man that, feeling himself out of his element, resolves to "bide his time" in patience until chance may throw him among more congenial associates. Mickey Free, who was himself no mean proficient in reading a character, at one glance saw his man, and began hammering his brains to see if he could not overreach him. The small portmanteau which contained Billy's wardrobe bore the conspicuous announcement of his name; and as Mickey could read, this was one important step already gained.

He accordingly took the first opportunity of seating himself beside him, and opened the conversation by some very polite observation upon the other's wearing apparel, which is always in the west considered a piece of very courteous attention. By degrees the dialogue prospered, and Mickey began to make some very important revelations about himself and his master, intimating that the "state of the country" was such that a man of his way of thinking had no peace or quiet in it.

"That's him there, forenent ye," said Mickey, "and a better Protestant never hated Mass. Ye understand."

"What!" said Billy, unbuttoning the collar of his coat to get a fairer view at his companion; "why, I thought you were—"

Here he made some resemblance of the usual manner of blessing oneself.

"Me, devil a more nor yourself, Mr. Crow."

"Why, do you know me, too?"

"Troth, more knows you than you think."

Billy looked very much puzzled at all this; at last he said,—

"And ye tell me that your master there's the right sort?"

"Thrue blue," said Mike, with a wink, "and so is his uncles."

"And where are they, when they are at home?"

"In Galway, no less; but they're here now."

"Where?"

"Here."

At these words he gave a knock of his heel to the coach, as if to intimate their "whereabouts."

"You don't mean in the coach, do ye?"

"To be sure I do; and troth you can't know much of the west, av ye don't know the three Mr. Trenches of Tallybash!—them's they."

"You don't say so?"

"Faix, but I do."

"May I never drink the 12th of July if I didn't think they were priests."

"Priests!" said Mickey, in a roar of laughter,—"priests!"

"Just priests!"

"Be-gorra, though, ye had better keep that to yourself; for they're not the men to have that same said to them."

"Of course I wouldn't offend them," said Mr. Crow; "faith, it's not me would cast reflections upon such real out-and-outers as they are. And where are they going now?"

"To Dublin straight; there's to be a grand lodge next week. But sure Mr. Crow knows better than me."

Billy after this became silent. A moody revery seemed to steal over him; and he was evidently displeased with himself for his want of tact in not discovering the three Mr. Trenches of Tallybash, though he only caught sight of their backs.

Mickey Free interrupted not the frame of mind in which he saw conviction was slowly working its way, but by gently humming in an undertone the loyal melody of "Croppies Lie Down," fanned the flame he had so dexterously kindled. At length they reached the small town of Kinnegad. While the coach changed horses, Mr. Crow lost not a moment in descending from the top, and rushing into the little inn, disappeared for a few moments. When he again issued forth, he carried a smoking tumbler of whiskey punch, which he continued to stir with a spoon. As he approached the coach-door he tapped gently with his knuckles; upon which the reverend prelate of Maronia, or Mesopotamia, I forget which, inquired what he wanted.

"I ask your pardon, gentlemen," said Billy, "but I thought I'd make bold to ask you to take something warm this cold day."

"Many thanks, my good friend; but we never do," said a bland voice from within.

"I understand," said Billy, with a sly wink; "but there are circumstances now and then,—and one might for the honor of the cause, you know. Just put it to your lips, won't you?"

"Excuse me," said a very rosy-cheeked little prelate, "but nothing stronger than water—"

"Botheration," thought Billy, as he regarded the speaker's nose. "But I thought," said he, aloud, "that you would not refuse this."

Here he made a peculiar manifestation in the air, which, whatever respect and reverence it might carry to the honest brethren of 13,476, seemed only to increase the wonder and astonishment of the bishops.

"What does he mean?" said one.

"Is he mad?" said another.

"Tear and ages," said Mr. Crow, getting quite impatient at the slowness of his friends' perception,—"tear and ages, I'm one of yourselves."

"One of us," said the three in chorus,—"one of us?"

"Ay, to be sure," here he took a long pull at the punch,—"to be sure I am; here's 'No surrender,' your souls! whoop—" a loud yell accompanying the toast as he drank it.

"Do you mean to insult us?" said Father P———. "Guard, take the fellow."

"Are we to be outraged in this manner?" chorussed the priests.

"'July the 1st, in Oldbridge town,'" sang Billy, "and here it is, 'The glorious, pious, and immortal memory of the great and good—'"

"Guard! Where is the guard?"

"'And good King William, that saved us from Popery—'"

"Coachman! Guard!" screamed Father ———.

"'Brass money—'"

"Policeman! policeman!" shouted the priests.

"'Brass money and wooden shoes;' devil may care who hears me!" said Billy, who, supposing that the three Mr. Trenches were skulking the avowal of their principles, resolved to assert the pre-eminence of the great cause single-handed and alone.

"'Here's the Pope in the pillory, and the Devil pelting him with priests.'"

At these words a kick from behind apprised the loyal champion that a very ragged auditory, who for some time past had not well understood the gist of his eloquence, had at length comprehended enough to be angry. *Ce n'est que le premier pas qui coûte*, certainly, in an Irish row. "The merest urchin may light the train; one handful of mud often ignites a shindy that ends in a most bloody battle."

And here, no sooner did the *vis-a-tergo* impel Billy forward than a severe rap of a closed fist in the eye drove him back, and in one instant he became the centre to a periphery of kicks, cuffs, pullings, and haulings that left the poor deputy-grand not only orange, but blue.

He fought manfully, but numbers carried the day; and when the coach drove off, which it did at last without him, the last thing visible to the outsides was the figure of Mr. Crow,—whose hat, minus the crown, had been driven over his head down upon his neck, where it remained like a dress cravat,—buffeting a mob of ragged vagabonds who had so completely metamorphosed the unfortunate man with mud and bruises that a committee of the grand lodge might actually have been unable to identify him.

As for Mickey and his friends behind, their mirth knew no bounds; and except the respectable insides, there was not an individual about the coach who ceased to think of and laugh at the incident till we arrived in Dublin and drew up at the Hibernian in Dawson Street.

CHAPTER XIV.

DUBLIN.

No sooner had I arrived in Dublin than my first care was to present myself to Dr. Mooney, by whom I was received in the most cordial manner. In fact, in my utter ignorance of such persons, I had imagined a college fellow to be a character necessarily severe and unbending; and as the only two very great people I had ever seen in my life were the Archbishop of Tuam and the chief-baron when on circuit, I pictured to myself that a university fellow was, in all probability, a cross between the two, and feared him accordingly.

The doctor read over my uncle's letter attentively, invited me to partake of his breakfast, and then entered upon something like an account of the life before me; for which Sir Harry Boyle had, however, in some degree prepared me.

"Your uncle, I find, wishes you to live in college,—perhaps it is better, too,—so that I must look out for chambers for you. Let me see: it will be rather difficult, just now, to find them." Here he fell for some moments into a musing fit, and merely muttered a few broken sentences, as: "To be sure, if other chambers could be had—but then—and after all, perhaps, as he is young—besides, Frank will certainly be expelled before long, and then he will have them all to himself. I say, O'Malley, I believe I must quarter you for the present with a rather wild companion; but as your uncle says you're a prudent fellow,"—here he smiled very much, as if my uncle had not said any such thing,—"why, you must only take the better care of yourself until we can make some better arrangement. My pupil, Frank Webber, is at this moment in want of a 'chum,' as the phrase is,—his last three having only been domesticated with him for as many weeks; so that until we find you a more quiet resting-place, you may take up your abode with him."

During breakfast, the doctor proceeded to inform me that my destined companion was a young man of excellent family and good fortune who, with very considerable talents and acquirements, preferred a life of rackety and careless dissipation to prospects of great success in public life, which his connection and family might have secured for him. That he had been originally entered at Oxford, which he was obliged to leave; then tried Cambridge, from which he escaped expulsion by being rusticated,—that is, having incurred a sentence of temporary banishment; and lastly, was endeavoring, with what he himself believed to be a total reformation, to stumble on to a degree in the "silent sister."

"This is his third year," said the doctor, "and he is only a freshman, having lost every examination, with abilities enough to sweep the university of its prizes. But come over now, and I'll present you to him."

I followed him down-stairs, across the court to an angle of the old square where, up the first floor left, to use the college direction, stood the name of Mr. Webber, a large No. 2 being conspicuously painted in the middle of the door and not over it, as is usually the custom. As we reached the spot, the observations of my companion were lost to me in the tremendous noise and uproar that resounded from within. It seemed as if a number of people were fighting pretty much as a banditti in a melodrama do, with considerable more of confusion than requisite; a fiddle and a French horn also lent their assistance to shouts and cries which, to say the best, were not exactly the aids to study I expected in such a place.

Three times was the bell pulled with a vigor that threatened its downfall, when at last, as the jingle of it rose above all other noises, suddenly all became hushed and still; a momentary pause succeeded, and the door was opened by a very respectable looking servant who, recognizing the doctor, at once introduced us into the apartment where Mr. Webber was sitting.

In a large and very handsomely furnished room, where Brussels carpeting and softly cushioned sofas contrasted strangely with the meagre and comfortless chambers of the doctor, sat a young man at a small breakfast-table beside the fire. He was attired in a silk dressing-gown and black velvet slippers, and supported his forehead upon a hand of most lady-like whiteness, whose fingers were absolutely covered with rings of great beauty and price. His long silky brown hair fell in rich profusion upon the back of his neck and over his arm, and the whole air and attitude was one which a painter might have copied. So intent was he upon the volume before him that he never raised his head at our approach, but continued to read aloud, totally unaware of our presence.

"Dr. Mooney, sir," said the servant.

"Ton dapamey hominos, prosephe, crione Agamemnon" repeated the student, in an ecstasy, and not paying the slightest attention to the announcement.

"Dr. Mooney, sir," repeated the servant, in a louder tone, while the doctor looked around on every side for an explanation of the late uproar, with a face of the most puzzled astonishment.

"Be dakiown para thina dolekoskion enkos" said Mr. Webber, finishing a cup of coffee at a draught.

"Well, Webber, hard at work I see," said the doctor.

"Ah, Doctor, I beg pardon! Have you been long here?" said the most soft and insinuating voice, while the speaker passed his taper fingers across his brow, as if to dissipate the traces of deep thought and study.

47

While the doctor presented me to my future companion, I could perceive, in the restless and searching look he threw around, that the fracas he had so lately heard was still an unexplained and *vexata questio* in his mind.

"May I offer you a cup of coffee, Mr. O'Malley?" said the youth, with an air of almost timid bashfulness. "The doctor, I know, breakfasts at a very early hour."

"I say, Webber," said the doctor, who could no longer restrain his curiosity, "what an awful row I heard here as I came up to the door. I thought Bedlam was broke loose. What could it have been?"

"Ah, you heard it too, sir," said Mr. Webber, smiling most benignly.

"Hear it? To be sure I did. O'Malley and I could not hear ourselves talking with the uproar."

"Yes, indeed, it is very provoking; but then, what's to be done? One can't complain, under the circumstances."

"Why, what do you mean?" said Mooney, anxiously.

"Nothing, sir; nothing. I'd much rather you'd not ask me; for after all, I'll change my chambers."

"But why? Explain this at once. I insist upon it."

"Can I depend upon the discretion of your young friend?" said Mr. Webber, gravely.

"Perfectly," said the doctor, now wound up to the greatest anxiety to learn a secret.

"And you'll promise not to mention the thing except among your friends?"

"I do," said the doctor.

"Well, then," said he, in a low and confident whisper, "it's the dean."

"The dean!" said Mooney, with a start. "The dean! Why, how can it be the dean?"

"Too true," said Mr. Webber, making a sign of drinking,—"too true, Doctor. And then, the moment he is so, he begins smashing the furniture. Never was anything heard like it. As for me, as I am now become a reading man, I must go elsewhere."

Now, it so chanced that the worthy dean, who albeit a man of most abstemious habits, possessed a nose which, in color and development, was a most unfortunate witness to call to character, and as Mooney heard Webber narrate circumstantially the frightful excesses of the great functionary, I saw that something like conviction was stealing over him.

"You'll, of course, never speak of this except to your most intimate friends," said Webber.

"Of course not," said the doctor, as he shook his hand warmly, and prepared to leave the room. "O'Malley, I leave you here," said he; "Webber and you can talk over your arrangements."

Webber followed the doctor to the door, whispered something in his ear, to which the other replied, "Very well, I will write; but if your father sends the money, I must insist—" The rest was lost in protestations and professions of the most fervent kind, amidst which the door was shut, and Mr. Webber returned to the room.

Short as was the interspace from the door without to the room within, it was still ample enough to effect a very thorough and remarkable change in the whole external appearance of Mr. Frank Webber; for scarcely had the oaken panel shut out the doctor, when he appeared no longer the shy, timid, and silvery-toned gentleman of five minutes before, but dashing boldly forward, he seized a key-bugle that lay hid beneath a sofa-cushion and blew a tremendous blast.

"Come forth, ye demons of the lower world," said he, drawing a cloth from a large table, and discovering the figures of three young men coiled up beneath. "Come forth, and fear not, most timorous freshmen that ye are," said he, unlocking a pantry, and liberating two others. "Gentlemen, let me introduce to your acquaintance Mr. O'Malley. My chum, gentlemen. Mr. O'Malley, that is Harry Nesbitt, who has been in college since the days of old Perpendicular, and numbers more cautions than any man who ever had his name on the books. Here is my particular friend, Cecil Cavendish, the only man who could ever devil kidneys. Captain Power, Mr. O'Malley, a dashing dragoon, as you see; aide-de-camp to his Excellency the Lord Lieutenant, and love-maker-general to Merrion Square West. These," said he, pointing to the late denizens of the pantry, "are jibs whose names are neither known to the proctor nor the police-office; but with due regard to their education and morals, we don't despair."

"By no means," said Power; "but come, let us resume our game." At these words he took a folio atlas of maps from a small table, and displayed beneath a pack of cards, dealt as if for whist. The two gentlemen to whom I was introduced by name returned to their places; the unknown two put on their boxing gloves, and all resumed the hilarity which Dr. Mooney's advent had so suddenly interrupted.

"Where's Moore?" said Webber, as he once more seated himself at his breakfast.

"Making a spatch-cock, sir," said the servant.

At the same instant, a little, dapper, jovial-looking personage appeared with the dish in question.

"Mr. O'Malley, Mr. Moore, the gentleman who, by repeated remonstrances to the board, has succeeded in getting eatable food for the inhabitants of this penitentiary, and has the honored reputation of reforming the commons of college."

"Anything to Godfrey O'Malley, may I ask, sir?" said Moore.

"His nephew," I replied.

"Which of you winged the gentleman the other day for not passing the decanter, or something of that sort?"

"If you mean the affair with Mr. Bodkin, it was I."

"Glorious, that; begad, I thought you were one of us. I say, Power, it was he pinked Bodkin."

"Ah, indeed," said Power, not turning his head from his game, "a pretty shot, I heard,—two by honors,—and hit him fairly,—the odd trick. Hammersley mentioned the thing to me."

"Oh, is he in town?" said I.

"No; he sailed for Portsmouth yesterday. He is to join the llth—game. I say, Webber, you've lost the rubber."

"Double or quit, and a dinner at Dunleary," said Webber. "We must show O'Malley,—confound the Mister!—something of the place."

"Agreed."

The whist was resumed; the boxers, now refreshed by a leg of the spatch-cock, returned to their gloves; Mr. Moore took up his violin; Mr. Webber his French horn; and I was left the only unemployed man in the company.

"I say, Power, you'd better bring the drag over here for us; we can all go down together."

"I must inform you," said Cavendish, "that, thanks to your philanthropic efforts of last night, the passage from Grafton Street to Stephen's Green is impracticable." A tremendous roar of laughter followed this announcement; and though at the time the cause was unknown to me, I may as well mention it here, as I subsequently learned it from my companions.

Among the many peculiar tastes which distinguished Mr. Francis Webber was an extraordinary fancy for street-begging. He had, over and over, won large sums upon his success in that difficult walk; and so perfect were his disguises,—both of dress, voice, and manner,—that he actually at one time succeeded in obtaining charity from his very opponent in the wager. He wrote ballads with the greatest facility, and sang them with infinite pathos and humor; and the old woman at the corner of College Green was certain of an audience when the severity of the night would leave all other minstrelsy deserted. As these feats of *jonglerie* usually terminated in a row, it was a most amusing part of the transaction to see the singer's part taken by the mob against the college men, who, growing impatient to carry him off to supper somewhere, would invariably be obliged to have a fight for the booty.

Now it chanced that a few evenings before, Mr. Webber was returning with a pocket well lined with copper from a musical *reunion* he had held at the corner of York Street, when the idea struck him to stop at the end of Grafton Street, where a huge stone grating at that time exhibited—perhaps it exhibits still—the descent to one of the great main sewers of the city.

The light was shining brightly from a pastrycook's shop, and showed the large bars of stone between which the muddy water was rushing rapidly down and plashing in the torrent that ran boisterously several feet beneath.

To stop in the street of any crowded city is, under any circumstances, an invitation to others to do likewise which is rarely unaccepted; but when in addition to this you stand fixedly in one spot and regard with stern intensity any object near you, the chances are ten to one that you have several companions in your curiosity before a minute expires.

Now, Webber, who had at first stood still without any peculiar thought in view, no sooner perceived that he was joined by others than the idea of making something out of it immediately occurred to him.

"What is it, agra?" inquired an old woman, very much in his own style of dress, pulling at the hood of his cloak. "And can't you see for yourself, darling?" replied he, sharply, as he knelt down and looked most intensely at the sewer.

"Are ye long there, avick?" inquired he of an imaginary individual below, and then waiting as if for a reply, said,

"Two hours! Blessed Virgin, he's two hours in the drain!"

By this time the crowd had reached entirely across the street, and the crushing and squeezing to get near the important spot was awful.

"Where did he come from?" "Who is he?" "How did he get there?" were questions on every side; and various surmises were afloat till Webber, rising from his knees, said, in a

49

mysterious whisper, to those nearest him, "He's made his escape to-night out o' Newgate by the big drain, and lost his way; he was looking for the Liffey, and took the wrong turn."

To an Irish mob what appeal could equal this? A culprit at any time has his claim upon their sympathy; but let him be caught in the very act of cheating the authorities and evading the law, and his popularity knows no bounds. Webber knew this well, and as the mob thickened around him sustained an imaginary conversation that Savage Landor might have envied, imparting now and then such hints concerning the runaway as raised their interest to the highest pitch, and fifty different versions were related on all sides,—of the crime he was guilty of, the sentence that was passed on him, and the day he was to suffer.

"Do you see the light, dear?" said Webber, as some ingeniously benevolent individual had lowered down a candle with a string,—"do ye see the light? Oh, he's fainted, the creature!" A cry of horror burst forth from the crowd at these words, followed by a universal shout of, "Break open the street."

Pickaxes, shovels, spades, and crowbars seemed absolutely the walking accompaniments of the crowd, so suddenly did they appear upon the field of action; and the work of exhumation was begun with a vigor that speedily covered nearly half of the street with mud and paving-stones. Parties relieved each other at the task, and ere half an hour a hole capable of containing a mail-coach was yawning in one of the most frequented thoroughfares of Dublin. Meanwhile, as no appearance of the culprit could be had, dreadful conjectures as to his fate began to gain ground. By this time the authorities had received intimation of what was going forward, and attempted to disperse the crowd; but Webber, who still continued to conduct the prosecution, called on them to resist the police and save the poor creature. And now began a most terrific fray: the stones, forming a ready weapon, were hurled at the unprepared constables, who on their side fought manfully, but against superior numbers; so that at last it was only by the aid of a military force the mob could be dispersed, and a riot which had assumed a very serious character got under. Meanwhile Webber had reached his chambers, changed his costume, and was relating over a supper-table the narrative of his philanthropy to a very admiring circle of his friends.

Such was my chum, Frank Webber; and as this was the first anecdote I had heard of him, I relate it here that my readers may be in possession of the grounds upon which my opinion of that celebrated character was founded, while yet our acquaintance was in its infancy.

CHAPTER XV.
CAPTAIN POWER.

Within a few weeks after my arrival in town I had become a matriculated student of the university, and the possessor of chambers within its walls in conjunction with the sage and prudent gentleman I have introduced to my readers in the last chapter. Had my intentions on entering college been of the most studious and regular kind, the companion into whose society I was then immediately thrown would have quickly dissipated them. He voted morning chapels a bore, Greek lectures a humbug, examinations a farce, and pronounced the statute-book, with its attendant train of fines and punishment, an "unclean thing." With all my country habits and predilections fresh upon me, that I was an easily-won disciple to his code need not be wondered at; and indeed ere many days had passed over, my thorough indifference to all college rules and regulations had given me a high place in the esteem of Webber and his friends. As for myself, I was most agreeably surprised to find that what I had looked forward to as a very melancholy banishment, was likely to prove a most agreeable sojourn. Under Webber's directions there was no hour of the day that hung heavily upon our hands. We rose about eleven and breakfasted, after which succeeded fencing, sparring, billiards, or tennis in the park; about three, got on horseback, and either cantered in the Phoenix or about the squares till visiting time; after which, made our calls, and then dressed for dinner, which we never thought of taking at commons, but had it from Morrison's,—we both being reported sick in the dean's list, and thereby exempt from the routine fare of the fellows' table. In the evening our occupations became still more pressing; there were balls, suppers, whist parties, rows at the theatre, shindies in the street, devilled drumsticks at Hayes's, select oyster parties at the Carlingford,—in fact, every known method of remaining up all night, and appearing both pale and penitent the following morning.

Webber had a large acquaintance in Dublin, and soon made me known to them all. Among others, the officers of the —th Light Dragoons, in which regiment Power was captain, were his particular friends; and we had frequent invitations to dine at their mess. There it was first that military life presented itself to me in its most attractive possible form, and heightened the passion I had already so strongly conceived for the army. Power, above all others, took my fancy. He was a gay, dashing-looking, handsome fellow of about eight-and-twenty, who had already seen some service, having joined while his regiment was in Portugal; was in heart and soul a soldier; and had that species of pride and enthusiasm in all that regarded a military career that forms no small part of the charm in the character of a young officer.

I sat near him the second day we dined at the mess, and was much pleased at many slight attentions in his manner towards me.

"I called on you to-day, Mr. O'Malley," said he, "in company with a friend who is most anxious to see you."

"Indeed," said I, "I did not hear of it."

"We left no cards, either of us, as we were determined to make you out on another day; my companion has most urgent reasons for seeing you. I see you are puzzled," said he; "and although I promised to keep his secret, I must blab. It was Sir George Dashwood was with me; he told us of your most romantic adventure in the west,—and faith there is no doubt you saved the lady's life."

"Was she worth the trouble of it?" said the old major, whose conjugal experiences imparted a very crusty tone to the question.

"I think," said I, "I need only tell her name to convince you of it."

"Here's a bumper to her," said Power, filling his glass; "and every true man will follow my example."

When the hip-hipping which followed the toast was over, I found myself enjoying no small share of the attention of the party as the deliverer of Lucy Dashwood.

"Sir George is cudgelling his brain to show his gratitude to you," said Power.

"What a pity, for the sake of his peace of mind, that you're not in the army," said another; "it's so easy to show a man a delicate regard by a quick promotion."

"A devil of a pity for his own sake, too," said Power, again; "they're going to make a lawyer of as strapping a fellow as ever carried a sabretasche."

"A lawyer!" cried out half a dozen together, pretty much with the same tone and emphasis as though he had said a twopenny postman; "the devil they are."

"Cut the service at once; you'll get no promotion in it," said the colonel; "a fellow with a black eye like you would look much better at the head of a squadron than of a string of witnesses. Trust me, you'd shine more in conducting a picket than a prosecution."

"But if I can't?" said I.

"Then take my plan," said Power, "and make it cut *you*."

"Yours?" said two or three in a breath,—"yours?"

"Ay, mine; did you never know that I was bred to the bar? Come, come, if it was only for O'Malley's use and benefit, as we say in the parchments, I must tell you the story."

The claret was pushed briskly round, chairs drawn up to fill any vacant spaces, and Power began his story.

"As I am not over long-winded, don't be scared at my beginning my history somewhat far back. I began life that most unlucky of all earthly contrivances for supplying casualties in case anything may befall the heir of the house,—a species of domestic jury-mast, only lugged out in a gale of wind,—a younger son. My brother Tom, a thick-skulled, pudding-headed dog, that had no taste for anything save his dinner, took it into his wise head one morning that he would go into the army, and although I had been originally destined for a soldier, no sooner was his choice made than all regard for my taste and inclination was forgotten; and as the family interest was only enough for one, it was decided that I should be put in what is called a 'learned profession,' and let push my fortune. 'Take your choice, Dick,' said my father, with a most benign smile,—'take your choice, boy: will you be a lawyer, a parson, or a doctor?'

"Had he said, 'Will you be put in the stocks, the pillory, or publicly whipped?' I could not have looked more blank than at the question.

"As a decent Protestant, he should have grudged me to the Church; as a philanthropist, he might have scrupled at making me a physician; but as he had lost deeply by law-suits, there looked something very like a lurking malice in sending me to the bar. Now, so far, I concurred with him; for having no gift for enduring either sermons or senna, I thought I'd make a bad administrator of either, and as I was ever regarded in the family as rather of a shrewd and quick turn, with a very natural taste for roguery, I began to believe he was right, and that Nature intended me for the circuit.

"From the hour my vocation was pronounced, it had been happy for the family that they could have got rid of me. A certain ambition to rise in my profession laid hold on me, and I meditated all day and night how I was to get on. Every trick, every subtle invention to cheat the enemy that I could read of, I treasured up carefully, being fully impressed with the notion that roguery meant law, and equity was only another name for odd and even.

"My days were spent haranguing special juries of housemaids and laundresses, cross-examining the cook, charging the under-butler, and passing sentence of death upon the pantry boy, who, I may add, was invariably hanged when the court rose.

"If the mutton were overdone, or the turkey burned, I drew up an indictment against old Margaret, and against the kitchen-maid as accomplice, and the family hungered while I harangued; and, in fact, into such disrepute did I bring the legal profession, by the score of annoyance of which I made it the vehicle, that my father got a kind of holy horror of law courts, judges, and crown solicitors, and absented himself from the assizes the same year, for which, being a high sheriff, he paid a penalty of five hundred pounds.

"The next day I was sent off in disgrace to Dublin to begin my career in college, and eat the usual quartos and folios of beef and mutton which qualify a man for the woolsack.

"Years rolled over, in which, after an ineffectual effort to get through college, the only examination I ever got being a jubilee for the king's birthday, I was at length called to the Irish bar, and saluted by my friends as Counsellor Power. The whole thing was so like a joke to me that it kept me in laughter for three terms; and in fact it was the best thing could happen me, for I had nothing else to do. The hall of the Four Courts was a very pleasant lounge; plenty of agreeable fellows that never earned sixpence or were likely to do so. Then the circuits were so many country excursions, that supplied fun of one kind or other, but no profit. As for me, I was what was called a good junior. I knew how to look after the waiters, to inspect the decanting of the wine and the airing of the claret, and was always attentive to the father of the circuit,—the crossest old villain that ever was a king's counsel. These eminent qualities, and my being able to sing a song in honor of our own bar, were recommendations enough to make me a favorite, and I was one.

"Now, the reputation I obtained was pleasant enough at first, but I began to wonder that I never got a brief. Somehow, if it rained civil bills or declarations, devil a one would fall upon my head; and it seemed as if the only object I had in life was to accompany the circuit, a kind of deputy-assistant commissary-general, never expected to come into action. To be sure, I was not alone in misfortune; there were several promising youths, who cut great figures in Trinity, in the same predicament, the only difference being, that they attributed to jealousy what I suspected was forgetfulness, for I don't think a single attorney in Dublin knew one of us.

"Two years passed over, and then I walked the hall with a bag filled with newspapers to look like briefs, and was regularly called by two or three criers from one court to the other. It never took. Even when I used to seduce a country friend to visit the courts, and get him into an animated conversation in a corner between two pillars, devil a one would believe him to be a client, and I was fairly nonplussed.

"'How is a man ever to distinguish himself in such a walk as this?' was my eternal question to myself every morning, as I put on my wig. 'My face is as well known here as Lord Manners's.' Every one says, 'How are you, Dick?' 'How goes it, Power?' But except Holmes, that said one morning as he passed me, 'Eh, always busy?' no one alludes to the possibility of my having anything to do.

"'If I could only get a footing,' thought I, 'Lord, how I'd astonish them! As the song says:—

"*Perhaps a recruit   Might chance to shoo   Great General Buonaparté.*"

So,' said I to myself, 'I'll make these halls ring for it some day or other, if the occasion ever present itself.' But, faith, it seemed as if some cunning solicitor overheard me and told his associates, for they avoided me like a leprosy. The home circuit I had adopted for some time past, for the very palpable reason that being near town it was least costly, and it had all the advantages of any other for me in getting me nothing to do. Well, one morning we were in Philipstown; I was lying awake in bed, thinking how long it would be before I'd sum up resolution to cut the bar, where certainly my prospects were not the most cheering, when some one tapped gently at my door.

"'Come in,' said I.

"The waiter opened gently, and held out his hand with a large roll of paper tied round with a piece of red tape.

"'Counsellor,' said he, 'handsel.'

"'What do you mean?' said I, jumping out of bed. 'What is it, you villain?'

"'A brief.'

"'A brief. So I see; but it's for Counsellor Kinshella, below stairs.' That was the first name written on it.

"'Bethershin,' said he, 'Mr. M'Grath bid me give it to you carefully.'

"By this time I had opened the envelope and read my own name at full length as junior counsel in the important case of Monaghan *v.* M'Shean, to be tried in the Record Court at

Ballinasloe. 'That will do,' said I, flinging it on the bed with a careless air, as if it were a very every-day matter with me.

"'But Counsellor, darlin', give us a thrifle to dhrink your health with your first cause, and the Lord send you plenty of them!'

"'My first,' said I, with a smile of most ineffable compassion at his simplicity; 'I'm worn out with them. Do you know, Peter, I was thinking seriously of leaving the bar, when you came into the room? Upon my conscience, it's in earnest I am.'

"Peter believed me, I think, for I saw him give a very peculiar look as he pocketed his half-crown and left the room.

"The door was scarcely closed when I gave way to the free transport of my ecstasy; there it lay at last, the long looked-for, long wished-for object of all my happiness, and though I well knew that a junior counsel has about as much to do in the conducting of a case as a rusty handspike has in a naval engagement, yet I suffered not such thoughts to mar the current of my happiness. There was my name in conjunction with the two mighty leaders on the circuit; and though they each pocketed a hundred, I doubt very much if they received their briefs with one half the satisfaction. My joy at length a little subdued, I opened the roll of paper and began carefully to peruse about fifty pages of narrative regarding a watercourse that once had turned a mill; but, from some reasons doubtless known to itself or its friends, would do so no longer, and thus set two respectable neighbors at loggerheads, and involved them in a record that had been now heard three several times.

"Quite forgetting the subordinate part I was destined to fill, I opened the case in a most flowery oration, in which I descanted upon the benefits accruing to mankind from water-communication since the days of Noah; remarking upon the antiquity of mills, and especially of millers, and consumed half an hour in a preamble of generalities that I hoped would make a very considerable impression upon the court. Just at the critical moment when I was about to enter more particularly into the case, three or four of the great unbriefed came rattling into my room, and broke in upon the oration.

"'I say, Power,' said one, 'come and have an hour's skating on the canal; the courts are filled, and we sha'n't be missed.'

"'Skate, my dear friend,' said I, in a most dolorous tone, 'out of the question; see, I am chained to a devilish knotty case with Kinshella and Mills.'

"'Confound your humbugging,' said another, 'that may do very well in Dublin for the attorneys, but not with us.'

"'I don't well understand you,' I replied; 'there is the brief. Hennesy expects me to report upon it this evening, and I am so hurried.'

"Here a very chorus of laughing broke forth, in which, after several vain efforts to resist, I was forced to join, and kept it up with the others.

"When our mirth was over, my friends scrutinized the red-tape-tied packet, and pronounced it a real brief, with a degree of surprise that certainly augured little for their familiarity with such objects of natural history.

"When they had left the room, I leisurely examined the all-important document, spreading it out before me upon the table, and surveying it as a newly-anointed sovereign might be supposed to contemplate a map of his dominions.

"'At last,' said I to myself,—'at last, and here is the footstep to the woolsack.' For more than an hour I sat motionless, my eyes fixed upon the outspread paper, lost in a very maze of revery. The ambition which disappointments had crushed, and delay had chilled, came suddenly back, and all my day-dreams of legal success, my cherished aspirations after silk gowns and patents of precedence, rushed once more upon me, and I was resolved to do or die. Alas, a very little reflection showed me that the latter was perfectly practicable; but that, as a junior counsel, five minutes of very common-place recitation was all my province, and with the main business of the day I had about as much to do as the call-boy of a playhouse has with the success of a tragedy.

"'My Lord, this is an action brought by Timothy Higgin,' etc., and down I go, no more to be remembered and thought of than if I had never existed. How different it would be if I were the leader! Zounds, how I would worry the witnesses, browbeat the evidence, cajole the jury, and soften the judges! If the Lord were, in His mercy, to remove old Mills and Kinshella before Tuesday, who knows but my fortune might be made? This supposition once started, set me speculating upon all the possible chances that might cut off two king's counsel in three days, and left me fairly convinced that my own elevation was certain,·were they only removed from my path.

"For two whole days the thought never left my mind; and on the evening of the second day, I sat moodily over my pint of port, in the Clonbrock Arms, with my friend Timothy Casey, Captain in the North Cork Militia, for my companion.

"'Dick,' said Tim, 'take off your wine, man. When does this confounded trial come on?'

"'To-morrow,' said I, with a deep groan.

"'Well, well, and if it does, what matter?' he said; 'you'll do well enough, never be afraid.'

"'Alas!' said I, 'you don't understand the cause of my depression.' I here entered upon an account of my sorrows, which lasted for above an hour, and only concluded just as a tremendous noise in the street without announced an arrival. For several minutes such was the excitement in the house, such running hither and thither, such confusion, and such hubbub, that we could not make out who had arrived.

"At last a door opened quite near us, and we saw the waiter assisting a very portly-looking gentleman off with his great-coat, assuring him the while that if he would only walk into the coffee-room for ten minutes, the fire in his apartment should be got ready. The stranger accordingly entered and seated himself at the fireplace, having never noticed that Casey and myself, the only persons there, were in the room.

"'I say, Phil, who is he?' inquired Casey of the waiter.

"'Counsellor Mills, Captain,' said the waiter, and left the room.

"'That's your friend,' said Casey.

"'I see,' said I; 'and I wish with all my heart he was at home with his pretty wife, in Leeson Street.'

"'Is she good-looking?' inquired Tim.

"'Devil a better,' said I; 'and he's as jealous as old Nick.'

"'Hem,' said Tim, 'mind your cue, and I'll give him a start.' Here he suddenly changed his whispering tone for one in a louder key, and resumed: 'I say, Power, it will make some work for you lawyers. But who can she be? that's the question.' Here he took a much crumpled letter from his pocket, and pretended to read: '"A great sensation was created in the neighborhood of Merrion Square, yesterday, by the sudden disappearance from her house of the handsome Mrs. ———." Confound it!—what's the name? What a hand he writes! Hill, or Miles, or something like that,—"the lady of an eminent barrister, now on circuit. The gay Lothario is, they say, the Hon. George ———.'" I was so thunderstruck at the rashness of the stroke, I could say nothing; while the old gentleman started as if he had sat down on a pin. Casey, meanwhile, went on.

"'Hell and fury!' said the king's counsel, rushing over, 'what is it you're saying?'

"'You appear warm, old gentleman,' said Casey, putting up the letter and rising from the table.

"'Show me that letter!—show me that infernal letter, sir, this instant!'

"'Show you my letter,' said Casey; 'cool, that, anyhow. You are certainly a good one.'

"'Do you know me, sir? Answer me that,' said the lawyer, bursting with passion.

"'Not at present,' said Tim, quietly; 'but I hope to do so in the morning in explanation of your language and conduct.' A tremendous ringing of the bell here summoned the waiter to the room.

"'Who is that—' inquired the lawyer. The epithet he judged it safe to leave unsaid, as he pointed to my friend Casey.

"'Captain Casey, sir, the commanding officer here.'

"'Just so,' said Casey. 'And very much, at your service any hour after five in the morning.'

"'Then you refuse, sir, to explain the paragraph I have just heard you read?'

"'Well done, old gentleman; so you have been listening to a private conversation I held with my friend here. In that case we had better retire to our room.' So saying, he ordered the waiter to send a fresh bottle and glasses to No. 14, and taking my arm, very politely wished Mr. Mills good-night, and left the coffee-room.

"Before we had reached the top of the stairs the house was once more in commotion. The new arrival had ordered out fresh horses, and was hurrying every one in his impatience to get away. In ten minutes the chaise rolled off from the door; and Casey, putting his head out of the window, wished him a pleasant journey; while turning to me, he said,—

"'There's one of them out of the way for you, if we are even obliged to fight the other.'

"The port was soon despatched, and with it went all the scruples of conscience I had at first felt for the cruel *ruse* we had just practised. Scarcely was the other bottle called for when we heard the landlord calling out in a stentorian voice,—

"'Two horses for Goran Bridge to meet Counsellor Kinshella.'

"'That's the other fellow?' said Casey.

"'It is,' said I.

"'Then we must be stirring,' said he. 'Waiter, chaise and pair in five minutes,—d'ye hear? Power, my boy, I don't want you; stay here and study your brief. It's little trouble Counsellor Kinshella will give you in the morning.'

"All he would tell me of his plans was that he didn't mean any serious bodily harm to the counsellor, but that certainly he was not likely to be heard of for twenty-four hours.

"'Meanwhile, Power, go in and win, my boy,' said he; 'such another walk over may never occur.'

"I must not make my story longer. The next morning the great record of Monaghan *v.* M'Shean was called on; and as the senior counsel were not present, the attorney wished a postponement. I, however, was firm; told the court I was quite prepared, and with such an air of assurance that I actually puzzled the attorney. The case was accordingly opened by me in a very brilliant speech, and the witnesses called; but such was my unlucky ignorance of the whole matter that I actually broke down the testimony of our own, and fought like a Trojan, for the credit and character of the perjurers against us! The judge rubbed his eyes; the jury looked amazed; and the whole bar laughed outright. However, on I went, blundering, floundering, and foundering at every step; and at half-past four, amidst the greatest and most uproarious mirth of the whole court, heard the jury deliver a verdict against us, just as old Kinshella rushed into the court covered with mud and spattered with clay. He had been sent for twenty miles to make a will for Mr. Daly, of Daly's Mount, who was supposed to be at the point of death, but who, on his arrival, threatened to shoot him for causing an alarm to his family by such an imputation.

"The rest is soon told. They moved for a new trial, and I moved out of the profession. I cut the bar, for it cut me. I joined the gallant 14th as a volunteer; and here I am without a single regret, I must confess, that I didn't succeed in the great record of Monaghan *v.* M'Shean."

Once more the claret went briskly round, and while we canvassed Power's story, many an anecdote of military life was told, as every instant increased the charm of that career I longed for.

"Another cooper, Major," said Power.

"With all my heart," said the rosy little officer, as he touched the bell behind him; "and now let's have a song."

"Yes, Power," said three or four together; "let us have 'The Irish Dragoon,' if it's only to convert your friend O'Malley there."

"Here goes, then," said Dick, taking off a bumper as he began the following chant to the air of "Love is the Soul of a gay Irishman":—

THE IRISH DRAGOON.   *Oh, love is the soul of an Irish dragoon   In battle, in bivouac, or in saloon,   From the tip of his spur to his bright sabretasche.   With his soldierly gait and his bearing so high, His gay laughing look and his light speaking eye,   He frowns at his rival, he ogles his wench,   He springs in his saddle and chases the French,   With his jingling spur and his bright sabretasche.   His spirits are high, and he little knows care,   Whether sipping his claret or charging a square,   With his jingling spur and his bright sabretasche.   As ready to sing or to skirmish he's found,   To take off his wine or to take up his ground; When the bugle may call him, how little he fears   To charge forth in column and beat the Mounseers,   With his jingling spur and his bright sabretasche.   When the battle is over, he gayly rides back   To cheer every soul in the night bivouac,   With his jingling spur and his bright sabretasche.   Oh, there you may see him in full glory crowned,   As he sits 'midst his friends on the hardly won ground,   And hear with what feeling the toast he will give,   As he drinks to the land where all Irishmen live,   With his jingling spur and his bright sabretasche.*

It was late when we broke up; but among all the recollections of that pleasant evening none clung to me so forcibly, none sank so deeply in my heart, as the gay and careless tone of Power's manly voice; and as I fell asleep towards morning, the words of "The Irish Dragoon" were floating through my mind and followed me in my dreams.

CHAPTER XVI.

THE VICE-PROVOST.

I had now been for some weeks a resident within the walls of the university, and yet had never presented my letter of introduction to Dr. Barret. Somehow, my thoughts and occupations had left me little leisure to reflect upon my college course, and I had not felt the necessity suggested by my friend Sir Harry, of having a supporter in the very learned and gifted individual to whom I was accredited. How long I might have continued in this state of indifference it is hard to say, when chance brought about my acquaintance with the doctor.

Were I not inditing a true history in this narrative of my life, to the events and characters of which so many are living witnesses, I should certainly fear to attempt anything like a description of this very remarkable man; so liable would any sketch, however faint and imperfect, be to the accusation of caricature, when all was so singular and so eccentric.

Dr. Barret was, at the time I speak of, close upon seventy years of age, scarcely five feet in height, and even that diminutive stature lessened by a stoop. His face was thin, pointed, and russet-colored; his nose so aquiline as nearly to meet his projecting chin, and his small gray eyes, red and bleary, peered beneath his well-worn cap with a glance of mingled fear and suspicion. His dress was a suit of the rustiest black, threadbare, and patched in several places, while a pair of large brown leather slippers, far too big for his feet, imparted a sliding motion to his walk that added an air of indescribable meanness to his appearance; a gown that had been worn for twenty years, browned and coated with the learned dust of the *Fagel*, covered his rusty habiliments, and completed the equipments of a figure that it was somewhat difficult for the young student to recognize as the vice-provost of the university. Such was he in externals. Within, a greater or more profound scholar never graced the walls of the college; a distinguished Grecian, learned in all the refinements of a hundred dialects; a deep Orientalist, cunning in all the varieties of Eastern languages, and able to reason with a Moonshee, or chat with a Persian ambassador. With a mind that never ceased acquiring, he possessed a memory ridiculous for its retentiveness, even of trifles; no character in history, no event in chronology was unknown to him, and he was referred to by his contemporaries for information in doubtful and disputed cases, as men consult a lexicon or dictionary. With an intellect thus stored with deep and far-sought knowledge, in the affairs of the world he was a child. Without the walls of the college, for above forty years, he had not ventured half as many times, and knew absolutely nothing of the busy, active world that fussed and fumed so near him; his farthest excursion was to the Bank of Ireland, to which he made occasional visits to fund the ample income of his office, and add to the wealth which already had acquired for him a well-merited repute of being the richest man in college.

His little intercourse with the world had left him, in all his habits and manners, in every respect exactly as when he entered college nearly half a century before; and as he had literally risen from the ranks in the university, all the peculiarities of voice, accent, and pronunciation which distinguished him as a youth, adhered to him in old age. This was singular enough, and formed a very ludicrous contrast with the learned and deep-read tone of his conversation; but another peculiarity, still more striking, belonged to him. When he became a fellow, he was obliged, by the rules of the college, to take holy orders as a *sine qua non* to his holding his fellowship. This he did, as he would have assumed a red hood or blue one, as bachelor of laws or doctor of medicine, and thought no more of it; but frequently, in his moments of passionate excitement, the venerable character with which he was invested was quite forgotten, and he would utter some sudden and terrific oath, more productive of mirth to his auditors than was seemly, and for which, once spoken, the poor doctor felt the greatest shame and contrition. These oaths were no less singular than forcible; and many a trick was practised, and many a plan devised, that the learned vice-provost might be entrapped into his favorite exclamation of, "May the devil admire me!" which no place or presence could restrain.

My servant, Mike, who had not been long in making himself acquainted with all the originals about him, was the cause of my first meeting the doctor, before whom I received a summons to appear on the very serious charge of treating with disrespect the heads of the college.

The circumstances were shortly these: Mike had, among the other gossip of the place, heard frequent tales of the immense wealth and great parsimony of the doctor, and of his anxiety to amass money on all occasions, and the avidity with which even the smallest trifle was added to his gains. He accordingly resolved to amuse himself at the expense of this trait, and proceeded thus. Boring a hole in a halfpenny, he attached a long string to it, and having dropped it on the doctor's step stationed himself on the opposite side of the court, concealed from view by the angle of the Commons' wall. He waited patiently for the chapel bell, at the first toll of which the door opened, and the doctor issued forth. Scarcely was his foot upon the step, when he saw the piece of money, and as quickly stooped to seize it; but just as his finger had nearly touched it, it evaded his grasp and slowly retreated. He tried again, but with the like success. At last, thinking he had miscalculated the distance, he knelt leisurely down, and put forth his hand, but lo! it again escaped him; on which, slowly rising from his posture, he shambled on towards the chapel, where, meeting the senior lecturer at the door, he cried out, "H——— to my soul, Wall, but I saw the halfpenny walk away!"

For the sake of the grave character whom he addressed, I need not recount how such a speech was received; suffice it to say, that Mike had been seen by a college porter, who reported him as my servant.

I was in the very act of relating the anecdote to a large party at breakfast in my rooms, when a summons arrived, requiring my immediate attendance at the board, then sitting in solemn conclave at the examination hall.

I accordingly assumed my academic costume as speedily as possible, and escorted by that most august functionary, Mr. M'Alister, presented myself before the seniors.

The members of the board, with the provost at their head, were seated at a long oak table covered with books, papers, etc., and from the silence they maintained as I walked up the hall, I augured that a very solemn scene was before me.

"Mr. O'Malley," said the dean, reading my name from a paper he held in his hand, "you have been summoned here at the desire of the vice-provost, whose questions you will reply to."

I bowed. A silence of a few minutes followed, when, at length, the learned doctor, hitching up his nether garments with both hands, put his old and bleary eyes close to my face, while he croaked out, with an accent that no hackney-coachman could have exceeded in vulgarity,—

"Eh, O'Malley, you're *quartus*, I believe; a'n't you?"

"I believe not. I think I am the only person of that name now on the books."

"That's thrue; but there were three O'Malleys before you. Godfrey O'Malley, that construed *Calve Neroni* to Nero the Calvinist,—ha! ha! ha!—was cautioned in 1788."

"My uncle, I believe, sir."

"More than likely, from what I hear of you,—*Ex uno*, etc. I see your name every day on the punishment roll. Late hours, never at chapel, seldom at morning lecture. Here ye are, sixteen shillings, wearing a red coat."

"Never knew any harm in that, Doctor."

"Ay, but d'ye see me, now? 'Grave raiment,' says the statute. And then, ye keep numerous beasts of prey, dangerous in their habits, and unseemly to behold."

"A bull terrier, sir, and two game-cocks, are, I assure you, the only animals in my household."

"Well. I'll fine you for it."

"I believe, Doctor," said the dean, interrupting in an undertone, "that you cannot impose a penalty in this matter."

"Ay, but I can. 'Singing-birds,' says the statute, 'are forbidden within the wall.'"

"And then, ye dazzled my eyes at Commons with a bit of looking-glass, on Friday. I saw you. May the devil!—ahem! As I was saying, that's casting *reflections* on the heads of the college; and your servant it was, *Michaelis Liber*, Mickey Free,—may the flames of!—ahem!—an insolent varlet! called me a sweep."

"You, Doctor; impossible!" said I, with pretended horror.

"Ay, but d'ye see me, now? It's thrue, for I looked about me at the time, and there wasn't another sweep in the place but myself. Hell to!—I mean—God forgive me for swearing! but I'll fine you a pound for this."

As I saw the doctor was getting on at such a pace, I resolved, notwithstanding the august presence of the board, to try the efficacy of Sir Harry's letter of introduction, which I had taken in my pocket in the event of its being wanted.

"I beg your pardon, sir, if the time be an unsuitable one; but may I take the opportunity of presenting this letter to you?"

"Ha! I know the hand—Boyle's. *Boyle secundus.* Hem, ha, ay! 'My young friend; and assist him by your advice.' To be sure! Oh, of course. Eh, tell me, young man, did Boyle say nothing to you about the copy of Erasmus, bound in vellum, that I sold him in Trinity term, 1782?"

"I rather think not, sir," said I, doubtfully.

"Well, then, he might. He owes me two-and-fourpence of the balance."

"Oh, I beg pardon, sir; I now remember he desired me to repay you that sum; but he had just sealed the letter when he recollected it."

"Better late than never," said the doctor, smiling graciously. "Where's the money? Ay! half-a-crown. I haven't twopence—never mind. Go away, young man; the case is dismissed. *Vehementer miror quare huc venisti.* You're more fit for anything than a college life. Keep good hours; mind the terms; and dismiss *Michaelis Liber*. Ha, ha, ha! May the devil!—hem!—that is do—" So saying, the little doctor's hand pushed me from the hall, his mind evidently relieved of all the griefs from which he had been suffering, by the recovery of his long-lost two-and-fourpence.

Such was my first and last interview with the vice-provost, and it made an impression upon me that all the intervening years have neither dimmed nor erased.

CHAPTER XVII.

TRINITY COLLEGE.—A LECTURE.

I had not been many weeks a resident of Old Trinity ere the flattering reputation my chum, Mr. Francis Webber, had acquired, extended also to myself; and by universal consent, we were acknowledged the most riotous, ill-conducted, disorderly men on the books of the university. Were the lamps of the squares extinguished, and the college left in total darkness, we were summoned before the dean; was the vice-provost serenaded with a chorus of trombones and French horns, to our taste in music was the attention ascribed; did a sudden alarm of fire disturb the congregation at morning chapel, Messrs. Webber and O'Malley were brought before the board,—and I must do them the justice to say that the most trifling circumstantial evidence was ever sufficient to bring a conviction. Reading men avoided the building where we resided as they would have done the plague. Our doors, like those of a certain classic precinct commemorated by a Latin writer, lay open night and day, while mustached dragoons, knowingly dressed four-in-hand men, fox-hunters in pink, issuing forth to the Dubber or returning splashed from a run with the Kildare hounds, were everlastingly seen passing and repassing. Within, the noise and confusion resembled rather the mess-room of a regiment towards eleven at night than the chambers of a college student; while, with the double object of affecting to be in ill-health, and to avoid the reflections that daylight occasionally inspires, the shutters were never opened, but lamps and candles kept always burning. Such was No. 2, Old Square, in the goodly days I write of. All the terrors of fines and punishments fell scatheless on the head of my worthy chum. In fact, like a well-known political character, whose pleasure and amusement it has been for some years past to drive through acts of Parliament and deride the powers of the law, so did Mr. Webber tread his way, serpenting through the statute-book, ever grazing, but rarely trespassing upon some forbidden ground which might involve the great punishment of expulsion. So expert, too, had he become in his special pleadings, so dexterous in the law of the university, that it was no easy matter to bring crime home to him; and even when this was done, his pleas of mitigation rarely failed of success.

There was a sweetness of demeanor, a mild, subdued tone about him, that constantly puzzled the worthy heads of the college how the accusations ever brought against him could be founded on truth; that the pale, delicate-looking student, whose harsh, hacking cough terrified the hearers, could be the boisterous performer upon a key-bugle, or the terrific assailant of watchmen, was something too absurd for belief. And when Mr. Webber, with his hand upon his heart, and in his most dulcet accents, assured them that the hours he was not engaged in reading for the medal were passed in the soothing society of a few select and intimate friends of literary tastes and refined minds, who, knowing the delicacy of his health,—here he would cough,—were kind enough to sit up with him for an hour or so in the evening, the delusion was perfect; and the story of the dean's riotous habits having got abroad, the charge was usually suppressed.

Like most idle men, Webber never had a moment to spare. Except read, there was nothing he did not do; training a hack for a race in the Phoenix, arranging a rowing-match, getting up a mock duel between two white-feather acquaintances, were his almost daily avocations. Besides that, he was at the head of many organized societies, instituted for various benevolent purposes. One was called "The Association for Discountenancing Watchmen;" another, "The Board of Works," whose object was principally devoted to the embellishment of the university, in which, to do them justice, their labors were unceasing, and what with the assistance of some black paint, a ladder, and a few pounds of gunpowder, they certainly contrived to effect many important changes. Upon an examination morning, some hundred luckless "jibs" might be seen perambulating the courts, in the vain effort to discover their tutors' chambers, the names having undergone an alteration that left all trace of their original proprietors unattainable: Doctor Francis Mooney having become Doctor Full Moon; Doctor Hare being, by the change of two letters, Doctor Ape; Romney Robinson, Romulus and Remus, etc. While, upon occasions like these, there could be but little doubt of Master Frank's intentions, upon many others, so subtle were his inventions, so well-contrived his plots, it became a matter of considerable difficulty to say whether the mishap which befell some luckless acquaintance were the result of design or mere accident; and not unfrequently well-disposed individuals were found condoling with "Poor Frank" upon his ignorance of some college rule or etiquette, his breach of which had been long and deliberately planned. Of this latter description was a circumstance which occurred about this time, and which some who may throw an eye over these pages will perhaps remember.

The dean, having heard (and, indeed, the preparations were not intended to secure secrecy) that Webber destined to entertain a party of his friends at dinner on a certain day, sent a peremptory order for his appearance at Commons, his name being erased from the sick list, and a pretty strong hint conveyed to him that any evasion upon his part would be certainly followed by an inquiry into the real reasons for his absence. What was to be done? That was the very day he had destined for his dinner. To be sure, the majority of his guests were college men, who would understand the difficulty at once; but still there were some others, officers of the 14th, with whom he was constantly dining, and whom he could not so easily put off. The affair was difficult, but still Webber was the man for a difficulty; in fact, he rather liked one. A very brief consideration accordingly sufficed, and he sat down and wrote to his friends at the Royal Barracks thus:—

Saturday. DEAR POWER,—I have a better plan for Tuesday than that I had proposed. Lunch here at three (we'll call it dinner), in the hall with the great guns. I can't say much for the grub; but the company—glorious! After that we'll start for Lucan in the drag; take our coffee, strawberries, etc., and return to No. 2 for supper at ten. Advertise your fellows of this change, and believe me, Most unchangeably yours, FRANK WEBBER.

Accordingly, as three o'clock struck, six dashing-looking light dragoons were seen slowly sauntering up the middle of the dining-hall, escorted by Webber, who, in full academic costume, was leisurely ciceroning his friends, and expatiating upon the excellences of the very remarkable portraits which graced the walls.

The porters looked on with some surprise at the singular hour selected for sight-seeing; but what was their astonishment to find that the party, having arrived at the end of the hall, instead of turning back again, very composedly unbuckled their belts, and having disposed of their sabres in a corner, took their places at the Fellows' table, and sat down amidst the collective wisdom of Greek lecturers and Regius professors, as though they had been mere mortals like themselves.

Scarcely was the long Latin grace concluded, when Webber, leaning forward, enjoined his friends, in a very audible whisper, that if they intended to dine no time was to be lost.

"We have but little ceremony here, gentlemen, and all we ask is a fair start," said he, as he drew over the soup, and proceeded to help himself.

The advice was not thrown away; for each man, with an alacrity a campaign usually teaches, made himself master of some neighboring dish, a very quick interchange of good things speedily following the appropriation. It was in vain that the senior lecturer looked aghast, that the professor of astronomy frowned. The whole table, indeed, were thunderstruck, even to the poor vice-provost himself, who, albeit given to the comforts of the table, could not lift a morsel to his mouth, but muttered between his teeth, "May the devil admire me, but they're dragoons!" The first shock of surprise over, the porters proceeded to inform them that except Fellows of the University or Fellow-commoners, none were admitted to the table. Webber however assured them that it was a mistake, there being nothing in the statute to exclude the 14th Light Dragoons, as he was prepared to prove. Meanwhile dinner proceeded, Power and his party performing with great self-satisfaction upon the sirloins and saddles about them, regretting only, from time to time, that there was a most unaccountable absence of wine, and suggesting the propriety of napkins whenever they should dine there again. Whatever chagrin these unexpected guests caused among their entertainers of the upper table, in the lower part of the hall the laughter was loud and unceasing; and long before the hour concluded, the Fellows took their departure, leaving to Master Frank Webber the task of doing the honors alone and unassisted. When summoned before the board for the offence on the following morning, Webber excused himself by throwing the blame upon his friends, with whom, he said, nothing short of a personal quarrel—a thing for a reading man not to be thought of—could have prevented intruding in the manner related. Nothing less than *his* tact could have saved him on this occasion, and at last he carried the day; while by an act of the board the 14th Light Dragoons were pronounced the most insolent corps in the service.

An adventure of his, however, got wind about this time, and served to enlighten many persons as to his real character, who had hitherto been most lenient in their expressions about him. Our worthy tutor, with a zeal for our welfare far more praiseworthy than successful, was in the habit of summoning to his chambers, on certain mornings of the week, his various pupils, whom he lectured in the books for the approaching examinations. Now, as these séances were held at six o'clock in winter as well as summer, in a cold fireless chamber,—the lecturer lying snug amidst his blankets, while we stood shivering around the walls,—the ardor of learning must indeed have proved strong that prompted a regular attendance. As to Frank, he would have as soon thought of attending chapel as of presenting himself on such an occasion. Not so with me. I had not yet grown hackneyed enough to fly in the face of authority, and I frequently left the whist-table, or broke off in a song, to hurry over to the doctor's chambers and spout Homer and

Hesiod. I suffered on in patience, till at last the bore became so insupportable that I told my sorrows to my friend, who listened to me out, and promised me succor.

It so chanced that upon some evening in each week Dr. Mooney was in the habit of visiting some friends who resided a short distance from town, and spending the night at their house. He, of course, did not lecture the following morning,—a paper placard, announcing no lecture, being affixed to the door on such occasions. Frank waited patiently till he perceived the doctor affixing this announcement upon his door one evening; and no sooner had he left the college than he withdrew the paper and departed.

On the next morning he rose early, and concealing himself on the staircase, waited the arrival of the venerable damsel who acted as servant to the doctor. No sooner had she opened the door and groped her way into the sitting-room than Frank crept forward, and stealing gently into the bedroom, sprang into the bed and wrapped himself up in the blankets. The great bell boomed forth at six o'clock, and soon after the sounds of the feet were heard upon the stairs. One by one they came along, and gradually the room was filled with cold and shivering wretches, more than half asleep, and trying to arouse themselves into an approach to attention.

"Who's there?" said Frank, mimicking the doctor's voice, as he yawned three or four times in succession and turned in the bed.

"Collisson, O'Malley, Nesbitt," etc., said a number of voices, anxious to have all the merit such a penance could confer.

"Where's Webber?"

"Absent, sir," chorussed the whole party.

"Sorry for it," said the mock doctor. "Webber is a man of first-rate capacity; and were he only to apply, I am not certain to what eminence his abilities might raise him. Come, Collisson, any three angles of a triangle are equal to—are equal to—what are they equal to?" Here he yawned as though he would dislocate his jaw.

"Any three angles of a triangle are equal to two right angles," said Collisson, in the usual sing-song tone of a freshman.

As he proceeded to prove the proposition, his monotonous tone seemed to have lulled the doctor into a doze, for in a few minutes a deep, long-drawn snore announced from the closed curtains that he listened no longer. After a little time, however, a short snort from the sleeper awoke him suddenly, and he called out, "Go on, I'm waiting. Do you think I can arouse at this hour of the morning for nothing but to listen to your bungling? Can no one give me a free translation of the passage?"

This digression from mathematics to classics did not surprise the hearers, though it somewhat confused them, no one being precisely aware what the line in question might be.

"Try it, Nesbitt,—you, O'Malley. Silent all? Really this is too bad!" An indistinct muttering here from the crowd was followed by an announcement from the doctor that the speaker was an ass, and his head a turnip! "Not one of you capable of translating a chorus from Euripides,—'Ou, ou, papai, papai,' etc.; which, after all, means no more than, 'Oh, whilleleu, murder, why did you die!' etc. What are you laughing at, gentlemen? May I ask, does it become a set of ignorant, ill-informed savages—yes, savages, I repeat the word—to behave in this manner? Webber is the only man I have with common intellect,—the only man among you capable of distinguishing himself. But as for you, I'll bring you before the board; I'll write to your friends; I'll stop your college indulgences; I'll confine you to the walls; I'll be damned, eh—"

This lapse confused him. He stammered, stuttered, endeavored to recover himself; but by this time we had approached the bed, just at the moment when Master Frank, well knowing what he might expect if detected, had bolted from the blankets and rushed from the room. In an instant we were in pursuit; but he regained his chambers, and double-locked the door before we could overtake him, leaving us to ponder over the insolent tirade we had so patiently submitted to.

That morning the affair got wind all over college. As for us, we were scarcely so much laughed at as the doctor; the world wisely remembering, if such were the nature of our morning's orisons, we might nearly as profitably have remained snug in our quarters.

Such was our life in Old Trinity; and strange enough it is that one should feel tempted to the confession, but I really must acknowledge these were, after all, happy times, and I look back upon them with mingled pleasure and sadness. The noble lord who so pathetically lamented that the devil was not so strong in him as he used to be forty years before, has an echo in my regrets that the student is not as young in me as when these scenes were enacting of which I write.

CHAPTER XVIII.

THE INVITATION.—THE WAGER.

I was sitting at breakfast with Webber, a few mornings after the mess dinner I have spoken of, when Power came in hastily.

"Ha, the very man!" said he. "I say, O'Malley, here's an invitation for you from Sir George, to dine on Friday. He desired me to say a thousand civil things about his not having made you out, regrets that he was not at home when you called yesterday, and all that. By Jove, I know nothing like the favor you stand in; and as for Miss Dashwood, faith! the fair Lucy blushed, and tore her glove in most approved style, when the old general began his laudation of you."

"Pooh, nonsense," said I; "that silly affair in the west."

"Oh, very probably; there's reason the less for you looking so excessively conscious. But I must tell you, in all fairness, that you have no chance; nothing short of a dragoon will go down."

"Be assured," said I, somewhat nettled, "my pretensions do not aspire to the fair Miss Dashwood."

"*Tant mieux et tant pis, mon cher.* I wish to Heaven mine did; and, by Saint Patrick, if I only played the knight-errant half as gallantly as yourself, I would not relinquish my claims to the Secretary at War himself."

"What the devil brought the old general down to your wild regions?" inquired Webber.

"To contest the county."

"A bright thought, truly. When a man was looking for a seat, why not try a place where the law is occasionally heard of?"

"I'm sure I can give you no information on that head; nor have I ever heard how Sir George came to learn that such a place as Galway existed."

"I believe I can enlighten you," said Power. "Lady Dashwood—rest her soul!—came west of the Shannon; she had a large property somewhere in Mayo, and owned some hundred acres of swamp, with some thousand starving tenantry thereupon, that people dignified as an estate in Connaught. This first suggested to him the notion of setting up for the county, probably supposing that the people who never paid in rent might like to do so in gratitude. How he was undeceived, O'Malley there can inform us. Indeed, I believe the worthy general, who was confoundedly hard up when he married, expected to have got a great fortune, and little anticipated the three chancery suits he succeeded to, nor the fourteen rent-charges to his wife's relatives that made up the bulk of the dower. It was an unlucky hit for him when he fell in with the old 'maid' at Bath; and had she lived, he must have gone to the colonies. But the Lord took her one day, and Major Dashwood was himself again. The Duke of York, the story goes, saw him at Hounslow during a review, was much struck with his air and appearance, made some inquiries, found him to be of excellent family and irreproachable conduct, made him an aide-de-camp, and, in fact, made his fortune. I do not believe that, while doing so kind, he could by possibility have done a more popular thing. Every man in the army rejoiced at his good fortune; so that, after all, though he has had some hard rubs, he has come well through, the only vestige of his unfortunate matrimonial connection being a correspondence kept up by a maiden sister of his late wife's with him. She insists upon claiming the ties of kindred upon about twenty family eras during the year, when she regularly writes a most loving and ill-spelled epistle, containing the latest information from Mayo, with all particulars of the Macan family, of which she is a worthy member. To her constant hints of the acceptable nature of certain small remittances, the poor general is never inattentive; but to the pleasing prospect of a visit in the flesh from Miss Judy Macan, the good man is dead. In fact, nothing short of being broke by general court-martial could complete his sensations of horror at such a stroke of fortune; and I am not certain, if choice were allowed him, that he would not prefer the latter."

"Then he has never yet seen her?" said Webber.

"Never," replied Power; "and he hopes to leave Ireland without that blessing, the prospect of which, however remote and unlikely, has, I know well, more than once terrified him since his arrival."

"I say, Power, and has your worthy general sent me a card for his ball?"

"Not through me, Master Frank."

"Well, now, I call that devilish shabby, do you know. He asks O'Malley there from *my* chambers, and never notices the other man, the superior in the firm. Eh, O'Malley, what say you?"

"Why, I didn't know you were acquainted."

"And who said we were? It was his fault, though, entirely, that we were not. I am, as I have ever been, the most easy fellow in the world on that score, never give myself airs to military people, endure anything, everything, and you see the result; hard, ain't it?"

"But, Webber, Sir George must really be excused in this matter. He has a daughter, a most attractive, lovely daughter, just at that budding, unsuspecting age when the heart is most susceptible of impressions; and where, let me ask, could she run such a risk as in the chance of a casual meeting with the redoubted lady-killer, Master Frank Webber? If he has not sought you out, then here be his apology."

"A very strong case, certainly," said Frank; "but, still, had he confided his critical position to my honor and secrecy, he might have depended on me; now, having taken the other line—"

"Well, what then?"

"Why, he must abide the consequences. I'll make fierce love to Louisa; isn't that the name?"

"Lucy, so please you."

"Well, be it so,—to Lucy,—talk the little girl into a most deplorable attachment for me."

"But, how, may I ask, and when?"

"I'll begin at the ball, man."

"Why, I thought you said you were not going?"

"There you mistake seriously. I merely said that I had not been invited."

"Then, of course," said I, "Webber, you can't think of going, in any case, on *my* account."

"My very dear friend, I go entirely upon my own. I not only shall go, but I intend to have most particular notice and attention paid me. I shall be prime favorite with Sir George, kiss Lucy—"

"Come, come, this is too strong."

"What do you bet I don't? There, now, I'll give you a pony apiece, I do. Do you say done?"

"That you kiss Miss Dashwood, and are not kicked down-stairs for your pains; are those the terms of the wager?" inquired Power.

"With all my heart. That I kiss Miss Dashwood, and am not kicked down-stairs for my pains."

"Then, I say, done."

"And with you, too, O'Malley?"

"I thank you," said I, coldly; "I am not disposed to make such a return for Sir George Dashwood's hospitality as to make an insult to his family the subject of a bet."

"Why, man, what are you dreaming of? Miss Dashwood will not refuse my chaste salute. Come, Power, I'll give you the other pony."

"Agreed," said he. "At the same time, understand me distinctly, that I hold myself perfectly eligible to winning the wager by my own interference; for if you do kiss her, by Jove! I'll perform the remainder of the compact."

"So I understand the agreement," said Webber, arranging his curls before the looking-glass. "Well, now, who's for Howth? The drag will be here in half an hour."

"Not I," said Power; "I must return to the barracks."

"Nor I," said I, "for I shall take this opportunity of leaving my card at Sir George Dashwood's."

"I have won my fifty, however," said Power, as we walked out in the courts.

"I am not quite certain—"

"Why, the devil, he would not risk a broken neck for that sum; besides, if he did, he loses the bet."

"He's a devilish keen fellow."

"Let him be. In any case I am determined to be on my guard here."

So chatting, we strolled along to the Royal Hospital, when, having dropped my pasteboard, I returned to the college.

CHAPTER XIX

THE BALL.

I have often dressed for a storming party with less of trepidation than I felt on the evening of Sir George Dashwood's ball. Since the eventful day of the election I had never seen Miss Dashwood; therefore, as to what precise position I might occupy in her favor was a matter of great doubt in my mind, and great import to my happiness. That I myself loved her, was a matter of which all the badinage of my friends regarding her made me painfully conscious; but that, in our relative positions, such an attachment was all but hopeless, I could not disguise from myself. Young as I was, I well knew to what a heritage of debt, lawsuit, and difficulty I was born to succeed. In my own resources and means of advancement I had no confidence whatever, had even the profession to which I was destined been more of my choice. I daily felt that it demanded greater exertions, if not far greater abilities, than I could command, to make success at all likely; and then, even if such a result were in store, years, at least, must elapse before it could happen; and where would she then be, and where should I? Where the ardent affection I now felt and gloried in,—perhaps all the more for its desperate hopelessness,—when the sanguine and buoyant spirit to combat with difficulties which youth suggests, and which, later, manhood refuses, should have passed away? And even if all these survived the toil and labor of anxious days and painful nights, what of her? Alas, I now reflected that, although only of my own age, her manner to me had taken all that tone of superiority and patronage which an elder assumes towards one younger, and which, in the spirit of protection it proceeds upon, essentially bars up every inlet to a dearer or warmer feeling,—at least, when the lady plays the former part. "What, then, is to be done?" thought I. "Forget her?—but how? How shall I renounce all my plans, and unweave the web of life I have been spreading around me for many a day, without that one golden thread that lent it more than half its brilliancy and all its attraction? But then the alternative is even worse, if I encourage expectations and nurture hopes never to be realized. Well, we meet to-night, after a long and eventful absence; let my future fate be ruled by the results of this meeting. If Lucy Dashwood does care for me, if I can detect in her manner enough to show me that my affection may meet a return, the whole effort of my life shall be to make her mine; if not, if my own feelings be all that I have to depend upon to extort a reciprocal affection, then shall I take my last look of her, and with it the first and brightest dream of happiness my life has hitherto presented."

It need not be wondered at if the brilliant *coup d'oeil* of the ball-room, as I entered, struck me with astonishment, accustomed as I had hitherto been to nothing more magnificent than an evening party of squires and their squiresses or the annual garrison ball at the barracks. The glare of wax-lights, the well-furnished saloons, the glitter of uniforms, and the blaze of plumed and jewelled dames, with the clang of military music, was a species of enchanted atmosphere which, breathing for the first time, rarely fails to intoxicate. Never before had I seen so much beauty. Lovely faces, dressed in all the seductive flattery of smiles, were on every side; and as I walked from room to room, I felt how much more fatal to a man's peace and heart's ease the whispered words and silent glances of those fair damsels, than all the loud gayety and boisterous freedom of our country belles, who sought to take the heart by storm and escalade.

As yet I had seen neither Sir George nor his daughter, and while I looked on every side for Lucy Dashwood, it was with a beating and anxious heart I longed to see how she would bear comparison with the blaze of beauty around.

Just at this moment a very gorgeously dressed hussar stepped from a doorway beside me, as if to make a passage for some one, and the next moment she appeared leaning upon the arm of another lady. One look was all that I had time for, when she recognized me.

"Ah, Mr. O'Malley, how happy—has Sir George—has my father seen you?"

"I have only arrived this moment; I trust he is quite well?"

"Oh, yes, thank you—"

"I beg your pardon with all humility, Miss Dashwood," said the hussar, in a tone of the most knightly courtesy, "but they are waiting for us."

"But, Captain Fortescue, you must excuse me one moment more. Mr. Lechmere, will you do me the kindness to find out Sir George? Mr. O'Malley—Mr. Lechmere." Here she said something in French to her companion, but so rapidly that I could not detect what it was, but merely heard the reply, *"Pas mal!"*—which, as the lady continued to canvass me most deliberately through her eye-glass, I supposed referred to me. "And now, Captain Fortescue—" And with a look of most courteous kindness to me she disappeared in the crowd.

The gentleman to whose guidance I was entrusted was one of the aides-de-camp, and was not long in finding Sir George. No sooner had the good old general heard my name, than he held out both his hands and shook mine most heartily.

"At last, O'Malley; at last I am able to thank you for the greatest service ever man rendered me. He saved Lucy, my Lord; rescued her under circumstances where anything short of his courage and determination must have cost her her life."

"Ah, very pretty indeed," said a stiff old gentleman addressed, as he bowed a most superbly powdered scalp before me; "most happy to make your acquaintance."

"Who is he?" added he, in nearly as loud a tone to Sir George.

"Mr. O'Malley, of O'Malley Castle."

"True, I forgot; why is he not in uniform?"

"Because, unfortunately, my Lord, we don't own him; he's not in the army."

"Ha! ha! thought he was."

"You dance, O'Malley, I suppose? I'm sure you'd rather be over there than hearing all my protestations of gratitude, sincere and heartfelt as they really are."

"Lechmere, introduce my friend, Mr. O'Malley; get him a partner."

I had not followed my new acquaintance many steps, when Power came up to me. "I say, Charley," cried he, "I have been tormented to death by half the ladies in the room to present you to them, and have been in quest of you this half-hour. Your brilliant exploit in savage land has made you a regular *preux chevalier*; and if you don't trade on that adventure to your most lasting profit, you deserve to be—a lawyer. Come along here! Lady Muckleman, the adjutant-general's lady and chief, has four Scotch daughters you are to dance with; then I am to introduce you in all form to the Dean of Something's niece,—she is a good-looking girl, and has two livings in a safe county. Then there's the town-major's wife; and, in fact, I have several engagements from this to supper-time."

"A thousand thanks for all your kindness in prospective, but I think, perhaps, it were right I should ask Miss Dashwood to dance, if only as a matter of form,—you understand?"

"And if Miss Dashwood should say, 'With pleasure, sir,' only as a matter of form,—you understand?" said a silvery voice beside me. I turned, and saw Lucy Dashwood, who, having overheard my free-and-easy suggestion, replied to me in this manner.

I here blundered out my excuses. What I said, and what I did not say, I do not now remember; but certainly, it was her turn now to blush, and her arm trembled within mine as I led her to the top of the room. In the little opportunity which our quadrille presented for conversation, I could not help remarking that, after the surprise of her first meeting with me, Miss Dashwood's manner became gradually more and more reserved, and that there was an evident struggle between her wish to appear grateful for what had occurred, with a sense of the necessity of not incurring a greater degree of intimacy. Such was my impression, at least, and such the conclusion I drew from a certain quiet tone in her manner that went further to wound my feelings and mar my happiness than any other line of conduct towards me could possibly have effected.

Our quadrille over, I was about to conduct her to a seat, when Sir George came hurriedly up, his face greatly flushed, and betraying every semblance of high excitement.

"Dear Papa, has anything occurred? Pray what is it?" inquired she.

He smiled faintly, and replied, "Nothing very serious, my dear, that I should alarm you in this way; but certainly, a more disagreeable *contretemps* could scarcely occur."

"Do tell me: what can it be?"

"Read this," said he, presenting a very dirty-looking note which bore the mark of a red wafer most infernally plain upon its outside.

Miss Dashwood unfolded the billet, and after a moment's silence, instead of participating, as he expected, in her father's feeling of distress, burst out a-laughing, while she said: "Why, really, Papa, I do not see why this should put you out much, after all. Aunt may be somewhat of a character, as her note evinces, but after a few days—"

"Nonsense, child; there's nothing in this world I have such a dread of as that confounded woman,—and to come at such a time."

"When does she speak of paying her visit?"

"I knew you had not read the note," said Sir George, hastily; "she's coming here to-night,—is on her way this instant, perhaps. What is to be done? If she forces her way in here, I shall go deranged outright; O'Malley, my boy, read this note, and you will not feel surprised if I appear in the humor you see me."

I took the billet from the hands of Miss Dashwood, and read as follows:—

DEAR BROTHER,—*When this reaches your hand, I'll not be far off. I'm on my way up to town, to be under Dr. Dease for the ould complaint. Cowley mistakes my case entirely; he says it's nothing but religion and wind. Father Magrath, who understands a good deal about females, thinks otherwise; but God knows who's right. Expect me to tea, and, with love to Lucy, Believe me, yours in haste,* JUDITH MACAN.

Let the sheets be well aired in my room; and if you have a spare bed, perhaps we could prevail upon Father Magrath to stop too.

I scarcely could contain my laughter till I got to the end of this very free-and-easy epistle; when at last I burst forth in a hearty fit, in which I was joined by Miss Dashwood.

From the account Power had given me in the morning, I had no difficulty in guessing that the writer was the maiden sister of the late Lady Dashwood; and for whose relationship Sir George had ever testified the greatest dread, even at the distance of two hundred miles; and for whom, in any nearer intimacy, he was in no wise prepared.

"I say, Lucy," said he, "there's only one thing to be done: if this horrid woman does arrive, let her be shown to her room; and for the few days of her stay in town, we'll neither see nor be seen by any one."

Without waiting for a reply, Sir George was turning away to give the necessary instructions, when the door of the drawing-room was flung open, and the servant announced, in his loudest voice, "Miss Macan." Never shall I forget the poor general's look of horror as the words reached him; for as yet, he was too far to catch even a glimpse of its fair owner. As for me, I was already so much interested in seeing what she was like, that I made my way through the crowd towards the door. It is no common occurrence that can distract the various occupations of a crowded ball-room, where, amidst the crash of music and the din of conversation, goes on the soft, low voice of insinuating flattery, or the light flirtation of a first acquaintance; every clique, every coterie, every little group of three or four has its own separate and private interests, forming a little world of its own, and caring for and heeding nothing that goes on around; and even when some striking character or illustrious personage makes his *entrée*, the attention he attracts is so momentary, that the buzz of conversation is scarcely, if at all, interrupted, and the business of pleasure continues to flow on. Not so now, however. No sooner had the servant pronounced the magical name of Miss Macan, than all seemed to stand still. The spell thus exercised over the luckless general seemed to have extended to his company; for it was with difficulty that any one could continue his train of conversation, while every eye was directed towards the door. About two steps in advance of the servant, who still stood door in hand, was a tall, elderly lady, dressed in an antique brocade silk, with enormous flowers gaudily embroidered upon it. Her hair was powdered and turned back in the fashion of fifty years before; while her high-pointed and heeled shoes completed a costume that had not been seen for nearly a century. Her short, skinny arms were bare and partly covered by a falling flower of old point lace, while on her hands she wore black silk mittens; a pair of green spectacles scarcely dimmed the lustre of a most piercing pair of eyes, to whose effect a very palpable touch of rouge on the cheeks certainly added brilliancy. There stood this most singular apparition, holding before her a fan about the size of a modern tea-tray; while at each repetition of her name by the servant, she curtesied deeply, bestowing the while upon the gay crowd before her a very curious look of maidenly modesty at her solitary and unprotected position.

As no one had ever heard of the fair Judith, save one or two of Sir George's most intimate friends, the greater part of the company were disposed to regard Miss Macan as some one who had mistaken the character of the invitation, and had come in a fancy dress. But this delusion was but momentary, as Sir George, armed with the courage of despair, forced his way through the crowd, and taking her hand affectionately, bid her welcome to Dublin. The fair Judy, at this, threw her arms about his neck, and saluted him with a hearty smack that was heard all over the room.

"Where's Lucy, Brother? Let me embrace my little darling," said the lady, in an accent that told more of Miss Macan than a three-volume biography could have done. "There she is, I'm sure; kiss her, my honey."

This office Miss Dashwood performed with an effort at courtesy really admirable; while, taking her aunt's arm, she led her to a sofa.

It needed all the poor general's tact to get over the sensation of this most *malapropos* addition to his party; but by degrees the various groups renewed their occupations, although many a smile, and more than one sarcastic glance at the sofa, betrayed that the maiden aunt had not escaped criticism.

Power, whose propensity for fun very considerably out-stripped his sense of decorum to his commanding officer, had already made his way towards Miss Dashwood, and succeeded in obtaining a formal introduction to Miss Macan.

"I hope you will do me the favor to dance next set with me, Miss Macan?"

"Really, Captain, it's very polite of you, but you must excuse me. I was never anything great in quadrilles; but if a reel or a jig—"

"Oh, dear Aunt, don't think of it, I beg of you."

"Or even Sir Roger de Coverley," resumed Miss Macan.

"I assure you, quite equally impossible."

"Then I'm certain you waltz," said Power.

"What do you take me for, young man? I hope I know better. I wish Father Magrath heard you ask me that question, and for all your laced jacket—"

"Dearest Aunt, Captain Power didn't mean to offend you; I'm certain he—"

"Well, why did he dare to [*sob, sob*]—did he see anything light about me, that he [*sob, sob, sob*]—oh, dear! oh, dear! is it for this I came up from my little peaceful place in the west [*sob, sob,*

sob]?—General, George, dear; Lucy, my love, I'm taken bad. Oh, dear! oh, dear! is there any whiskey negus?"

Whatever sympathy Miss Macan's sufferings might have excited in the crowd about her before, this last question totally routed them, and a most hearty fit of laughter broke forth from more than one of the bystanders.

At length, however, she was comforted, and her pacification completely effected by Sir George setting her down to a whist-table. From this moment I lost sight of her for above two hours. Meanwhile I had little opportunity of following up my intimacy with Miss Dashwood, and as I rather suspected that, on more than one occasion, she seemed to avoid our meeting, I took especial care on my part, to spare her the annoyance.

For one instant only had I any opportunity of addressing her, and then there was such an evident embarrassment in her manner that I readily perceived how she felt circumstanced, and that the sense of gratitude to one whose further advances she might have feared, rendered her constrained and awkward. "Too true," said I, "she avoids me. My being here is only a source of discomfort and pain to her; therefore, I'll take my leave, and whatever it may cost me, never to return." With this intention, resolving to wish Sir George a very good night, I sought him out for some minutes. At length I saw him in a corner, conversing with the old nobleman to whom he had presented me early in the evening.

"True, upon my honor, Sir George," said he; "I saw it myself, and she did it just as dexterously as the oldest blackleg in Paris."

"Why, you don't mean to say that she cheated?"

"Yes, but I do, though,—turned the ace every time. Lady Herbert said to me, 'Very extraordinary it is,—four by honors again.' So I looked, and then I perceived it,—a very old trick it is; but she did it beautifully. What's her name?"

"Some western name; I forget it," said the poor general, ready to die with shame.

"Clever old woman, very!" said the old lord, taking a pinch of snuff; "but revokes too often."

Supper was announced at this critical moment, and before I had further thought of my determination to escape, I felt myself hurried along in the crowd towards the staircase. The party immediately in front of me were Power and Miss Macan, who now appeared reconciled, and certainly testified most openly their mutual feelings of good-will.

"I say, Charley," whispered Power, as I came along, "it is capital fun,—never met anything equal to her; but the poor general will never live through it, and I'm certain of ten day's arrest for this night's proceeding."

"Any news of Webber?" I inquired.

"Oh, yes, I fancy I can tell something of him; for I heard of some one presenting himself, and being refused the *entrée*, so that Master Frank has lost his money. Sit near us, I pray you, at supper. We must take care of the dear aunt for the niece's sake, eh?"

Not seeing the force of this reasoning, I soon separated myself from them, and secured a corner at a side-table. Every supper on such an occasion as this is the same scene of solid white muslin, faded flowers, flushed faces, torn gloves, blushes, blanc-mange, cold chicken, jelly, sponge cakes, spooney young gentlemen doing the attentive, and watchful mammas calculating what precise degree of propinquity in the crush is safe or seasonable for their daughters to the mustached and unmarrying lovers beside them. There are always the same set of gratified elders, like the benchers in King's Inn, marched up to the head of the table, to eat, drink, and be happy, removed from the more profane looks and soft speeches of the younger part of the creation. Then there are the *hoi polloi* of outcasts, younger sons of younger brothers, tutors, governesses, portionless cousins, and curates, all formed in phalanx round the side-tables, whose primitive habits and simple tastes are evinced by their all eating off the same plate and drinking from nearly the same wine-glass,—too happy if some better-off acquaintance at the long table invites them to "wine," though the ceremony on their part is limited to the pantomime of drinking. To this miserable *tiers etat* I belonged, and bore my fate with unconcern; for, alas, my spirits were depressed and my heart heavy. Lucy's treatment of me was every moment before me, contrasted with her gay and courteous demeanor to all save myself, and I longed for the moment to get away.

Never had I seen her looking so beautiful; her brilliant eyes were lit with pleasure, and her smile was enchantment itself. What would I not have given for one moment's explanation, as I took my leave forever!—one brief avowal of my unalterable, devoted love; for which I sought not nor expected return, but merely that I might not be forgotten.

Such were my thoughts, when a dialogue quite near me aroused me from my revery. I was not long in detecting the speakers, who, with their backs turned to us, were seated at the great table discussing a very liberal allowance of pigeon-pie, a flask of champagne standing between them.

"Don't now! don't I tell ye; it's little ye know Galway, or ye wouldn't think to make up to me, squeezing my foot."

"Upon my soul, you're an angel, a regular angel. I never saw a woman suit my fancy before."

"Oh, behave now. Father Magrath says—"

"Who's he?"

"The priest; no less."

"Oh, confound him!"

"Confound Father Magrath, young man?"

"Well, then, Judy, don't be angry; I only meant that a dragoon knows rather more of these matters than a priest."

"Well, then, I'm not so sure of that. But anyhow, I'd have you to remember it ain't a Widow Malone you have beside you."

"Never heard of the lady," said Power.

"Sure, it's a song,—poor creature,—it's a song they made about her in the North Cork, when they were quartered down in our county."

"I wish to Heaven you'd sing it."

"What will you give me, then, if I do?"

"Anything,—everything; my heart, my life."

"I wouldn't give a trauneen for all of them. Give me that old green ring on your finger, then."

"It's yours," said Power, placing it gracefully upon Miss Macan's finger; "and now for your promise."

"May be my brother might not like it."

"He'd be delighted," said Power; "he dotes on music."

"Does he now?"

"On my honor, he does."

"Well, mind you get up a good chorus, for the song has one, and here it is."

"Miss Macan's song!" said Power, tapping the table with his knife.

"Miss Macan's song!" was re-echoed on all sides; and before the luckless general could interfere, she had begun. How to explain the air I know not, for I never heard its name; but at the end of each verse a species of echo followed the last word that rendered it irresistibly ridiculous.

THE WIDOW MALONE.

Did ye hear of the Widow Malone, Ohone! Who lived in the town of Athlone, Alone? Oh, she melted the hearts Of the swains in them parts, So lovely the Widow Malone, Ohone! So lovely the Widow Malone. Of lovers she had a full score, Or more; And fortunes they all had galore, In store; From the minister down To the clerk of the crown, All were courting the Widow Malone, Ohone! All were courting the Widow Malone. But so modest was Mrs. Malone, 'T was known No one ever could see her alone, Ohone! Let them ogle and sigh, They could ne'er catch her eye, So bashful the Widow Malone, Ohone! So bashful the Widow Malone. Till one Mister O'Brien from Clare, How quare! It's little for blushin' they care Down there; Put his arm round her waist, Gave ten kisses at laste, "Oh," says he, "you're my Molly Malone, My own; Oh," says he, "you're my Molly Malone." And the widow they all thought so shy, My eye! Ne'er thought of a simper or sigh, For why? But "Lucius," says she, "Since you've made now so free, You may marry your Mary Malone, Ohone! You may marry your Mary Malone." There's a moral contained in my song, Not wrong; And one comfort it's not very long, But strong; If for widows you die, Larn to kiss, not to sigh, For they're all like sweet Mistress Malone, Ohone! Oh, they're very like Mistress Malone.

Never did song create such a sensation as Miss Macan's; and certainly her desires as to the chorus were followed to the letter, for "The Widow Malone, ohone!" resounded from one end of the table to the other, amidst one universal shout of laughter. None could resist the ludicrous effect of her melody; and even poor Sir George, sinking under the disgrace of his relationship, which she had contrived to make public by frequent allusions to her "dear brother the general," yielded at last, and joined in the mirth around him.

"I insist upon a copy of 'The Widow,' Miss Macan," said Power.

"To be sure; give me a call to-morrow,—let me see,—about two. Father Magrath won't be at home," said she, with a coquettish look.

"Where, pray, may I pay my respects?"

"No. 22 South Anne Street,—very respectable lodgings. I'll write the address in your pocket-book."

Power produced a card and pencil, while Miss Macan wrote a few lines, saying, as she handed it:—

"There, now, don't read it here before the people; they'll think it mighty indelicate in me to make an appointment."

Power pocketed the card, and the next minute Miss Macan's carriage was announced.

Sir George Dashwood, who little flattered himself that his fair guest had any intention of departure, became now most considerately attentive, reminded her of the necessity of muffling against the night air, hoped she would escape cold, and wished her a most cordial good-night, with a promise of seeing her early the following day.

Notwithstanding Power's ambition to engross the attention of the lady, Sir George himself saw her to her carriage, and only returned to the room as a group was collecting around the gallant captain, to whom he was relating some capital traits of his late conquest,—for such he dreamed she was.

"Doubt it who will," said he, "she has invited me to call on her to-morrow, written her address on my card, told me the hour she is certain of being alone. See here!" At these words he pulled forth the card, and handed it to Lechmere.

Scarcely were the eyes of the other thrown upon the writing, when he said, "So, this isn't it, Power."

"To be sure it is, man," said Power. "Anne Street is devilish seedy, but that's the quarter."

"Why, confound it, man!" said the other; "there's not a word of that here."

"Read it out," said Power. "Proclaim aloud my victory."

Thus urged, Lechmere read:—

DEAR P.,— Please pay to my credit,—and soon, mark ye!—the two ponies lost this evening. I have done myself the pleasure of enjoying your ball, kissed the lady, quizzed the papa, and walked into the cunning Fred Power. Yours, FRANK WEBBER. "The Widow Malone, ohone!" is at your service.

Had a thunderbolt fallen at his feet, his astonishment could not have equalled the result of this revelation. He stamped, swore, raved, laughed, and almost went deranged. The joke was soon spread through the room, and from Sir George to poor Lucy, now covered with blushes at her part in the transaction, all was laughter and astonishment.

"Who is he? That is the question," said Sir George, who, with all the ridicule of the affair hanging over him, felt no common relief at the discovery of the imposition.

"A friend of O'Malley's," said Power, delighted, in his defeat, to involve another with himself.

"Indeed!" said the general, regarding me with a look of a very mingled cast.

"Quite true, sir," said I, replying to the accusation that his manner implied; "but equally so, that I neither knew of his plot nor recognized him when here."

"I am perfectly sure of it, my boy," said the general; "and, after all, it was an excellent joke,—carried a little too far, it's true; eh, Lucy?"

But Lucy either heard not, or affected not to hear; and after some little further assurance that he felt not the least annoyed, the general turned to converse with some other friends; while I, burning with indignation against Webber, took a cold farewell of Miss Dashwood, and retired.

CHAPTER XX.
THE LAST NIGHT IN TRINITY.

How I might have met Master Webber after his impersonation of Miss Macan, I cannot possibly figure to myself. Fortunately, indeed, for all parties, he left town early the next morning; and it was some weeks ere he returned. In the meanwhile I became a daily visitor at the general's, dined there usually three or four times a week, rode out with Lucy constantly, and accompanied her every evening either to the theatre or into society. Sir George, possibly from my youth, seemed to pay little attention to an intimacy which he perceived every hour growing closer, and frequently gave his daughter into my charge in our morning excursions on horseback. As for me, my happiness was all but perfect. I loved, and already began to hope that I was not regarded with indifference; for although Lucy's manner never absolutely evinced any decided preference towards me, yet many slight and casual circumstances served to show me that my attentions to her were neither unnoticed nor uncared for. Among the many gay and dashing companions of our rides, I remarked that, however anxious for such a distinction, none ever seemed to make any way in her good graces; and I had already gone far in my self-deception that I was destined for good fortune, when a circumstance which occurred one morning at length served to open my eyes to the truth, and blast by one fatal breath the whole harvest of my hopes.

We were about to set out one morning on a long ride, when Sir George's presence was required by the arrival of an officer who had been sent from the Horse Guards on official business. After half an hour's delay, Colonel Cameron, the officer in question, was introduced, and entered into conversation with our party. He had only landed in England from the Peninsula a few days before, and had abundant information of the stirring events enacting there. At the conclusion of an anecdote,—I forget what,—he turned suddenly round to Miss Dashwood, who was standing beside me, and said in a low voice:—

"And now, Miss Dashwood, I am reminded of a commission I promised a very old brother officer to perform. Can I have one moment's conversation with you in the window?"

As he spoke, I perceived that he crumpled beneath his glove something like a letter.

"To me?" said Lucy, with a look of surprise that sadly puzzled me whether to ascribe it to coquetry or innocence,—"to me?"

"To you," said the colonel, bowing; "and I am sadly deceived by my friend Hammersley—"

"Captain Hammersley?" said she, blushing deeply as she spoke.

I heard no more. She turned towards the window with the colonel, and all I saw was that he handed her a letter, which, having hastily broken open and thrown her eyes over, she grew at first deadly pale, then red, and while her eyes filled with tears, I heard her say, "How like him! How truly generous this is!" I listened for no more; my brain was wheeling round and my senses reeling. I turned and left the room; in another moment I was on my horse, galloping from the spot, despair, in all its blackness, in my heart, and in my broken-hearted misery, wishing for death.

I was miles away from Dublin ere I remembered well what had occurred, and even then not over clearly. The fact that Lucy Dashwood, whom I imagined to be my own in heart, loved another, was all that I really knew. That one thought was all my mind was capable of, and in it my misery, my wretchedness were centred.

Of all the grief my life has known, I have had no moments like the long hours of that dreary night. My sorrow, in turn, took every shape and assumed every guise. Now I remembered how the Dashwoods had courted my intimacy and encouraged my visits,—how Lucy herself had evinced in a thousand ways that she felt a preference for me. I called to mind the many unequivocal proofs I had given her that my feeling at least was no common one; and yet, how had she sported with my affections, and jested with my happiness! That she loved Hammersley I had now a palpable proof. That this affection must have been mutual, and prosecuted at the very moment I was not only professing my own love for her, but actually receiving all but an avowal of its return,—oh, it was too, too base! and in my deepest heart I cursed my folly, and vowed never to see her more.

It was late on the next day ere I retraced my steps towards town, my heart sad and heavy, careless what became of me for the future, and pondering whether I should not at once give up my college career and return to my uncle. When I reached my chambers, all was silent and comfortless; Webber had not returned; my servant was from home; and I felt myself more than ever wretched in the solitude of what had been so oft the scene of noisy and festive gayety. I sat some hours in a half-musing state, every sad depressing thought that blighted hopes can conjure up rising in turn before me. A loud knocking at the door at length aroused me. I got up and opened it. No one was there. I looked around as well as the coming gloom of evening would permit, but saw nothing. I listened, and heard, at some distance off, my friend Power's manly voice as he sang,—

"Oh, love is the soul of an Irish dragoon!"

I hallooed out, "Power!"

"Eh, O'Malley, is that you?" inquired he. "Why, then, it seems it required some deliberation whether you opened your door or not. Why, man, you can have no great gift of prophecy, or you wouldn't have kept me so long there."

"And have you been so?"

"Only twenty minutes; for as I saw the key in the lock, I had determined to succeed if noise would do it."

"How strange! I never heard it."

"Glorious sleeper you must be; but come, my dear fellow, you don't appear altogether awake yet."

"I have not been quite well these few days."

"Oh, indeed! The Dashwoods thought there must have been something of that kind the matter by your brisk retreat. They sent me after you yesterday; but wherever you went, Heaven knows. I never could come up with you; so that your great news has been keeping these twenty-four hours longer than need be."

"I am not aware what you allude to."

"Well, you are not over likely to be the wiser when you hear it, if you can assume no more intelligent look than that. Why, man, there's great luck in store for you."

"As how, pray? Come, Power, out with it; though I can't pledge myself to feel half as grateful for my good fortune as I should do. What is it?"

"You know Cameron?"

"I have seen him," said I, reddening.

"Well, old Camy, as we used to call him, has brought over, among his other news, your gazette."

"My gazette! What do you mean?"

"Confound your uncommon stupidity this evening! I mean, man, that you are one of us,—gazetted to the 14th Light,—the best fellows for love, war, and whiskey that ever sported a sabretasche.

'Oh, love is the soul of an Irish dragoon!'

By Jove, I am as delighted to have rescued you from the black harness of the King's Bench as though you had been a prisoner there! Know, then, friend Charley, that on Wednesday we proceed to Fermoy, join some score of gallant fellows,—all food for powder,—and, with the aid of a rotten transport and the stormy winds that blow, will be bronzing our beautiful faces in Portugal before the month's out. But come, now, let's see about supper. Some of ours are coming over here at eleven, and I promised them a devilled bone; and as it's your last night among these classic precincts, let us have a shindy of it."

While I despatched Mike to Morrison's to provide supper, I heard from Power that Sir George Dashwood had interested himself so strongly for me that I had obtained my cornetcy in the 14th; that, fearful lest any disappointment might arise, he had never mentioned the matter to me, but that he had previously obtained my uncle's promise to concur in the arrangement if his negotiation succeeded. It had so done, and now the long-sought-for object of many days was within my grasp. But, alas, the circumstance which lent it all its fascinations was a vanished dream; and what but two days before had rendered my happiness perfect, I listened to listlessly and almost without interest. Indeed, my first impulse at finding that I owed my promotion to Sir George was to return a positive refusal of the cornetcy; but then I remembered how deeply such conduct would hurt my poor uncle, to whom I never could give an adequate explanation. So I heard Power in silence to the end, thanked him sincerely for his own good-natured kindness in the matter, which already, by the interest he had taken in me, went far to heal the wounds that my own solitary musings were deepening in my heart. At eighteen, fortunately, consolations are attainable that become more difficult at eight-and-twenty, and impossible at eight-and-thirty.

While Power continued to dilate upon the delights of a soldier's life—a theme which many a boyish dream had long since made hallowed to my thoughts—I gradually felt my enthusiasm rising, and a certain throbbing at my heart betrayed to me that, sad and dispirited as I felt, there was still within that buoyant spirit which youth possesses as its privilege, and which answers to the call of enterprise as the war-horse to the trumpet. That a career worthy of manhood, great, glorious, and inspiriting, opened before me, coming so soon after the late downfall of my hopes, was in itself a source of such true pleasure that ere long I listened to my friend, and heard his narrative with breathless interest. A lingering sense of pique, too, had its share in all this. I longed to come forward in some manly and dashing part, where my youth might not be ever remembered against me, and when, having brought myself to the test, I might no longer be looked upon and treated as a boy.

We were joined at length by the other officers of the 14th, and, to the number of twelve, sat down to supper.

It was to be my last night in Old Trinity, and we resolved that the farewell should be a solemn one. Mansfield, one of the wildest young fellows in the regiment, had vowed that the leave-taking should be commemorated by some very decisive and open expressions of our feelings, and had already made some progress in arrangements for blowing up the great bell, which had more than once obtruded upon our morning convivialities; but he was overruled by his more discreet associates, and we at length assumed our places at table, in the midst of which stood a *hecatomb* of all my college equipments, cap, gown, bands, etc. A funeral pile of classics was arrayed upon the hearth, surmounted by my "Book on the Cellar," and a punishment-roll waved its length, like a banner, over the doomed heroes of Greece and Rome.

It is seldom that any very determined attempt to be gay *par excellence* has a perfect success, but certainly upon this evening ours had. Songs, good stories, speeches, toasts, high visions of the campaign before us, the wild excitement which such a meeting cannot be free from, gradually, as the wine passed from hand to hand, seized upon all, and about four in the morning, such was the uproar we caused, and so terrific the noise of our proceedings, that the accumulated force of porters, sent one by one to demand admission, was now a formidable body at the door, and Mike at last came in to assure us that the bursar,—the most dread official of all collegians,—was without, and insisted, with a threat of his heaviest displeasure in case of refusal, that the door should be opened.

A committee of the whole house immediately sat upon the question; and it was at length resolved, *nemine contradicente*, that the request should be complied with. A fresh bowl of punch, in honor of our expected guest, was immediately concocted, a new broil put on the gridiron, and having seated ourselves with as great a semblance of decorum as four bottles a man admits of, Curtis the junior captain, being most drunk, was deputed to receive the bursar at the door, and introduce him to our august presence.

Mike's instructions were, that immediately on Dr. Stone the bursar entering, the door was to be slammed to, and none of his followers admitted. This done, the doctor was to be ushered in and left to our polite attentions.

A fresh thundering from without scarcely left time for further deliberation; and at last Curtis moved towards the door in execution of his mission.

"Is there any one there?" said Mike, in a tone of most unsophisticated innocence, to a rapping that, having lasted three quarters of an hour, threatened now to break in the panel. "Is there any one there?"

"Open the door this instant,—the senior bursar desires you,—this instant."

"Sure it's night, and we're all in bed," said Mike.

"Mr. Webber, Mr. O'Malley," said the bursar, now boiling with indignation, "I summon you, in the name of the board, to admit me."

"Let the gemman in," hiccoughed Curtis; and at the same instant the heavy bars were withdrawn, and the door opened, but so sparingly as with difficulty to permit the passage of the burly figure of the bursar.

Forcing his way through, and regardless of what became of the rest, he pushed on vigorously through the antechamber, and before Curtis could perform his functions of usher, stood in the midst of us. What were his feelings at the scene before him, Heaven knows. The number of figures in uniform at once betrayed how little his jurisdiction extended to the great mass of the company, and he immediately turned towards me.

"Mr. Webber—"

"O'Malley, if you please, Mr. Bursar," said I, bowing with, most ceremonious politeness.

"No matter, sir; *arcades ambo*, I believe."

"Both archdeacons," said Melville, translating, with a look of withering contempt upon the speaker.

The doctor continued, addressing me,—

"May I ask, sir, if you believe yourself possessed of any privilege for converting this university into a common tavern?"

"I wish to Heaven he did," said Curtis; "capital tap your old commons would make."

"Really, Mr. Bursar," replied I, modestly, "I had begun to flatter myself that our little innocent gayety had inspired you with the idea of joining our party."

"I humbly move that the old cove in the gown do take the chair," sang out one. "All who are of this opinion say, 'Ay.'" A perfect yell of ayes followed this. "All who are of the contrary say, 'No.' The ayes have it."

Before the luckless doctor had a moment for thought, his legs were lifted from under him, and he was jerked, rather than placed, upon a chair, and put sitting upon the table.

"Mr. O'Malley, your expulsion within twenty-four hours—"

"Hip, hip, hurra, hurra, hurra!" drowned the rest, while Power, taking off the doctor's cap, replaced it by a foraging cap, very much to the amusement of the party.

"There is no penalty the law permits of that I shall not—"

"Help the doctor," said Melville, placing a glass of punch in his unconscious hand.

"Now for a 'Viva la Compagnie!'" said Telford, seating himself at the piano, and playing the first bars of that well-known air, to which, in our meetings, we were accustomed to improvise a doggerel in turn.

"I drink to the graces, Law, Physic, Divinity,   *Viva la Compagnie! And here's to the worthy old Bursar of Trinity,*   *Viva la Compagnie!"*

"Viva, viva la va!" etc., were chorussed with a shout that shook the old walls, while Power took up the strain:

"Though with lace caps and gowns they look so like asses,   *Viva la Compagnie!*   *They'd rather have punch than the springs of Parnassus,*   *Viva la*

Compagnie!   What a nose the old gentleman has, by the way,   Viva la Compagnie!
Since he smelt out the Devil from Botany Bay, /1/   Viva la Compagnie!

[Footnote:1 Botany Bay was the slang name given by college men to a new square rather remotely situated from the remainder of the college.]

Words cannot give even the faintest idea of the poor bursar's feelings while these demoniacal orgies were enacting around him. Held fast in his chair by Lechmere and another, he glowered on the riotous mob around like a maniac, and astonishment that such liberties could be taken with one in his situation seemed to have surpassed even his rage and resentment; and every now and then a stray thought would flash across his mind that we were mad,—a sentiment which, unfortunately, our conduct was but too well calculated to inspire.

"So you're the morning lecturer, old gentleman, and have just dropped in here in the way of business; pleasant life you must have of it," said Casey, now by far the most tipsy man present.

"If you think, Mr. O'Malley, that the events of this evening are to end here—"

"Very far from it, Doctor," said Power; "I'll draw up a little account of the affair for 'Saunders.' They shall hear of it in every corner and nook of the kingdom."

"The bursar of Trinity shall be a proverb for a good fellow that loveth his lush," hiccoughed out Fegan.

"And if you believe that such conduct is academical," said the doctor, with a withering sneer.

"Perhaps not," lisped Melville, tightening his belt; "but it's devilish convivial,—eh, Doctor?"

"Is that like him?" said Moreton, producing a caricature which he had just sketched.

"Capital,—very good,—perfect. M'Cleary shall have it in his window by noon to-day," said Power.

At this instant some of the combustibles disposed among the rejected habiliments of my late vocation caught fire, and squibs, crackers, and detonating shots went off on all sides. The bursar, who had not been deaf to several hints and friendly suggestions about setting fire to him, blowing him up, etc., with one vigorous spring burst from his antagonists, and clearing the table at a bound, reached the floor. Before he could be seized, he had gained the door, opened it, and was away. We gave chase, yelling like so many devils. But wine and punch, songs and speeches, had done their work, and more than one among the pursuers measured his length upon the pavement; while the terrified bursar, with the speed of terror, held on his way, and gained his chambers by about twenty yards in advance of Power and Melville, whose pursuit only ended when the oaken panel of the door shut them out from their victim. One loud cheer beneath his window served for our farewell to our friend, and we returned to my rooms. By this time a regiment of those classic functionaries yclept porters had assembled around the door, and seemed bent upon giving battle in honor of their maltreated ruler; but Power explained to them, in a neat speech replete with Latin quotations, that their cause was a weak one, that we were more than their match, and finally proposed to them to finish the punch-bowl, to which we were really incompetent,—a motion that met immediate acceptance; and old Duncan, with his helmet in one hand and a goblet in the other, wished me many happy days and every luck in this life as I stepped from the massive archway, and took my last farewell of Old Trinity.

Should any kind reader feel interested as to the ulterior course assumed by the bursar, I have only to say that the terrors of the "Board" were never fulminated against me, harmless and innocent as I should have esteemed them. The threat of giving publicity to the entire proceedings by the papers, and the dread of figuring in a sixpenny caricature in M'Cleary's window, were too much for the worthy doctor, and he took the wiser course under the circumstances, and held his peace about the matter. I, too, have done so for many a year, and only now recall the scene among the wild transactions of early days and boyish follies.

CHAPTER XXI

THE PHOENIX PARK.

What a glorious thing it is when our first waking thoughts not only dispel some dark, depressing dream, but arouse us to the consciousness of a new and bright career suddenly opening before us, buoyant in hope, rich in promise for the future! Life has nothing better than this. The bold spring by which the mind clears the depth that separates misery from happiness is ecstasy itself; and then what a world of bright visions come teeming before us,—what plans we form; what promises we make to ourselves in our own hearts; how prolific is the dullest imagination; how excursive the tamest fancy, at such a moment! In a few short and fleeting seconds, the events of a whole life are planned and pictured before us. Dreams of happiness and visions of bliss, of which all our after-years are insufficient to eradicate the *prestige*, come in myriads about us; and from that narrow aperture through which this new hope pierces into our heart, a flood of light is poured that illumines our path to the very verge of the grave. How many a success in after-days is reckoned but as one step in that ladder of ambition some boyish review has framed, perhaps, after all, destined to be the first and only one! With what triumph we hail some goal attained, some object of our wishes gained, less for its present benefit, than as the accomplishment of some youthful prophecy, when picturing to our hearts all that we would have in life, we whispered within us the flattery of success.

Who is there who has not had some such moment; and who would exchange it, with all the delusive and deceptive influences by which it comes surrounded, for the greatest actual happiness he has partaken of? Alas, alas, it is only in the boundless expanse of such imaginations, unreal and fictitious as they are, that we are truly blessed! Our choicest blessings in life come even so associated with some sources of care that the cup of enjoyment is not pure but dregged in bitterness.

To such a world of bright anticipation did I awake on the morning after the events I have detailed in the last chapter. The first thing my eyes fell upon was an official letter from the Horse Guards:—

"*The commander of the forces desires that Mr. O'Malley will report himself, immediately on the receipt of this letter, at the headquarters of the regiment to which he is gazetted.*"

Few and simple as the lines were, how brimful of pleasure they sounded to my ears. The regiment to which I was gazetted! And so I was a soldier at last! The first wish of my boyhood was then really accomplished. And my uncle, what will he say; what will he think?

"A letter, sir, by the post," said Mike, at the moment.

I seized it eagerly; it came from home, but was in Considine's handwriting. How my heart failed me as I turned to look at the seal. "Thank God!" said I, aloud, on perceiving that it was a red one. I now tore it open and read:—

My Dear Charley,—Godfrey, being laid up with the gout, has desired me to write to you by this day's post. Your appointment to the 14th, notwithstanding all his prejudices about the army, has given him sincere pleasure. I believe, between ourselves, that your college career, of which he has heard something, convinced him that your forte did not lie in the classics; you know I said so always, but nobody minded me. Your new prospects are all that your best friends could wish for you: you begin early; your corps is a crack one; you are ordered for service. What could you have more? Your uncle hopes, if you can get a few days' leave, that you will come down here before you join, and I hope so too; for he is unusually low-spirited, and talks about his never seeing you again, and all that sort of thing. I have written to Merivale, your colonel, on this subject, as well as generally on your behalf. We were cornets together forty years ago. A strict fellow you'll find him, but a trump on service. If you can't manage the leave, write a long letter home at all events. And so, God bless you, and all success! Yours sincerely, W. Considine. I had thought of writing you a long letter of advice for your new career; and, indeed, half accomplished one. After all, however, I can tell you little that your own good sense will not teach you as you go on; and experience is ever better than precept. I know of but one rule in life which admits of scarcely any exception, and having followed it upwards of sixty years, approve of it only the more: Never quarrel when you can help it; but meet any man,—your tailor, your hairdresser,—if he wishes to have you out. W. C.

I had scarcely come to the end of this very characteristic epistle, when two more letters were placed upon my table. One was from Sir George Dashwood, inviting me to dinner to meet some of my "brother officers." How my heart beat at the expression. The other was a short note, marked "Private," from my late tutor, Dr. Mooney, saying, "that if I made a suitable apology to the bursar for the late affair at my room, he might probably be induced to abandon any further step; otherwise—" then followed innumerable threats about fine, penalties, expulsion, etc., that fell most harmlessly upon my ears. I accepted the invitation; declined the apology; and having ordered my horse, cantered off to the barracks to consult my friend Power as to all the minor details of my career.

As the dinner hour grew near, my thoughts became again fixed upon Miss Dashwood; and a thousand misgivings crossed my mind as to whether I should have nerve enough to meet her, without disclosing in my manner the altered state of my feelings; a possibility which I now dreaded fully as much as I had longed some days before to avow my affection for her, however slight its prospect of return. All my valiant resolves and well-contrived plans for appearing unmoved and indifferent in her presence, with which I stored my mind while dressing and when on the way to dinner, were, however, needless, for it was a party exclusively of men; and as the coffee was served in the dining-room, no move was made to the drawing-room by any of the company. "Quite as well as it is!" was my muttered opinion, as I got into my cab at the door. "All is at an end as regards me in her esteem, and I must not spend my days sighing for a young lady that cares for another." Very reasonable, very proper resolutions these; but, alas! I went home to bed, only to think half the night long of the fair Lucy, and dream of her the remainder of it.

When morning dawned my first thought was, Shall I see her once more? Shall I leave her forever thus abruptly? Or, rather, shall I not unburden my bosom of its secret, confess my love, and say farewell? I felt such a course much more in unison with my wishes than the day before; and as Power had told me that before a week we should present ourselves at Fermoy, I knew that no time was to be lost.

My determination was taken. I ordered my horse, and early as it was, rode out to the Royal Hospital. My heart beat so strongly as I rode up to the door that I half resolved to return. I rang the bell. Sir George was in town. Miss Dashwood had just gone, five minutes before, to spend some days at Carton. "It is fate!" thought I as I turned from the spot and walked slowly beside my horse towards Dublin.

In the few days that intervened before my leaving town, my time was occupied from morning to night; the various details of my uniform, outfit, etc., were undertaken for me by Power. My horses were sent for to Galway; and I myself, with innumerable persons to see, and a mass of business to transact, contrived at least three times a day to ride out to the Royal Hospital, always to make some trifling inquiry for Sir George, and always to hear repeated that Miss Dashwood had not returned.

Thus passed five of my last six days in Dublin; and as the morning of the last opened, it was with a sorrowing spirit that I felt my hour of departure approach without one only opportunity of seeing Lucy, even to say good-by. While Mike was packing in one corner, and I in another was concluding a long letter to my poor uncle, my door opened and Webber entered.

"Eh, O'Malley, I'm only in time to say adieu, it seems. To my surprise this morning I found you had cut the 'Silent Sister.' I feared I should be too late to catch one glimpse of you ere you started for the wars."

"You are quite right, Master Frank, and I scarcely expected to have seen you. Your last brilliant achievement at Sir George's very nearly involved me in a serious scrape."

"A mere trifle. How confoundedly silly Power must have looked, eh? Should like so much to have seen his face. He booked up next day,—very proper fellow. By-the-bye, O'Malley, I rather like the little girl; she is decidedly pretty, and her foot,—did you remark her foot?—capital."

"Yes, she's very good-looking," said I, carelessly.

"I'm thinking of cultivating her a little," said Webber, pulling up his cravat and adjusting his hair at the glass. "She's spoiled by all the tinsel vaporing of her hussar and aide-de-camp acquaintances; but something may be done for her, eh?"

"With your most able assistance and kind intentions."

"That's what I mean exactly. Sorry you're going,—devilish sorry. You served out Stone gloriously: perhaps it's as well, though,—you know they'd have expelled you; but still something might turn up. Soldiering is a bad style of thing, eh? How the old general did take his sister-in-law's presence to heart! But he must forgive and forget, for I am going to be very great friends with him and Lucy. Where are you going now?"

"I am about to try a new horse before troops," said I. "He's stanch enough with the cry of the fox-pack in his ears; but I don't know how he'll stand a peal of artillery."

"Well, come along," said Webber; "I'll ride with you." So saying, we mounted and set off to the Park, where two regiments of cavalry and some horse artillery were ordered for inspection.

The review was over when we reached the exercising ground, and we slowly walked our horses towards the end of the Park, intending to return to Dublin by the road. We had not proceeded far, when, some hundred yards in advance, we perceived an officer riding with a lady, followed by an orderly dragoon.

"There he goes," said Webber; "I wonder if he'd ask me to dinner, if I were to throw myself in his way?"

"Who do you mean?" said I.

"Sir George Dashwood, to be sure, and, *la voilà*, Miss Lucy. The little darling rides well, too; how squarely she sits her horse. O'Malley, I've a weakness there; upon my soul I have."

"Very possible," said I; "I am aware of another friend of mine participating in the sentiment."

"One Charles O'Malley, of his Majesty's—"

"Nonsense, man; no, no. I mean a very different person, and, for all I can see, with some reason to hope for success."

"Oh, as to that, we flatter ourselves the thing does not present any very considerable difficulties."

"As how, pray?"

"Why, of course, like all such matters, a very decisive determination to be, to do, and to suffer, as Lindley Murray says, carries the day. Tell her she's an angel every day for three weeks. She may laugh a little at first, but she'll believe it in the end. Tell her that you have not the slightest prospect of obtaining her affections, but still persist in loving her. That, finally, you must die from the effects of despair, etc., but rather like the notion of it than otherwise. That you know she has no fortune; that you haven't a sixpence; and who should marry, if people whose position in the world was similar did not?"

"But halt; pray, how are you to get time and place for all such interesting conversations?"

"Time and place! Good Heavens, what a question! Is not every hour of the twenty-four the fittest? Is not every place the most suitable? A sudden pause in the organ of St. Patrick's did, it is true, catch me once in a declaration of love, but the choir came in to my aid and drowned the lady's answer. My dear O'Malley, what could prevent you this instant, if you are so disposed, from doing the amiable to the darling Lucy there?"

"With the father for an umpire in case we disagreed," said I.

"Not at all. I should soon get rid of him."

"Impossible, my dear friend."

"Come now, just for the sake of convincing your obstinacy. If you like to say good-by to the little girl without a witness, I'll take off the he-dragon."

"You don't mean—"

"I do, man; I do mean it." So saying, he drew a crimson silk handkerchief from his pocket, and fastened it round his waist like an officer's sash. This done, and telling me to keep in their wake for some minutes, he turned from me, and was soon concealed by a copse of white-thorn near us.

I had not gone above a hundred yards farther when I heard Sir George's voice calling for the orderly. I looked and saw Webber at a considerable distance in front, curvetting and playing all species of antics. The distance between the general and myself was now so short that I overheard the following dialogue with his sentry:—

"He's not in uniform, then?"

"No, sir; he has a round hat."

"A round hat!"

"His sash—"

"A sword and sash. This is too bad. I'm determined to find him out."

"How d'ye do, General?" cried Webber, as he rode towards the trees.

"Stop, sir!" shouted Sir George.

"Good-day, Sir George," replied Webber, retiring.

"Stay where you are, Lucy," said the general as, dashing spurs into his horse, he sprang forward at a gallop, incensed beyond endurance that his most strict orders should be so openly and insultingly transgressed.

Webber led on to a deep hollow, where the road passed between two smooth slopes, covered with furze-bushes, and from which it emerged afterwards in the thickest and most intricate part of the Park. Sir George dashed boldly after, and in less than half a minute both were lost to my view, leaving me in breathless amazement at Master Frank's ingenuity, and some puzzle as to my own future movements.

"Now then, or never!" said I, as I pushed boldly forward, and in an instant was alongside of Miss Dashwood. Her astonishment at seeing me so suddenly increased the confusion from which I felt myself suffering, and for some minutes I could scarcely speak. At last I plucked up courage a little, and said:—

"Miss Dashwood, I have looked most anxiously, for the last four days, for the moment which chance has now given me. I wished, before I parted forever with those to whom I owe already so much, that I should at least speak my gratitude ere I said good-by."

"But when do you think of going?"

"To-morrow. Captain Power, under whose command I am, has received orders to embark immediately for Portugal."

I thought—perhaps it was but a thought—that her cheek grew somewhat paler as I spoke; but she remained silent; and I, scarcely knowing what I had said, or whether I had finished, spoke not either.

"Papa, I'm sure, is not aware," said she, after a long pause, "of your intention of leaving so soon, for only last night he spoke of some letters he meant to give you to some friends in the Peninsula; besides, I know," here she smiled faintly,—"that he destined some excellent advice for your ears, as to your new path in life, for he has an immense opinion of the value of such to a young officer."

"I am, indeed, most grateful to Sir George, and truly never did any one stand more in need of counsel than I do." This was said half musingly, and not intended to be heard.

"Then, pray, consult papa," said she, eagerly; "he is much attached to you, and will, I am certain, do all in his power—"

"Alas! I fear not, Miss Dashwood."

"Why, what can you mean. Has anything so serious occurred?"

"No, no; I'm but misleading you, and exciting your sympathy with false pretences. Should I tell you all the truth, you would not pardon, perhaps not hear me."

"You have, indeed, puzzled me; but if there is anything in which my father—"

"Less him than his daughter," said I, fixing my eyes full upon her as I spoke. "Yes, Lucy, I feel I must confess it, cost what it may; I love you. Stay, hear me out; I know the fruitlessness, the utter despair, that awaits such a sentiment. My own heart tells me that I am not, cannot be, loved in return; yet would I rather cherish in its core my affection, slighted and unblessed, such as it is, than own another heart. I ask for nothing, I hope for nothing; I merely entreat that, for my truth, I may meet belief, and for my heart's worship of her whom alone I can love, compassion. I see that you at least pity me. Nay, one word more; I have one favor more to ask,—it is my last, my only one. Do not, when time and distance may have separated us, perhaps forever, think that the expressions I now use are prompted by a mere sudden ebullition of boyish feeling; do not attribute to the circumstance of my youth alone the warmth of the attachment I profess,—for I swear to you, by every hope that I have, that in my heart of hearts my love to you is the source and spring of every action in my life, of every aspiration in my heart; and when I cease to love you, I shall cease to feel."

"And now, farewell,—farewell forever!" I pressed her hand to my lips, gave one long, last look, turned my horse rapidly away, and ere a minute was far out of sight of where I had left her.

CHAPTER XXII.

THE ROAD.

Power was detained in town by some orders from the adjutant-general, so that I started for Cork the next morning with no other companion than my servant Mike. For the first few stages upon the road, my own thoughts sufficiently occupied me to render me insensible or indifferent to all else. My opening career, the prospects my new life as a soldier held out, my hopes of distinction, my love of Lucy with all its train of doubts and fears, passed in review before me, and I took no note of time till far past noon. I now looked to the back part of the coach, where Mike's voice had been, as usual, in the ascendant for some time, and perceived that he was surrounded by an eager auditory of four raw recruits, who, under the care of a sergeant, were proceeding to Cork to be enrolled in their regiment. The sergeant, whose minutes of wakefulness were only those when the coach stopped to change horses, and when he got down to mix a "summat hot," paid little attention to his followers, leaving them perfectly free in all their movements, to listen to Mike's eloquence and profit by his suggestions, should they deem fit. Master Michael's services to his new acquaintances, I began to perceive, were not exactly of the same nature as Dibdin is reported to have rendered to our navy in the late war. Far from it. His theme was no contemptuous disdain for danger; no patriotic enthusiasm to fight for home and country; no proud consciousness of British valor, mingled with the appropriate hatred of our mutual enemies,—on the contrary, Mike's eloquence was enlisted for the defendant. He detailed, and in no unimpressive way either, the hardships of a soldier's life,—its dangers, its vicissitudes, its chances, its possible penalties, its inevitably small rewards; and, in fact, so completely did he work on the feelings of his hearers that I perceived more than one glance exchanged between the victims that certainly betokened anything save the resolve to fight for King George. It was at the close of a long and most powerful appeal upon the superiority of any other line in life, petty larceny and small felony inclusive, that he concluded with the following quotation:—

"Thrue for ye, boys!

'With your red scarlet coat,   You're as proud as a goat,   And your long cap and feather.'

But, by the piper that played before Moses! it's more whipping nor gingerbread is going on among them, av ye knew but all, and heerd the misfortune that happened to my father."

"And was he a sodger?" inquired one.

"Troth was he, more sorrow to him; and wasn't he a'most whipped one day for doing what he was bid?"

"Musha, but that was hard!"

"To be sure it was hard; but faix, when my father seen that they didn't know their own minds, he thought, anyhow, he knew his, so he ran away,—and devil a bit of him they ever cotch afther. May be ye might like to hear the story; and there's instruction in it for yez, too."

A general request to this end being preferred by the company, Mike took a shrewd look at the sergeant, to be sure that he was still sleeping, settled his coat comfortably across his knees, and began:—

Well, it's a good many years ago my father 'listed in the North Cork, just to oblige Mr. Barry, the landlord there. 'For,' says he, 'Phil,' says he, 'it's not a soldier ye'll be at all, but my own man, to brush my clothes and go errands, and the like o' that; and the king, long life to him! will help to pay ye for your trouble. Ye understand me?' Well, my father agreed, and Mr. Barry was as good as his word. Never a guard did my father mount, nor as much as a drill had he, nor a roll-call, nor anything at all, save and except wait on the captain, his master, just as pleasant as need be, and no inconvenience in life.

"Well, for three years this went on as I am telling, and the regiment was ordered down to Bantry, because of a report that the 'boys' was rising down there; and the second evening there was a night party patrolling with Captain Barry for six hours in the rain, and the captain, God be marciful to him! tuk could and died. More by token, they said it was drink, but my father says it wasn't: 'for' says he, 'after he tuk eight tumblers comfortable,' my father mixed the ninth, and the captain waived his hand this way, as much as to say he'd have no more. 'Is it that ye mean?' says my father; and the captain nodded. 'Musha, but it's sorry I am,' says my father, 'to see you this way; for ye must be bad entirely to leave off in the beginning of the evening.' And thrue for him, the captain was dead in the morning.

"A sorrowful day it was for my father when he died. It was the finest place in the world; little to do, plenty of diversion, and a kind man he was,—when he was drunk. Well, then, when the captain was buried and all was over, my father hoped they'd be for letting him away, as he said, 'Sure, I'm no use in life to anybody, save the man that's gone, for his ways are all I know, and I never was a sodger.' But, upon my conscience, they had other thoughts in their heads, for they ordered him into the ranks to be drilled just like the recruits they took the day before.

"'Musha, isn't this hard?' said my father. 'Here I am, an ould vitrin that ought to be discharged on a pension with two-and-sixpence a day, obliged to go capering about the barrack-yard, practising the goose-step, or some other nonsense not becoming my age nor my habits.' But so it was. Well, this went on for some time, and sure, if they were hard on my father, hadn't he his revenge; for he nigh broke their hearts with his stupidity. Oh, nothing in life could equal him! Devil a thing, no matter how easy, he could learn at all; and so far from caring for being in confinement, it was that he liked best. Every sergeant in the regiment had a trial of him, but all to no good; and he seemed striving so hard to learn all the while that they were loath to punish him, the ould rogue!

"This was going on for some time, when, one day, news came in that a body of the rebels, as they called them, was coming down from the Gap of Mulnavick to storm the town and burn all before them. The whole regiment was of coorse under arms, and great preparations was made for a battle. Meanwhile patrols were ordered to scour the roads, and sentries posted at every turn of the way and every rising ground to give warning when the boys came in sight; and my father was placed at the Bridge of Drumsnag, in the wildest and bleakest part of the whole country, with nothing but furze mountains on every side, and a straight road going over the top of them.

"'This is pleasant,' says my father, as soon as they left him there alone by himself, with no human creature to speak to, nor a whiskey-shop within ten miles of him; 'cowld comfort,' says he, 'on a winter's day; and faix, but I have a mind to give ye the slip.'

"Well, he put his gun down on the bridge, and he lit his pipe, and he sat down under an ould tree and began to ruminate upon his affairs.

"'Oh, then, it's wishing it well I am,' says he, 'for sodgering; and bad luck to the hammer that struck the shilling that 'listed me, that's all,' for he was mighty low in his heart.

"Just then a noise came rattling down near him. He listened, and before he could get on his legs, down comes' the general, ould Cohoon, with an orderly after him.

"'Who goes there?' says my father.

"'The round,' says the general, looking about all the time to see where was the sentry, for my father was snug under the tree.

"'What round?' says my father.

"'The grand round,' says the general, more puzzled than afore.

"'Pass on, grand round, and God save you kindly!' says my father, putting his pipe in his mouth again, for he thought all was over.

77

"'D—n your soul, where are you?' says the general, for sorrow bit of my father could he see yet.

"'It's here I am,' says he, 'and a cowld place I have of it; and if it wasn't for the pipe I'd be lost entirely.'

"The words wasn't well out of his mouth when the general began laughing, till ye'd think he'd fall off his horse; and the dragoon behind him—more by token, they say it wasn't right for him—laughed as loud as himself.

"'Yer a droll sentry,' says the general, as soon as he could speak.

"'Be-gorra, it's little fun there's left in me,' says my father, 'with this drilling, and parading, and blackguarding about the roads all night.'

"'And is this the way you salute your officer?' says the general.

"'Just so,' says my father; 'devil a more politeness ever they taught me.'

"'What regiment do you belong to?' says the general.

"'The North Cork, bad luck to them!' says my father, with a sigh.

"'They ought to be proud of ye,' says the general.

"'I'm sorry for it,' says my father, sorrowfully, 'for may be they'll keep me the longer.'

"'Well, my good fellow,' says the general, 'I haven't more time to waste here; but let me teach you something before I go. Whenever your officer passes, it's your duty to present to him.'

"'Arrah, it's jokin' ye are,' says my father.

"'No, I'm in earnest,' says he, 'as ye might learn, to your cost, if I brought you to a court-martial.'

"'Well, there's no knowing,' says my father, 'what they'd be up to; but sure, if that's all, I'll do it, with all "the veins," whenever yer coming this way again.'

"The general began to laugh again here; but said,—

'I'm coming back in the evening,' says he, 'and mind you don't forget your respect to your officer.'

"'Never fear, sir,' says my father; 'and many thanks to you for your kindness for telling me.'

"Away went the general, and the orderly after him, and in ten minutes they were out of sight.

"The night was falling fast, and one half of the mountain was quite dark already, when my father began to think they were forgetting him entirely. He looked one way, and he looked another, but sorra bit of a sergeant's guard was coming to relieve him. There he was, fresh and fasting, and daren't go for the bare life. 'I'll give you a quarter of an hour more,' says my father, 'till the light leaves that rock up there; after that,' says he, 'by the Mass! I'll be off, av it cost me what it may.'

"Well, sure enough, his courage was not needed this time; for what did he see at the same moment but a shadow of something coming down the road opposite the bridge. He looked again; and then he made out the general himself, that was walking his horse down the steep part of the mountain, followed by the orderly. My father immediately took up his musket off the wall, settled his belts, shook the ashes out of his pipe and put it into his pocket, making himself as smart and neat-looking as he could be, determining, when ould Cohoon came up, to ask him for leave to go home, at least for the night. Well, by this time the general was turning a sharp part of the cliff that looks down upon the bridge, from where you might look five miles round on every side. 'He sees me,' says my father; 'but I'll be just as quick as himself.' No sooner said than done; for coming forward to the parapet of the bridge, he up with his musket to his shoulder, and presented it straight at the general. It wasn't well there, when the officer pulled up his horse quite short, and shouted out, 'Sentry! sentry!'

"'Anan?' says my father, still covering him.

"'Down with your musket you rascal. Don't you see it's the grand round?'

"'To be sure I do,' says my father, never changing for a minute.

"'The ruffian will shoot me,' says the general.

"'Devil a fear,' says my father, 'av it doesn't go off of itself.'

"'What do you mean by that, you villian?' says the general, scarcely able to speak with fright, for every turn he gave on his horse, my father followed with the gun,—what do you mean?'

"'Sure, ain't I presenting?' says my father. 'Blood an ages! do you want me to fire next?'

"With that the general drew a pistol from his holster, and took deliberate aim at my father; and there they both stood for five minutes, looking at each other, the orderly all the while breaking his heart laughing behind a rock; for, ye see, the general knew av he retreated that my father might fire on purpose, and av he came on, that he might fire by chance,—and sorra bit he knew what was best to be done.

"'Are ye going to pass the evening up there, grand round?' says my father; 'for it's tired I'm getting houldin' this so long.'

"'Port arms!' shouted the general, as if on parade.

"'Sure I can't, till yer past,' says my father, angrily; 'and my hands trembling already.'

"'By Heavens! I shall be shot,' says the general.

"'Be-gorra, it's what I'm afraid of,' says my father; and the words wasn't out of his mouth before off went the musket, bang!—and down fell the general, smack on the ground, senseless. Well the orderly ran out at this, and took him up and examined his wound; but it wasn't a wound at all, only the wadding of the gun. For my father—God be kind to him!—ye see, could do nothing right; and so he bit off the wrong end of the cartridge when he put it in the gun, and, by reason, there was no bullet in it. Well, from that day after they never got a sight of him; for the instant that the general dropped, he sprang over the bridge-wall and got away; and what, between living in a lime-kiln for two months, eating nothing but blackberries and sloes, and other disguises, he never returned to the army, but ever after took to a civil situation, and drive a hearse for many years."

How far Mike's narrative might have contributed to the support of his theory, I am unable to pronounce; for his auditory were, at some distance from Cork, made to descend from their lofty position and join a larger body of recruits, all proceeding to the same destination, under a strong escort of infantry. For ourselves, we reached the "beautiful city" in due time, and took up our quarters at the Old George Hotel.

CHAPTER XXIII.

CORK.

The undress rehearsal of a new piece, with its dirty-booted actors, its cloaked and hooded actresses *en papillote*, bears about the same relation to the gala, wax-lit, and bespangled ballet, as the raw young gentleman of yesterday to the epauletted, belted, and sabretasched dragoon, whose transformation is due to a few hours of head-quarters, and a few interviews with the adjutant.

So, at least, I felt it; and it was with a very perfect concurrence in his Majesty's taste in a uniform, and a most entire approval of the regimental tailor, that I strutted down George's Street a few days after my arrival in Cork. The transports had not as yet come round; there was a great doubt of their doing so for a week or so longer; and I found myself as the dashing cornet, the centre of a thousand polite attentions and most kind civilities.

The officer under whose orders I was placed for the time was a great friend of Sir George Dashwood's, and paid me, in consequence, much attention. Major Dalrymple had been on the staff from the commencement of his military career, had served in the commissariat for some time, was much on foreign stations; but never, by any of the many casualties of his life, had he seen what could be called service. His ideas of the soldier's profession were, therefore, what might almost be as readily picked up by a commission in the battle-axe guards, as one in his Majesty's Fiftieth. He was now a species of district paymaster, employed in a thousand ways, either inspecting recruits, examining accounts, revising sick certificates, or receiving contracts for mess beef. Whether the nature of his manifold occupations had enlarged the sphere of his talents and ambition, or whether the abilities had suggested the variety of his duties, I know not, but truly the major was a man of all work. No sooner did a young ensign join his regiment at Cork, than Major Dalrymple's card was left at his quarters; the next day came the major himself; the third brought an invitation to dinner; on the fourth he was told to drop in, in the evening; and from thenceforward, he was the *ami de la maison*, in company with numerous others as newly-fledged and inexperienced as himself.

One singular feature of the society at the house was that although the major was as well known as the flag on Spike Island, yet somehow, no officer above the rank of an ensign was ever to be met with there. It was not that he had not a large acquaintance; in fact, the "How are you, Major?" "How goes it, Dalrymple?" that kept everlastingly going on as he walked the streets, proved the reverse; but strange enough, his predilections leaned towards the newly gazetted, far before the bronzed and seared campaigners who had seen the world, and knew more about it. The reasons for this line of conduct were twofold. In the first place, there was not an article of outfit, from a stock to a sword-belt, that he could not and did not supply to the young officer,— from the gorget of the infantry to the shako of the grenadier, all came within his province; not that he actually kept a *magasin* of these articles, but he had so completely interwoven his interests with those of numerous shopkeepers in Cork that he rarely entered a shop over whose door Dalrymple & Co. might not have figured on the sign-board. His stables were filled with a perfect infirmary of superannuated chargers, fattened and conditioned up to a miracle, and groomed to perfection. He could get you—*only you*—about three dozen of sherry to take out with you as seastore; he knew of such a servant; he chanced upon such a camp-furniture yesterday in his walks; in fact, why want for anything? His resources were inexhaustible; his kindness unbounded.

Then money was no object,—hang it, you could pay when you liked; what signified it? In other words, a bill at thirty-one days, cashed and discounted by a friend of the major's, would always do. While such were the unlimited advantages his acquaintance conferred, the sphere of his benefits took another range. The major had two daughters; Matilda and Fanny were as well known in the army as Lord Fitzroy Somerset, or Picton, from the Isle of Wight to Halifax, from Cape Coast to Chatham, from Belfast to the Bermudas. Where was the subaltern who had not knelt at the shrine of one or the other, if not of both, and vowed eternal love until a change of quarters? In plain words, the major's solicitude for the service was such, that, not content with providing the young officer with all the necessary outfit of his profession, he longed also to supply him with a comforter for his woes, a charmer for his solitary hours, in the person of one of his amiable daughters. Unluckily, however, the necessity for a wife is not enforced by "general orders," as is the cut of your coat, or the length of your sabre; consequently, the major's success in the home department of his diplomacy was not destined for the same happy results that awaited it when engaged about drill trousers and camp kettles, and the Misses Dalrymple remained misses through every clime and every campaign. And yet, why was it so? It is hard to say. What would men have? Matilda was a dark-haired, dark-eyed, romantic-looking girl, with a tall figure and a slender waist, with more poetry in her head than would have turned any ordinary brain; always unhappy, in need of consolation, never meeting with the kindred spirit that understood her, destined to walk the world alone, her fair thoughts smothered in the recesses of her own heart. Devilish hard to stand this, when you began in a kind of platonic friendship on both sides. More than one poor fellow nearly succumbed, particularly when she came to quote Cowley, and told him, with tears in her eyes,—

"There are hearts that live and love alone," etc.

I'm assured that this *coup-de-grace* rarely failed in being followed by a downright avowal of open love, which, somehow, what between the route coming, what with waiting for leave from home, etc., never got further than a most tender scene, and exchange of love tokens; and, in fact, such became so often the termination, that Power swears Matty had to make a firm resolve about cutting off any more hair, fearing a premature baldness during the recruiting season.

Now, Fanny had selected another arm of the service. Her hair was fair; her eyes blue, laughing, languishing,—mischief-loving blue, with long lashes, and a look in them that was wont to leave its impression rather longer than you exactly knew of; then, her figure was *petite*, but perfect; her feet Canova might have copied; and her hand was a study for Titian; her voice, too, was soft and musical, but full of that *gaieté de coeur* that never fails to charm. While her sister's style was *il penseroso*, hers was *l'allegro*; every imaginable thing, place, or person supplied food for her mirth, and her sister's lovers all came in for their share. She hunted with Smith Barry's hounds; she yachted with the Cove Club; she coursed, practised at a mark with a pistol, and played chicken hazard with all the cavalry,—for, let it be remarked as a physiological fact, Matilda's admirers were almost invariably taken from the infantry, while Fanny's adorers were as regularly dragoons. Whether the former be the romantic arm of the service, and the latter be more adapted to dull realities, or whether the phenomenon had any other explanation, I leave to the curious. Now, this arrangement, proceeding upon that principle which has wrought such wonders in Manchester and Sheffield,—the division of labor,—was a most wise and equitable one, each having her one separate and distinct field of action, interference was impossible; not but that when, as in the present instance, cavalry was in the ascendant, Fanny would willingly spare a dragoon or two to her sister, who likewise would repay the debt when occasion offered.

The mamma—for it is time I should say something of the head of the family—was an excessively fat, coarse-looking, dark-skinned personage, of some fifty years, with a voice like a boatswain in a quinsy. Heaven can tell, perhaps, why the worthy major allied his fortunes with hers, for she was evidently of a very inferior rank in society, could never have been aught than downright ugly, and I never heard that she brought him any money. "Spoiled five," the national amusement of her age and sex in Cork, scandal, the changes in the army list, the failures in speculation of her luckless husband, the forlorn fortunes of the girls, her daughters, kept her in occupation, and her days were passed in one perpetual, unceasing current of dissatisfaction and ill-temper with all around, that formed a heavy counterpoise to the fascinations of the young ladies. The repeated jiltings to which they had been subject had blunted any delicacy upon the score of their marriage; and if the newly-introduced cornet or ensign was not coming forward, as became him, at the end of the requisite number of days, he was sure of receiving a very palpable admonition from Mrs. Dalrymple. Hints, at first dimly shadowed, that Matilda was not in spirits this morning; that Fanny, poor child, had a headache,—directed especially at the culprit in question,—grew gradually into those little motherly fondnesses in mamma, that, like the fascination of the rattlesnake, only lure on to ruin. The doomed man was pressed to dinner when all others were permitted to take their leave; he was treated like one of the family, God help him! After dinner, the major would keep him an hour over his wine, discussing the misery of an ill-assorted marriage; detailing his own happiness in marrying a woman like the Tonga Islander I have mentioned; hinting that girls should be brought up, not only to become companions to their husbands, but with ideas fitting their station; if his auditor were a military man, that none but an old officer (like him) could know how to educate girls (like his); and that feeling he possessed two such treasures, his whole aim in life was to guard and keep them,—a difficult task, when proposals of the most flattering kind were coming constantly before him. Then followed a fresh bottle, during which the major would consult his young friend upon a very delicate affair,—no less than a proposition for the hand of Miss Matilda, or Fanny, whichever he was supposed to be soft upon. This was generally a *coup-de-maître*; should he still resist, he was handed over to Mrs. Dalrymple, with a strong indictment against him, and rarely did he escape a heavy sentence. Now, is it not strange that two really pretty girls, with fully enough of amiable and pleasing qualities to have excited the attention and won the affections of many a man, should have gone on for years,—for, alas! they did so in every climate, under every sun,—to waste their sweetness in this miserable career of intrigue and man-trap, and yet nothing come of it? But so it was. The first question a newly-landed regiment was asked, if coming from where they resided, was, "Well, how are the girls?" "Oh, gloriously. Matty is there." "Ah, indeed! poor thing." "Has Fan sported a new habit?" "Is it the old gray with the hussar braiding? Confound it, that was seedy when I saw them in Corfu. And Mother Dal as fat and vulgar as ever?" "Dawson of ours was the last, and was called up for sentence when we were ordered away; of course, he bolted," etc. Such was the invariable style of question and answer concerning them; and although some few, either from good feeling or fastidiousness, relished but little the mode in which it had become habitual to treat them, I grieve to say that, generally, they were pronounced fair game for every species of flirtation and love-making without any "intentions" for the future. I should not have trespassed so far upon my readers' patience, were I not, in recounting these traits of my friends above, narrating matters of history. How many are there who may cast their eyes upon these pages, that will say, "Poor Matilda! I knew her at Gibraltar. Little Fanny was the life and soul of us all in Quebec."

"Mr. O'Malley," said the adjutant, as I presented myself in the afternoon of my arrival in Cork to a short, punchy, little red-faced gentleman, in a short jacket and ducks, "you are, I perceive, appointed to the 14th; you will have the goodness to appear on parade to-morrow morning. The riding-school hours are——. The morning drill is——; evening drill——. Mr. Minchin, you are a 14th man, I believe? No, I beg pardon! a carbineer; but no matter. Mr. O'Malley, Mr. Minchin; Captain Dounie, Mr. O'Malley. You'll dine with us to-day, and to-morrow you shall be entered at the mess."

"Yours are at Santarem, I believe?" said an old, weather-beaten looking officer with one arm.

"I'm ashamed to say, I know nothing whatever of them; I received my gazette unexpectedly enough."

"Ever in Cork before, Mr. O'Malley?"

"Never," said I.

"Glorious place," lisped a white-eyelashed, knocker-kneed ensign; "splendid *gals*, eh?"

"Ah, Brunton," said Minchin, "you may boast a little; but we poor devils—"

"Know the Dals?" said the hero of the lisp, addressing me.

"I haven't that honor," I replied, scarcely able to guess whether what he alluded to were objects of the picturesque or a private family.

"Introduce him, then, at once," said the adjutant; "we'll all go in the evening. What will the old squaw think?"

"Not I," said Minchin. "She wrote to the Duke of York about my helping Matilda at supper, and not having any honorable intentions afterwards."

"We dine at 'The George' to-day, Mr. O'Malley, sharp seven. Until then—"

So saying, the little man bustled back to his accounts, and I took my leave with the rest, to stroll about the town till dinner-time.

CHAPTER XXIV.
THE ADJUTANT'S DINNER.

The adjutant's dinner was as professional an affair as need be. A circuit or a learned society could not have been more exclusively devoted to their own separate and immediate topics than were we. Pipeclay in all its varieties came on the *tapis*; the last regulation cap, the new button, the promotions, the general orders, the colonel and the colonel's wife, stoppages, and the mess fund were all well and ably discussed; and strange enough, while the conversation took this wide range, not a chance allusion, not one stray hint ever wandered to the brave fellows who were covering the army with glory in the Peninsula, nor one souvenir of him that, was even then enjoying a fame as a leader second to none in Europe. This surprised me not a little at the time; but I have since that learned how little interest the real services of an army possess for the ears of certain officials, who, stationed at home quarters, pass their inglorious lives in the details of drill, parade, mess-room gossip, and barrack scandal. Such, in fact, were the dons of the present dinner. We had a commissary-general, an inspecting brigade-major of something, a physician to the forces, the adjutant himself, and Major Dalrymple; the *hoi polloi* consisting of the raw ensign, a newly-fledged cornet (Mr. Sparks), and myself.

The commissary told some very pointless stories about his own department; the doctor read a dissertation upon Walcheren fever; the adjutant got very stupidly tipsy; and Major Dalrymple succeeded in engaging the three juniors of the party to tea, having previously pledged us to purchase nothing whatever of outfit without his advice, he well knowing (which he did) how young fellows like us were cheated, and resolving to be a father to us (which he certainly tried to be).

As we rose from the table, about ten o'clock, I felt how soon a few such dinners would succeed in disenchanting me of all my military illusions; for, young as I was, I saw that the commissary was a vulgar bore, the doctor a humbug, the adjutant a sot, and the major himself I greatly suspected to be an old rogue.

"You are coming with us, Sparks?" said Major Dalrymple, as he took me by one arm and the ensign by the other. "We are going to have a little tea with the ladies; not five minutes' walk."

"Most happy, sir," said Mr. Sparks, with a very flattered expression of countenance.

"O'Malley, you know Sparks, and Burton too."

This served for a species of triple introduction, at which we all bowed, simpered, and bowed again. We were very happy to have the pleasure, etc.

"How pleasant to get away from these fellows!" said the major, "they are so uncommonly prosy! That commissary, with his mess beef, and old Pritchard, with black doses and rigors,— nothing so insufferable! Besides, in reality, a young officer never needs all that nonsense. A little medicine chest—I'll get you one each to-morrow for five pounds—no, five pounds ten—the same thing—that will see you all through the Peninsula. Remind me of it in the morning." This we all promised to do, and the major resumed: "I say, Sparks, you've got a real prize in that gray horse,—such a trooper as he is! O'Malley, you'll be wanting something of that kind, if we can find it for you."

"Many thanks, Major; but my cattle are on the way here already. I've only three horses, but I think they are tolerably good ones."

The major now turned to Burton and said something in a low tone, to which the other replied, "Well, if you say so, I'll get it; but it's devilish dear."

"Dear, my young friend! Cheap, dog cheap."

"Only think, O'Malley, a whole brass bed, camp-stool, basin-stand, all complete, for sixty pounds! If it was not that a widow was disposing of it in great distress, one hundred could not buy it. Here we are; come along,—no ceremony. Mind the two steps; that's it, Mrs. Dalrymple, Mr. O'Malley; Mr. Sparks, Mr. Burton, my daughters. Is tea over, girls?"

"Why, Papa, it's nearly eleven o'clock," said Fanny, as she rose to ring the bell, displaying in so doing the least possible portion of a very well-turned ankle.

Miss Matilda Dal laid down her book, but seemingly lost in abstraction, did not deign to look at us. Mrs. Dalrymple, however, did the honors with much politeness, and having by a few adroit and well-put queries ascertained everything concerning our rank and position, seemed perfectly satisfied that our intrusion was justifiable.

While my *confrère*, Mr. Sparks, was undergoing his examination I had time to look at the ladies, whom I was much surprised at finding so very well looking; and as the ensign had opened a conversation with Fanny, I approached my chair towards the other, and having carelessly turned over the leaves of the book she had been reading, drew her on to talk of it. As my acquaintance with young ladies hitherto had been limited to those who had "no soul," I felt some difficulty at first in keeping up with the exalted tone of my fair companion, but by letting her take the lead for some time, I got to know more of the ground. We went on tolerably together, every moment increasing my stock of technicals, which were all that was needed to sustain the conversation. How often have I found the same plan succeed, whether discussing a question of law or medicine, with a learned professor of either! or, what is still more difficult, canvassing the merits of a preacher or a doctrine with a serious young lady, whose "blessed privileges" were at first a little puzzling to comprehend.

I so contrived it, too, that Miss Matilda should seem as much to be making a convert to her views as to have found a person capable of sympathizing with her; and thus, long before the little supper, with which it was the major's practice to regale his friends every evening, made its appearance, we had established a perfect understanding together,—a circumstance that, a bystander might have remarked, was productive of a more widely diffused satisfaction than I could have myself seen any just cause for. Mr. Burton was also progressing, as the Yankees say, with the sister; Sparks had booked himself as purchaser of military stores enough to make the campaign of the whole globe; and we were thus all evidently fulfilling our various vocations, and affording perfect satisfaction to our entertainers.

Then came the spatch-cock, and the sandwiches, and the negus, which Fanny first mixed for papa, and subsequently, with some little pressing, for Mr. Burton; Matilda the romantic assisted *me*; Sparks helped himself. Then we laughed, and told stories; pressed Sparks to sing, which, as he declined, we only pressed the more. How, invariably, by-the-bye, is it the custom to show one's appreciation of anything like a butt by pressing him for a song! The major was in great spirits; told us anecdotes of his early life in India, and how he once contracted to supply the troops with milk, and made a purchase, in consequence, of some score of cattle, which turned out to be bullocks. Matilda recited some lines from Pope in my ear. Fanny challenged Burton to a rowing match. Sparks listened to all around him, and Mrs. Dalrymple mixed a very little weak punch, which Dr. Lucas had recommended to her to take the last thing at night,—*Noctes coenoeque* etc. Say what you will, these were very jovial little *réunions*. The girls were decidedly very pretty. We were in high favor; and when we took leave at the door, with a very cordial shake hands, it was with no *arrière pensée* we promised to see them in the morning.

CHAPTER XXV.

THE ENTANGLEMENT.

When we think for a moment over all the toils, all the anxieties, all the fevered excitement of a *grande passion*, it is not a little singular that love should so frequently be elicited by a state of mere idleness; and yet nothing, after all, is so predisposing a cause as this. Where is the man between eighteen and eight-and-thirty—might I not say forty—who, without any very pressing duns, and having no taste for strong liquor and *rouge-et-noir*, can possibly lounge through the long hours of his day without at least fancying himself in love? The thousand little occupations it suggests become a necessity of existence; its very worries are like the wholesome opposition that purifies and strengthens the frame of a free state. Then, what is there half so sweet as the reflective flattery which results from our appreciation of an object who in return deems us the *ne plus ultra* of perfection? There it is, in fact; that confounded bump of self-esteem does it all, and has more imprudent matches to answer for than all the occipital protuberances that ever scared poor Harriet Martineau.

Now, to apply my moralizing. I very soon, to use the mess phrase, got "devilish spooney" about the "Dals." The morning drill, the riding-school, and the parade were all most fervently consigned to a certain military character that shall be nameless, as detaining me from some appointment made the evening before; for as I supped there each night, a party of one kind or another was always planned for the day following. Sometimes we had a boating excursion to Cove, sometimes a picnic at Foaty; now a rowing party to Glanmire, or a ride, at which I furnished the cavalry. These doings were all under my especial direction, and I thus became speedily the organ of the Dalrymple family; and the simple phrase, "It was Mr. O'Malley's arrangement," "Mr. O'Malley wished it," was like the *Moi le roi* of Louis XIV.

Though all this while we continued to carry on most pleasantly, Mrs. Dalrymple, I could perceive, did not entirely sympathize with our projects of amusement. As an experienced engineer might feel when watching the course of some storming projectile—some brilliant congreve—flying over a besieged fortress, yet never touching the walls nor harming the inhabitants, so she looked on at all these demonstrations of attack with no small impatience, and wondered when would the breach be reported practicable. Another puzzle also contributed its share of anxiety,—which of the girls was it? To be sure, he spent three hours every morning with Fanny; but then, he never left Matilda the whole evening. He had given his miniature to one; a locket with his hair was a present to the sister. The major thinks he saw his arm round Matilda's waist in the garden; the housemaid swears she saw him kiss Fanny in the pantry. Matilda smiles when we talk of his name with her sister's; Fanny laughs outright, and says, "Poor Matilda! the man never dreamed of her." This is becoming uncomfortable. The major must ask his intentions. It is certainly one or the other; but then, we have a right to know which. Such was a very condensed view of Mrs. Dalrymple's reflections on this important topic,—a view taken with her usual tact and clear-sightedness.

Matters were in this state when Power at length arrived in Cork, to take command of our detachment and make the final preparations for our departure. I had been, as usual, spending the evening at the major's, and had just reached my quarters, when I found my friend sitting at my fire, smoking his cigar and solacing himself with a little brandy-and-water.

"At last," said he, as I entered,—"at last! Why, where the deuce have you been till this hour,—past two o'clock? There is no ball, no assembly going on, eh?"

"No," said I, half blushing at the eagerness of the inquiry; "I've been spending the evening with a friend."

"Spending the evening! Say, rather, the night! Why, confound you, man, what is there in Cork to keep you out of bed till near three?"

"Well, if you must know, I have been supping at a Major Dalrymple's,—a devilish good fellow, with two such daughters!"

"Ahem!" said Power, shutting one eye knowingly, and giving a look like a Yorkshire horse-dealer. "Go on."

"Why, what do you mean?"

"Go on; continue."

"I've finished; I've nothing more to tell."

"So, they're here, are they?" said he, reflectingly.

"Who?" said I.

"Matilda and Fanny, to be sure."

"Why, you know them, then?"

"I should think I do."

"Where have you met them?"

"Where have I not? When I was in the Rifles they were quartered at Zante. Matilda was just then coming it rather strong with Villiers, of ours, a regular greenhorn. Fanny, also, nearly did for Harry Nesbitt, by riding a hurdle race. Then they left for Gibraltar, in the year,—what year was it?"

"Come, come," said I, "this is a humbug; the girls are quite young; you just have heard their names."

"Well, perhaps so; only tell me which is your peculiar weakness, as they say in the west, and may be I'll convince you."

"Oh, as to that," said I, laughing, "I'm not very far gone on either side."

"Then, Matilda, probably, has not tried you with Cowley, eh?—you look a little pink—'There are hearts that live and love alone.' Oh, poor fellow, you've got it! By Jove, how you've been coming it, though, in ten days! She ought not to have got to that for a month, at least; and how like a young one it was, to be caught by the poetry. Oh, Master Charley, I thought that the steeple-chaser might have done most with your Galway heart,—the girl in the gray habit, that sings 'Moddirederoo,' ought to have been the prize! Halt! by Saint George, but that tickles you also! Why, zounds, if I go on, probably, at this rate, I'll find a tender spot occupied by the 'black lady' herself."

It was no use concealing, or attempting to conceal, anything from my inquisitive friend; so I mixed my grog, and opened my whole heart; told how I had been conducting myself for the entire preceding fortnight; and when I concluded, sat silently awaiting Power's verdict, as though a jury were about to pronounce upon my life.

"Have you ever written?"

"Never; except, perhaps, a few lines with tickets for the theatre, or something of that kind."

"Have you copies of your correspondence?"

"Of course not. Why, what do you mean?"

"Has Mrs. Dal ever been present; or, as the French say, has she assisted at any of your tender interviews with the young ladies?"

"I'm not aware that one kisses a girl before mamma."

"I'm not speaking of that; I merely allude to an ordinary flirtation."

"Oh, I suppose she has seen me attentive."

"Very awkward, indeed! There is only one point in your favor; for as your attentions were not decided, and as the law does not, as yet, permit polygamy—"

"Come, come, you know I never thought of marrying."

"Ah, but they did."

"Not a bit of it."

"Ay, but they did. What do you wager but that the major asks your intentions, as he calls it, the moment he hears the transport has arrived?"

"By Jove! now you remind me, he asked this evening, when he could have a few minutes' private conversation with me to-morrow, and I thought it was about some confounded military chest or sea-store, or one of his infernal contrivances that he every day assures me are indispensable; though, if every officer had only as much baggage as I have got, under his directions, it would take two armies, at least, to carry the effects of the fighting one."

"Poor fellow!" said he, starting upon his legs; "what a burst you've made of it!" So saying, he began in a nasal twang,—

"I publish the banns of marriage between Charles O'Malley, late of his Majesty's 14th Dragoons, and ―――― Dalrymple, spinster, of this city—"

"I'll be hanged if you do, though," said I, seeing pretty clearly, by this time, something of the estimation my friends were held in. "Come, Power, pull me through, like a good fellow,—pull me through, without doing anything to hurt the girls' feelings."

"Well, we'll see about it," said he,—"we'll see about it in the morning; but, at the same time, let me assure you, the affair is not so easy as you may at first blush suppose. These worthy people have been so often 'done'—to use the cant phrase—before, that scarcely a *ruse* remains untried. It is of no use pleading that your family won't consent; that your prospects are null; that you are ordered for India; that you are engaged elsewhere; that you have nothing but your pay; that you are too young or too old,—all such reasons, good and valid with any other family, will avail you little here. Neither will it serve your cause that you may be warranted by a doctor as subject to periodical fits of insanity; monomaniacal tendencies to cut somebody's throat, etc. Bless your heart, man, they have a soul above such littlenesses! They care nothing for consent of friends, means, age, health, climate, prospects, or temper. Firmly believing matrimony to be a lottery, they are not superstitious about the number they pitch upon; provided only that they get a ticket, they are content."

"Then it strikes me, if what you say is correct, that I have no earthly chance of escape, except some kind friend will undertake to shoot me."

"That has been also tried."

"Why, how do you mean?"

"A mock duel, got up at mess,—we had one at Malta. Poor Vickers was the hero of that affair. It was right well planned, too. One of the letters was suffered, by mere accident, to fall into Mrs. Dal's hands, and she was quite prepared for the event when he was reported shot the next morning. Then the young lady, of course, whether she cared or not, was obliged to be perfectly unconcerned, lest the story of engaged affections might get wind and spoil another market. The thing went on admirably, till one day, some few months later, they saw, in a confounded army-list, that the late George Vickers was promoted to the 18th Dragoons, so that the trick was discovered, and is, of course, stale at present."

"Then could I not have a wife already, and a large family of interesting babies?"

"No go,—only swell the damages, when they come to prosecute. Besides, your age and looks forbid the assumption of such a fact. No, no; we must go deeper to work."

"But where shall we go?" said I, impatiently; "for it appears to me these good people have been treated to every trick and subterfuge that ever ingenuity suggested."

"Come, I think I have it; but it will need a little more reflection. So, now, let us to bed. I'll give you the result of my lucubrations at breakfast; and, if I mistake not, we may get you through this without any ill-consequences. Good-night, then, old boy; and now dream away of your lady-love till our next meeting."

CHAPTER XXVI.

THE PREPARATION.

To prevent needless repetitions in my story, I shall not record here the conversation which passed between my friend Power and myself on the morning following at breakfast. Suffice it to say, that the plan proposed by him for my rescue was one I agreed to adopt, reserving to myself, in case of failure, a *pis aller* of which I knew not the meaning, but of whose efficacy Power assured me I need not doubt.

"If all fail," said he,—"if every bridge break down beneath you, and no road of escape be left, why, then, I believe you must have recourse to another alternative. Still I should wish to avoid it, if possible, and I put it to you, in honor, not to employ it unless as a last expedient. You promise me this?"

"Of course," said I, with great anxiety for the dread final measure. "What is it?"

He paused, smiled dubiously, and resumed,—

"And, after all,—but, to be sure, there will not be need for it,—the other plan will do,—must do. Come, come, O'Malley, the admiralty say that nothing encourages drowning in the navy like a life-buoy. The men have such a prospect of being picked up that they don't mind falling overboard; so, if I give you this life-preserver of mine, you'll not swim an inch. Is it not so, eh?"

"Far from it," said I. "I shall feel in honor bound to exert myself the more, because I now see how much it costs you to part with it."

"Well, then, hear it. When everything fails; when all your resources are exhausted; when you have totally lost your memory, in fact, and your ingenuity in excuses say,—but mind, Charley, not till then,—say that you must consult your friend, Captain Power, of the 14th; that's all."

"And is this it?" said I, quite disappointed at the lame and impotent conclusion to all the high-sounding exordium; "is this all?"

"Yes," said he, "that is all. But stop, Charley; is not that the major crossing the street there? Yes, to be sure it is; and, by Jove! he has got on the old braided frock this morning. Had you not told me one word of your critical position, I should have guessed there was something in the wind from that. That same vestment has caused many a stout heart to tremble that never quailed before a shot or shell."

"How can that be? I should like to hear."

"Why, my dear boy, that's his explanation coat, as we called it at Gibraltar. He was never known to wear it except when asking some poor fellow's 'intentions.' He would no more think of sporting it as an every-day affair, than the chief-justice would go cook-shooting in his black cap and ermine. Come, he is bound for your quarters, and as it will not answer our plans to let him see you now, you had better hasten down-stairs, and get round by the back way into George's Street, and you'll be at his house before he can return."

Following Power's directions, I seized my foraging-cap and got clear out of the premises before the major had reached them. It was exactly noon as I sounded my loud and now well-known summons at the major's knocker. The door was quickly opened; but instead of dashing up-stairs, four steps at a time, as was my wont, to the drawing-room, I turned short into the dingy-looking little parlor on the right, and desired Matthew, the venerable servitor of the house, to say that I wished particularly to see Mrs. Dalrymple for a few minutes, if the hour were not inconvenient.

There was something perhaps of excitement in my manner, some flurry in my look, or some trepidation in my voice, or perhaps it was the unusual hour, or the still more remarkable circumstance of my not going at once to the drawing-room, that raised some doubts in Matthew's mind as to the object of my visit; and instead of at once complying with my request to inform Mrs. Dalrymple that I was there, he cautiously closed the door, and taking a quick but satisfactory glance round the apartment to assure himself that we were alone, he placed his back against it and heaved a deep sigh.

We were both perfectly silent: I in total amazement at what the old man could possibly mean; he, following up the train of his own thoughts, comprehended little or nothing of my surprise, and evidently was so engrossed by his reflections that he had neither ears nor eyes for aught around him. There was a most singular semi-comic expression in the old withered face that nearly made me laugh at first; but as I continued to look steadily at it, I perceived that, despite the long-worn wrinkles that low Irish drollery and fun had furrowed around the angles of his mouth, the real character of his look was one of sorrowful compassion.

Doubtless, my readers have read many interesting narratives wherein the unconscious traveller in some remote land has been warned of a plan to murder him, by some mere passing wink, a look, a sign, which some one, less steeped in crime, less hardened in iniquity than his fellows, has ventured for his rescue. Sometimes, according to the taste of the narrator, the interesting individual is an old woman, sometimes a young one, sometimes a black-bearded bandit, sometimes a child; and not unfrequently, a dog is humane enough to do this service. One thing, however, never varies,—be the agent biped or quadruped, dumb or speechful, young or old, the stranger invariably takes the hint, and gets off scott free for his sharpness. This never-varying trick on the doomed man, I had often been sceptical enough to suspect; however, I had not been many minutes a spectator of the old man's countenance, when I most thoroughly recanted my errors, and acknowledged myself wrong. If ever the look of a man conveyed a warning, his did; but there was more in it than even that,—there was a tone of sad and pitiful compassion, such as an old gray-bearded rat might be supposed to put on at seeing a young and inexperienced one opening the hinge of an iron trap, to try its efficacy upon his neck. Many a little occasion had presented itself, during my intimacy with the family, of doing Matthew some small services, of making him some trifling presents; so that, when he assumed before me the gesture and look I have mentioned, I was not long in deciphering his intentions.

"Matthew!" screamed a sharp voice which I recognized at once for that of Mrs. Dalrymple. "Matthew! Where is the old fool?"

But Matthew heard not, or heeded not.

"Matthew! Matthew! I say."

"I'm comin', ma'am," said he, with a sigh, as, opening the parlor-door, he turned upon me one look of such import that only the circumstances of my story can explain its force, or my reader's own ingenious imagination can supply.

"Never fear, my good old friend," said I, grasping his hand warmly, and leaving a guinea in the palm,—"never fear."

"God grant it, sir!" said he, setting on his wig in preparation for his appearance in the drawing-room.

"Matthew! The old wretch!"

"Mr. O'Malley," said the often-called Matthew, as opening the door, he announced me unexpectedly among the ladies there assembled, who, not hearing of my approach, were evidently not a little surprised and astonished. Had I been really the enamored swain that the Dalrymple family were willing to believe, I half suspect that the prospect before me might have cured me of my passion. A round bullet-head, *papilloté*, with the "Cork Observer," where still-born babes and maids-of-all-work were descanted upon in very legible type, was now the substitute for the classic front and Italian ringlets of *la belle* Matilda; while the chaste Fanny herself, whose feet had been a fortune for a statuary, was, in the most slatternly and slipshod attire, pacing the room in a towering rage, at some thing, place, or person, unknown (to me). If the ballet-master at the *Académie* could only learn to get his imps, demons, angels, and goblins "off" half as rapidly as the two young ladies retreated on my being announced, I answer for the piece so brought out having a run for half the season. Before my eyes had regained their position parallel to the plane of the horizon, they were gone, and I found myself alone with Mrs. Dalrymple. Now, she stood her ground, partly to cover the retreat of the main body, partly, too, because—representing the baggage wagons, ammunition stores, hospital, staff, etc.—her retirement from the field demanded more time and circumspection than the light brigade.

Let not my readers suppose that the *mère* Dalrymple was so perfectly faultless in costume that her remaining was a matter of actual indifference; far from it. She evidently had a struggle for it; but a sense of duty decided her, and as Ney doggedly held back to cover the retreating forces on the march from Moscow, so did she resolutely lurk behind till the last flutter of the last petticoat assured her that the fugitives were safe. Then did she hesitate for a moment what course to take; but as I assumed my chair beside her, she composedly sat down, and crossing her hands before her, waited for an explanation of this ill-timed visit.

Had the Horse Guards, in the plenitude of their power and the perfection of their taste, ordained that the 79th and 42d Regiments should in future, in lieu of their respective tartans, wear flannel kilts and black worsted hose, I could readily have fallen into the error of mistaking Mrs. Dalrymple for a field officer in the new regulation dress; the philabeg finding no mean representation in a capacious pincushion that hung down from her girdle, while a pair of shears, not scissors, corresponded to the dirk. After several ineffectual efforts on her part to make her vestment (I know not its fitting designation) cover more of her legs than its length could possibly effect, and after some most bland smiles and half blushes at *dishabille*, etc., were over, and that I had apologized most humbly for the unusually early hour of my call, I proceeded to open my negotiations, and unfurl my banner for the fray.

"The old 'Racehorse' has arrived at last," said I, with a half-sigh, "and I believe that we shall not obtain a very long time for our leave-taking; so that, trespassing upon your very great kindness, I have ventured upon an early call."

"The 'Racehorse,' surely can't sail to-morrow," said Mrs. Dalrymple, whose experience of such matters made her a very competent judge; "her stores—"

"Are taken in already," said I; "and an order from the Horse Guards commands us to embark in twenty-four hours; so that, in fact, we scarcely have time to look about us."

"Have you seen the major?" inquired Mrs. Dalrymple, eagerly.

"Not to-day," I replied, carelessly; "but, of course, during the morning we are sure to meet. I have many thanks yet to give him for all his most kind attentions."

"I know he is most anxious to see you," said Mrs. Dalrymple, with a very peculiar emphasis, and evidently desiring that I should inquire the reasons of this anxiety. I, however, most heroically forbore indulging my curiosity, and added that I should endeavor to find him on my way to the barracks; and then, hastily looking at my watch, I pronounced it a full hour later than it really was, and promising to spend the evening—my last evening—with them, I took my leave and hurried away, in no small flurry to be once more out of reach of Mrs. Dalrymple's fire, which I every moment expected to open upon me.

CHAPTER XXVII.
THE SUPPER.

Power and I dined together *tête-à-tête* at the hotel, and sat chatting over my adventures with the Dalrymples till nearly nine o'clock.

"Come, Charley," said he, at length, "I see your eye wandering very often towards the timepiece; another bumper, and I'll let you off. What shall it be?"

"What you like," said I, upon whom a share of three bottles of strong claret had already made a very satisfactory impression.

"Then champagne for the *coup-de-grace*. Nothing like your *vin mousseux* for a critical moment,—every bubble that rises sparkling to the surface prompts some bright thought, or elicits some brilliant idea, that would only have been drowned in your more sober fluids. Here's to the girl you love, whoever she be."

"To her bright eyes, then, be it," said I, clearing off a brimming goblet of nearly half the bottle, while my friend Power seemed multiplied into any given number of gentlemen standing amidst something like a glass manufactory of decanters.

"I hope you feel steady enough for this business," said my friend, examining me closely with the candle.

"I'm an archdeacon," muttered I, with one eye involuntarily closing.

"You'll not let them double on you!"

"Trust me, old boy," said I, endeavoring to look knowing.

"I think you'll do," said he, "so now march. I'll wait for you here, and we'll go on board together; for old Bloater the skipper says he'll certainly weigh by daybreak."

"Till then," said I, as opening the door, I proceeded very cautiously to descend the stairs, affecting all the time considerable *nonchalance*, and endeavoring, as well as my thickened utterance would permit, to hum:—

"*Oh, love is the soul of an Irish dragoon.*"

If I was not in the most perfect possession of my faculties in the house, the change to the open air certainly but little contributed to their restoration; and I scarcely felt myself in the street when my brain became absolutely one whirl of maddened and confused excitement. Time and space are nothing to a man thus enlightened, and so they appeared to me; scarcely a second had elapsed when I found myself standing in the Dalrymples' drawing-room.

If a few hours had done much to metamorphose *me*, certes, they had done something for my fair friends also; anything more unlike what they appeared in the morning can scarcely be imagined. Matilda in black, with her hair in heavy madonna bands upon her fair cheek, now paler even than usual, never seemed so handsome; while Fanny, in a light-blue dress, with blue flowers in her hair, and a blue sash, looked the most lovely piece of coquetry ever man set his eyes upon. The old major, too, was smartened up, and put into an old regimental coat that he had worn during the siege of Gibraltar; and lastly, Mrs. Dalrymple herself was attired in a very imposing costume that made her, to my not over-accurate judgment, look very like an elderly bishop in a flame-colored cassock. Sparks was the only stranger, and wore upon his countenance, as I entered, a look of very considerable embarrassment that even my thick-sightedness could not fail of detecting.

Parlez-moi de l'amitié, my friends. Talk to me of the warm embrace of your earliest friend, after years of absence; the cordial and heartfelt shake hands of your old school companion, when in after years, a chance meeting has brought you together, and you have had time and opportunity for becoming distinguished and in repute, and are rather a good hit to be known to than otherwise; of the close grip you give your second when he comes up to say, that the gentleman with the loaded detonator opposite won't fire, that he feels he's in the wrong. Any or all of these together, very effective and powerful though they be, are light in the balance when compared with the two-handed compression you receive from the gentleman that expects you to marry one of his daughters.

"My dear O'Malley, how goes it? Thought you'd never come," said he, still holding me fast and looking me full in the face, to calculate the extent to which my potations rendered his flattery feasible.

"Hurried to death with preparations, I suppose," said Mrs. Dalrymple, smiling blandly. "Fanny dear, some tea for him."

"Oh, Mamma, he does not like all that sugar; surely not," said she, looking up with a most sweet expression, as though to say, "I at least know his tastes."

"I believed you were going without seeing us," whispered Matilda, with a very glassy look about the corner of her eyes.

Eloquence was not just then my forte, so that I contented myself with a very intelligible look at Fanny, and a tender squeeze of Matilda's hand, as I seated myself at the table.

Scarcely had I placed myself at the tea-table, with Matilda beside and Fanny opposite me, each vying with the other in their delicate and kind attentions, when I totally forgot all my poor friend Power's injunctions and directions for my management. It is true, I remembered that there was a scrape of some kind or other to be got out of, and one requiring some dexterity, too; but what or with whom I could not for the life of me determine. What the wine had begun, the bright eyes completed; and amidst the witchcraft of silky tresses and sweet looks, I lost all my reflection, till the impression of an impending difficulty remained fixed in my mind, and I tortured my poor, weak, and erring intellect to detect it. At last, and by a mere chance, my eyes fell upon Sparks; and by what mechanism I contrived it, I know not, but I immediately saddled him with the whole of my annoyances, and attributed to him and to his fault any embarrassment I labored under.

The physiological reason of the fact I'm very ignorant of, but for the truth and frequency I can well vouch, that there are certain people, certain faces, certain voices, certain whiskers, legs, waistcoats, and guard-chains, that inevitably produce the most striking effects upon the brain of a gentleman already excited by wine, and not exactly cognizant of his own peculiar fallacies.

These effects are not produced merely among those who are quarrelsome in their cups, for I call the whole 14th to witness that I am not such; but to any person so disguised, the inoffensiveness of the object is no security on the other hand,—for I once knew an eight-day clock kicked down a barrack stairs by an old Scotch major, because he thought it was laughing at him. To this source alone, whatever it be, can I attribute the feeling of rising indignation with which I contemplated the luckless cornet, who, seated at the fire, unnoticed and uncared for, seemed a very unworthy object to vent anger or ill-temper upon.

"Mr. Sparks, I fear," said I, endeavoring at the time to call up a look of very sovereign contempt,—"Mr. Sparks, I fear, regards my visit here in the light of an intrusion."

Had poor Mr. Sparks been told to proceed incontinently up the chimney before him, he could not have looked more aghast. Reply was quite out of his power. So sudden and unexpectedly was this charge of mine made that he could only stare vacantly from one to the other; while I, warming with my subject, and perhaps—but I'll not swear it—stimulated by a gentle pressure from a soft hand near me, continued:—

"If he thinks for one moment that my attentions in this family are in any way to be questioned by him, I can only say—"

"My dear O'Malley, my dear boy!" said the major, with the look of a father-in-law in his eye.

"The spirit of an officer and a gentleman spoke there," said Mrs. Dalrymple, now carried beyond all prudence by the hope that my attack might arouse my dormant friend into a counter-declaration; nothing, however, was further from poor Sparks, who began to think he had been unconsciously drinking tea with five lunatics.

"If he supposes," said I, rising from my chair, "that his silence will pass with me as any palliation—"

"Oh, dear! oh, dear! there will be a duel. Papa, dear, why don't you speak to Mr. O'Malley?"

"There now, O'Malley, sit down. Don't you see he is quite in error?"

"Then let him say so," said I, fiercely.

"Ah, yes, to be sure," said Fanny. "Do say it; say anything he likes, Mr. Sparks."

"I must say," said Mrs. Dalrymple, "however sorry I may feel in my own house to condemn any one, that Mr. Sparks is very much in the wrong."

Poor Sparks looked like a man in a dream.

"If he will tell Charles,—Mr. O'Malley, I mean," said Matilda, blushing scarlet, "that he meant nothing by what he said—"

"But I never spoke, never opened my lips!" cried out the wretched man, at length sufficiently recovered to defend himself.

"Oh, Mr. Sparks!"

"Oh, Mr. Sparks!"

"Oh, Mr. Sparks!" chorussed the three ladies.

While the old major brought up the rear with an "Oh, Sparks, I must say—"

"Then, by all the saints in the calendar, I must be mad," said he; "but if I have said anything to offend you, O'Malley, I am sincerely sorry for it."

"That will do, sir," said I, with a look of royal condescension at the *amende* I considered as somewhat late in coming, and resumed my seat.

This little *intermezzo*, it might be supposed, was rather calculated to interrupt the harmony of our evening. Not so, however. I had apparently acquitted myself like a hero, and was evidently in a white heat, in which I could be fashioned into any shape. Sparks was humbled so far that he would probably feel it a relief to make any proposition; so that by our opposite courses we had both arrived at a point at which all the dexterity and address of the family had been long since aiming without success. Conversation then resumed its flow, and in a few minutes every trace of our late *fracas* had disappeared.

By degrees I felt myself more and more disposed to turn my attention towards Matilda, and dropping my voice into a lower tone, opened a flirtation of a most determined kind. Fanny had, meanwhile, assumed a place beside Sparks, and by the muttered tones that passed between them, I could plainly perceive they were similarly occupied. The major took up the "Southern Reporter," of which he appeared deep in the contemplation, while Mrs. Dal herself buried her head in her embroidery and neither heard nor saw anything around her.

I know, unfortunately, but very little what passed between myself and my fair companion; I can only say that when supper was announced at twelve (an hour later than usual), I was sitting upon the sofa with my arm round her waist, my cheek so close that already her lovely tresses brushed my forehead, and her breath fanned my burning brow.

"Supper, at last," said the major, with a loud voice, to arouse us from our trance of happiness without taking any mean opportunity of looking unobserved. "Supper, Sparks, O'Malley; come now, it will be some time before we all meet this way again."

"Perhaps not so long, after all," said I, knowingly.

"Very likely not," echoed Sparks, in the same key.

"I've proposed for Fanny," said he, whispering in my ear.

"Matilda's mine," replied I, with the look of an emperor.

"A word with you, Major," said Sparks, his eye flashing with enthusiasm, and his cheek scarlet. "One word,—I'll not detain you."

They withdrew into a corner for a few seconds, during which Mrs. Dalrymple amused herself by wondering what the secret could be, why Mr. Sparks couldn't tell her, and Fanny meanwhile pretended to look for something at a side table, and never turned her head round.

"Then give me your hand," said the major, as he shook Sparks's with a warmth of whose sincerity there could be no question. "Bess, my love," said he, addressing his wife. The remainder was lost in a whisper; but whatever it was, it evidently redounded to Sparks's credit, for the next moment a repetition of the hand-shaking took place, and Sparks looked the happiest of men.

"*A mon tour*," thought I, "now," as I touched the major's arm, and led him towards the window. What I said may be one day matter for Major Dalrymple's memoirs, if he ever writes them; but for my part I have not the least idea. I only know that while I was yet speaking he called over Mrs. Dal, who, in a frenzy of joy, seized me in her arms and embraced me. After which, I kissed her, shook hands with the major, kissed Matilda's hand, and laughed prodigiously, as though I had done something confoundedly droll,—a sentiment evidently participated in by Sparks, who laughed too, as did the others; and a merrier, happier party never sat down to supper.

"Make your company pleased with themselves," says Mr. Walker, in his *Original* work upon dinner-giving, "and everything goes on well." Now, Major Dalrymple, without having read the authority in question, probably because it was not written at the time, understood the principle fully as well as the police-magistrate, and certainly was a proficient in the practice of it.

To be sure, he possessed one grand requisite for success,—he seemed most perfectly happy himself. There was that *air dégagé* about him which, when an old man puts it on among his juniors, is so very attractive. Then the ladies, too, were evidently well pleased; and the usually austere mamma had relaxed her "rigid front" into a smile in which any *habitué* of the house could have read our fate.

We ate, we drank, we ogled, smiled, squeezed hands beneath the table, and, in fact, so pleasant a party had rarely assembled round the major's mahogany. As for me, I made a full disclosure of the most burning love, backed by a resolve to marry my fair neighbor, and settle upon her a considerably larger part of my native county than I had ever even rode over. Sparks, on the other side, had opened his fire more cautiously, but whether taking courage from my boldness, or perceiving with envy the greater estimation I was held in, was now going the pace fully as fast as myself, and had commenced explanations of his intentions with regard to Fanny that evidently satisfied her friends. Meanwhile the wine was passing very freely, and the hints half uttered an hour before began now to be more openly spoken and canvassed.

Sparks and I hob-nobbed across the table and looked unspeakable things at each other; the girls held down their heads; Mrs. Dal wiped her eyes; and the major pronounced himself the happiest father in Europe.

It was now wearing late, or rather early; some gray streaks of dubious light were faintly forcing their way through the half-closed curtains, and the dread thought of parting first presented itself. A cavalry trumpet, too, at this moment sounded a call that aroused us from our trance of pleasure, and warned us that our moments were few. A dead silence crept over all; the solemn feeling which leave-taking ever inspires was uppermost, and none spoke. The major was the first to break it.

"O'Malley, my friend, and you, Mr. Sparks; I must have a word with you, boys, before we part."

"Here let it be, then, Major," said I, holding his arm as he turned to leave the room,—"here, now; we are all so deeply interested, no place is so fit."

"Well, then," said the major, "as you desire it, now that I'm to regard you both in the light of my sons-in-law,—at least, as pledged to become so,—it is only fair as respects—"

"I see,—I understand perfectly," interrupted I, whose passion for conducting the whole affair myself was gradually gaining on me. "What you mean is, that we should make known our intentions before some mutual friends ere we part; eh, Sparks? eh, Major?"

"Right, my boy,—right on every point."

"Well, then, I thought of all that; and if you'll just send your servant over to my quarters for our captain,—he's the fittest person, you know, at such a time—"

"How considerate!" said Mrs. Dalrymple.

"How perfectly just his idea is!" said the major.

"We'll then, in his presence, avow our present and unalterable determination as regards your fair daughters; and as the time is short—"

Here I turned towards Matilda, who placed her arm within mine; Sparks possessed himself of Fanny's hand, while the major and his wife consulted for a few seconds.

"Well, O'Malley, all you propose is perfect. Now, then, for the captain. Who shall he inquire for?"

"Oh, an old friend of yours," said I, jocularly; "you'll be glad to see him."

"Indeed!" said all together.

"Oh, yes, quite a surprise, I'll warrant it."

"Who can it be? Who on earth is it?"

"You can't guess," added I, with a very knowing look. "Knew you at Corfu; a very intimate friend, indeed, if he tell the truth."

A look of something like embarrassment passed around the circle at these words, while I, wishing to end the mystery, resumed:—

"Come, then, who can be so proper for all parties, at a moment like this, as our mutual friend Captain Power?"

Had a shell fallen into the cold grouse pie in the midst of us, scattering death and destruction on every side, the effect could scarcely have been more frightful than that my last words produced. Mrs. Dalrymple fell with a sough upon the floor, motionless as a corpse; Fanny threw herself, screaming, upon a sofa; Matilda went off into strong hysterics upon the hearth-rug; while the major, after giving me a look a maniac might have envied, rushed from the room in search of his pistols with a most terrific oath to shoot somebody, whether Sparks or myself, or both of us, on his return, I cannot say. Fanny's sobs and Matilda's cries, assisted by a drumming process by Mrs. Dal's heels upon the floor, made a most infernal concert and effectually prevented anything like thought or reflection; and in all probability so overwhelmed was I at the sudden catastrophe I had so innocently caused, I should have waited in due patience for the major's return, had not Sparks seized my arm, and cried out,—

"Run for it, O'Malley; cut like fun, my boy, or we're done for."

"Run; why? What for? Where?" said I, stupefied by the scene before me.

"Here he is!" called out Sparks, as throwing up the window, he sprang out upon the stone sill, and leaped into the street. I followed mechanically, and jumped after him, just as the major had reached the window. A ball whizzed by me, that soon determined my further movements; so, putting on all speed, I flew down the street, turned the corner, and regained the hotel breathless and without a hat, while Sparks arrived a moment later, pale as a ghost, and trembling like an aspen-leaf.

"Safe, by Jove!" said Sparks, throwing himself into a chair, and panting for breath.

"Safe, at last," said I, without well knowing why or for what.

"You've had a sharp run of it, apparently," said Power, coolly, and without any curiosity as to the cause; "and now, let us on board; there goes the trumpet again. The skipper is a surly old fellow, and we must not lose his tide for him." So saying, he proceeded to collect his cloaks, cane, etc., and get ready for departure.

CHAPTER XXVIII

THE VOYAGE.

When I awoke from the long, sound sleep which succeeded my last adventure, I had some difficulty in remembering where I was or how I had come there. From my narrow berth I looked out upon the now empty cabin, and at length some misty and confused sense of my situation crept slowly over me. I opened the little shutter beside me and looked out. The bold headlands of the southern coast were frowning in sullen and dark masses about a couple of miles distant, and I perceived that we were going fast through the water, which was beautifully calm and still. I now looked at my watch; it was past eight o'clock; and as it must evidently be evening, from the appearance of the sky, I felt that I had slept soundly for above twelve hours.

In the hurry of departure the cabin had not been set to rights, and there lay every species of lumber and luggage in all imaginable confusion. Trunks, gun-cases, baskets of eggs, umbrellas, hampers of sea-store, cloaks, foraging-caps, maps, and sword-belts were scattered on every side,—while the *débris* of a dinner, not over-remarkable for its propriety in table equipage, added to the ludicrous effect. The heavy tramp of a foot overhead denoted the step of some one taking his short walk of exercise; while the rough voice of the skipper, as he gave the word to "Go about!" all convinced me that we were at last under way, and off to "the wars."

The confusion our last evening on shore produced in my brain was such that every effort I made to remember anything about it only increased my difficulty, and I felt myself in a web so tangled and inextricable that all endeavor to escape free was impossible. Sometimes I thought that I had really married Matilda Dalrymple; then, I supposed that the father had called me out, and wounded me in a duel; and finally, I had some confused notion about a quarrel with Sparks, but what for, when, and how it ended, I knew not. How tremendously tipsy I must have been! was the only conclusion I could draw from all these conflicting doubts; and after all, it was the only thing like fact that beamed upon my mind. How I had come on board and reached my berth was a matter I reserved for future inquiry, resolving that about the real history of my last night on shore I would ask no questions, if others were equally disposed to let it pass in silence.

I next began to wonder if Mike had looked after all my luggage, trunks, etc., and whether he himself had been forgotten in our hasty departure. About this latter point I was not destined for much doubt; for a well-known voice, from the foot of the companion-ladder, at once proclaimed my faithful follower, and evidenced his feelings at his departure from his home and country.

Mr. Free was, at the time I mention, gathered up like a ball opposite a small, low window that looked upon the bluff headlands now fast becoming dim and misty as the night approached. He was apparently in low spirits, and hummed in a species of low, droning voice, the following ballad, at the end of each verse of which came an Irish chorus which, to the erudite in such matters, will suggest the air of Moddirederoo:—

MICKEY FREE'S LAMENT. Then fare ye well, ould Erin dear; To part, my heart does ache well: From Carrickfergus to Cape Clear, I'll never see your equal. And though to foreign parts we're bound, Where cannibals may ate us, We'll ne'er forget the holy ground Of potteen and potatoes. Moddirederoo aroo, aroo, etc. When good Saint Patrick banished frogs, And shook them from his garment, He never thought we'd go abroad, To live upon such varmint; Nor quit the land where whiskey grew To wear King George's button, Take vinegar for mountain dew, And toads for mountain mutton. Moddirederoo aroo, aroo, etc.

"I say, Mike, stop that confounded keen, and tell me where are we?"

"Off the ould head of Kinsale, sir."

"Where is Captain Power?"

"Smoking a cigar on deck, with the captain, sir."

"And Mr. Sparks?"

"Mighty sick in his own state-room. Oh, but it's himself has enough of glory—bad luck to it!—by this time. He'd make your heart break to look at him."

"Who have you got on board besides?"

"The adjutant's here, sir; and an old gentleman they call the major."

"Not Major Dalrymple?" said I, starting up with terror at the thought, "eh, Mike?"

"No, sir, another major; his name is Mulroon, or Mundoon, or something like that."

"Monsoon, you son of a lumper potato," cried out a surly, gruff voice from a berth opposite. "Monsoon. Who's at the other side?"

"Mr. O'Malley, 14th," said I, by way of introduction.

"My service to you, then," said the voice. "Going to join your regiment?"

"Yes; and you, are you bound on a similar errand?"

"No, Heaven be praised! I'm attached to the commissariat, and only going to Lisbon. Have you had any dinner?"

"Not a morsel; have you?"

"No more than yourself; but I always lie by for three or four days this way, till I get used to the confounded rocking and pitching, and with a little grog and some sleep, get over the time gayly enough. Steward, another tumbler like the last; there—very good—that will do. Your good health, Mr.—what was it you said?"

"O'Malley."

"O'Malley—your good health! Good-night." And so ended our brief colloquy, and in a few minutes more, a very decisive snore pronounced my friend to be fulfilling his precept for killing the hours.

I now made the effort to emancipate myself from my crib, and at last succeeded in getting on the floor, where, after one *chassez* at a small looking-glass opposite, followed by a very impetuous rush at a little brass stove, in which I was interrupted by a trunk and laid prostrate, I finally got my clothes on, and made my way to the deck. Little attuned as was my mind at the moment to admire anything like scenery, it was impossible to be unmoved by the magnificent prospect before me. It was a beautiful evening in summer; the sun had set above an hour before, leaving behind him in the west one vast arch of rich and burnished gold, stretching along the whole horizon, and tipping all the summits of the heavy rolling sea, as it rolled on, unbroken by foam or ripple, in vast moving mountains, from the far coast of Labrador. We were already in blue water, though the bold cliffs that were to form our departing point were but a few miles to leeward. There lay the lofty bluff of Old Kinsale, whose crest, overhanging, peered from a summit of some hundred feet into the deep water that swept its rocky base, many a tangled lichen and straggling bough trailing in the flood beneath. Here and there upon the coast a twinkling gleam proclaimed the hut of the fisherman, whose swift hookers had more than once shot by us and disappeared in a moment. The wind, which began to fall at sunset, freshened as the moon rose; and the good ship, bending to the breeze, lay gently over, and rushed through the waters with a sound of gladness. I was alone upon the deck. Power and the captain, whom I expected to have found, had disappeared somehow, and I was, after all, not sorry to be left to my own reflections uninterrupted.

My thoughts turned once more to my home,—to my first, my best, earliest friend, whose hearth I had rendered lonely and desolate, and my heart sank within me as I remembered it. How deeply I reproached myself for the selfish impetuosity with which I had ever followed any rising fancy, any new and sudden desire, and never thought of him whose every hope was in, whose every wish was for me. Alas! alas, my poor uncle! how gladly would I resign every prospect my soldier's life may hold out, with all its glittering promise, and all the flattery of success, to be once more beside you; to feel your warm and manly grasp; to see your smile; to hear your voice; to be again where all our best feelings are born and nurtured, our cares assuaged, our joys more joyed in, and our griefs more wept,—at home! These very words have more music to my ears than all the softest strains that ever siren sung. They bring us back to all we have loved, by ties that are never felt but through such simple associations. And in the earlier memories called up, our childish feelings come back once more to visit us like better spirits, as we walk amidst the dreary desolation that years of care and uneasiness have spread around us.

Wretched must he be who ne'er has felt such bliss; and thrice happy he who, feeling it, knows that still there lives for him that same early home, with all its loved inmates, its every dear and devoted object waiting his coming and longing for his approach.

Such were my thoughts as I stood gazing at the bold line of coast now gradually growing more and more dim while evening fell, and we continued to stand farther out to sea. So absorbed was I all this time in my reflections, that I never heard the voices which now suddenly burst upon my ears quite close beside me. I turned, and saw for the first time that at the end of the quarter-deck stood what is called a roundhouse, a small cabin, from which the sounds in question proceeded. I walked gently forward and peeped in, and certainly anything more in contrast with my late revery need not be conceived. There sat the skipper, a bluff, round-faced, jolly-looking little tar, mixing a bowl of punch at a table, at which sat my friend Power, the adjutant, and a tall, meagre-looking Scotchman, whom I once met in Cork, and heard that he was the doctor of some infantry regiment. Two or three black bottles, a paper of cigars, and a tallow candle were all the table equipage; but certainly the party seemed not to want for spirits and fun, to judge from the hearty bursts of laughing that every moment pealed forth, and shook the little building that held them. Power, as usual with him, seemed to be taking the lead, and was evidently amusing himself with the peculiarities of his companions.

"Come, Adjutant, fill up; here's to the campaign before us. We, at least, have nothing but pleasure in the anticipation; no lovely wife behind; no charming babes to fret and be fretted for, eh?"

"Vara true," said the doctor, who was mated with a *tartar*, "ye maun have less regrets at leaving hame; but a married man is no' entirely denied his ain consolations."

"Good sense in that," said the skipper; "a wide berth and plenty of sea room are not bad things now and then."

"Is that your experience also?" said Power, with a knowing look. "Come, come, Adjutant, we're not so ill off, you see; but, by Jove, I can't imagine how it is a man ever comes to thirty without having at least one wife,—without counting his colonial possessions of course."

"Yes," said the adjutant, with a sigh, as he drained his glass to the bottom. "It is devilish strange,—woman, lovely woman!" Here he filled and drank again, as though he had been proposing a toast for his own peculiar drinking.

"I say, now," resumed Power, catching at once that there was something working in his mind,—"I say, now, how happened it that you, a right good-looking, soldier-like fellow, that always made his way among the fair ones, with that confounded roguish eye and slippery tongue,—how the deuce did it come to pass that you never married?"

"I've been more than once on the verge of it," said the adjutant, smiling blandly at the flattery.

"And nae bad notion yours just to stay there," said the doctor, with a very peculiar contortion of countenance.

"No pleasing you, no contenting a fellow like you," said Power, returning to the charge; "that's the thing; you get a certain ascendancy; you have a kind of success that renders you, as the French say, *tête montée*, and you think no woman rich enough or good-looking enough or big enough."

"No; by Jove you're wrong," said the adjutant, swallowing the bait, hook and all,—"quite wrong there; for some how, all my life, I was decidedly susceptible. Not that I cared much for your blushing sixteen, or budding beauties in white muslin, fresh from a back-board and a governess; no, my taste inclined rather to the more sober charms of two or three-and-thirty, the *embonpoint*, a good foot and ankle, a sensible breadth about the shoulders—"

"Somewhat Dutch-like, I take it," said the skipper, puffing out a volume of smoke; "a little bluff in the bows, and great stowage, eh?"

"You leaned then towards the widows?" said Power.

"Exactly; I confess, a widow always was my weakness. There was something I ever liked in the notion of a woman who had got over all the awkward girlishness of early years, and had that self-possession which habit and knowledge of the world confer, and knew enough of herself to understand what she really wished, and where she would really go."

"Like the trade winds," puffed the skipper.

"Then, as regards fortune, they have a decided superiority over the spinster class. I defy any man breathing,—let him be half police-magistrate, half chancellor,—to find out the figure of a young lady's dower. On your first introduction to the house, some kind friend whispers, 'Go it, old boy; forty thousand, not a penny less.' A few weeks later, as the siege progresses, a maiden aunt, disposed to puffing, comes down to twenty; this diminishes again one half, but then 'the money is in bank stock, hard Three-and-a-Half.' You go a little farther, and as you sit one day over your wine with papa, he certainly promulgates the fact that his daughter has five thousand pounds, two of which turn out to be in Mexican bonds, and three in an Irish mortgage."

"Happy for you," interrupted Power, "that it be not in Galway, where a proposal to foreclose, would be a signal for your being called out and shot without benefit of clergy."

"Bad luck to it, for Galway," said the adjutant. "I was nearly taken in there once to marry a girl that her brother-in-law swore had eight hundred a year; and it came out afterwards that so she had, but it was for one year only; and he challenged me for doubting his word too."

"There's an old formula for finding out an Irish fortune," says Power, "worth, all the algebra they ever taught in Trinity. Take the half of the assumed sum, and divide it by three; the quotient will be a flattering representative of the figure sought for."

"Not in the north," said the adjutant, firmly,—"not in the north, Power. They are all well off there. There's a race of canny, thrifty, half-Scotch niggers,—your pardon, Doctor, they are all Irish,—linen-weaving, Presbyterian, yarn-factoring, long-nosed, hard-drinking fellows, that lay by rather a snug thing now and then. Do you know, I was very near it once in the north. I've half a mind to tell you the story; though, perhaps, you'll laugh at me."

The whole party at once protested that nothing could induce them to deviate so widely from the line of propriety; and the skipper having mixed a fresh bowl and filled all the glasses round, the cigars were lighted, and the adjutant began.

CHAPTER XXIX.
THE ADJUTANT'S STORY.—LIFE IN DERBY.

"It is now about eight, may be ten, years since we were ordered to march from Belfast and take up our quarters in Londonderry. We had not been more than a few weeks altogether in Ulster when the order came; and as we had been, for the preceding two years, doing duty in the south and west, we concluded that the island was tolerably the same in all parts. We opened our campaign in the maiden city exactly as we had been doing with 'unparalleled success' in Cashel, Fermoy, Tuam, etc.,—that is to say, we announced garrison balls and private theatricals; offered a cup to be run for in steeple-chase; turned out a four-in-hand drag, with mottled grays; and brought over two Deal boats to challenge the north."

"The 18th found the place stupid," said his companions.

"To be sure, they did; slow fellows like them must find any place stupid. No dinners; but they gave none. No fun; but they had none in themselves. In fact, we knew better; we understood how the thing was to be done, and resolved that, as a mine of rich ore lay unworked, it was reserved for us to produce the shining metal that others, less discerning, had failed to discover. Little we knew of the matter; never was there a blunder like ours. Were you ever in Derry?"

"Never," said the three listeners.

"Well, then, let me inform you that the place has its own peculiar features. In the first place, all the large towns in the south and west have, besides the country neighborhood that surrounds them, a certain sprinkling of gentlefolk, who, though with small fortunes and not much usage of the world, are still a great accession to society, and make up the blank which, even in the most thickly peopled country, would be sadly felt without them. Now, in Derry, there is none of this. After the great guns—and, *per Baccho!* what great guns they are!—you have nothing but the men engaged in commerce,—sharp, clever, shrewd, well-informed fellows; they are deep in flax-seed, cunning in molasses, and not to be excelled in all that pertains to coffee, sassafras, cinnamon, gum, oakum, and elephants' teeth. The place is a rich one, and the spirit of commerce is felt throughout it. Nothing is cared for, nothing is talked of, nothing alluded to, that does not bear upon this; and, in fact, if you haven't a venture in Smyrna figs, Memel timber, Dutch dolls, or some such commodity, you are absolutely nothing, and might as well be at a ball with a cork leg, or go deaf to the opera."

"Now, when I've told thus much, I leave you to guess what impression our triumphal entry into the city produced. Instead of the admiring crowds that awaited us elsewhere, as we marched gayly into quarters, here we saw nothing but grave, sober-looking, and, I confess it, intelligent-looking faces, that scrutinized our appearance closely enough, but evidently with no great approval and less enthusiasm. The men passed on hurriedly to the counting-houses and wharves; the women, with almost as little interest, peeped at us from the windows, and walked away again. Oh, how we wished for Galway, glorious Galway, that paradise of the infantry that lies west of the Shannon! Little we knew, as we ordered the band, in lively anticipation of the gayeties before us, to strike up 'Payne's first set,' that, to the ears of the fair listeners in Ship Quay Street, the rumble of a sugar hogshead or the crank of a weighing crane were more delightful music."

"By Jove!" interrupted Power, "you are quite right. Women are strongly imitative in their tastes. The lovely Italian, whose very costume is a natural following of a Raphael, is no more like the pretty Liverpool damsel than Genoa is to Glasnevin; and yet what the deuce have they, dear souls, with their feet upon a soft carpet and their eyes upon the pages of Scott or Byron, to do with all the cotton or dimity that ever was printed? But let us not repine; that very plastic character is our greatest blessing."

"I'm not so sure that it always exists," said the doctor, dubiously, as though his own experience pointed otherwise.

"Well, go ahead!" said the skipper, who evidently disliked the digression thus interrupting the adjutant's story.

"Well, we marched along, looking right and left at the pretty faces—and there were plenty of them, too—that a momentary curiosity drew to the windows; but although we smiled and ogled and leered as only a newly arrived regiment can smile, ogle, or leer, by all that's provoking we might as well have wasted our blandishments upon the Presbyterian meeting-house, that frowned upon us with its high-pitched roof and round windows.

"'Droll people, these,' said one; 'Rayther rum ones,' cried another; 'The black north, by Jove!' said a third: and so we went along to the barracks, somewhat displeased to think that, though the 18th were slow, they might have met their match.

"Disappointed, as we undoubtedly felt, at the little enthusiasm that marked our *entrée*, we still resolved to persist in our original plan, and accordingly, early the following morning, announced our intention of giving amateur theatricals. The mayor, who called upon our colonel, was the first to learn this, and received the information with pretty much the same kind of look the Archbishop of Canterbury might be supposed to assume if requested by a a friend to ride 'a Derby.' The incredulous expression of the poor man's face, as he turned from one of us to the other, evidently canvassing in his mind whether we might not, by some special dispensation of Providence, be all insane, I shall never forget.

"His visit was a very short one; whether concluding that we were not quite safe company, or whether our notification was too much for his nerves, I know not.

"We were not to be balked, however. Our plans for gayety, long planned and conned over, were soon announced in all form; and though we made efforts almost super-human in the cause, our plays were performed to empty benches, our balls were unattended, our picnic invitations politely declined, and, in a word, all our advances treated with a cold and chilling politeness that plainly said, 'We'll none of you.'

"Each day brought some new discomfiture, and as we met at mess, instead of having, as heretofore, some prospect of pleasure and amusement to chat over, it was only to talk gloomily over our miserable failures, and lament the dreary quarters that our fates had doomed us to.

"Some months wore on in this fashion, and at length—what will not time do?—we began, by degrees, to forget our woes. Some of us took to late hours and brandy-and-water; others got sentimental, and wrote journals and novels and poetry; some made acquaintances among the townspeople, and out in to a quiet rubber to pass the evening; while another detachment, among which I was, got up a little love affair to while away the tedious hours, and cheat the lazy sun.

"I have already said something of my taste in beauty; now, Mrs. Boggs was exactly the style of woman I fancied. She was a widow; she had black eyes,—not your jet-black, sparkling, Dutch-doll eyes, that roll about and twinkle, but mean nothing; no, hers had a soft, subdued, downcast, pensive look about them, and were fully as melting a pair of orbs as any blue eyes you ever looked at.

"Then, she had a short upper lip, and sweet teeth; by Jove, they were pearls! and she showed them too, pretty often. Her figure was well-rounded, plump, and what the French call*nette*. To complete all, her instep and ankle were unexceptional; and lastly, her jointure was seven hundred pounds per annum, with a trifle of eight thousand more that the late lamented Boggs bequeathed, when, after four months of uninterrupted bliss, he left Derry for another world.

"When chance first threw me in the way of the fair widow, some casual coincidence of opinion happened to raise me in her estimation, and I soon afterwards received an invitation to a small evening party at her house, to which I alone of the regiment was asked.

"I shall not weary you with the details of my intimacy; it is enough that I tell you I fell desperately in love. I began by visiting twice or thrice a week, and in less than two months, spent every morning at her house, and rarely left it till the 'Roast beef' announced mess.

"I soon discovered the widow's cue; she was serious. Now, I had conducted all manner of flirtatious in my previous life; timid young ladies, manly young ladies, musical, artistical, poetical, and hysterical,—bless you, I knew them all by heart; but never before had I to deal with a serious one, and a widow to boot. The case was a trying one. For some weeks it was all very up-hill work; all the red shot of warm affection I used to pour in on other occasions was of no use here. The language of love, in which I was no mean proficient, availed me not. Compliments and flattery, those rare skirmishers before the engagement, were denied me; and I verily think that a tender squeeze of the hand would have cost me my dismissal.

"'How very slow, all this!' thought I, as, at the end of two months siege, I still found myself seated in the trenches, and not a single breach in the fortress; 'but, to be sure, it's the way they have in the north, and one must be patient.'

"While thus I was in no very sanguine frame of mind as to my prospects, in reality my progress was very considerable. Having become a member of Mr. M'Phun's congregation, I was gradually rising in the estimation of the widow and her friends, whom my constant attendance at meeting, and my very serious demeanor had so far impressed that very grave deliberation was held whether I should not be made an elder at the next brevet.

"If the widow Boggs had not been a very lovely and wealthy widow; had she not possessed the eyes, lips, hips, ankles, and jointure aforesaid,—I honestly avow that neither the charms of that sweet man Mr. M'Phun's eloquence, nor even the flattering distinction in store for me, would have induced me to prolong my suit. However, I was not going to despair when in sight of land. The widow was evidently softened. A little time longer, and the most scrupulous moralist, the most rigid advocate for employing time wisely, could not have objected to my daily system of courtship. I was none of your sighing, dying, ogling, hand-squeezing, waist-pressing, oath-swearing, everlasting-adoring affairs, with an interchange of rings and lockets; not a bit of it. It was confoundedly like a controversial meeting at the Rotundo, and I myself had a far greater resemblance to Father Tom Maguire than a gay Lothario.

"After all, when mess-time came, when the 'Roast beef' played, and we assembled at dinner, and the soup and fish had gone round, with two glasses of sherry in, my spirits rallied, and a very jolly evening consoled me for all my fatigues and exertions, and supplied me with energy for the morrow; for, let me observe here, that I only made love before dinner. The evenings I reserved for myself, assuring Mrs. Boggs that my regimental duties required all my time after mess hour, in which I was perfectly correct: for at six we dined; at seven I opened the claret No. 1; at eight I had uncorked my second bottle; by half-past eight I was returning to the sherry; and at ten, punctual to the moment, I was repairing to my quarters on the back of my servant, Tim Daly, who had carried me safely for eight years, without a single mistake, as the fox-hunters say. This was a way we had in the —th. Every man was carried away from mess, some sooner, some later. I was always an early riser, and went betimes.

"Now, although I had very abundant proof, from circumstantial evidence, that I was nightly removed from the mess-room to my bed in the mode I mention, it would have puzzled me sorely to prove the fact in any direct way; inasmuch as by half-past nine, as the clock chimed, and Tim entered to take me, I was very innocent of all that was going on, and except a certain vague sense of regret at leaving the decanter, felt nothing whatever.

"It so chanced—what mere trifles are we ruled by in our destiny!—that just as my suit with the widow had assumed its most favorable footing, old General Hinks, that commanded the district, announced his coming over to inspect our regiment. Over he came accordingly, and to be sure, we had a day of it. We were paraded for six mortal hours; then we were marching and countermarching, moving into line, back again into column, now forming open column, then into square; till at last, we began to think that the old general was like the Flying Dutchman, and was probably condemned to keep on drilling us to the day of judgment. To be sure, he enlivened the proceeding to me by pronouncing the regiment the worst-drilled and appointed corps in the service, and the adjutant (me!) the stupidest dunderhead—these were his words—he had ever met with.

"'Never mind,' thought I; 'a few days more, and it's little I'll care for the eighteen manoeuvres. It's small trouble your eyes right or your left, shoulders forward, will give me. I'll sell out, and with the Widow Boggs and seven hundred a year,—but no matter.'

"This confounded inspection lasted till half-past five in the afternoon; so that our mess was delayed a full hour in consequence, and it was past seven as we sat down to dinner. Our faces were grim enough as we met together at first; but what will not a good dinner and good wine do for the surliest party? By eight o'clock we began to feel somewhat more convivially disposed; and before nine, the decanters were performing a quick-step round the table, in a fashion very exhilarating and very jovial to look at.

"'No flinching to-night,' said the senior major. 'We've had a severe day; let us also have a merry evening.'

"'By Jove! Ormond,' cried another, 'we must not leave this to-night. Confound the old humbugs and their musty whist party; throw them over.'

"'I say, Adjutant,' said Forbes; addressing me, 'you've nothing particular to say to the fair widow this evening? You'll not bolt, I hope?'

"'That he sha'n't,' said one near me; 'he must make up for his absence to-morrow, for to-night we all stand fast.'

"'Besides,' said another, 'she's at meeting by this. Old—what-d'ye-call-him?—is at fourteenthly before now.'

"'A note for you, sir,' said the mess waiter, presenting me with a rose-colored three-cornered billet. It was from *la chère* Boggs herself, and ran thus:—

DEAR SIR,—*Mr. M'Phun and a few friends are coming to tea at   my house after meeting; perhaps you will also favor us with your   company. Yours truly,   ELIZA BOGGS.*

"What was to be done? Quit the mess; leave a jolly party just at the jolliest moment; exchange Lafitte and red hermitage for a *soirée* of elders, presided over by that sweet man, Mr. M'Phun! It was too bad!—but then, how much was in the scale! What would the widow say if I declined? What would she think? I well knew that the invitation meant nothing less than a full-dress parade of me before her friends, and that to decline was perhaps to forfeit all my hopes in that quarter forever.

"'Any answer, sir?' said the waiter.

"'Yes,' said I, in a half-whisper, 'I'll go,—tell the servant, I'll go.'

"At this moment my tender epistle was subtracted from before me, and ere I had turned round, had made the tour of half the table. I never perceived the circumstance, however, and filling my glass, professed my resolve to sit to the last, with a mental reserve to take my departure at the very first opportunity. Ormond and the paymaster quitted the room for a moment, as if to give orders for a broil at twelve, and now all seemed to promise a very convivial and well-sustained party for the night.

"'Is that all arranged?' inquired the major, as Ormond entered.

"'All right,' said he; 'and now let us have a bumper and a song. Adjutant, old boy, give us a chant.'

"'What shall it be, then?' inquired I, anxious to cover my intended retreat by any appearance of joviality.

"'Give us—
"'When I was in the Fusiliers   Some fourteen years ago.'"

"'No, no; confound it! I've heard nothing else since I joined the regiment. Let us have the "Paymaster's Daughter."'

"'Ah! that's pathetic; I like that,' lisped a young ensign.

"'If I'm to have a vote,' grunted out the senior major, 'I pronounce for "West India Quarters."'

"'Yes, yes,' said half-a-dozen voices together; 'let's have "West India Quarters." Come, give him a glass of sherry, and let him begin.'

"I had scarcely finished off my glass, and cleared my throat for my song, when the clock on the chimney-piece chimed half-past nine, and the same instant I felt a heavy hand fall upon my shoulder. I turned and beheld my servant Tim. This, as I have already mentioned, was the hour at which Tim was in the habit of taking me home to my quarters; and though we had dined an hour later, he took no notice of the circumstance, but true to his custom, he was behind my chair. A very cursory glance at my 'familiar' was quite sufficient to show me that we had somehow changed sides; for Tim, who was habitually the most sober of mankind, was, on the present occasion, exceedingly drunk, while I, a full hour before that consummation, was perfectly sober.

"'What d'ye want, sir?' inquired I, with something of severity in my manner.

"'Come home,' said Tim, with a hiccough that set the whole table in a roar.

"'Leave the room this instant,' said I, feeling wrath at being thus made a butt of for his offences. 'Leave the room, or I'll kick you out of it.' Now, this, let me add in a parenthesis, was somewhat of a boast, for Tim was six feet three, and strong in proportion, and when in liquor, fearless as a tiger.

"'You'll kick me out of the room, eh, will you? Try, only try it, that's all.' Here a new roar of laughter burst forth, while Tim, again placing an enormous paw upon my shoulder, continued, 'Don't be sitting there, making a baste of yourself, when you've got enough. Don't you see you're drunk?'

"I sprang to my legs on this, and made a rush to the fireplace to secure the poker; but Tim was beforehand with me, and seizing me by the waist with both hands, flung me across his shoulders as though I were a baby, saying, at the same time, 'I'll take you away at half-past eight to-morrow, as you're as rampageous again.' I kicked, I plunged, I swore, I threatened, I even begged and implored to be set down; but whether my voice was lost in the uproar around me, or that Tim only regarded my denunciations in the light of cursing, I know not, but he carried me bodily down the stairs, steadying himself by one hand on the banisters, while with the other he held me as in a vice. I had but one consolation all this while; it was this, that as my quarters lay immediately behind the mess-room, Tim's excursion would soon come to an end, and I should be free once more; but guess my terror to find that the drunken scoundrel, instead of going as usual to the left, turned short to the right hand, and marched boldly into Ship Quay Street. Every window in the mess-room was filled with our fellows, absolutely shouting with laughter. 'Go it Tim! That's the fellow! Hold him tight! Never let go!' cried a dozen voices; while the wretch, with the tenacity of drunkenness, gripped me still harder, and took his way down the middle of the street.

"It was a beautiful evening in July, a soft summer night, as I made this pleasing excursion down the most frequented thoroughfare in the maiden city, my struggles every moment exciting

98

roars of laughter from an increasing crowd of spectators, who seemed scarcely less amused than puzzled at the exhibition. In the midst of a torrent of imprecations against my torturer, a loud noise attracted me. I turned my head, and saw,—horror of horrors!—the door of the meeting-house just flung open, and the congregation issuing forth *en masse*. Is it any wonder if I remember no more? There I was, the chosen one of the widow Boggs, the elder elect, the favored friend and admired associate of Mr. M'Phun, taking an airing on a summer's evening on the back of a drunken Irishman. Oh, the thought was horrible! and certainly the short and pithy epithets by which I was characterized in the crowd, neither improved my temper nor assuaged my wrath, and I feel bound to confess that my own language was neither serious nor becoming. Tim, however, cared little for all this, and pursued the even tenor of his way through the whole crowd, nor stopped till, having made half the circuit of the wall, he deposited me safe at my own door; adding, as he set me down, 'Oh, av you're as throublesome every evening, it's a wheelbarrow I'll be obleeged to bring for you!'

"The next day I obtained a short leave of absence, and ere a fortnight expired, exchanged into the —th, preferring Halifax itself to the ridicule that awaited me in Londonderry."

CHAPTER XXX.
FRED POWER'S ADVENTURE IN PHILIPSTOWN.

The lazy hours of the long summer day crept slowly over. The sea, unbroken by foam or ripple, shone like a broad blue mirror, reflecting here and there some fleecy patches of snow-white cloud as they stood unmoved in the sky. The good ship rocked to and fro with a heavy and lumbering motion, the cordage rattled, the bulkheads creaked, the sails flapped lazily against the masts, the very sea-gulls seemed to sleep as they rested on the long swell that bore them along, and everything in sea and sky bespoke the calm. No sailor trod the deck; no watch was stirring; the very tiller ropes were deserted; and as they traversed backwards and forwards with every roll of the vessel, told that we had no steerage-way, and lay a mere log upon the water.

I sat alone in the bow, and fell into a musing fit upon the past and the future. How happily for us is it ordained that in the most stirring existences there are every here and there such little resting-spots of reflection, from which, as from some eminence, we look back upon the road we have been treading in life, and cast a wistful glance at the dark vista before us! When first we set out upon our worldly pilgrimage, these are indeed precious moments, when with buoyant heart and spirit high, believing all things, trusting all things, our very youth comes back to us, reflected from every object we meet; and like Narcissus, we are but worshipping our own image in the water. As we go on in life, the cares, the anxieties, and the business of the world engross us more and more, and such moments become fewer and shorter. Many a bright dream has been dissolved, many a fairy vision replaced, by some dark reality; blighted hopes, false friendships have gradually worn callous the heart once alive to every gentle feeling, and time begins to tell upon us,—yet still, as the well-remembered melody to which we listened with delight in infancy brings to our mature age a touch of early years, so will the very association of these happy moments recur to us in our revery, and make us young again in thought. Then it is that, as we look back upon our worldly career, we become convinced how truly is the child the father of the man, how frequently are the projects of our manhood the fruit of some boyish predilection; and that in the emulative ardor that stirs the schoolboy's heart, we may read the *prestige* of that high daring that makes a hero of its possessor.

These moments, too, are scarcely more pleasurable than they are salutary to us. Disengaged for the time from every worldly anxiety, we pass in review before our own selves, and in the solitude of our own hearts are we judged. That still small voice of conscience, unheard and unlistened to amidst the din and bustle of life, speaks audibly to us now; and while chastened on one side by regrets, we are sustained on the other by some approving thought; and with many a sorrow for the past, and many promise for the future, we begin to feel "how good it is for us to be here."

The evening wore later; the red sun sank down upon the sea, growing larger and larger; the long line of mellow gold that sheeted along the distant horizon grew first of a dark ruddy tinge, then paler and paler, till it became almost gray; a single star shone faintly in the east, and darkness soon set in. With night came the wind, for almost imperceptibly the sails swelled slowly out, a slight rustle at the bow followed, the ship lay gently over, and we were once more in motion. It struck four bells; some casual resemblance in the sound of the old pendulum that marked the hour at my uncle's house startled me so that I actually knew not where I was. With lightning speed my once home rose up before me with its happy hearts; the old familiar faces were there; the gay laugh was in my ears; there sat my dear old uncle, as with bright eye and mellow voice he looked a very welcome to his guests; there Boyle; there Considine; there the grim-visaged portraits that graced the old walls whose black oak wainscot stood in broad light and shadow, as the blazing turf fire shone upon it; there was my own place, now vacant; methought my uncle's eye was turned towards it and that I heard him say, "My poor boy! I wonder where is he now!" My heart swelled, my chest heaved, the tears coursed slowly down my cheeks, as I asked myself, "Shall I ever see them more?" Oh, how little, how very little to us are the accustomed blessings of our life till some change has robbed us of them, and how dear are they when lost to us! My uncle's dark foreboding that we should never meet again on earth, came for the first time forcibly to my mind, and my heart was full to bursting. What could repay me for the agony of that moment as I thought of him, my first, my best, my only friend, whom I had deserted? And how gladly would I have resigned my bright day-dawn of ambition to be once more beside his chair, to hear his voice, to see his smile, to feel his love for me! A loud laugh from the cabin roused me from my sad, depressing revery, and at the same instant Mike's well-known voice informed me that the captain was looking for me everywhere, as supper was on the table. Little as I felt disposed to join the party at such a moment, as I knew there was no escaping Power, I resolved to make the best of matters; so after a few minutes I followed Mickey down the companion and entered the cabin.

The scene before me was certainly not calculated to perpetuate depressing thoughts. At the head of a rude old-fashioned table, upon which figured several black bottles and various ill-looking drinking vessels of every shape and material, sat Fred Power; on his right was placed the skipper, on his left the doctor,—the bronzed, merry-looking, weather-beaten features of the one contrasting ludicrously with the pale, ascetic, acute-looking expression of the other. Sparks, more than half-drunk, with the mark of a red-hot cigar upon his nether lip, was lower down; while Major Monsoon, to preserve the symmetry of the party, had protruded his head, surmounted by a huge red nightcap, from the berth opposite, and held out his goblet to be replenished from the punch-bowl.

"Welcome, thrice welcome, thou man of Galway!" cried out Power, as he pointed to a seat, and pushed a wine-glass towards me. "Just in time, too, to pronounce upon a new brewery. Taste that; a little more of the lemon you would say, perhaps? Well, I agree with you. Rum and brandy, glenlivet and guava jelly, limes, green tea, and a slight suspicion of preserved ginger,— nothing else, upon honor,—and the most simple mixture for the cure, the radical cure, of blue devils and debt I know of; eh, Doctor? You advise it yourself, to be taken before bed-time; nothing inflammatory in it, nothing pugnacious; a mere circulation of the better juices and more genial spirits of the marly clay, without arousing any of the baser passions; whiskey is the devil for that."

"I canna say that I dinna like whiskey toddy," said the doctor; "in the cauld winter nights it's no sae bad."

"Ah, that's it," said Power; "there's the pull you Scotch have upon us poor Patlanders,— cool, calculating, long-headed fellows, you only come up to the mark after fifteen tumblers; whereas we hot-brained devils, with a blood at 212 degrees of Fahrenheit and a high-pressure engine of good spirits always ready for an explosion, we go clean mad when tipsy; not but I am fully convinced that a mad Irishman is worth two sane people of any other country under heaven."

"If you mean by that insin—insin—sinuation to imply any disrespect to the English," stuttered out Sparks, "I am bound to say that I for one, and the doctor, I am sure, for another—"

"Na, na," interrupted the doctor, "ye mauna coont upon me; I'm no disposed to fetch ower our liquor."

"Then, Major Monsoon, I'm certain—"

"Are ye, faith?" said the major, with a grin; "blessed are they who expect nothing,—of which number you are not,—for most decidedly you shall be disappointed."

"Never mind, Sparks, take the whole fight to your own proper self, and do battle like a man; and here I stand, ready at all arms to prove my position,—that we drink better, sing better, court better, fight better, and make better punch than every John Bull, from Berwick to the Land's End."

Sparks, however, who seemed not exactly sure how far his antagonist was disposed to quiz, relapsed into a half-tipsy expression of contemptuous silence, and sipped his liquor without reply.

"Yes," said Power, after a pause, "bad luck to it for whiskey; it nearly got me broke once, and poor Tom O'Reilly of the 5th, too, the best-tempered fellow in the service. We were as near it as touch and go; and all for some confounded Loughrea spirits that we believed to be perfectly innocent, and used to swill away freely without suspicion of any kind."

"Let's hear the story," said I, "by all means."

"It's not a long one," said Power, "so I don't care if I tell it; and besides, if I make a clean breast of my own sins, I'll insist upon Monsoon's telling you afterwards how he stocked his cellar in Cadiz. Eh, Major; there's worse tipple than the King of Spain's sherry?"

"You shall judge for yourself, old boy," said Monsoon, good-humoredly; "and as for the narrative, it is equally at your service. Of course it goes no further. The commander-in-chief, long life to him! is a glorious fellow; but he has no more idea of a joke than the Archbishop of Canterbury, and it might chance to reach him."

"Recount, and fear not!" cried Power; "we are discreet as the worshipful company of apothecaries."

"But you forget you are to lead the way."

"Here goes, then," said the jolly captain; "not that the story has any merit in it, but the moral is beautiful.

"Ireland, to be sure, is a beautiful country; but somehow it would prove a very dull one to be quartered in, if it were not that the people seem to have a natural taste for the army. From the belle of Merrion Square down to the inn-keeper's daughter in Tralee, the loveliest part of the creation seem to have a perfect appreciation of our high acquirements and advantages; and in no other part of the globe, the Tonga Islands included, is a red-coat more in favor. To be sure, they would be very ungrateful if it were not the case; for we, upon our side, leave no stone unturned to make ourselves agreeable. We ride, drink, play, and make love to the ladies from Fairhead to Killarney, in a way greatly calculated to render us popular; and as far as making the time pass pleasantly, we are the boys for the 'greatest happiness' principle. I repeat it; we deserve our popularity. Which of us does not get head and ears in debt with garrison balls and steeple-chases, picnics, regattas, and the thousand-and-one inventions to get rid of one's spare cash,—so called for being so sparingly dealt out by our governors? Now and then, too, when all else fails, we take a newly-joined ensign and make him marry some pretty but penniless lass in a country town, just to show the rest that we are not joking, but have serious ideas of matrimony in the midst of all our flirtations. If it were all like this, the Green Isle would be a paradise; but unluckily every now and then one is condemned to some infernal place where there is neither a pretty face nor tight ankle, where the priest himself is not a good fellow, and long, ill-paved, straggling streets, filled on market days with booths of striped calico and soapy cheese, is the only promenade, and a ruinous barrack, with mouldy walls and a tumbling chimney, the only quarters.

"In vain, on your return from your morning stroll or afternoon canter, you look on the chimney-piece for a shower of visiting-cards and pink notes of invitation; in vain you ask your servant, Has any one called. Alas, your only visitor has been the ganger, to demand a party to assist in still-hunting amidst that interesting class of the population who, having nothing to eat, are engaged in devising drink, and care as much for the life of a red-coat as you do for that of a crow or a curlew. This may seem overdrawn; but I would ask you, Were you ever for your sins quartered in that capital city of the Bog of Allen they call Philipstown? Oh, but it is a romantic spot! They tell us somewhere that much of the expression of the human face divine depends upon the objects which constantly surround us. Thus the inhabitants of mountain districts imbibe, as it were, a certain bold and daring character of expression from the scenery, very different from the placid and monotonous look of those who dwell in plains and valleys; and I can certainly credit the theory in this instance, for every man, woman, and child you meet has a brown, baked, scruffy, turf-like face, that fully satisfies you that if Adam were formed of clay the Philipstown people were worse treated and only made of bog mould.

"Well, one fine morning poor Tom and myself were marched off from Birr, where one might 'live and love forever,' to take up our quarters at this sweet spot. Little we knew of Philipstown; and like my friend the adjutant there, when he laid siege to Deny, we made our *entrée* with all the pomp we could muster, and though we had no band, our drums and fifes did duty for it; and we brushed along through turf-creels and wicker-baskets of new brogues that obstructed the street till we reached the barrack,—the only testimony of admiration we met with being, I feel bound to admit, from a ragged urchin of ten years, who, with a wattle in his hand, imitated me as I marched along, and when I cried halt, took his leave of us by dexterously fixing his thumb to the side of his nose and outstretching his fingers, as if thus to convey a very strong hint that we were not half so fine fellows as we thought ourselves. Well, four mortal summer months of hot sun and cloudless sky went over, and still we lingered in that vile village, the everlasting monotony of our days being marked by the same brief morning drill, the same blue-legged chicken dinner, the same smoky Loughrea whiskey, and the same evening stroll along the canal bank to watch for the Dublin packet-boat, with its never-varying cargo of cattle-dealers, priests, and peelers on their way to the west country, as though the demand for such colonial productions in these parts was insatiable. This was pleasant, you will say; but what was to be done? We had nothing else. Now, nothing saps a man's temper like *ennui*. The cranky, peevish people one meets with would be excellent folk, if they only had something to do. As for us, I'll venture to say two men more disposed to go pleasantly down the current of life it were hard to meet with; and yet, such was the consequence of these confounded four months' sequestration from all other society, we became sour and cross-grained, everlastingly disputing about trifles, and continually arguing about matters which neither were interested in, nor, indeed, knew anything about. There were, it is true, few topics to discuss; newspapers we never saw; sporting there was none,—but then, the drill, the return of duty, the probable chances of our being ordered for service, were all daily subjects to be talked over, and usually with considerable asperity and bitterness. One point, however, always served us when hard pushed for a bone of contention; and which, begun by a mere accident at first, gradually increased to a sore and peevish subject, and finally led to the consequences which I have hinted at in the beginning. This was no less than the respective merits of our mutual servants; each everlastingly indulging in a tirade against the other for awkwardness, incivility, unhandiness,—charges, I am bound to confess, most amply proved on either side.

"'Well, I am sure, O'Reilly, if you can stand that fellow, it's no affair of mine; but such an ungainly savage I never met,' I would say.

"To which he would reply, 'Bad enough he is, certainly; but, by Jove! when I only think of your Hottentot, I feel grateful for what I've got.'

"Then ensued a discussion, with attack, rejoinder, charge, and recrimination till we retired for the night, wearied with our exertions, and not a little ashamed of ourselves at bottom for our absurd warmth and excitement. In the morning the matter would be rigidly avoided by each party until some chance occasion had brought it on the *tapis*, when hostilities would be immediately renewed, and carried on with the same vigor, to end as before.

"In this agreeable state of matters we sat one warm summer evening before the mess-room, under the shade of a canvas awning, discussing, by way of refrigerant, our eighth tumbler of whiskey punch. We had, as usual, been jarring away about everything under heaven. A lately arrived post-chaise, with an old, stiff-looking gentleman in a queue, had formed a kind of 'godsend' for debate, as to who he was, whither he was going, whether he really had intended to spend the night there, or that he only put up because the chaise was broken; each, as was customary, maintaining his own opinion with an obstinacy we have often since laughed at, though, at the time, we had few mirthful thoughts about the matter.

"As the debate waxed warm, O'Reilly asserted that he positively knew the individual in question to be a United Irishman, travelling with instructions from the French government; while I laughed him to scorn by swearing that he was the rector of Tyrrell's Pass, that I knew him well, and, moreover, that he was the worst preacher in Ireland. Singular enough it was that all this while the disputed identity was himself standing coolly at the inn window, with his snuff-box in his hand, leisurely surveying us as we sat, appearing, at least, to take a very lively interest in our debate.

"'Come, now,' said O'Reilly, 'there's only one way to conclude this, and make you pay for your obstinacy. What will you bet that he's the rector of Tyrrell's Pass?'

"'What odds will you take that he's Wolfe Tone?' inquired I, sneeringly.

"'Five to one against the rector,' said he, exultingly.

"'An elephant's molar to a toothpick against Wolfe Tone,' cried I.

"'Ten pounds even that I'm nearer the mark than you,' said Tom, with a smash of his fist upon the table.

"'Done,' said I,—'done. But how are we to decide the wager?'

"'That's soon done,' said he. At the same instant he sprang to his legs and called out: 'Pat, I say, Pat, I want you to present my respects to—'

"'No, no, I bar that; no *ex parte* statements. Here, Jem, do you simply tell that—'

"'That fellow can't deliver a message. Do come here, Pat. Just beg of—'

"'He'll blunder it, the confounded fool; so, Jem, do you go.'

"The two individuals thus addressed were just in the act of conveying a tray of glasses and a spiced round of beef for supper into the mess-room; and as I may remark that they fully entered into the feelings of jealousy their respective masters professed, each eyed the other with a look of very unequivocal dislike.

"'Arrah! you needn't be pushing me that way,' said Pat, 'an' the round o' beef in my hands.'

"'Devil's luck to ye, it's the glasses you'll be breaking with your awkward elbow!'

"'Then, why don't ye leave the way? Ain't I your superior?'

"'Ain't I the captain's own man?'

"'Ay, and if you war. Don't I belong to his betters? Isn't my master the two liftenants?'

"This, strange as it may sound, was so far true, as I held a commission in an African corps, with my lieutenancy in the 5th.

"'Be-gorra, av he was six—There now, you done it!'

"At the same moment, a tremendous crash took place and the large dish fell in a thousand pieces on the pavement, while the spiced round rolled pensively down the yard.

"Scarcely was the noise heard when, with one vigorous kick, the tray of glasses was sent spinning into the air, and the next moment the disputants were engaged in bloody battle. It was at this moment that our attention was first drawn towards them, and I need not say with what feelings of interest we looked on.

"'Hit him, Pat—there, Jem, under the guard! That's it—go in! Well done, left hand! By Jove! that was a facer! His eye's closed—he's down! Not a bit of it-how do you like that? Unfair, unfair! No such thing! I say it was! Not at all—I deny it!'

"By this time we had approached the combatants, each man patting his own fellow on the back, and encouraging him by the most lavish promises. Now it was, but in what way I never could exactly tell, that I threw out my right hand to stop a blow that I saw coming rather too near me, when, by some unhappy mischance, my doubled fist lighted upon Tom O'Reilly's nose. Before I could express my sincere regret for the accident, the blow was returned with double force, and the next moment we were at it harder than the others. After five minutes' sharp work, we both stopped for breath, and incontinently burst out a-laughing. There was Tom, with a nose as large as three, a huge cheek on one side, and the whole head swinging round like a harlequin's; while I, with one eye closed, and the other like a half-shut cockle-shell, looked scarcely less rueful. We had not much time for mirth, for at the same instant a sharp, full voice called out close beside us—

"To your quarters, sirs. I put you both under arrest, from which you are not to be released until the sentence of a court-martial decide if conduct such as this becomes officers and gentlemen.'

"I looked round, and saw the old fellow in the queue.

"'Wolfe Tone, by all that's unlucky!' said I, with an attempt at a smile.

"'The rector of Tyrrell's Pass,' cried out Tom, with a snuffle; 'the worst preacher in Ireland—eh, Fred?'

"We had not much time for further commentaries upon our friend, for he at once opened his frock coat, and displayed to our horrified gaze the uniform of a general officer.

"'Yes, sir, General Johnson, if you will allow me to present him to your acquaintance; and now, guard, turn out.'

"In a few minutes more the orders were issued, and poor Tom and myself found ourselves fast confined to our quarters, with a sentinel at the door, and the pleasant prospect that, in the space of about ten days, we should be broke, and dismissed the service; which verdict, as the general order would say, the commander of the forces has been graciously pleased to approve.

"However, when morning came the old general, who was really a trump, inquired a little further into the matter, saw it was partly accidental, and after a severe reprimand, and a caution about Loughrea whiskey after the sixth tumbler, released us from arrest, and forgave the whole affair."

CHAPTER XXXI.
THE VOYAGE CONTINUED.

Ugh, what a miserable thing is a voyage! Here we are now eight days at sea, the eternal sameness of all around growing every hour less supportable. Sea and sky are beautiful things when seen from the dark woods and waving meadows on shore; but their picturesque effect is sadly marred from want of contrast. Besides that, the "*toujours* pork," with crystals of salt as long as your wife's fingers; the potatoes that seemed varnished in French polish; the tea seasoned with geological specimens from the basin of London, ycleped maple sugar; and the butter—ye gods, the butter! But why enumerate these smaller features of discomfort and omit the more glaring ones?—the utter selfishness which blue water suggests, as inevitably as the cold fit follows the ague. The good fellow that shares his knapsack or his last guinea on land, here forages out the best corner to hang his hammock; jockeys you into a comfortless crib, where the uncalked deck-butt filters every rain from heaven on your head; votes you the corner at dinner, not only that he may place you with your back to the thorough-draught of the gangway ladder, but that he may eat, drink, and lie down before you have even begun to feel the qualmishness that the dinner of a troop-ship is well calculated to suggest; cuts his pencil with your best razor; wears your shirts, as washing is scarce; and winds up all by having a good story of you every evening for the edification of the other "sharp gentlemen," who, being too wide awake to be humbugged themselves, enjoy his success prodigiously. This, gentle reader, is neither confession nor avowal of mine. The passage I have here presented to you I have taken from the journal of my brother officer, Mr. Sparks, who, when not otherwise occupied, usually employed his time in committing to paper his thoughts upon men, manners, and things at sea in general; though, sooth to say, his was not an idle life. Being voted by unanimous consent "a junior," he was condemned to offices that the veriest fag in Eton or Harrow had rebelled against. In the morning, under the pseudonym of *Mrs.* Sparks, he presided at breakfast, having previously made tea, coffee, and chocolate for the whole cabin, besides boiling about twenty eggs at various degrees of hardness; he was under heavy recognizances to provide a plate of buttered toast of very alarming magnitude, fried ham, kidneys, etc., to no end. Later on, when others sauntered about the deck, vainly endeavoring to fix their attention upon a novel or a review, the poor cornet might be seen with a white apron tucked gracefully round his spare proportions, whipping eggs for pancakes, or, with upturned shirt-sleeves, fashioning dough for a pudding. As the day waned, the cook's galley became his haunt, where, exposed to a roasting fire, he inspected the details of a *cuisine*; for which, whatever his demerits, he was sure of an ample remuneration in abuse at dinner. Then came the dinner itself, that dread ordeal, where nothing was praised and everything censured. This was followed by the punch-making, where the tastes of six different and differing individuals were to be exclusively consulted in the self-same beverage; and lastly, the supper at night, when Sparkie, as he was familiarly called, towards evening grown quite exhausted, became the subject of unmitigated wrath and most unmeasured reprobation.

"I say, Sparks, it's getting late. The spatch-cock, old boy. Don't be slumbering."

"By-the-bye, Sparkie, what a mess you made of that pea-soup to-day! By Jove, I never felt so ill in my life!"

"Na, na; it was na the soup. It was something he pit in the punch, that's burning me ever since I tuk it. Ou, man, but ye're an awfu' creature wi' vittals!"

"He'll improve, Doctor; he'll improve. Don't discourage him; the boy's young. Be alive now, there. Where's the toast?—confound you, where's the toast?"

"There, Sparks, you like a drumstick, I know. Mustn't muzzle the ox, eh? Scripture for you, old boy. Eat away; hang the expense. Hand him over the jug. Empty—eh, Charley? Come, Sparkie, bear a hand; the liquor's out."

"But won't you let me eat?"

"Eat! Heavens, what a fellow for eating! By George, such an appetite is clean against the articles of war! Come, man, it's drink we're thinking of. There's the rum, sugar, limes; see to the hot water. Well, Skipper, how are we getting on?"

"Lying our course; eight knots off the log. Pass the rum. Why, Mister Sparks!"

"Eh, Sparks, what's this?"

"Sparks, my man, confound it!"

And then, *omnes* chorussing "Sparks!" in every key of the gamut, the luckless fellow would be obliged to jump up from his meagre fare and set to work at a fresh brewage of punch for the others. The bowl and the glasses filled, by some little management on Power's part our friend the cornet would be *drawn out*, as the phrase is, into some confession of his early years, which seemed to have been exclusively spent in love-making,—devotion to the fair being as integral a portion of his character as tippling was of the worthy major's.

Like most men who pass their lives in over-studious efforts to please,—however ungallant the confession be,—the amiable Sparks had had little success. His love, if not, as it generally happened, totally unrequited, was invariably the source of some awkward catastrophe, there being no imaginable error he had not at some time or other fallen into, nor any conceivable mischance to which he had not been exposed. Inconsolable widows, attached wives, fond mothers, newly-married brides, engaged young ladies were by some*contretemps* continually the subject of his attachments; and the least mishap which followed the avowal of his passion was to be heartily laughed at and obliged to leave the neighborhood. Duels, apologies, actions at law, compensations, etc., were of every-day occurrence, and to such an extent, too, that any man blessed with a smaller bump upon the occiput would eventually have long since abandoned the pursuit, and taken to some less expensive pleasure. But poor Sparks, in the true spirit of a martyr, only gloried the more, the more he suffered; and like the worthy man who continued to purchase tickets in the lottery for thirty years, with nothing but a succession of blanks, he ever imagined that Fortune was only trying his patience, and had some cool forty thousand pounds of happiness waiting his perseverance in the end. Whether this prize ever did turn up in the course of years, I am unable to say; but certainly, up to the period of his history I now speak of, all had been as gloomy and unrequiting as need be. Power, who knew something of every man's adventures, was aware of so much of poor Sparks's career, and usually contrived to lay a trap for a confession that generally served to amuse us during an evening,—as much, I acknowledge, from the manner of the recital as anything contained in the story. There was a species of serious matter-of-fact simplicity in his detail of the most ridiculous scenes that left you convinced that his bearing upon the affair in question must have greatly heightened the absurdity,—nothing, however comic or droll in itself, ever exciting in him the least approach to a smile. He sat with his large light-blue eyes, light hair, long upper lip, and retreating chin, lisping out an account of an adventure, with a look of Listen about him that was inconceivably amusing.

"Come, Sparks," said Power, "I claim a promise you made me the other night, on condition we let you off making the oyster-patties at ten o'clock; you can't forget what I mean." Here the captain knowingly touched the tip of his ear, at which signal the cornet colored slightly, and drank off his wine in a hurried, confused way. "He promised to tell us, Major, how he lost the tip of his left ear. I have myself heard hints of the circumstance, but would much rather hear Sparks's own version of it."

"Another love story," said the doctor, with a grin, "I'll be bound."

"Shot off in a duel?" said I, inquiringly. "Close work, too."

"No such thing," replied Power; "but Sparks will enlighten you. It is, without exception, the most touching and beautiful thing I ever heard. As a simple story, it beats the 'Vicar of Wakefield' to sticks."

"You don't say so?" said poor Sparks, blushing.

"Ay, that I do; and maintain it, too. I'd rather be the hero of that little adventure, and be able to recount it as you do,—for, mark me, that's no small part of the effect,—than I'd be full colonel of the regiment. Well, I am sure I always thought it affecting. But, somehow, my dear friend, you don't know your powers; you have that within you would make the fortune of half the periodicals going. Ask Monsoon or O'Malley there if I did not say so at breakfast, when you were grilling the old hen,—which, by-the-bye, let me remark, was not one of your *chefs-d'oeuvre*."

"A tougher beastie I never put a tooth in."

"But the story, the story," said I.

"Yes," said Power, with a tone of command, "the story, Sparks."

"Well, if you really think it worth telling, as I have always felt it a very remarkable incident, here goes."

CHAPTER XXXII

MR. SPARKS'S STORY.

"I sat at breakfast one beautiful morning at the Goat Inn at Barmouth, looking out of a window upon the lovely vale of Barmouth, with its tall trees and brown trout-stream struggling through the woods, then turning to take a view of the calm sea, that, speckled over with white-sailed fishing-boats, stretched away in the distance. The eggs were fresh; the trout newly caught; the cream delicious. Before me lay the 'Plwdwddlwn Advertiser,' which, among the fashionable arrivals at the seaside, set forth Mr. Sparks, nephew of Sir Toby Sparks, of Manchester,—a paragraph, by the way, I always inserted. The English are naturally an aristocratic people, and set a due value upon a title."

"A very just observation," remarked Power, seriously, while Sparks continued.

"However, as far as any result from the announcement, I might as well have spared myself the trouble, for not a single person called. Not one solitary invitation to dinner, not a picnic, not a breakfast, no, nor even a tea-party, was heard of. Barmouth, at the time I speak of, was just in that transition state at which the caterpillar may be imagined, when, having abandoned his reptile habits, he still has not succeeded in becoming a butterfly. In fact, it had ceased to be a fishing village, but had not arrived at the dignity of a watering-place. Now, I know nothing as bad as this. You have not, on one hand, the quiet retirement of a little peaceful hamlet, with its humble dwellings and cheap pleasures, nor have you the gay and animated tableau of fashion in miniature, on the other; but you have noise, din, bustle, confusion, beautiful scenery and lovely points of view marred and ruined by vulgar associations. Every bold rock and jutting promontory has its citizen occupants; every sandy cove or tide-washed bay has its myriads of squalling babes and red baize-clad bathing women,—those veritable descendants of the nymphs of old. Pink parasols, donkey-carts, baskets of bread-and-butter, reticules, guides to Barmouth, specimens of ore, fragments of gypsum meet you at every step, and destroy every illusion of the picturesque."

"'I shall leave this,' thought I. 'My dreams, my long-cherished dreams of romantic walks upon the sea-shore, of evening strolls by moonlight, through dell and dingle, are reduced to a

105

short promenade through an alley of bathing-boxes, amidst a screaming population of nursery-maids and sick children, with a thorough-bass of "Fresh shrimps!" discordant enough to frighten the very fish from the shores. There is no peace, no quiet, no romance, no poetry, no love.' Alas, that most of all was wanting! For, after all, what is it which lights up the heart, save the flame of a mutual attachment? What gilds the fair stream of life, save the bright ray of warm affection? What—"

"In a word," said Power, "it is the sugar in the punch-bowl of our existence. *Perge*, Sparks; push on."

"I was not long in making up my mind. I called for my bill; I packed my clothes; I ordered post-horses; I was ready to start; one item in the bill alone detained me. The frequent occurrence of the enigmatical word 'crw,' following my servant's name, demanded an explanation, which I was in the act of receiving, when a chaise-and-four drove rapidly up to the house. In a moment the blinds were drawn up, and such a head appeared at the window! Let me pause for one moment to drink in the remembrance of that lovely being,—eyes where heaven's own blue seemed concentrated were shaded by long, deep lashes of the darkest brown; a brow fair, noble, and expansive, at each side of which masses of dark-brown hair waved half in ringlets, half in loose falling bands, shadowing her pale and downy cheek, where one faint rosebud tinge seemed lingering; lips slightly parted, as though to speak, gave to the features all the play of animation which completed this intellectual character, and made up—"

"What I should say was a devilish pretty girl," interrupted Power.

"Back the widow against her at long odds, any day," murmured the adjutant.

"She was an angel! an angel!" cried Sparks with enthusiasm.

"So was the widow, if you go to that," said the adjutant, hastily.

"And so is Matilda Dalrymple," said Power, with a sly look at me. "We are all honorable men; eh, Charley?"

"Go ahead with the story," said the skipper; "I'm beginning to feel an interest in it."

"'Isabella,' said a man's voice, as a large, well-dressed personage assisted her to alight,—'Isabella, love, you must take a little rest here before we proceed farther.'

"'I think she had better, sir,' said a matronly-looking woman, with a plaid cloak and a black bonnet.

"They disappeared within the house, and I was left alone. The bright dream was past: she was there no longer; but in my heart her image lived, and I almost felt she was before me. I thought I heard her voice, I saw her move; my limbs trembled; my hands tingled; I rang the bell, ordered my trunks back again to No. 5, and as I sank upon the sofa, murmured to myself, 'This is indeed love at first sight.'"

"How devilish sudden it was," said the skipper.

"Exactly like camp fever," responded the doctor. "One moment ye are vara well; the next ye are seized wi' a kind of shivering; then comes a kind of mandering, dandering, travelling a'overness."

"D—— the camp fever," interrupted Power.

"Well, as I observed, I fell in love; and here let me take the opportunity of observing that all that we are in the habit of hearing about single or only attachments is mere nonsense. No man is so capable of feeling deeply as he who is in the daily practice of it. Love, like everything else in this world, demands a species of cultivation. The mere tyro in an affair of the heart thinks he has exhausted all its pleasures and pains; but only he who has made it his daily study for years, familiarizing his mind with every phase of the passion, can properly or adequately appreciate it. Thus, the more you love, the better you love; the more frequently has your heart yielded—"

"It's vara like the mucous membrane," said the doctor.

"I'll break your neck with the decanter if you interrupt him again!" exclaimed Power.

"For days I scarcely ever left the house," resumed Sparks, "watching to catch one glance of the lovely Isabella. My farthest excursion was to the little garden of the inn, where I used to set every imaginable species of snare, in the event of her venturing to walk there. One day I would leave a volume of poetry; another, a copy of Paul and Virginia with a marked page; sometimes my guitar, with a broad, blue ribbon, would hang pensively from a tree,—but, alas! all in vain; she never appeared. At length I took courage to ask the waiter about her. For some minutes he could not comprehend what I meant; but, at last, discovering my object, he cried out, 'Oh, No. 8, sir; it is No. 8 you mean?'

"'It may be,' said I. 'What of her, then?'

"'Oh, sir, she's gone these three days.'

"'Gone!' said I, with a groan.

"'Yes, sir; she left this early on Tuesday with the same old gentleman and the old woman in a chaise-and-four. They ordered horses at Dolgelly to meet them; but I don't know which road they took afterwards.'

"I fell back on my chair unable to speak. Here was I enacting Romeo for three mortal days to a mere company of Welsh waiters and chamber-maids, sighing, serenading, reciting, attitudinizing, rose-plucking, soliloquizing, half-suiciding, and all for the edification of a set of savages, with about as much civilization as their own goats.

"'The bill,' cried I, in a voice of thunder; 'my bill this instant.'

"I had been imposed upon shamefully, grossly imposed upon, and would not remain another hour in the house. Such were my feelings at least, and so thinking, I sent for my servant, abused him for not having my clothes ready packed. He replied; I reiterated, and as my temper mounted, vented every imaginable epithet upon his head, and concluded by paying him his wages and sending him about his business. In one hour more I was upon the road.

"'What road, sir,' said the postilion, as he mounted into the saddle.

"'To the devil, if you please,' said I, throwing myself back in the carriage.

"'Very well, sir,' replied the boy, putting spurs to his horse.

"That evening I arrived in Bedgellert.

"The little humble inn of Bedgellert, with its thatched roof and earthen floor, was a most welcome sight to me, after eleven hours' travelling on a broiling July day. Behind the very house itself rose the mighty Snowdon, towering high above the other mountains, whose lofty peaks were lost amidst the clouds; before me was the narrow valley—"

"Wake me up when he's under way again," said the skipper, yawning fearfully.

"Go on, Sparks," said Power, encouragingly; "I was never more interested in my life; eh, O'Malley?"

"Quite thrilling," responded I, and Sparks resumed.

"Three weeks did I loiter about that sweet spot, my mind filled with images of the past and dreams of the future, my fishing-rod my only companion. Not, indeed, that I ever caught anything; for, somehow, my tackle was always getting foul of some willow-tree or water-lily, and at last, I gave up even the pretence of whipping the streams. Well, one day—I remember it as well as though it were but yesterday, it was the 4th of August—I had set off upon an excursion to Llanberris. I had crossed Snowdon early, and reached the little lake on the opposite side by breakfast time. There I sat down near the ruined tower of Dolbadern, and opening my knapsack, made a hearty meal. I have ever been a day-dreamer; and there are few things I like better than to lie, upon some hot and sunny day, in the tall grass beneath the shade of some deep boughs, with running water murmuring near, hearing the summer bee buzzing monotonously, and in the distance, the clear, sharp tinkle of the sheep-bell. In such a place, at such a time, one's fancy strays playfully, like some happy child, and none but pleasant thoughts present themselves. Fatigued by my long walk, and overcome by heat, I fell asleep. How long I lay there I cannot tell, but the deep shadows were half way down the tall mountain when I awoke. A sound had startled me; I thought I heard a voice speaking close to me. I looked up, and for some seconds I could not believe that I was not dreaming. Beside me, within a few paces, stood Isabella, the beautiful vision that I had seen at Barmouth, but far, a thousand times, more beautiful. She was dressed in something like a peasant's dress, and wore the round hat which, in Wales at least, seems to suit the character of the female face so well; her long and waving ringlets fell carelessly upon her shoulders, and her cheek flushed from walking. Before I had a moment's notice to recover my roving thought, she spoke; her voice was full and round, but soft and thrilling, as she said,—

"'I beg pardon, sir, for having disturbed you unconsciously; but, having done so, may I request you will assist me to fill this pitcher with water?'

"She pointed at the same time to a small stream which trickled down a fissure in the rock, and formed a little well of clear water beneath. I bowed deeply, and murmuring something, I know not what, took the pitcher from her hand, and scaling the rocky cliff, mounted to the clear source above, where having filled the vessel, I descended. When I reached the ground beneath, I discovered that she was joined by another person whom, in an instant, I recognized to be the old gentleman I had seen with her at Barmouth, and who in the most courteous manner apologized for the trouble I had been caused, and informed me that a party of his friends were enjoying a little picnic quite near, and invited me to make one of them.

"I need not say that I accepted the invitation, nor that with delight I seized the opportunity of forming an acquaintance with Isabella, who, I must confess, upon her part showed no disinclination to the prospect of my joining the party.

"After a few minutes' walking, we came to a small rocky point which projected for some distance into the lake, and offered a view for several miles of the vale of Llanberris. Upon this lovely spot we found the party assembled; they consisted of about fourteen or fifteen persons, all busily engaged in the arrangement of a very excellent cold dinner, each individual having some peculiar province allotted to him or her, to be performed by their own hands. Thus, one elderly gentlemen was whipping cream under a chestnut-tree, while a very fashionably-dressed young man was washing radishes in the lake; an old lady with spectacles was frying salmon over a wood-fire, opposite to a short, pursy man with a bald head and drab shorts, deep in the mystery of a chicken salad, from which he never lifted his eyes when I came up. It was thus I found how the fair Isabella's lot had been cast, as a drawer of water; she, with the others, contributing her share of exertion for the common good. The old gentleman who accompanied her seemed the only unoccupied person, and appeared to be regarded as the ruler of the feast; at least, they all called him general, and implicitly followed every suggestion he threw out. He was a man of a certain grave and quiet manner, blended with a degree of mild good-nature and courtesy, that struck me much at first, and gained greatly on me, even in the few minutes I conversed with him as we came along. Just before he presented me to his friends, he gently touched my arm, and drawing me aside, whispered in my ear:—

"'Don't be surprised at anything you may hear to-day here; for I must inform you this is a kind of club, as I may call it, where every one assumes a certain character, and is bound to sustain it under a penalty. We have these little meetings every now and then; and as strangers are never present, I feel some explanation necessary, that you may be able to enjoy the thing,—you understand?'

"'Oh, perfectly,' said I, overjoyed at the novelty of the scene, and anticipating much pleasure from my chance meeting with such very original characters.

"'Mr. Sparks, Mrs. Winterbottom. Allow me to present Mr. Sparks.'

"'Any news from Batavia, young gentleman?' said the sallow old lady addressed. 'How is coffee!'

"The general passed on, introducing me rapidly as he went.

"'Mr. Doolittle, Mr. Sparks.'

"'Ah, how do you do, old boy?' said Mr. Doolittle; 'sit down beside me. We have forty thousand acres of pickled cabbage spoiling for want of a little vinegar.'

"'Fie, fie, Mr. Doolittle,' said the general, and passed on to another.

"'Mr. Sparks, Captain Crosstree.'

"'Ah, Sparks, Sparks! son of old Blazes! ha, ha, ha!' and the captain fell back into an immoderate fit of laughter.

"'*Le Rio est serci*,' said the thin meagre figure in nankeens, bowing, cap in hand, before the general; and accordingly, we all assumed our places upon the grass.

"'Say it again! Say it again, and I'll plunge this dagger in your heart!' said a hollow voice, tremulous with agitation and rage, close beside me. I turned my head, and saw an old gentleman with a wart on his nose, sitting opposite a meat-pie, which he was contemplating with a look of fiery indignation. Before I could witness the sequel of the scene, I felt a soft hand pressed upon mine. I turned. It was Isabella herself, who, looking at me with an expression I shall never forget, said:—

"'Don't mind poor Faddy; he never hurts any one.'

"Meanwhile the business of dinner went on rapidly. The servants, of whom enormous numbers were now present, ran hither and thither; and duck, ham, pigeon-pie, cold veal, apple tarts, cheese, pickled salmon, melon, and rice pudding, flourished on every side. As for me, whatever I might have gleaned from the conversation around under other circumstances, I was too much occupied with Isabella to think of any one else. My suit—for such it was—progressed rapidly. There was evidently something favorable in the circumstances we last met under; for her manner had all the warmth and cordiality of old friendship. It is true that, more than once, I caught the general's eye fixed upon us with anything but an expression of pleasure, and I thought that Isabella blushed and seemed confused also. 'What care I?' however, was my reflection; 'my views are honorable; and the nephew and heir of Sir Toby Sparks—' Just in the very act of making this reflection, the old man in the shorts hit me in the eye with a roasted apple, calling out at the moment:—

"'When did you join, thou child of the pale-faces?'

"'Mr. Murdocks!' cried the general, in a voice of thunder; and the little man hung down his head, and spoke not.

"'A word with you, young gentleman,' said a fat old lady, pinching my arm above the elbow.

"'Never mind her,' said Isabella, smiling; 'poor dear old Dorking, she thinks she's an hour-glass. How droll, isn't it?'

"'Young man, have you any feelings of humanity?' inquired the old lady, with tears in her eyes as she spoke; 'will you, dare you assist a fellow-creature under my sad circumstances?'

"'What can I do for you, Madam?' said I, really feeling for her distress.

"'Just like a good dear soul, just turn me up, for I'm nearly run out.'

"Isabella burst out a laughing at the strange request,—an excess which, I confess, I was unable myself to repress; upon which the old lady, putting on a frown of the most ominous blackness, said:—

"'You may laugh, Madam; but first before you ridicule the misfortunes of others, ask yourself are you, too, free from infirmity? When did you see the ace of spades, Madam? Answer me that.'

"Isabella became suddenly pale as death; her very lips blanched, and her voice, almost inaudible, muttered:—

"'Am I, then, deceived? Is not this he?' So saying, she placed her hand upon my shoulder.

"'That the ace of spades?' exclaimed the old lady, with a sneer,—'that the ace of spades!'

"'Are you, or are you not, sir?' said Isabella, fixing her deep and languid eyes upon me. 'Answer me, as you are honest; are you the ace of spades?'

"'He is the King of Tuscarora. Look at his war paint!' cried an elderly gentleman, putting a streak of mustard across my nose and cheek.

"'Then am I deceived,' said Isabella. And flying at me, she plucked a handful of hair out of my whiskers.

"'Cuckoo, cuckoo!' shouted one; 'Bow-wow-wow!' roared another; 'Phiz!' went a third; and in an instant, such a scene of commotion and riot ensued. Plates, dishes, knives, forks, and decanters flew right and left; every one pitched into his neighbor with the most fearful cries, and hell itself seemed broke loose. The hour-glass and the Moulah of Oude had got me down and were pummelling me to death, when a short, thickset man came on all fours slap down upon them shouting out, 'Way, make way for the royal Bengal tiger!' at which they both fled like lightning, leaving me to the encounter single-handed. Fortunately, however, this was not of very long duration, for some well-disposed Christians pulled him from off me; not, however, before he had seized me in his grasp, and bitten off a portion of my left ear, leaving me, as you see, thus mutilated for the rest of my days."

"What an extraordinary club," broke in the doctor.

"Club, sir, club! it was a lunatic asylum. The general was no other than the famous Dr. Andrew Moorville, that had the great madhouse at Bangor, and who was in the habit of giving his patients every now and then a kind of country party; it being one remarkable feature of their malady that when one takes to his peculiar flight, whatever it be, the others immediately take the hint and go off at score. Hence my agreeable adventure: the Bengal tiger being a Liverpool merchant, and the most vivacious madman in England; while the hour-glass and the Moulah were both on an experimental tour to see whether they should not be pronounced totally incurable for life."

"And Isabella?" inquired Power.

"Ah, poor Isabella had been driven mad by a card-playing aunt at Bath, and was in fact the most hopeless case there. The last words I heard her speak confirmed my mournful impression of her case,—

"'Yes,' said she, as they removed her to her carriage, 'I must, indeed, have but a weak intellect, when I could have taken the nephew of a Manchester cotton-spinner, with a face like a printed calico, for a trump card, and the best in the pack!'"

Poor Sparks uttered these last words with a faltering accent, and finishing his glass at one draught withdrew without wishing us good-night.

CHAPTER XXXIII.

THE SKIPPER.

In such like gossipings passed our days away, for our voyage itself had nothing of adventure or incident to break its dull monotony; save some few hours of calm, we had been steadily following our seaward track with a fair breeze, and the long pennant pointed ever to the land where our ardent expectations were hurrying before it.

The latest accounts which had reached us from the Peninsula told that our regiment was almost daily engaged; and we burned with impatience to share with the others the glory they were reaping. Power, who had seen service, felt less on this score than we who had not "fleshed our maiden swords;" but even he sometimes gave way, and when the wind fell toward sunset, he would break out into some exclamation of discontent, half fearing we should be too late. "For," said he, "if we go on in this way the regiment will be relieved and ordered home before we reach it."

"Never fear, my boys, you'll have enough of it. Both sides like the work too well to give in; they've got a capital ground and plenty of spare time," said the major.

"Only to think," cried Power, "that we should be lounging away our idle hours when these gallant fellows are in the saddle late and early. It is too bad; eh, O'Malley? You'll not be pleased to go back with the polish on your sabre? What will Lucy Dashwood say?"

This was the first allusion Power had ever made to her, and I became red to the very forehead.

"By-the-bye," added he, "I have a letter for Hammersley, which should rather have been entrusted to your keeping."

At these words I felt cold as death, while he continued:—

"Poor fellow! certainly he is most desperately smitten; for, mark me, when a man at his age takes the malady, it is forty times as severe as with a younger fellow, like you. But then, to be sure, he began at the wrong end in the matter; why commence with papa? When a man has his own consent for liking a girl, he must be a contemptible fellow if he can't get her; and as to anything else being wanting, I don't understand it. But the moment you begin by influencing the heads of the house, good-by to your chances with the dear thing herself, if she have any spirit whatever. It is, in fact, calling on her to surrender without the honors of war; and what girl would stand that?"

"It's vara true," said the doctor; "there's a strong speerit of opposition in the sex, from physiological causes."

"Curse your physiology, old Galen; what you call opposition, is that piquant resistance to oppression that makes half the charm of the sex. It is with them—with reverence be it spoken—as with horses: the dull, heavy-shouldered ones, that bore away with the bit in their teeth, never caring whether you are pulling to the right or to the left, are worth nothing; the real luxury is in the management of your arching-necked curvetter, springing from side to side with every motion of your wrist, madly bounding at restraint, yet, to the practised hand, held in check with a silk tread. Eh, Skipper, am I not right?"

"Well, I can't say I've had much to do with horse-beasts, but I believe you're not far wrong. The lively craft that answers the helm quick, goes round well in stays, luffs up close within a point or two, when you want her, is always a good sea-boat, even though she pitches and rolls a bit; but the heavy lugger that never knows whether your helm is up or down, whether she's off the wind or on it, is only fit for firewood,—you can do nothing with a ship or a woman if she hasn't got steerage way on her."

"Come, Skipper, we've all been telling our stories; let us hear one of yours?"

"My yarn won't come so well after your sky-scrapers of love and courting and all that. But if you like to hear what happened to me once, I have no objection to tell you.

"I often think how little we know what's going to happen to us any minute of our lives. To-day we have the breeze fair in our favor, we are going seven knots, studding-sails set, smooth water, and plenty of sea-room; to-morrow the wind freshens to half a gale, the sea gets up, a rocky coast is seen from the lee bow, and may be—to add to all—we spring a leak forward; but then, after all, bad as it looks, mayhap, we rub through even this, and with the next day, the prospect is as bright and cheering as ever. You'll perhaps ask me what has all this moralizing to do with women and ships at sea? Nothing at all with them, except that I was a going to say, that when matters look worst, very often the best is in store for us, and we should never say strike when there is a timber together. Now for my story:—

"It's about four years ago, I was strolling one evening down the side of the harbor at Cove, with my hands in my pocket, having nothing to do, nor no prospect of it, for my last ship had been wrecked off the Bermudas, and nearly all the crew lost; and somehow, when a man is in misfortune, the underwriters won't have him at no price. Well, there I was, looking about me at the craft that lay on every side waiting for a fair wind to run down channel. All was active and busy; every one getting his vessel ship-shape and tidy,—tarring, painting, mending sails, stretching new bunting, and getting in sea-store; boats were plying on every side, signals flying, guns firing from the men-of-war, and everything was lively as might be,—all but me. There I was, like an old water-logged timber ship, never moving a spar, but looking for all the world as though I were a settling fast to go down stern foremost: may be as how I had no objection to that same; but that's neither here nor there. Well, I sat down on the fluke of an anchor, and began a thinking if it wasn't better to go before the mast than live on that way. Just before me, where I sat down, there was an old schooner that lay moored in the same place for as long as I could remember. She was there when I was a boy, and never looked a bit the fresher nor newer as long as I recollected; her old bluff bows, her high poop, her round stern, her flush deck, all Dutch-like, I knew them well, and many a time I delighted to think what queer kind of a chap he was that first set her on the stocks, and pondered in what trade she ever could have been. All the sailors about the port used to call her Noah's Ark, and swear she was the identical craft that he stowed away all the wild beasts in during the rainy season. Be that as it might, since I fell into misfortune, I got to feel a liking for the old schooner; she was like an old friend; she never changed to me, fair weather or foul; there she was, just the same as thirty years before, when all the world were forgetting and steering wide away from me. Every morning I used to go down to the harbor and have a look at her, just to see that all was right and nothing stirred; and if it blew very hard at night, I'd get up and go down to look how she weathered it, just as if I was at sea in her. Now and then I'd get some of the watermen to row me aboard of her, and leave me there for a few hours; when I used to be quite happy walking the deck, holding the old worm-eaten wheel, looking out ahead, and going down below, just as though I was in command of her. Day after day this habit grew on me, and at last my whole life was spent in watching her and looking after her,—-there was something so much alike in our fortunes, that I always thought of her. Like myself, she had had her day of life and activity; we had both braved the storm and the breeze; her shattered bulwarks and worn cutwater attested that she had, like myself, not escaped her calamities. We both had survived our dangers, to be neglected and forgotten, and to lie rotting on the stream of life till the crumbling hand of Time should break us up, timber by timber. Is it any wonder if I loved the old craft; nor if by any chance the idle boys would venture aboard of her to play and amuse themselves that I hallooed them away; or when a newly-arrived ship, not caring for the old boat, would run foul of her, and carry away some spar or piece of running rigging, I would suddenly call out to them to sheer off and not damage us? By degrees, they came all to notice this; and I found that they thought me out of my senses, and many a trick was played off upon old Noah, for that was the name the sailors gave me.

"Well, this evening, as I was saying, I sat upon the fluke of the anchor, waiting for a chance boat to put me aboard. It was past sunset, the tide was ebbing, and the old craft was surging to the fast current that ran by with a short, impatient jerk, as though she were well weary, and wished to be at rest; her loose stays creaked mournfully, and as she yawed over, the sea ran from many a breach in her worn sides, like blood trickling from a wound. 'Ay, ay,' thought I, 'the hour is not far off; another stiff gale, and all that remains of you will be found high and dry upon the shore.' My heart was very heavy as I thought of this; for in my loneliness, the old Ark—though that was not her name, as I'll tell you presently—was all the companion I had. I've heard of a poor prisoner who, for many and many years, watched a spider that wove his web within his window, and never lost sight of him from morning till night; and somehow, I can believe it well. The heart will cling to something, and if it has no living object to press to, it will find a lifeless one,—it can no more stand alone than the shrouds can without the mast. The evening wore on, as I was thinking thus; the moon shone out, but no boat came, and I was just determining to go home again for the night, when I saw two men standing on the steps of the wharf below me, and looking straight at the Ark. Now, I must tell you I always felt uneasy when any one came to look at her; for I began to fear that some shipowner or other would buy her to break up, though, except the copper fastenings, there was little of any value about her. Now, the moment I saw the two figures stop short, and point to her, I said to myself, 'Ah, my old girl, so they won't even let the blue water finish you, but they must set their carpenters and dockyard people to work upon you.' This thought grieved me more and more. Had a stiff sou'-wester laid her over, I should have felt it more natural, for her sand was run out; but just as this passed through my mind, I heard a voice from one of the persons, that I at once knew to be the port admiral's:—

"'Well, Dawkins,' said he to the other, 'if you think she'll hold together, I'm sure I've no objection. I don't like the job, I confess; but still the Admiralty must be obeyed.'

"'Oh, my lord,' said the other, 'she's the very thing; she's a rakish-looking craft, and will do admirably. Any repair we want, a few days will effect; secrecy is the great thing.'

"'Yes,' said the admiral, after a pause, 'as you observed, secrecy is the great thing.'

"'Ho! ho!' thought I, 'there's something in the wind, here;' so I laid myself out upon the anchor-stock, to listen better, unobserved.

"'We must find a crew for her, give her a few carronades, make her as ship-shape as we can, and if the skipper—'

"'Ay, but there is the real difficulty,' said the admiral, hastily; 'where are we to find a fellow that will suit us? We can't every day find a man willing to jeopardize himself in such a cause as this, even though the reward be a great one.'

"'Very true, my lord; but I don't think there is any necessity for our explaining to him the exact nature of the service.'

"'Come, come, Dawkins, you can't mean that you'll lead a poor fellow into such a scrape blindfolded?'

"'Why, my lord, you never think it requisite to give a plan of your cruise to your ship's crew before clearing out of harbor.'

"'This may be perfectly just, but I don't like it,' said the admiral.

"'In that case, my lord, you are imparting the secrets of the Admiralty to a party who may betray the whole plot.'

"'I wish, with all my soul, they'd given the order to any one else,' said the admiral, with a sigh; and for a few moments neither spoke a word.

"'Well, then, Dawkins, I believe there is nothing for it but what you say; meanwhile, let the repairs be got in hand, and see after a crew.'

"'Oh, as to that,' said the other, 'there are plenty of scoundrels in the fleet here fit for nothing else. Any fellow who has been thrice up for punishment in six months, we'll draft on board of her; the fellows who have only been once to the gangway, we'll make the officers.'

"'A pleasant ship's company,' thought I, 'if the Devil would only take the command.

"'And with a skipper proportionate to their merit,' said Dawkins.

"'Begad, I'll wish the French joy of them,' said the admiral.

"'Ho, ho!' thought I, 'I've found you out at last; so this is a secret expedition. I see it all; they're fitting her out as a fire-ship, and going to send her slap in among the French fleet at Brest. Well,' thought I, 'even that's better; that, at least, is a glorious end, though the poor fellows have no chance of escape.'

"'Now, then,' said the admiral, 'to-morrow you'll look out for the fellow to take the command. He must be a smart seaman, a bold fellow, too, otherwise the ruffianly crew will be too much for him; he may bid high, we'll come to his price.'

"'So you may,' thought I, 'when you're buying his life.'

"'I hope sincerely,' continued the admiral, 'that we may light upon some one without wife or child; I never could forgive myself—'

"'Never fear, my lord,' said the other; 'my care shall be to pitch upon one whose loss no one would feel; some one without friend or home, who, setting his life for nought, cares less for the gain than the very recklessness of the adventure.'

"'That's me,' said I, springing up from the anchor-stock, and springing between them; 'I'm that man.'

"Had the very Devil himself appeared at the moment, I doubt if they would have been more scared. The admiral started a pace or two backwards, while Dawkins, the first surprise over, seized me by the collar, and hold me fast.

"'Who are you, scoundrel, and what brings you here?' said he, in a voice hoarse with passion.

"'I'm old Noah,' said I; for somehow, I had been called by no other name for so long, I never thought of my real one.

"'Noah!' said the admiral,—'Noah! Well, but Noah, what were you doing here at this time of night?'

"'I was a watching the Ark, my lord,' said I, bowing, as I took off my hat.

"'I've heard of this fellow before, my lord,' said Dawkins; 'he's a poor lunatic that is always wandering about the harbor, and, I believe, has no harm in him.'

"'Yes, but he has been listening, doubtless, to our conversation,' said the admiral. 'Eh, have you heard all we have been saying?'

"'Every word of it, my lord.'

"At this the admiral and Dawkins looked steadfastly at each other for some minutes, but neither spoke; at last Dawkins said, 'Well, Noah, I've been told you are a man to be depended on; may we rely upon your not repeating anything you overheard this evening,—at least, for a year to come?'

"'You may,' said I.

"'But, Dawkins,' said the admiral, in a half-whisper, 'if the poor fellow be mad?'

"'My lord,' said I, boldly, 'I am not mad. Misfortune and calamity I have had enough of to make me so; but, thank God, my brain has been tougher than my poor heart. I was once the part-owner and commander of a goodly craft, that swept the sea, if not with a broad pennon at her mast-head, with as light a spirit as ever lived beneath one. I was rich, I had a home and a child; I am now poor, houseless, childless, friendless, and an outcast. If in my solitary wretchedness I have loved to look upon that old bark, it is because its fortune seemed like my own. It had outlived all that needed or cared for it. For this reason have they thought me mad, though there are those, and not few either, who can well bear testimony if stain or reproach lie at my door, and if I can be reproached with aught save bad luck. I have heard by chance what you have said this night. I know that you are fitting out a secret expedition; I know its dangers, its inevitable dangers, and I here offer myself to lead it. I ask no reward; I look for no price. Alas, who is left to me for whom I could labor now? Give me but the opportunity to end my clays with honor on board the old craft, where my heart still clings; give me but that. Well, if you will not do so much, let me serve among the crew; put me before the mast. My lord, you'll not refuse this. It is an old man asks; one whose gray hairs have floated many a year ago before the breeze.'

"'My poor fellow, you know not what you ask; this is no common case of danger.'

"'I know it all, my lord; I have heard it all.'

"'Dawkins, what is to be done here?' inquired the admiral.

"'I say, friend,' inquired Dawkins, laying his hand upon my arm, 'what is your real name? Are you he who commanded the "Dwarf" privateer in the Isle of France?'

"'The same.'

"'Then you are known to Lord Collingwood?'

"'He knows me well, and can speak to my character.'

"'What he says of himself is all true, my lord.'

"'True,' said I, 'true! You did not doubt it, did you?'

"'We,' said the admiral, 'must speak together again. Be here to-morrow night at this hour; keep your own counsel of what has passed, and now good-night.' So saying, the admiral took Dawkins by the arm and returned slowly towards the town, leaving me where I stood, meditating on this singular meeting and its possible consequences.

"The whole of the following day was passed by me in a state of feverish excitement which I cannot describe; this strange adventure breaking in so suddenly upon the dull monotony of my daily existence had so aroused and stimulated me that I could neither rest nor eat. How I longed for night to come; for sometimes, as the day wore later, I began to fear that the whole scene of my meeting with the admiral had been merely some excited dream of a tortured and fretted mind; and as I stood examining the ground where I believed the interview to have occurred, I endeavored to recall the position of different objects as they stood around, to corroborate my own failing remembrance.

"At last the evening closed in; but unlike the preceding one, the sky was covered with masses of dark and watery cloud that drifted hurriedly across; the air felt heavy and thick, and unnaturally still and calm; the water of the harbor looked of a dull, leaden hue, and all the vessels seemed larger than they were, and stood out from the landscape more clearly than usual; now and then a low rumbling noise was heard, somewhat alike in sound, but far too faint for distant thunder, while occasionally the boats and smaller craft rocked to and fro, as though some ground swell stirred them without breaking the languid surface of the sea above.

"A few drops of thick, heavy rain fell just as the darkness came on, and then all felt still and calm as before. I sat upon the anchor-stock, my eyes fixed upon the old Ark, until gradually her outline grew fainter and fainter against the dark sky, and her black hull could scarcely be distinguished from the water beneath. I felt that I was looking towards her; for long after I had lost sight of the tall mast and high-pitched bowsprit, I feared to turn away my head lest I should lose the place where she lay.

"The time went slowly on, and although in reality I had not been long there, I felt as if years themselves had passed over my head. Since I had come there my mind brooded over all the misfortunes of my life; as I contrasted its outset, bright with hope and rich in promise, with the sad reality, my heart grew heavy and my chest heaved painfully. So sunk was I in my reflections, so lost in thought, that I never knew that the storm had broken loose, and that the heavy rain was falling in torrents. The very ground, parched with long drought, smoked as it pattered upon it; while the low, wailing cry of the sea-gull, mingled with the deep growl of far-off thunder, told that the night was a fearful one for those at sea. Wet through and shivering, I sat still, now listening amidst the noise of the hurricane and the creaking of the cordage for any footstep to approach, and now relapsing back into half-despairing dread that my heated brain alone had conjured up the scene of the day before. Such were my dreary reflections when a loud crash aboard the schooner told me that some old spar had given way. I strained my eyes through the dark to see what had happened, but in vain; the black vapor, thick with falling rain, obscured everything, and all was hid from view. I could hear that she worked violently as the waves beat against her worn sides, and that her iron cable creaked as she pitched to the breaking sea. The wind was momentarily increasing, and I began to fear lest I should have taken my last look at the old craft, when my attention was called off by hearing a loud voice cry out, 'Halloo there! Where are you?'

"'Ay, ay, sir, I'm here.' In a moment the admiral and his friend were beside me.

"'What a night!' exclaimed the admiral, as he shook the rain from the heavy boat-cloak and cowered in beneath some tall blocks of granite near. 'I began half to hope that you might not have been here, my poor fellow,' said the admiral; 'it's a dreadful time for one so poorly clad for a storm. I say, Dawkins, let him have a pull at your flask.' The brandy rallied me a little, and I felt that it cheered my drooping courage.

"'This is not a time nor is it a place for much parley,' said the admiral, 'so that we must even make short work of it. Since we met here last night I have satisfied myself that you are to be trusted, that your character and reputation have nothing heavier against them than misfortune, which certainly, if I have been rightly informed, has been largely dealt out to you. Now, then, I am willing to accept of your offer of service if you are still of the same mind as when you made it, and if you are willing to undertake what we have to do without any question and inquiry as to points on which we must not and dare not inform you. Whatever you may have overheard last night may or may not have put you in possession of our secret. If the former, your determination can be made at once; if the latter, you have only to decide whether you are ready to go blindfolded in the business.'

"'I am ready, my lord,' said I.

"'You perhaps are then aware what is the nature of the service?'

"'I know it not,' said I. 'All that I heard, sir, leads me to suppose it one of danger, but that's all.'

"'I think, my lord,' said Dawkins, 'that no more need now be said. Cupples is ready to engage, we are equally so to accept; the thing is pressing. When can you sail?'

"'To-night,' said I, 'if you will.'

"'Really, Dawkins,' said the admiral, 'I don't see why—'

"'My lord, I beg of you,' said the other, interrupting, 'let me now complete the arrangement. This is the plan,' said he, turning towards me as he spoke: 'As soon as that old craft can be got ready for sea, or some other if she be not worth it, you will sail from this port with a strong crew, well armed and supplied with ammunition. Your destination is Malta, your object to deliver to the admiral stationed there the despatches with which you will be entrusted; they contain information of immense importance, which for certain reasons cannot be sent through a ship of war, but must be forwarded by a vessel that may not attract peculiar notice. If you be attacked, your orders are to resist; if you be taken, on no account destroy the papers, for the French vessel can scarcely escape capture from our frigates, and it is of great consequence these papers should remain. Such is a brief sketch of our plan; the details can be made known to you hereafter.'

"'I am quite ready, my lord. I ask for no terms; I make no stipulations. If the result be favorable it will be time enough to speak of that. When am I to sail?'

"As I spoke, the admiral turned suddenly round and said something in a whisper to Dawkins, who appeared to overrule it, whatever it might be, and finally brought him over to his own opinion.

"'Come, Cupples,' said Dawkins, 'the affair is now settled; to-morrow a boat will be in waiting for you opposite Spike Island to convey you on board the "Semiramis," where every step in the whole business shall be explained to you; meanwhile you have only to keep your own counsel and trust the secret to no one.'

"'Yes, Cupples,' said the admiral, 'we rely upon you for that, so good-night.' As he spoke he placed within my hands a crumpled note for ten pounds, and squeezing my fingers, departed.

"My yarn is spinning out to a far greater length than I intended, so I'll try and shorten it a bit. The next day I went aboard the 'Semiramis,' where, when I appeared upon the quarter-deck, I found myself an object of some interest. The report that I was the man about to command the 'Brian,'—that was the real name of the old craft,—had caused some curiosity among the officers, and they all spoke to me with great courtesy. After waiting a short time I was ordered to go below, where the admiral, his flag-captain, Dawkins, and the others were seated. They repeated at greater length the conversation of the night before, and finally decided that I was to sail in three weeks; for although the old schooner was sadly damaged, they had lost no time, but had her already high in dock, with two hundred ship-carpenters at work upon her.

"I do not shorten sail here to tell you what reports were circulated about Cove as to my extraordinary change in circumstances, nor how I bore my altered fortunes. It is enough if I say that in less than three weeks I weighed anchor and stood out to sea one beautiful morning in autumn, and set out upon my expedition.

"I have already told you something of the craft. Let me complete the picture by informing you that before twenty-four hours passed over I discovered that so ungainly, so awkward, so unmanageable a vessel never put to sea. In light winds she scarcely stirred or moved, as if she were waterlogged; if it came to blow upon the quarter, she fell off from her helm at a fearful rate; in wearing, she endangered every spar she had; and when you put her in stays, when half round she would fall back and nearly carry away every stitch of canvas with the shock. If the ship was bad, the crew was ten times worse. What Dawkins said turned out to be literally true. Every ill-conducted, disorderly fellow who had been up the gangway once a week or so, every unreclaimed landsman of bad character and no seamanship, was sent on board of us: and in fact, except that there was scarcely any discipline and no restraint, we appeared like a floating penitentiary of convicted felons.

So long as we ran down channel with a slack sea and fair wind, so long all went on tolerably well; to be sure they only kept watch when they were tired below, when they came up, reeled about the deck, did all just as they pleased, and treated me with no manner of respect. After some vain efforts to repress their excesses,—vain, for I had but one to second me,—I appeared to take no notice of their misconduct, and contented myself with waiting for the time when, my dreary voyage over, I should quit the command and part company with such associates forever. At last, however, it came on to blow, and the night we passed the Lizard was indeed a fearful one. As morning broke, a sea running mountains high, a wind strong from the northwest, was hurrying the old craft along at a rate I believed impossible. I shall not stop to recount the frightful scenes of anarchy, confusion, drunkenness, and insubordination which our crew exhibited,—the recollection is too bad already, and I would spare you and myself the recital; but on the fourth day from the setting in of the gale, as we entered the Bay of Biscay, some one aloft descried a strange sail to windward bearing down as if in pursuit of us. Scarcely did the news reach the deck when, bad as it was before, matters became now ten times worse, some resolving to give themselves up if the chase happened to be French, and vowing that before surrendering the spirit-room should be forced, and every man let drink as he pleased. Others proposed if there were anything like equality in the force, to attack, and convert the captured vessel, if they succeeded, into a slaver, and sail at once for Africa. Some were for blowing up the old 'Brian' with all on board; and in fact every counsel that drunkenness, insanity, and crime combined could suggest was offered and descanted on. Meanwhile the chase gained rapidly upon us, and before noon we discovered her to be a French letter-of-marque with four guns and a long brass swivel upon the poop deck. As for us, every sheet of canvas we could crowd was crammed on, but in vain. And as we labored through the heavy sea, our riotous crew grew every moment worse, and sitting down sulkily in groups upon the deck, declared that, come what might, they would neither work the ship nor fight her; that they had been sent to sea in a rotten craft merely to effect their destruction; and that they cared little for the disgrace of a flag they detested. Half furious with the taunting sarcasm I heard on every side, and nearly mad from passion, and bewildered, my first impulse was to run among them with my drawn cutlass, and ere I fell their victim, take heavy vengeance upon the ringleaders, when suddenly a sharp booming noise came thundering along, and a round shot went flying over our heads.

"'Down with the ensign; strike at once!' cried eight or ten voices together, as the ball whizzed through the rigging. Anticipating this, and resolving, whatever might happen, to fight her to the last, I had made the mate, a staunch-hearted, resolute fellow, to make fast the signal sailyard aloft, so that it was impossible for any one on deck to lower the bunting. Bang! went another gun; and before the smoke cleared away, a third, which, truer in its aim than the rest, went clean through the lower part of our mainsail.

"'Steady, then, boys, and clear for action,' said the mate.

'She's a French smuggling craft that will sheer off when we show fight, so that we must not fire a shot till she comes alongside.'

"'And harkee, lads,' said I, taking up the tone of encouragement he spoke with, 'if we take her, I promise to claim nothing of the prize. Whatever we capture you shall divide among yourselves.'

"'It's very easy to divide what we never had,' said one; 'Nearly as easy as to give it,' cried another; 'I'll never light match or draw cutlass in the cause,' said a third.

"'Surrender!' 'Strike the flag!' 'Down with the colors!' roared several voices together.

"By this time the Frenchman was close up, and ranging his long gun to sweep our decks; his crew were quite perceptible,—about twenty bronzed, stout-looking follows, stripped to the waist, and carrying pistols in broad flat belts slung over the shoulder.

"'Come, my lads,' said I, raising my voice, as I drew a pistol from my side and cocked it, 'our time is short now; I may as well tell you that the first shot that strikes us amidship blows up the whole craft and every man on board. We are nothing less than a fireship, destined for Brest harbor to blow up the French fleet. If you are willing to make an effort for your lives, follow me!'

"The men looked aghast. Whatever recklessness crime and drunkenness had given them, the awful feeling of inevitable death at once repelled. Short as was the time for reflection, they felt that there were many circumstances to encourage the assertion,—the nature of the vessel, her riotous, disorderly crew, the secret nature of the service, all confirmed it,—and they answered with a shout of despairing vengeance, 'We'll board her; lead us on!' As the cry rose up, the long swivel from the chase rang sharply in our ears, and a tremendous discharge of grape flew through our rigging. None of our men, however, fell; and animated now with the desire for battle, they sprang to the binnacle, and seized their arms.

"In an instant the whole deck became a scene of excited bustle; and scarcely was the ammunition dealt out, and the boarding party drawn up, when the Frenchman broached to and lashed his bowsprit to our own.

"One terrific yell burst from our fellows as they sprang from the rigging and the poop upon the astonished Frenchmen, who thought that the victory was already their own; with death and ruin behind, their only hope before, they dashed forward like madmen to the fray.

"The conflict was bloody and terrific, though not a long one. Nearly equal in number, but far superior in personal strength, and stimulated by their sense of danger, our fellows rushed onward, carrying all before them to the quarter-deck. Here the Frenchmen rallied, and for some minutes had rather the advantage, until the mate, turning one of their guns against them, prepared to sweep them down in a mass. Then it was that they ceased their fire and cried out for quarter,—all save their captain, a short, thick-set fellow, with a grizzly beard and mustache, who, seeing his men fall back, turned on them one glance of scowling indignation, and rushing forward, clove our boatswain to the deck with one blow. Before the example could have been followed, he lay a bloody corpse upon the deck; while our people, roused to madness by the loss of a favorite among the men, dashed impetuously forward, and dealing death on every side, left not one man living among their unresisting enemies. My story is soon told now. We brought our prize safe into Malta, which we reached in five days. In less than a week our men were drafted into different men-of-war on the station. I was appointed a warrant officer in the 'Sheerwater,' forty-four guns; and as the admiral opened the despatch, the only words he spoke puzzled me for many a day after.

"'You have accomplished your orders too well,' said he; 'that privateer is but a poor compensation for the whole French navy.'"

"Well," inquired Power, "and did you never hear the meaning of the words?"

"Yes," said he; "many years after I found out that our despatches were false ones, intended to have fallen into the hands of the French and mislead them as to Lord Nelson's fleet, which at that time was cruising to the southward to catch them. This, of course, explained what fate was destined for us,—a French prison, if not death; and after all, either was fully good enough for the crew that sailed in the old 'Brian.'"

CHAPTER XXXIV.
THE LAND.

It was late when we separated for the night, and the morning was already far advanced ere I awoke; the monotonous tramp overhead showed me that the others were stirring, and I gently moved the shutter of the narrow window beside me to look out.

The sea, slightly rippled upon its surface, shone like a plate of fretted gold,—not a wave, not a breaker appeared; but the rushing sound close by showed that we were moving fast through the water.

"Always calm hereabouts," said a gruff voice on deck, which I soon recognized as the skipper's; "no sea whatever."

"I can make nothing of it," cried out Power, from the forepart of the vessel. "It appears to me all cloud."

"No, no, sir, believe me; it's no fog-bank, that large dark mass to leeward there,—that's Cintra."

"Land!" cried I, springing up, and rushing upon deck; "where, Skipper,—where is the land?"

"I say, Charley," said Power, "I hope you mean to adopt a little more clothing on reaching Lisbon; for though the climate is a warm one—"

"Never mind, O'Malley," said the major, "the Portuguese will only be flattered by the attention, if you land as you are."

"Why, how so?"

"Surely, you remember what the niggers said when they saw the 79th Highlanders landing at St. Lucie. They had never seen a Scotch regiment before, and were consequently somewhat puzzled at the costume; till at last, one more cunning than the rest explained it by saying: 'They are in such a hurry to kill the poor black men that they came away without their breeches.'"

"Now, what say you?" cried the skipper, as he pointed with his telescope to a dark-blue mass in the distance; "see there!"

"Ah, true enough; that's Cintra!"

"Then we shall probably be in the Tagus River before morning?"

"Before midnight, if the wind holds," said the skipper. We breakfasted on deck beneath an awning. The vessel scarcely seemed to move as she cut her way through the calm water.

The misty outline of the coast grew gradually more defined, and at length the blue mountains could be seen; at first but dimly, but as the day wore on, their many-colored hues shone forth, and patches of green verdure, dotted with sheep or sheltered by dark foliage, met the eye. The bulwarks were crowded with anxious faces; each looked pointedly towards the shore, and many a stout heart beat high, as the land drew near, fated to cover with its earth more than one among us.

"And that's Portingale, Mister Charles," said a voice behind me. I turned and saw my man Mike, as with anxious joy, he fixed his eyes upon the shore.

"They tell me it's a beautiful place, with wine for nothing and spirits for less. Isn't it a pity they won't be raisonable and make peace with us?"

"Why, my good fellow, we are excellent friends; it's the French who want to beat us all."

"Upon my conscience, that's not right. There's an ould saying in Connaught, 'It's not fair for one to fall upon twenty.' Sergeant Haggarty says that I'll see none of the divarsion at all."

"I don't well understand—"

"He does be telling me that, as I'm only your footboy, he'll send me away to the rear, where there's nothing but wounded and wagons and women."

"I believe the sergeant is right there; but after all, Mike, it's a safe place."

"Ah, then, musha for the safety! I don't think much of it. Sure, they might circumvint us. And av it wasn't displazing to you, I'd rather list."

"Well, I've no objection, Mickey. Would you like to join my regiment?"

"By coorse, your honor. I'd like to be near yourself; bekase, too, if anything happens to you,—the Lord be betune us and harm," here he crossed himself piously,—"sure, I'd like to be able to tell the master how you died; and sure, there's Mr. Considine—God pardon him! He'll be beating my brains out av I couldn't explain it all."

"Well, Mike, I'll speak to some of my friends here about you, and we'll settle it all properly. Here's the doctor."

"Arrah, Mr. Charles, don't mind him. He's a poor crayture entirely. Devil a thing he knows."

"Why, what do you mean, man? He's physician to the forces."

"Oh, be-gorra, and so he may be!" said Mike, with a toss of his head. "Those army docthers isn't worth their salt. It's thruth I'm telling you. Sure, didn't he come to see me when I was sick below in the hould?

"'How do you feel?' says he.

"'Terribly dhry in the mouth,' says I.

"'But your bones,' says he; 'how's them?'

"'As if cripples was kicking me,' says I.

"Well, with that he wint away, and brought back two powders.

"'Take them,' says he, 'and you'll be cured in no time.'

"'What's them?' says I.

"'They're ematics,' says he.

"'Blood and ages!' says I, 'are they?'

"'Devil a lie,' says he; 'take them immediately.'

"And I tuk them; and would you believe me, Mister Charles?—it's thruth I'm telling you,—devil a one o' them would stay on my stomach. So you see what a docther he is!"

I could not help smiling at Mike's ideas of medicine, as I turned away to talk to the major, who was busily engaged beside me. His occupation consisted in furbishing up a very tarnished and faded uniform, whose white seams and threadbare lace betokened many years of service.

"Getting up our traps, you see, O'Malley," said he, as he looked with no small pride at the faded glories of his old vestment. "Astonish them at Lisbon, we flatter ourselves. I say, Power, what a bad style of dress they've got into latterly, with their tight waist and strapped trousers; nothing free, nothing easy, nothing *dégagé* about it. When in a campaign, a man ought to be able to stow prog for twenty-four hours about his person, and no one the wiser. A very good rule, I assure you, though it sometimes leads to awkward results. At Vimeira, I got into a sad scrape that way. Old Sir Harry, that commanded there, sent for the sick return. I was at dinner when the orderly came, so I packed up the eatables about me, and rode off. Just, however, as I came up to the quarters, my horse stumbled and threw me slap on my head.

"'Is he killed?' said Sir Harry.

"'Only stunned, your Excellency,' said some one.

"'Then he'll come to, I suppose. Look for the papers in his pocket.'

"So they turned me on my back, and plunged a hand into my side-pocket; but, the devil take it! they pulled out a roast hen. Well, the laugh was scarcely over at this, when another fellow dived into my coat behind, and lugged out three sausages; and so they went on, till the ground was covered with ham, pigeon-pie, veal, kidney, and potatoes; and the only thing like a paper was a mess-roll of the 4th, with a droll song about Sir Harry written in pencil on the back of it. Devil of a bad affair for me! I was nearly broke for it; but they only reprimanded me a little, and I was afterwards attached to the victualling department."

What an anxious thing is the last day of a voyage! How slowly creep the hours, teeming with memories of the past and expectations of the future!

Every plan, every well-devised expedient to cheat the long and weary days is at once abandoned; the chess-board and the new novel are alike forgotten, and the very quarter-deck walk, with its merry gossip and careless chit-chat, becomes distasteful. One blue and misty mountain, one faint outline of the far-off shore, has dispelled all thought of these; and with straining eye and anxious heart, we watch for land.

As the day wears on apace, the excitement increases; the faint and shadowy forms of distant objects grow gradually clearer. Where before some tall and misty mountain peak was seen, we now descry patches of deepest blue and sombre olive; the mellow corn and the waving woods, the village spire and the lowly cot, come out of the landscape; and like some well-remembered voice, they speak of home. The objects we have seen, the sounds we have heard a hundred times before without interest, become to us now things that stir the heart.

For a time the bright glare of the noonday sun dazzles the view and renders indistinct the prospect; but as evening falls, once more is all fair and bright and rich before us. Rocked by the long and rolling swell, I lay beside the bowsprit, watching the shore-birds that came to rest upon the rigging, or following some long and tangled seaweed as it floated by; my thoughts now wandering back to the brown hills and the broad river of my early home, now straying off in dreary fancies of the future.

How flat and unprofitable does all ambition seem at such moments as these; how valueless, how poor, in our estimation, those worldly distinctions we have so often longed and thirsted for, as with lowly heart and simple spirit we watch each humble cottage, weaving to ourselves some story of its inmates as we pass!

The night at length closed in, but it was a bright and starry one, lending to the landscape a hue of sombre shadow, while the outlines of the objects were still sharp and distinct as before. One solitary star twinkled near the horizon. I watched it as, at intervals disappearing, it would again shine out, marking the calm sea with a tall pillar of light.

"Come down, Mr. O'Malley," cried the skipper's well-known voice,—"come down below and join us in a parting glass; that's the Lisbon light to leeward, and before two hours we drop our anchor in the Tagus."

CHAPTER XXXV.

MAJOR MONSOON.

Of my travelling companions I have already told my readers something. Power is now an old acquaintance; to Sparks I have already presented them; of the adjutant they are not entirely ignorant; and it therefore only remains for me to introduce to their notice Major Monsoon. I should have some scruple for the digression which this occasions in my narrative, were it not that with the worthy major I was destined to meet subsequently; and indeed served under his orders for some months in the Peninsula. When Major Monsoon had entered the army or in what precise capacity, I never yet met the man who could tell. There were traditionary accounts of his having served in the East Indies and in Canada in times long past. His own peculiar reminiscences extended to nearly every regiment in the service, "horse, foot, and dragoons." There was not a clime he had not basked in; not an engagement he had not witnessed. His memory, or, if you will, his invention, was never at fault; and from the siege of Seringapatam to the battle of Corunna he was perfect. Besides this, he possessed a mind retentive of even the most trifling details of his profession,—from the formation of a regiment to the introduction of a new button, from the laying down of a parallel to the price of a camp-kettle, he knew it all. To be sure, he had served in the commissary-general's department for a number of years, and nothing instils such habits as this.

"The commissaries are to the army what the special pleaders are to the bar," observed my friend Power,—"dry dogs, not over creditable on the whole, but devilish useful."

The major had begun life a two-bottle man; but by a studious cultivation of his natural gifts, and a steady determination to succeed, he had, at the time I knew him, attained to his fifth.

It need not be wondered at, then, that his countenance bore some traces of his habits. It was of a deep sunset-purple, which, becoming tropical, at the tip of the nose verged almost upon a plum-color; his mouth was large, thick-lipped, and good-humored; his voice rich, mellow, and racy, and contributed, with the aid of a certain dry, chuckling laugh, greatly to increase the effect of the stories which he was ever ready to recount; and as they most frequently bore in some degree against some of what he called his little failings, they were ever well received, no man being so popular with the world as he who flatters its vanity at his own expense. To do this the major was ever ready, but at no time more so than when the evening wore late, and the last bottle of his series seemed to imply that any caution regarding the nature of his communication was perfectly unnecessary. Indeed, from the commencement of his evening to the close, he seemed to pass through a number of mental changes, all in a manner preparing him for this final consummation, when he confessed anything and everything; and so well regulated had those stages become, that a friend dropping in upon him suddenly could at once pronounce from the tone of his conversation on what precise bottle the major was then engaged.

Thus, in the outset he was gastronomic,—discussed the dinner from the soup to the Stilton; criticised the cutlets; pronounced upon the merits of the mutton; and threw out certain vague hints that he would one day astonish the world by a little volume upon cookery.

With bottle No. 2 he took leave of the *cuisine*, and opened his battery upon the wine. Bordeaux, Burgundy, hock, and hermitage, all passed in review before him,—their flavor discussed, their treatment descanted upon, their virtues extolled; from humble port to imperial tokay, he was thoroughly conversant with all, and not a vintage escaped as to when the sun had suffered eclipse, or when a comet had wagged his tail over it.

With No. 3 he became pipeclay,—talked army list and eighteen manoeuvres, lamented the various changes in equipments which modern innovation had introduced, and feared the loss of pigtails might sap the military spirit of the nation.

With No. 4 his anecdotic powers came into play,—he recounted various incidents of the war with his own individual adventures and experience, told with an honest *naïveté*, that proved personal vanity; indeed, self-respect never marred the interest of the narrative, besides, as he had ever regarded a campaign something in the light of a foray, and esteemed war as little else than a pillage excursion, his sentiments were singularly amusing.

With his last bottle, those feelings that seemed inevitably connected with whatever is last appeared to steal over him,—a tinge of sadness for pleasures fast passing and nearly passed, a kind of retrospective glance at the fallacy of all our earthly enjoyments, insensibly suggesting moral and edifying reflections, led him by degrees to confess that he was not quite satisfied with himself, though "not very bad for a commissary;" and finally, as the decanter waxed low, he would interlard his meditations by passages of Scripture, singularly perverted by his misconception from their true meaning, and alternately throwing out prospects of censure or approval. Such was Major Monsoon; and to conclude in his own words this brief sketch, he "would have been an excellent officer if Providence had not made him such a confounded, drunken, old scoundrel."

"Now, then, for the King of Spain's story. Out with it, old boy; we are all good men and true here," cried Power, as we slowly came along upon the tide up the Tagus, "so you've nothing to fear."

"Upon my life," replied the major, "I don't half like the tone of our conversation. There is a certain freedom young men affect now a-days regarding morals that is not at all to my taste. When I was five or six and twenty—"

"You were the greatest scamp in the service," cried Power.

"Fie, fie, Fred. If I was a little wild or so,"—here the major's eyes twinkled maliciously,—"it was the ladies that spoiled me; I was always something of a favorite, just like our friend Sparks there. Not that we fared very much alike in our little adventures; for somehow, I believe I was generally in fault in most of mine, as many a good man and many an excellent man has been before." Here his voice dropped into a moralizing key, as he added, "David, you know, didn't behave well to old Uriah. Upon my life he did not, and he was a very respectable man."

"The King of Spain's sherry! the sherry!" cried I, fearing that the major's digression might lose us a good story.

"You shall not have a drop of it," replied the major.

"But the story, Major, the story!"

"Nor the story, either."

"What," said Power, "will you break faith with us?"

"There's none to be kept with reprobates like you. Fill my glass."

"Hold there! stop!" cried Power. "Not a spoonful till he redeems his pledge."

119

"Well, then, if you must have a story,—for most assuredly I must drink,—I have no objection to give you a leaf from my early reminiscences; and in compliment to Sparks there, my tale shall be of love."

"I dinna like to lose the king's story. I hae my thoughts it was na a bad ane."

"Nor I neither, Doctor; but—"

"Come, come, you shall have that too, the first night we meet in a bivouac, and as I fear the time may not be very far distant, don't be impatient; besides a love-story—"

"Quite true," said Power, "a love-story claims precedence; *place aux dames*. There's a bumper for you, old wickedness; so go along."

The major cleared off his glass, refilled it, sipped twice, and ogled it as though he would have no peculiar objection to sip once more, took a long pinch of snuff from a box nearly as long as, and something the shape of a child's coffin, looked around to see that we were all attention, and thus began:—

"When I have been in a moralizing mood, as I very frequently am about this hour in the morning, I have often felt surprised by what little, trivial, and insignificant circumstances our lot in life seems to be cast; I mean especially as regards the fair sex. You are prospering, as it were, to-day; to-morrow a new cut of your whiskers, a novel tie of your cravat, mars your destiny and spoils your future, *varium et mutabile*, as Horace has it. On the other hand, some equally slight circumstance will do what all your ingenuity may have failed to effect. I knew a fellow who married the greatest fortune in Bath, from the mere habit he had of squeezing one's hand. The lady in question thought it particular, looked conscious, and all that; he followed up the blow; and, in a word, they were married in a week. So a friend of mine, who could not help winking his left eye, once opened a flirtation with a lively widow which cost him a special license and a settlement. In fact you are never safe. They are like the guerillas, and they pick you off when you least expect it, and when you think there is nothing to fear. Therefore, as young fellows beginning life, I would caution you. On this head you can never be too circumspect. Do you know, I was once nearly caught by so slight a habit as sitting thus, with my legs across."

Here the major rested his right foot on his left knee, in illustration, and continued:—

"We were quartered in Jamaica. I had not long joined, and was about as raw a young gentleman as you could see; the only very clear ideas in my head being that we were monstrous fine fellows in the 50th, and that the planters' daughters were deplorably in love with us. Not that I was much wrong on either side. For brandy-and-water, sangaree, Manilla cigars, and the ladies of color, I'd have backed the corps against the service. Proof was, of eighteen only two ever left the island; for what with the seductions of the coffee plantations, the sugar canes, the new rum, the brown skins, the rainy season, and the yellow fever, most of us settled there."

"It's very hard to leave the West Indies if once you've been quartered there."

"So I have heard," said Power.

"In time, if you don't knock under to the climate, you become soon totally unfit for living anywhere else. Preserved ginger, yams, flannel jackets, and grog won't bear exportation; and the free-and-easy chuck under the chin, cherishing, waist-pressing kind of way we get with the ladies would be quite misunderstood in less favored regions, and lead to very unpleasant consequences."

"It is a curious fact how much climate has to do with love-making. In our cold country the progress is lamentably slow. Fogs, east winds, sleet, storms, and cutting March weather nip many a budding flirtation; whereas warm, sunny days and bright moonlight nights, with genial air and balmy zephyrs, open the heart like the cup of a camelia, and let us drink in the soft dew of—"

"Devilish poetical, that," said Power, evolving a long blue line of smoke from the corner of his mouth.

"Isn't it, though?" said the major, smiling graciously. "'Pon my life, I thought so myself. Where was I?"

"Out of my latitude altogether," said the poor skipper, who often found it hard to follow the thread of a story.

"Yes, I remember. I was remarking that sangaree and calipash, mangoes and guava jelly, dispose the heart to love, and so they do. I was not more than six weeks in Jamaica when I felt it myself. Now, it was a very dangerous symptom, if you had it strong in you, for this reason. Our colonel, the most cross-grained old crabstick that ever breathed, happened himself to be taken in when young, and resolving, like the fox who lost his tail and said it was not the fashion to wear one, to pretend he did the thing for fun, determined to make every fellow marry upon the slightest provocation. Begad, you might as well enter a powder magazine with a branch of candles in your hand, as go into society in the island with a leaning towards the fair sex. Very hard this was for me particularly; for like poor Sparks there, my weakness was ever for the petticoats. I had, besides, no petty, contemptible prejudices as to nation, habits, language, color, or complexion; black, brown, or fair, from the Muscovite to the Malabar, from the voluptuous *embonpoint* of the adjutant's widow,—don't be angry old boy,—to the fairy form of Isabella herself, I loved them all round. But were I to give a preference anywhere I should certainly do so to the West Indians, if it were only for the sake of the planters' daughters. I say it fearlessly, these colonies are the brightest jewels in the crown. Let's drink their health, for I'm as husky as a lime-kiln."

This ceremony being performed with suitable enthusiasm, the major cried out, "Another cheer for Polly Hackett, the sweetest girl in Jamaica. By Jove, Power, if you only saw her as I did five and forty years ago, with eyes black as jet, twinkling, ogling, leering, teasing, and imploring, all at once, do you mind, and a mouthful of downright pearls pouting and smiling at you, why, man, you'd have proposed for her in the first half-hour, and shot yourself the next, when she refused you. She was, indeed, a perfect little beauty, *rayther* dark, to be sure,—a little upon the rosewood tinge, but beautifully polished, and a very nice piece of furniture for a cottage *orné*, as the French call it. Alas, alas, how these vanities do catch hold of us! My recollections have made me quite feverish and thirsty. Is there any cold punch in the bowl? Thank you, O'Malley, that will do,—merely to touch my lips. Well, well, it's all past and gone now; but I was very fond of Tolly Hackett, and she was of me. We used to take our little evening walks together through the coffee plantation: very romantic little strolls they were, she in white muslin with a blue sash and blue shoes; I in a flannel jacket and trousers, straw hat and cravat, a Virginia cigar as long as a walking-stick in my mouth, puffing and courting between times; then we'd take a turn to the refining-house, look in at the big boilers, quiz the niggers, and come back to Twangberry Moss to supper, where old Hackett, the father, sported a glorious table at eleven o'clock. Great feeding it was; you were always sure of a preserved monkey, a baked land-crab, or some such delicacy. And such Madeira; it makes me dry to think of it.

"Talk of West India slavery, indeed. It's the only land of liberty. There is nothing to compare with the perfect free-and-easy, devil-may-care-kind-of-a-take-yourself way that every one has there. If it would be any peculiar comfort for you to sit in the saddle of mutton, and put your legs in a soup tureen at dinner, there would be found very few to object to it. There is no nonsense of any kind about etiquette. You eat, drink, and are merry, or, if you prefer, are sad; just as you please. You may wear uniform, or you may not, it's your own affair; and consequently, it may be imagined how insensibly such privileges gain upon one, and how very reluctant we become ever to resign or abandon them.

"I was the man to appreciate it all. The whole course of proceeding seemed to have been invented for my peculiar convenience, and not a man in the island enjoyed a more luxurious existence than myself, not knowing all the while how dearly I was destined to pay for my little comforts. Among my plenary after-dinner indulgences I had contracted an inveterate habit of sitting cross-legged, as I showed you. Now, this was become a perfect necessity of existence to me. I could have dispensed with cheese, with my glass of port, my pickled mango, my olive, my anchovy toast, my nutshell of curaçoa, but not my favorite lounge. You may smile; but I've read of a man who could never dance except in a room with an old hair-brush. Now, I'm certain my stomach would not digest if my legs were perpendicular. I don't mean to defend the thing. The attitude was not graceful, it was not imposing; but it suited me somehow, and I liked it.

"From what I have already mentioned, you may suppose that West India habits exercised but little control over my favorite practice, which I indulged in every evening of my life. Well, one day old Hackett gave us a great blow-out,—a dinner of two-and-twenty souls; six days' notice; turtle from St. Lucie, guinea-fowl, claret of the year forty, Madeira *à discrétion*, and all that. Very well done the whole thing; nothing wrong, nothing wanting. As for me, I was in great feather. I took Polly in to dinner, greatly to the discomfiture of old Belson, our major, who was making up in that quarter; for you must know, she was an only daughter, and had a very nice thing of it in molasses and niggers. The papa preferred the major, but Polly looked sweetly upon me. Well, down we went, and really a most excellent feed we had. Now, I must mention here that Polly had a favorite Blenheim spaniel the old fellow detested; it was always tripping him up and snarling at him,—for it was, except to herself, a beast of rather vicious inclinations. With a true Jamaica taste, it was her pleasure to bring the animal always into the dinner-room, where, if papa discovered him, there was sure to be a row. Servants sent in one direction to hunt him out, others endeavoring to hide him, and so on; in fact, a tremendous hubbub always followed his introduction and accompanied his exit, upon which occasions I invariably exercised my gallantry by protecting the beast, although I hated him like the devil all the time.

"To return to our dinner. After two mortal hours of hard eating, the pace began to slacken, and as evening closed in, a sense of peaceful repose seemed to descend upon our labors. Pastels shed an aromatic vapor through the room. The well-iced decanters went with measured pace along; conversation, subdued to the meridian of after-dinner comfort, just murmured; the open *jalousies* displayed upon the broad veranda the orange-tree in full blossom, slightly stirring with the cool sea-breeze."

"And the piece of white muslin beside you, what of her?"

"Looked twenty times more bewitching than ever. Well, it was just the hour when, opening the last two buttons of your white waistcoat (remember we were in Jamaica), you stretch your legs to the full extent, throw your arm carelessly over the back of your chair, look contemplatively towards the ceiling, and wonder, within yourself, why it is not all 'after dinner' in this same world of ours. Such, at least, were my reflections as I assumed my attitude of supreme comfort, and inwardly ejaculated a health to Sneyd and Barton. Just at this moment I heard Polly's voice gently whisper,—

"'Isn't he a love? Isn't he a darling?'

"'Zounds!' thought I, as a pang of jealousy shot through my heart, 'is it the major she means?' For old Belson, with his bag wig and rouged cheeks, was seated on the other side of her.

"'What a dear thing it is!' said Polly.

"'Worse and worse,' said I; 'it must be him.'

"'I do so love his muzzy face.'

"'It is him!' said I, throwing off a bumper, and almost boiling over with passion at the moment.

"'I wish I could take one look at him,' said she, laying down her head as she spoke.

"The major whispered something in her ear, to which she replied,—

"'Oh, I dare not; papa will see me at once.'

"'Don't be afraid, Madam,' said I, fiercely; 'your father perfectly approves of your taste.'

"'Are you sure of it?' said she, giving me such a look.

"'I know it,' said I, struggling violently with my agitation.

"The major leaned over as if to touch her hand beneath the cloth. I almost sprang from my chair, when Polly, in her sweetest accents, said,—

"'You must be patient, dear thing, or you may be found out, and then there will be such a piece of work. Though I'm sure, Major, you would not betray me.' The major smiled till he cracked the paint upon his cheeks. 'And I am sure that Mr. Monsoon—'

"'You may rely upon me,' said I, half sneeringly.

"The major and I exchanged glances of defiance, while Polly continued,—

"'Now, come, don't be restless. You are very comfortable there. Isn't he, Major?' The major smiled again more graciously than before, as he added,—

"'May I take a look?'

"'Just one peep, then, no more!' said she, coquettishly; 'poor dear Wowski is so timid.'

"Scarcely had these words borne balm and comfort to my heart,—for I now knew that to the dog, and not to my rival, were all the flattering expressions applied,—when a slight scream from Polly, and a tremendous oath from the major, raised me from my dream of happiness.

"'Take your foot down, sir. Mr. Monsoon, how could you do so?' cried Polly.

"'What the devil, sir, do you mean?' shouted the major.

"'Oh, I shall die of shame,' sobbed she.

"'I'll shoot him like a riddle,' muttered old Belson.

"By this time the whole table had got at the story, and such peals of laughter, mingled with suggestions for my personal maltreatment, I never heard. All my attempts at explanation were in vain. I was not listened to, much less believed; and the old colonel finished the scene by ordering me to my quarters, in a voice I shall never forget, the whole room being, at the time I made my exit, one scene of tumultuous laughter from one end to the other. Jamaica after this became too hot for me. The story was repeated on every side; for, it seems, I had been sitting with my foot on Polly's lap; but so occupied was I with my jealous vigilance of the major I was not aware of the fact until she herself discovered it.

"I need not say how the following morning brought with it every possible offer of *amende* upon my part; anything from a written apology to a proposition to marry the lady I was ready for, and how the matter might have ended I know not; for in the middle of the negotiations, we were ordered off to Halifax where, be assured, I abandoned my Oriental attitude for many a long day after."

CHAPTER XXXVI.

THE LANDING.

What a contrast to the dull monotony of our life at sea did the scene present which awaited us on landing in Lisbon. The whole quay was crowded with hundreds of people eagerly watching the vessel which bore from her mast the broad ensign of Britain. Dark-featured, swarthy, mustached faces, with red caps rakishly set on one side, mingled with the Saxon faces and fair-haired natives of our own country. Men-of-war boats plied unceasingly to and fro across the tranquil river, some slender reefer in the stern-sheets, while behind him trailed the red pennon of some "tall admiral."

The din and clamor of a mighty city mingled with the far-off sounds of military music; and in the vistas of the opening street, masses of troops might be seen in marching order; and all betokened the near approach of war.

Our anchor had scarcely been dropped, when an eight-oar gig, with a midshipman steering, came alongside.

"Ship ahoy, there! You've troops on board?"

"Ay, ay, sir."

Before the answer could be spoken, he was on the deck.

"May I ask," said he, touching his cap slightly, "who is the officer in command of the detachment?"

"Captain Power; very much at your service," said Fred, returning the salute.

"Rear-Admiral Sir Edward Douglas requests that you will do him the favor to come on board immediately, and bring your despatches with you."

"I'm quite ready," said Power, as he placed his papers in his sabretasche; "but first tell us what's doing here. Anything new lately?"

"I have heard nothing, except of some affair with the Portuguese,—they've been drubbed again; but our people have not been engaged. I say, we had better get under way; there's our first lieutenant with his telescope up; he's looking straight at us. So, come along. Good-evening, gentlemen." And in another moment the sharp craft was cutting the clear water, while Power gayly waved us a good-by.

"Who's for shore?" said the skipper, as half-a-dozen boats swarmed around the side, or held on by their boat-hooks to the rigging.

"Who is not?" said Monsoon, who now appeared in his old blue frock covered with tarnished braiding, and a cocked hat that might have roofed a pagoda. "Who is not, my old boy? Is not every man among us delighted with the prospect of fresh prog, cool wine, and a bed somewhat longer than four feet six? I say, O'Malley! Sparks! Where's the adjutant? Ah, there he is! We'll not mind the doctor,—he's a very jovial little fellow, but a damned bore, *entre nous*; and we'll have a cosy little supper at the Rue di Toledo. I know the place well. Whew, now! Get away, boy. Sit steady, Sparks; she's only a cockleshell. There; that's the Plaza de la Regna,—there, to the left. There's the great cathedral,—you can't see it now. Another seventy-four! Why there's a whole fleet here! I wish old Power joy of his afternoon with old Douglas."

"Do you know him then, Major?"

"Do I?—I should rather think I do. He was going to put me in irons here in this river once. A great shame it was; but I'll tell you the story another time. There, gently now; that's it. Thank God! once more upon land. How I do hate a ship; upon my life, a sauce-boat is the only boat endurable in this world."

We edged our way with difficulty through the dense crowd, and at last reached the Plaza. Here the numbers were still greater, but of a different class: several pretty and well-dressed women, with their dark eyes twinkling above their black mantillas as they held them across their faces, watched with an intense curiosity one of the streets that opened upon the square.

In a few moments the band of a regiment was heard, and very shortly after the regular tramp of troops followed, as the Eighty-seventh marched into the Plaza, and formed a line.

The music ceased; the drums rolled along the line; and the next moment all was still. It was really an inspiriting sight to one whose heart was interested in the career, to see those gallant fellows, as, with their bronzed faces and stalwart frames, they stood motionless as a rock. As I continued to look, the band marched into the middle of the square, and struck up, "Garryowen." Scarcely was the first part played, when a tremendous cheer burst from the troop-ship in the river. The welcome notes had reached the poor fellows there; the well-known sounds that told of home and country met their ears; and the loud cry of recognition bespoke their hearts' fulness.

"There they go. Your wild countrymen have heard their *Ranz des vaches*, it seems. Lord! how they frightened the poor Portuguese; look how they're running!"

Such was actually the case. The loud cheer uttered from the river was taken up by others straggling on shore, and one universal shout betokened that fully one-third of the red-coats around came from the dear island, and in their enthusiasm had terrified the natives to no small extent.

"Is not that Ferguson there!" cried the major, as an officer passed us with his arm in a sling. "I say, Joe—Ferguson! oh, knew it was!"

"Monsoon, my hearty, how goes it?—only just arrived, I see. Delighted to meet you out here once more. Why, we've been as dull as a veteran battalion without you. These your friends? Pray present me." The ceremony of introduction over, the major invited Ferguson to join our party at supper. "No, not to-night, Major," said he, "you must be my guests this evening. My quarters are not five minutes' walk from this; I shall not promise you very luxurious fare."

"A carbonade with olives, a roast duck, a bowl of bishop, and, if you will, a few bottles of Burgundy," said the major; "don't put yourself out for us,—soldier's fare, eh?"

I could not help smiling at the *naïve* notion of simplicity so cunningly suggested by old Monsoon. As I followed the party through the streets, my step was light, my heart not less so; for what sensations are more delightful than those of landing after a voyage? The escape from the durance vile of shipboard, with its monotonous days and dreary nights, its ill-regulated appointments, its cramped accommodation, its uncertain duration, its eternal round of unchanging amusements, for the freedom of the shore, with a land breeze, and a firm footing to tread upon; and certainly, not least of all, the sight of that brightest part of creation, whose soft eyes and tight ankles are, perhaps, the greatest of all imaginable pleasures to him who has been the dweller on blue water for several weeks long.

"Here we are," cried out Ferguson, as we stopped at the door of a large and handsome house. We follow up a spacious stair into an ample room, sparingly, but not uncomfortably furnished: plans of sieges, maps of the seat of war, pistols, sabres, and belts decorated the white walls, and a few books and a stray army list betokened the habits of the occupant.

While Ferguson disappeared to make some preparations for supper, Monsoon commenced a congratulation to the party upon the good fortune that had befallen them. "Capital fellow is Joe; never without something good, and a rare one to pass the bottle. Oh, here he comes. Be alive there, Sparks, take a corner of the cloth; how deliciously juicy that ham looks. Pass the Madeira down there; what's under that cover,—stewed kidneys?" While Monsoon went on thus we took our places at the table, and set to with an appetite which only a newly-landed traveller ever knows.

"Another spoonful of the gravy? Thank you. And so they say we've not been faring over well latterly?" said the major.

"Not a word of truth in the report. Our people have not been engaged. The only thing lately was a smart brush we had at the Tamega. Poor Patrick, a countryman of ours, and myself were serving with the Portuguese brigade, when Laborde drove us back upon the town and actually routed us. The Portuguese general, caring little for anything save his own safety, was making at once for the mountains when Patrick called upon his battalion to face about and charge; and nobly they did it, too. Down they came upon the advancing masses of the French, and literally hurled them back upon the main body. The other regiments, seeing this gallant stand, wheeled about and poured in a volley, and then, fixing bayonets, stormed a little mount beside the hedge, which commanded the whole suburb of Villa Real. The French, who soon recovered their order, now prepared for a second attack, and came on in two dense columns, when Patrick, who had little confidence in the steadiness of his people for any lengthened resistance, resolved upon once more charging with the bayonet. The order was scarcely given when the French were upon us, their flank defended by some of La Houssaye's heavy dragoons. For an instant the conflict was doubtful, until poor Patrick fell mortally wounded upon the parapet; when the men, no longer hearing his bold cheer, nor seeing his noble figure in the advance, turned and fled, pell-mell, back upon the town. As for me, blocked up amidst the mass, I was cut down from the shoulder to the elbow by a young fellow of about sixteen, who galloped about like a schoolboy on a holiday. The wound was only dangerous from the loss of blood, and so I contrived to reach Amacante without much difficulty; from whence, with three or four others, I was ordered here until fit for service."

"But what news from our own head-quarters?" inquired I.

"All imaginable kind of rumors are afloat. Some say that Craddock is retiring; others, that a part of the army is in motion upon Caldas."

"Then we are not going to have a very long sojourn here, after all, eh, Major? Donna Maria de Tormes will be inconsolable. By-the-bye, their house is just opposite us. Have you never heard Monsoon mention his friends there?"

"Come, come, Joe, how can you be so foolish?"

"But, Major, my dear friend, what signifies your modesty? There is not a man in the service does not know it, save those in the last gazette."

"Indeed, Joe, I am very angry with you."

"Well, then, by Jove! I must tell it, myself; though, faith, lads, you lose not a little for want of Monsoon's tact in the narrative."

"Anything is better that trusting to such a biographer," cried the major; "so here goes:—

"When I was acting commissary-general to the Portuguese forces some few years ago, I obtained great experience of the habits of the people; for though naturally of an unsuspecting temperament myself, I generally contrive to pick out the little foibles of my associates, even upon a short acquaintance. Now, my appointment pleased me very much on this score,—it gave me little opportunities of examining the world. 'The greatest study of mankind is man,'—Sparks would say woman, but no matter.

"Now, I soon discovered that our ancient and very excellent allies, the Portuguese, with a beautiful climate, delicious wines, and very delightful wives and daughters, were the most infernal rogues and scoundrels ever met with. 'Make yourself thoroughly acquainted with the leading features of the natives,' said old Sir Harry to me in a despatch from head-quarters; and, faith, it was not difficult,—such open, palpable, undisguised rascals never were heard of. I thought I knew a thing or two myself, when I landed; but, Lord love you! I was a babe, I was an infant in swaddling clothes, compared with them; and they humbugged me,—ay, *me!*—till I began to suspect that I was only walking in my sleep.

"'Why, Monsoon,' said the general, 'they told me you were a sharp fellow, and yet the people here seem to work round you every day. This will never do. You must brighten up a little or I shall be obliged to send you back.'

"'General,' said I, 'they used to call me no fool in England; but, somehow, here—'

"'I understand,' said he; 'you don't know the Portuguese; there's but one way with them,—strike quickly, and strike home. Never give them time for roguery,—for if they have a moment's reflection, they'll cheat the devil himself; but when you see the plot working, come slap down and decide the thing your own way.'

"Well, now, there never was anything so true as this advice, and for the eighteen months I acted upon it, I never knew it to fail.

"'I want a thousand measures of wheat.'

"'Senhor Excellenza, the crops have been miserably deficient, and——'

"'Sergeant-major,' I would say, 'these poor people have no corn; it's a wine country,—let them make up the rations that way.'

"The wheat came in that evening.

"'One hundred and twenty bullocks wanted for the reserve.'

"'The cattle are all up the mountains.'

"'Let the alcalde catch them before night or I'll catch *him.*'

"Lord bless you! I had beef enough to feed the Peninsula. And in this way, while the forces were eating short allowance and half rations elsewhere, our brigade were plump as aldermen.

"When we lay in Andalusia this was easy enough. What a country, to be sure! Such vineyards, such gardens, such delicious valleys, waving with corn and fat with olives; actually, it seemed a kind of dispensation of Providence to make war in. There was everything you could desire; and then, the people, like all your wealthy ones, were so timid, and so easily frightened, you could get what you pleased out of them by a little terror. My scouts managed this very well.

"'He is coming,' they would say, 'after to-morrow.'

"'*Madre de Dios!*'

"'I hope he won't burn the village.'

"'*Questos infernales Ingleses!* how wicked they are.'

"You'd better try what a sack of moidores or doubloons might do with him; he may refuse them, but make the effort.'

"Ha!" said the major, with a long-drawn sigh, "those were pleasant times; alas, that they should ever come to an end! Well, among the old hidalgos I met there was one Don Emanuel Selvio de Tormes, an awful old miser, rich as Croesus, and suspicious as the arch-fiend himself. Lord, how I melted him down! I quartered two squadrons of horse and a troop of flying artillery upon him. How the fellows did eat! Such a consumption of wines was never heard of; and as they began to slacken a little, I took care to replace them by fresh arrivals,—fellows from the mountains, *caçadores* they call them. At last, my friend Don Emanuel could stand it no longer, and he sent me a diplomatic envoy to negotiate terms, which, upon the whole, I must say, were fair enough; and in a few days after, the *caçadores* were withdrawn, and I took up my quarters at the château. I have had various chances and changes in this wicked world, but I am free to confess that I never passed a more agreeable time than the seven weeks I spent there. Don Emanuel, when properly managed, became a very pleasant little fellow; Donna Maria, his wife, was a sweet creature. You need not be winking that way. Upon my life she was: rather fat, to be sure, and her age something verging upon the fifties; but she had such eyes, black as sloes, and luscious as ripe grapes; and she was always smiling and ogling, and looking so sweet. Confound me, if I think she wasn't the most enchanting being in this world, with about ten thousand pounds' worth of jewels upon her fingers and in her ears. I have her before me at this instant, as she used to sit in the little arbor in the garden, with a Manilla cigar in her mouth, and a little brandy-and-water—quite weak, you know—beside her.

"'Ah, General,' she used to say—she always called me general—'what a glorious career yours is! A soldier is *indeed* a man.'

"Then she would look at poor Emanuel, who used to sit in a corner, holding his hand to his face, for hours, calculating interest and cent per cent, till he fell asleep.

"Now, he labored under a very singular malady,—not that I ever knew it at the time,—a kind of luxation of the lower jaw, which, when it came on, happened somehow to press upon some vital nerve or other, and left him perfectly paralyzed till it was restored to its proper place. In fact, during the time the agony lasted, he was like one in a trance; for though he could see and hear, he could neither speak nor move, and looked as if he had done with both for many a day to come.

"Well, as I was saying, I knew nothing of all this till a slight circumstance made it known to me. I was seated one evening in the little arbor I mentioned, with Donna Maria. There was a little table before us covered with wines and fruits, a dish of olives, some Castile oranges, and a fresh pine. I remember it well: my eye roved over the little dessert set out in old-fashioned, rich silver dishes, then turned towards the lady herself, with rings and brooches, earrings and chains enough to reward one for sacking a town; and I said to myself, 'Monsoon, Monsoon, this is better than long marches in the Pyrenees, with a cork-tree for a bed-curtain, and wet grass for a mattress. How pleasantly one might jog on in this world with this little country-house for his abode, and Donna Maria for a companion!'

"I tasted the port; it was delicious. Now, I knew very little Portuguese, but I made some effort to ask if there was much of it in the cellar.

"She smiled, and said, 'Oh, yes.'

"'What a luxurious life one might lead here!' thought I; 'and after all, perhaps Providence might remove Don Emanuel.'

"I finished the bottle as I thus meditated. The next was, if possible, more crusty.

"'This is a delicious retreat,' said I, soliloquizing.

"Donna Maria seemed to know what was passing in my mind, for she smiled, too.

"'Yes,' said I, in broken Portuguese, 'one ought to be very happy here, Donna Maria.'

"She blushed, and I continued:—

"'What can one want for more in this life? All the charms that rendered Paradise what it was'—I took her hand here—'and made Adam blessed.'

"'Ah, General!' said she, with a sigh, 'you are such a flatterer.'

"'Who could flatter,' said I, with enthusiasm, 'when there are not words enough to express what he feels?' This was true, for my Portuguese was fast failing me, 'But if I ever was happy, it is now.'

"I took another pull at the port.

"'If I only thought,' said I, 'that my presence here was not thought unwelcome—'

"'Fie, General,' said she, 'how could you say such a thing?'

"'If I only thought I was not hated,' said I, tremblingly.

"'Oh!' said she, again.

"'Despised.'

"'Oh!'

"'Loathed.'

"She pressed my hand, I kissed hers; she hurriedly snatched it from me, and pointed towards a lime-tree near, beneath which, in the cool enjoyment of his cigar, sat the spare and detested figure of Don Emanuel.

"'Yes,' thought I, 'there he is,—the only bar to my good fortune; were it not for him, I should not be long before I became possessor of this excellent old château, with a most indiscretionary power over the cellar. Don Mauricius Monsoon would speedily assume his place among the grandees of Portugal.'

"I know not how long my revery lasted, nor, indeed, how the evening passed; but I remember well the moon was up, and a sky, bright with a thousand stars was shining, as I sat beside the fair Donna Maria, endeavoring, with such Portuguese as it had pleased fate to bestow on me, to instruct her touching my warlike services and deeds of arms. The fourth bottle of port was ebbing beneath my eloquence, as responsively her heart beat, when I heard a slight rustle in the branches near. I looked, and, Heavens, what a sight did I behold! There was little Don Emanuel stretched upon the grass with his mouth wide open, his face pale as death, his arms stretched out at either side, and his legs stiffened straight out. I ran over and asked if he were ill, but no answer came. I lifted up an arm, but it fell heavily upon the ground as I let it go; the leg did likewise. I touched his nose; it was cold.

"'Hollo,' thought I, 'is it so? This comes of mixing water with your sherry. I saw where it would end.'

"Now, upon my life! I felt sorry for the little fellow; but somehow, one gets so familiarized with this sort of thing in a campaign that one only half feels in a case like this.

"'Yes,' said I, 'man is but grass; but I for one must make hay when the sun shines. Now for the Donna Maria,'—for the poor thing was asleep in the arbor all this while.

"'Donna,' said I, shaking her by the elbow,—'Donna, don't be shocked at what I'm going to say.'

"'Ah, General,' said she, with a sigh, 'say no more; I must not listen to you.'

"'You don't know that,' said I, with a knowing look,—'you don't know that.'

"'Why, what can you mean?'

"'The little fellow is done for.' For the port was working strong now, and destroyed all my fine sensibility. 'Yes, Donna,' said I, 'you are free,'—here I threw myself upon my knees,—'free to make me the happiest of commissaries and the jolliest grandee of Portugal that ever—'

"'But Don Emanuel?'

"'Run out, dry, empty,' inverting a finished decanter to typify my words as I spoke.

"'He is not dead?' said she, with a scream.

"'Even so,' said I, with a hiccough! 'ordered for service in a better world, where there are neither inspections nor arrears.'

"Before the words were well out, she sprang from the bench and rushed over to the spot where the little don lay. What she said or did I know not, but the next moment he sat bolt upright on the grass, and as he held his jaw with one hand and supported himself on the other, vented such a torrent of abuse and insult at me, that, for want of Portuguese enough to reply, I rejoined in English, in which I swore pretty roundly for five minutes. Meanwhile the donna had summoned the servants, who removed Don Emanuel to the house, where on my return I found my luggage displayed before the door, with a civil hint to deploy in orderly time and take ground elsewhere.

"In a few days, however, his anger cooled down, and I received a polite note from Donna Maria, that the don at length began to understand the joke, and begged that I would return to the château, and that he would expect me at dinner the same day."

"With which, of course, you complied?"

"Which of course I did. Forgive your enemies, my dear boy,—it is only Christian-like; and really, we lived very happily ever after. The donna was a mighty clever woman, and a dear good soul besides."

It was late when the major concluded his story; so after wishing Ferguson a good-night, we took our leave, and retired for the night to our quarters.

CHAPTER XXXVII

LISBON.

The tramp of horses' feet and the sound of voices beneath my window roused me from a deep sleep. I sprang up and drew aside the curtain. What a strange confusion beset me as I looked forth! Before me lay a broad and tranquil river whose opposite shore, deeply wooded and studded with villas and cottages, rose abruptly from the water's edge; vessels of war lay tranquilly in the stream, their pennants trailing in the tide. The loud boom of a morning gun rolled along the surface, awaking a hundred echoes as it passed, and the lazy smoke rested for some minutes on the glassy water as it blended with the thin air of the morning.

"Where am I?" was my first question to myself, as I continued to look from side to side, unable to collect my scattered senses.

One word sufficed to recall me to myself, as I heard Power's voice, from without, call out, "Charley! O'Malley, I say! Come down here!"

I hurriedly threw on my clothes and went to the door.

"Well, Charley, I've been put in harness rather sooner than I expected. Here's old Douglas has been sitting up all night writing despatches; and I must hasten on to headquarters without a moment's delay. There's work before us, that's certain; but when, where, and how, of that I know nothing. You may expect the route every moment; the French are still advancing.

Meanwhile I have a couple of commissions for you to execute. First, here's a packet for Hammersley; you are sure to meet him with the regiment in a day or two. I have some scruples about asking you this; but, confound it! you're too sensible a fellow to care—" Here he hesitated; and as I colored to the eyes, for some minutes he seemed uncertain how to proceed. At length, recovering himself, he went on: "Now for the other. This is a most loving epistle from a poor devil of a midshipman, written last night by a tallow candle, in the cock-pit, containing vows of eternal adoration and a lock of hair. I promised faithfully to deliver it myself; for the 'Thunderer' sails for Gibraltar next tide, and he cannot go ashore for an instant. However, as Sir Arthur's billet may be of more importance than the reefer's, I must intrust its safe keeping to your hands. Now, then, don't look so devilish sleepy, but seem to understand what I am saying. This is the address: 'La Senhora Inez da Silviero, Rua Nuova, opposite the barber's.' You'll not neglect it. So now, my dear boy, till our next meeting, *adios!*"

"Stop! For Heaven's sake, not so fast, I pray! Where's the street?"

"The Rua Nuova. Remember Figaro, my boy. *Cinque perruche.*"

"But what am I to do?"

"To do! What a question! Anything; everything. Be a good diplomate. Speak of the torturing agony of the lover, for which I can vouch. The boy is only fifteen. Swear that he is to return in a month, first lieutenant of the 'Thunder Bomb,' with intentions that even Madame Dalrymple would approve."

"What nonsense," said I, blushing to the eyes.

"And if that suffice not, I know of but one resource."

"Which is?"

"Make love to her yourself. Ay, even so. Don't look so confoundedly vinegar; the girl, I hear, is a devilish pretty one, the house pleasant, and I sincerely wish I could exchange duties with you, leaving you to make your bows to his Excellency the C. O. F., and myself free to make mine to La Senhora. And now, push along, old red cap."

So saying, he made a significant cut of his whip at the Portuguese guide, and in another moment was out of sight.

My first thought was one of regret at Power's departure. For some time past we had been inseparable companions; and notwithstanding the reckless and wild gayety of his conduct, I had ever found him ready to assist me in every difficulty, and that with an address and dexterity a more calculating adviser might not have possessed. I was now utterly alone; for though Monsoon and the adjutant were still in Lisbon, as was also Sparks, I never could make intimates of them.

I ate my breakfast with a heavy heart, my solitary position again suggesting thoughts of home and kindred. Just at this moment my eyes fell upon the packet destined for Hammersley; I took it up and weighed it in my hand. "Alas!" thought I, "how much of my destiny may lie within that envelope! How fatally may my after-life be influenced by it!" It felt heavy as though there was something besides letters. True, too true; there was a picture, Lucy's portrait! The cold drops of perspiration stood upon my forehead as my fingers traced the outline of a miniature-case in the parcel. I became deadly sick, and sank, half-fainting, upon a chair. And such is the end of my first dream of happiness! How have I duped, how have I deceived myself! For, alas, though Lucy had never responded to my proffered vows of affection, yet had I ever nurtured in my heart a secret hope that I was not altogether uncared for. Every look she had given me, every word she had spoken, the tone of her voice, her step, her every gesture, were before me, all confirming my delusion, and yet,—I could bear no more, and burst into tears.

The loud call of a cavalry trumpet aroused me.

How long I had passed in this state of despondency I knew not; but it was long past noon when I rallied myself. My charger was already awaiting me; and a second blast of the trumpet told that the inspection in the Plaza was about to commence.

As I continued to dress, I gradually rallied from my depressing thoughts; and ere I belted my sabretasche, the current of my ideas had turned from their train of sadness to one of hardihood and daring. Lucy Dashwood had treated me like a wilful schoolboy. Mayhap, I may prove myself as gallant a soldier as even him she has preferred before me.

A third sound of the trumpet cut short my reflections, and I sprang into the saddle, and hastened towards the Plaza. As I dashed along the streets, my horse, maddened with the impulse that stirred my own heart, curvetted and plunged unceasingly. As I reached the Plaza, the crowd became dense, and I was obliged to pull up. The sound of the music, the parade, the tramp of the infantry, and the neighing of the horses, were, however, too much for my mettlesome steed, and he became nearly unmanageable; he plunged fearfully, and twice reared as though he would have fallen back. As I scattered the foot passengers right and left with terror, my eye fell upon one lovely girl, who, tearing herself from her companion, rushed wildly towards an open doorway for shelter; suddenly, however, changing her intention, she came forward a few paces, and then, as if overcome by fear, stood stock-still, her hands clasped upon her bosom, her eyes upturned, her features deadly pale, while her knees seemed bending beneath her. Never did I behold a more beautiful object. Her dark hair had fallen loose upon her shoulder, and she stood the very *idéal* of the "Madonna Supplicating." My glance was short as a lightning flash; for the same instant my horse swerved, and dashed forward right at the place where she was standing. One terrific cry rose from the crowd, who saw her danger. Beside her stood a muleteer who had drawn up his mule and cart close beside the footway for safety; she made one effort to reach it, but her outstretched arms alone moved, and paralyzed by terror, she sank motionless upon the pavement. There was but one course open to me now; so collecting myself for the effort, I threw my horse upon his haunches, and then, dashing the spurs into his flanks, breasted him at the mule cart. With one spring he rose, and cleared it at a bound, while the very air rang with the acclamations of the multitude, and a thousand bravos saluted me as I alighted upon the opposite side.

"Well done, O'Malley!" sang out the little adjutant, as I flew past and pulled up in the middle of the Plaza.

"Something devilish like Galway in that leap," said a very musical voice beside me; and at the same instant a tall, soldier-like man, in an undress dragoon frock, touched his cap, and said, "A 14th man, I perceive, sir. May I introduce myself? Major O'Shaughnessy."

I bowed, and shook the major's proffered hand, while he continued,—

"Old Monsoon mentioned your name to us this morning. You came out together, if I mistake not?"

"Yes; but somehow, I've missed the major since my landing."

"Oh, you'll see him presently; he'll be on parade. By-the-bye, he wishes particularly to meet you. We dine to-day at the 'Quai de Soderi,' and if you're not engaged—Yes, this is the person," said he, turning at the moment towards a servant, who, with a card in his hand, seemed to search for some one in the crowd.

The man approached, and handed it to me.

"What can this mean?" said I. "Don Emanuel de Blacas y Silviero, Rua Nuova."

"Why, that's the great Portuguese contractor, the intendant of half the army, the richest fellow in Lisbon. Have you known him long?"

"Never heard of him till now."

"By Jove, you're in luck! No man gives such dinners; he has such a cellar! I'll wager a fifty it was his daughter you took in the flying leap a while ago. I hear she is a beautiful creature."

"Yes," thought I, "that must be it; and yet, strange enough, I think the name and address are familiar to me."

"Ten to one, you've heard Monsoon speak of him; he's most intimate there. But here comes the major."

And as he spoke, the illustrious commissary came forward holding a vast bundle of papers in one hand, and his snuff-box in the other, followed by a long string of clerks, contractors, assistant-surgeons, paymasters, etc., all eagerly pressing forward to be heard.

"It's quite impossible; I can't do it to-day. Victualling and physicking are very good things, but must be done in season. I have been up all night at the accounts,—haven't I, O'Malley?" here he winked at me most significantly; "and then I have the forage and stoppage fund to look through ['we dine at six, sharp,' said he, *sotto voce*], which will leave me without one minute unoccupied for the next twenty-four hours. Look to your toggery this evening; I've something in my eye for you, O'Malley."

"Officers unattached to their several corps will fall into the middle of the Plaza," said a deep voice among the crowd; and in obedience to the order I rode forward and placed myself with a number of others, apparently newly joined, in the open square. A short, gray-haired old colonel, with a dark, eagle look, proceeded to inspect us, reading from a paper as he came along,—

"Mr. Hepton, 6th Foot; commission bearing date 11th January; drilled, proceed to Ovar, and join his regiment.

"Mr. Gronow, Fusilier Guards, remains with the depot.

"Captain Mortimer, 1st Dragoons, appointed aide-de-camp to the general commanding the cavalry brigade.

"Mr. Sparks,—where is Mr. Sparks? Mr. Sparks absent from parade; make a note of it.

"Mr. O'Malley, 14th Light Dragoons. Mr. O'Malley,—oh, I remember! I have received a letter from Sir George Dashwood concerning you. You will hold yourself in readiness to march. Your friends desire that before you may obtain any staff appointment, you should have the opportunity of seeing some service. Am I to understand such is your wish?"

"Most certainly."

"May I have the pleasure of your company at dinner to-day?"

"I regret that I have already accepted an invitation to dine with Major Monsoon."

"With Major Monsoon? Ah, indeed! Perhaps it might be as well I should mention,—but no matter. I wish you good-morning."

So saying, the little colonel rode off, leaving me to suppose that my dinner engagement had not raised me in his estimation, though why, I could not exactly determine.

CHAPTER XXXVIII.
THE RUA NUOVA.

Our dinner was a long and uninteresting one, and as I found that the major was likely to prefer his seat as chairman of the party to the seductions of ladies' society, I took the first opportunity of escaping and left the room.

It was a rich moonlight night as I found myself in the street. My way, which led along the banks of the Tagus, was almost as light as in daytime, and crowded with walking parties, who sauntered carelessly along in the enjoyment of the cool, refreshing night-air. On inquiring, I discovered that the Rua Nuova was at the extremity of the city; but as the road led along by the river I did not regret the distance, but walked on with increasing pleasure at the charms of so heavenly a climate and country.

After three quarters of an hour's walk, the streets became by degrees less and less crowded. A solitary party passed me now and then; the buzz of distant voices succeeded to the gay laughter and merry tones of the passing groups, and at length my own footsteps alone awoke the echoes along the deserted pathway. I stopped every now and then to gaze upon the tranquil river, whose eddies were circling in the pale silver of the moonlight. I listened with attentive ear as the night breeze wafted to me the far-off sounds of a guitar, and the deep tones of some lover's serenade; while again the tender warbling of the nightingale came borne across the stream on a wind rich with the odor of the orange-tree.

As thus I lingered on my way the time stole on, and it was near midnight ere I had roused myself from the revery surrounding objects had thrown about me. I stopped suddenly, and for some minutes I struggled with myself to discover if I was really awake. As I walked along, lost in my reflections, I had entered a little garden beside the river. Fragrant plants and lovely flowers bloomed on every side; the orange, the camelia, the cactus, and the rich laurel of Portugal were blending their green and golden hues around me, while the very air was filled with delicious music. "Was it a dream? Could such ecstasy be real?" I asked myself, as the rich notes swelled upwards in their strength, and sank in soft cadence to tones of melting harmony; now bursting forth in the full force of gladness, the voices blended together in one stream of mellow music, and suddenly ceasing, the soft but thrilling shake of a female voice rose upon the air, and in its plaintive beauty stirred the very heart. The proud tramp of martial music succeeded to the low wailing cry of agony; then came the crash of battle, the clang of steel; the thunder of the fight rolled on in all its majesty, increasing in its maddening excitement till it ended in one loud shout of victory.

All was still; not a breath moved, not a leaf stirred, and again was I relapsing into my dreamy scepticism, when again the notes swelled upwards in concert. But now their accents were changed, and in low, subdued tones, faintly and slowly uttered, the prayer of thanksgiving rose to Heaven and spoke their gratefulness. I almost fell upon my knees, and already the tears filled my eyes as I drank in the sounds. My heart was full to bursting, and even now as I write it my pulse throbs as I remember the hymn of the Abencerrages.

When I rallied from my trance of excited pleasure, my first thought was, where was I, and how came I there? Before I could resolve my doubts upon the question, my attention was turned in another direction, for close beside me the branches moved forward, and a pair of arms were thrown around my neck, while a delicious voice cried out in an accent of childish, delight, "*Trovado!*" At the same instant a lovely head sank upon my shoulder, covering it with tresses of long brown hair. The arms pressed me still more closely, till I felt her very heart beating against my side.

"*Mio fradre*," said a soft, trembling voice, as her fingers played in my hair and patted my temples.

What a situation mine! I well knew that some mistaken identity had been the cause, but still I could not repress my inclination to return the embrace, as I pressed my lips upon the fair forehead that leaned upon my bosom; at the same moment she threw back her head, as if to look me more fully in the face. One glance sufficed; blushing deeply over her cheeks and neck, she sprang from my arms, and uttering a faint cry, staggered against a tree. In an instant I saw it was the lovely girl I had met in the morning; and without losing a second I poured out apologies for my intrusion with all the eloquence I was master of, till she suddenly interrupted me by asking if I spoke French. Scarcely had I recommenced my excuses in that language, when a third party appeared upon the stage. This was a short, elderly man, in a green uniform, with several decorations upon his breast, and a cocked hat with a most flowing plume in his right hand.

"May I beg to know whom I have the honor of receiving?" inquired he, in very excellent English, as he advanced with a look of very ceremonious and distant politeness.

I immediately explained that, presuming upon the card which his servant had presented me, I had resolved on paying my respects when a mistake had led me accidentally into his garden.

My apologies had not come to an end when he folded me in his arms and overwhelmed me with thanks, at the same time saying a few words in Portuguese to his daughter. She stooped down, and taking my hand gently within her own, touched it with her lips.

This piece of touching courtesy,—which I afterwards found meant little or nothing,—affected me deeply at the time, and I felt the blood rush to my face and forehead, half in pride, half in a sense of shame. My confusion was, however, of short duration; for taking my arm, the old gentleman led me along a few paces, and turning round a small clump of olives, entered a little summer-house. Here a considerable party were assembled, which for their picturesque effect could scarcely have been better managed on the stage.

Beneath the mild lustre of a large lamp of stained glass, half hid in the overhanging boughs, was spread a table covered with vessels of gold and silver plate of gorgeous richness; drinking cups and goblets of antique pattern shone among cups of Sèvres china or Venetian glass; delicious fruit, looking a thousand times more tempting for being contained in baskets of silver foliage, peeped from amidst a profusion of fresh flowers, whose odor was continually shed around by a slight *jet d'eau* that played among the leaves. Around upon the grass, seated upon cushions or reclining on Genoa carpets, were several beautiful girls in most becoming costumes, their dark locks and darker eyes speaking of "the soft South," while their expressive gestures and animated looks betokened a race whose temperament was glowing as their clime. There were several men also, the greater number of whom appeared in uniform,—bronzed, soldier-like fellows, who had the jaunty air and easy carriage of their calling,—among whom was one Englishman, or at least so I guessed from his wearing the uniform of a heavy dragoon regiment.

"This is my daughter's *fête*," said Don Emanuel, as he ushered me into the assembly,—"her birthday; a sad day it might have been for us had it not been for your courage and forethought." So saying, he commenced a recital of my adventure to the bystanders, who overwhelmed me with civil speeches and a shower of soft looks that completed the fascination of the fairy scene. Meanwhile the fair Inez had made room for me beside her, and I found myself at once the lion of the party, each vying with her neighbor who should show me most attention, La Senhora herself directing her conversation exclusively to me,—a circumstance which, considering the awkwardness of our first meeting, I felt no small surprise at, and which led me, somewhat maliciously I confess, to make a half allusion to it, feeling some interest in ascertaining for whom the flattering reception was really intended.

"I thought you were Charles," said she, blushing, in answer to my question.

"And you are right," said I; "I am Charles."

"Nay, but I meant *my* Charles."

There was something of touching softness in the tone of these few words that made me half wish I were *her* Charles. Whether my look evinced as much or not, I cannot tell, but she speedily added,—

"He is my brother; he is a captain in the caçadores, and I expected him here this evening. Some one saw a figure pass the gate and conceal himself in the trees, and I was sure it was he."

"What a disappointment!" said I.

"Yes; was it not?" said she, hurriedly; and then, as if remembering how ungracious was the speech, she blushed more deeply and hung down her head.

Just at this moment, as I looked up, I caught the eye of the English officer fixed steadfastly upon me. He was a tall, fine-looking fellow, of about two or three and thirty, with marked and handsome features, which, however, conveyed an expression of something sneering and sinister that struck me the moment I saw him. His glass was fixed in his eye, and I perceived that he regarded us both with a look of no common interest. My attention did not, however, dwell long upon the circumstance, for Don Emanuel, coming behind my shoulder, asked me if I would not take out his daughter in the bolero they were just forming.

To my shame I was obliged to confess that I had not even seen the dance; and while I continued to express my resolve to correct the errors of my education, the Englishman came up and asked the senhora to be his partner. This put the very keystone upon my annoyance, and I half turned angrily away from the spot, when I heard her decline his invitation, and avow her determination not to dance.

There was something which pleased me so much at this refusal, that I could not help turning upon her a look of most grateful acknowledgment; but as I did so, I once more encountered the gaze of the Englishman, whose knitted brows and compressed lips were bent upon me in a manner there was no mistaking. This was neither the fitting time nor place to seek any explanation of the circumstance, so, wisely resolving to wait a better occasion, I turned away and resumed my attentions towards my fair companion.

"Then you don't care for the bolero?" said I, as she reseated herself upon the grass.

"Oh, I delight in it!" said she, enthusiastically.

"But you refused to dance?"

She hesitated, blushed, tried to mutter something, and was silent.

"I had determined to learn it," said I, half jestingly; "but if you will not dance with me—"

"Yes; that I will,—indeed I will."

"But you declined my countryman. Is it because he is inexpert?"

The senhora hesitated, looked confused for some minutes; at length, coloring slightly, she said: "I have already made one rude speech to you this evening; I fear lest I should make a second. Tell me, is Captain Trevyllian your friend?"

"If you mean that gentleman yonder, I never saw him before."

"Nor heard of him?"

"Nor that either. We are total strangers to each other."

"Well, then, I may confess it. I do not like him. My father prefers him to any one else, invites him here daily, and, in fact, instals him as his first favorite. But still, I cannot like him; and yet I have done my best to do so."

"Indeed!" said I, pointedly. "What are his chief demerits? Is he not agreeable? Is he not clever?"

"Oh, on the contrary, most agreeable, fascinating, I should say, in conversation; has travelled, seen a great deal of the world, is very accomplished, and has distinguished himself on several occasions. He wears, as you see, a Portuguese order."

"And with all that—"

"And with all that, I cannot bear him. He is a duellist, a notorious duellist. My brother, too, knows more of him, and avoids him. But let us not speak further. I see his eyes are again fixed on us; and somehow, I fear him, without well knowing wherefore."

A movement among the party, shawls and mantillas were sought for on all sides; and the preparations for leave-taking appeared general. Before, however, I had time to express my thanks for my hospitable reception, the guests had assembled in a circle around the senhora, and toasting her with a parting bumper, they commenced in concert a little Portuguese song of farewell, each verse concluding with a good-night, which, as they separated and held their way homewards, might now and then be heard rising upon the breeze and wafting their last thoughts back to her. The concluding verse, which struck me much, I have essayed to translate. It ran somehow thus:—

"The morning breezes chill   Now close our joyous scene,   And yet we linger still,   Where we've so happy been.   How blest were it to live   With hearts like ours so light,   And only part to give   One long and last good-night!   Good-night!"

With many an invitation to renew my visit, most kindly preferred by Don Emanuel and warmly seconded by his daughter, I, too, wished my good-night and turned my steps homeward.

CHAPTER XXXIX

THE VILLA.

The first object which presented itself to my eye the next morning was the midshipman's packet intrusted to my care by Power. I turned it over to read the address more carefully, and what was my surprise to find that the name was that of my fair friend Donna Inez.

"This certainly thickens the plot," thought I. "And so I have now fallen upon the real Simon Pure, and the reefer has had the good fortune to distance the dragoon. Well, thus far, I cannot say that I regret it. Now, however, for the parade, and then for the villa."

"I say, O'Malley," cried out Monsoon, as I appeared on the Plaza, "I have accepted an invitation for you to-day. We dine across the river. Be at my quarters a little before six, and we'll go together."

I should rather have declined the invitation; but not well knowing why, and having no ready excuse, acceded, and promised to be punctual.

"You were at Don Emanuel's last night. I heard of you!"

"Yes; I spent a most delightful evening."

"That's your ground, my boy. A million of moidores, and such a campagna in Valencia. A better thing than the Dalrymple affair. Don't blush. I know it all. But stay; here they come."

As he spoke, the general commanding, with a numerous staff, rode forward. As they passed, I recognized a face which I had certainly seen before, and in a moment remembered it was that of the dragoon of the evening before. He passed quite close, and fixing his eyes steadfastly on me, evinced no sign of recognition.

The parade lasted above two hours; and it was with a feeling of impatience I mounted a fresh horse to canter out to the villa. When I arrived, the servant informed me that Don Emanuel was in the city, but that the senhora was in the garden, offering, at the same time, to escort me. Declining this honor, I intrusted my horse to his keeping and took my way towards the arbor where last I had seen her.

I had not walked many paces, when the sound of a guitar struck on my ear. I listened. It was the senhora's voice. She was singing a Venetian canzonetta in a low, soft, warbling tone, as one lost in a revery; as though the music was a mere accompaniment to some pleasant thought. I peeped through the dense leaves, and there she sat upon a low garden seat, an open book on the rustic table before her, beside her, embroidery, which seemed only lately abandoned. As I looked, she placed her guitar upon the ground and began to play with a small spaniel that seemed to have waited with impatience for some testimony of favor. A moment more, and she grew weary of this; then, heaving a long but gentle sigh, leaned back upon her chair and seemed lost in thought. I now had ample time to regard her, and certainly never beheld anything more lovely. There was a character of classic beauty, and her brow, though fair and ample, was still strongly marked upon the temples; the eyes, being deep and squarely set, imparted a look of intensity to her features which their own softness subdued; while the short upper lip, which trembled with every passing thought, spoke of a nature tender and impressionable, and yet impassioned. Her foot and ankle peeped from beneath her dark robe, and certainly nothing could be more faultless; while her hand, fair as marble, blue-veined and dimpled, played amidst the long tresses of her hair, that, as if in the wantonness of beauty, fell carelessly upon her shoulders.

It was some time before I could tear myself away from the fascination of so much beauty, and it needed no common effort to leave the spot. As I made a short *détour* in the garden before approaching the arbor, she saw me as I came forward, and kissing her hand gayly, made room for me beside her.

"I have been fortunate in finding you alone, Senhora," said I, as I seated myself by her side, "for I am the bearer of a letter to you. How far it may interest you, I know not, but to the writer's feelings I am bound to testify."

"A letter to me? You jest, surely?"

"That I am in earnest, this will show," said I, producing the packet.

She took it from my hands, turned it about and about, examined the seal; while, half doubtingly, she said:—

"The name is mine; but still—"

"You fear to open it; is it not so? But after all, you need not be surprised if it's from Howard; that's his name, I think."

"Howard! from little Howard!" exclaimed she, enthusiastically; and tearing open the letter, she pressed it to her lips, her eyes sparkling with pleasure and her cheek glowing as she read. I watched her as she ran rapidly over the lines; and I confess that, more than once, a pang of discontent shot through my heart that the midshipman's letter could call up such interest,—not that I was in love with her myself, but yet, I know not how it was, I had fancied her affections unengaged; and without asking myself wherefore, I wished as much.

"Poor dear boy!" said she, as she came to the end. How these few and simple words sank into my heart, as I remembered how they had once been uttered to myself, and in perhaps no very dissimilar circumstances.

"But where is the souvenir he speaks of?" said she.

"The souvenir. I'm not aware—"

"Oh, I hope you've not lost the lock of hair he sent me!" I was quite dumfounded at this, and could not remember whether I had received it from Power or not, so answered, at random,—

"Yes; I must have left it on my table."

"Promise me, then, to bring it to-morrow with you?"

"Certainly," said I, with something of pique in my manner. "If I find such a means of making my visit an agreeable one, I shall certainly not omit it."

"You are quite right," said she, either not noticing or not caring for the tone of my reply. "You will, indeed, be a welcome messenger. Do you know, he was one of my lovers?"

"One of them, indeed! Then pray how many do you number at this moment?"

"What a question; as if I could possibly count them! Besides, there are so many absent,—some on leave, some deserters, perhaps,—that I might be reckoning among my troops, but who, possibly, form part of the forces of the enemy. Do you know little Howard?"

"I cannot say that we are personally acquainted, but I am enabled through the medium of a friend to say that his sentiments are not strange to me. Besides, I have really pledged myself to support the prayer of his petition."

"How very good of you! For which reason you've forgotten, if not lost, the lock of hair."

"That you shall have to-morrow," said I, pressing my hand solemnly to my heart.

"Well, then, don't forget it. But hush; here comes Captain Trevyllian. So you say Lisbon really pleases you?" said she, in a tone of voice totally changed, as the dragoon of the preceding evening approached.

"Mr. O'Malley, Captain Trevyllian."

We bowed stiffly and haughtily to each other, as two men salute who are unavoidably obliged to bow, with every wish on either side to avoid acquaintance. So, at least, I construed his bow; so I certainly intended my own.

It requires no common tact to give conversation the appearance of unconstraint and ease when it is evident that each person opposite is laboring under excited feelings; so that, notwithstanding the senhora's efforts to engage our attention by the commonplaces of the day, we remained almost silent, and after a few observations of no interest, took our several leaves. Here again a new source of awkwardness arose; for as we walked together towards the house, where our horses stood, neither party seemed disposed to speak.

"You are probably returning to Lisbon?" said he, coldly.

I assented by a bow; upon which, drawing his bridle within his arm, he bowed once more, and turned away in an opposite direction; while I, glad to be relieved of an unsought-for companionship, returned alone to the town.

CHAPTER XL

THE DINNER.

It was with no peculiar pleasure that I dressed for our dinner party. Major O'Shaughnessy, our host, was one of that class of my countrymen I cared least for,—a riotous, good-natured, noisy, loud-swearing, punch-drinking western; full of stories of impossible fox hunts, and unimaginable duels, which all were acted either by himself or some member of his family. The company consisted of the adjutant, Monsoon, Ferguson, Trevyllian, and some eight or ten officers with whom I was acquainted. As is usual on such occasions, the wine circulated freely, and amidst the din and clamor of excited conversation, the fumes of Burgundy, and the vapor of cigar smoke, we most of us became speedily mystified. As for me, my evil destiny would have it that I was placed exactly opposite Trevyllian, with whom upon more than one occasion I happened to differ in opinion, and the question was in itself some trivial and unimportant one; yet the tone which he assumed, and of which I, too, could not divest myself in reply, boded anything rather than an amicable feeling between us. The noise and turmoil about prevented the others remarking the circumstance; but I could perceive in his manner what I deemed a studied determination to promote a quarrel, while I felt within myself a most unchristian-like desire to indulge his fancy.

"Worse fellows at passing the bottle than Trevyllian and O'Malley there I have rarely sojourned with," cried the major; "look if they haven't got eight decanters between them, and here we are in a state of African thirst."

"How can you expect him to think of thirst when such perfumed billets as that come showering upon him?" said the adjutant, alluding to a rose-colored epistle a servant had placed within my hands.

"Eight miles of a stone-wall country in fifteen minutes,—devil a lie in it!" said O'Shaughnessy, striking the table with his clinched fist; "show me the man would deny it."

"Why, my dear fellow—"

"Don't be dearing me. Is it 'no' you'll be saying me?"

"Listen, now; there's O'Reilly, there—"

"Where is he?"

"He's under the table."

"Well, it's the same thing. His mother had a fox—bad luck to you, don't scald me with the jug—his mother had a fox-cover in Shinrohan."

When O'Shaughnessy had got thus far in his narrative, I had the opportunity of opening my note, which merely contained the following words: "Come to the ball at the Casino, and bring the Cadeau you promised."

I had scarcely read this over once, when a roar of laughter at something said attracted my attention. I looked up, and perceived Trevyllian's eyes bent upon me with the fierceness of a tiger; the veins in his forehead were swollen and distorted, and the whole expression of his face betokened rage and passion. Resolved no longer to submit to such evident determination to insult, I was rising from my place at table, when, as if anticipating my intention, he pushed back his chair and left the room. Fearful of attracting attention by immediately following him, I affected to join in the conversation around me, while my temples throbbed, and my hands tingled with impatience to get away.

"Poor McManus," said O'Shaughnessy, "rest his soul! he'd have puzzled the bench of bishops for hard words. Upon my conscience, I believe he spent his mornings looking for them in the Old Testament. Sure ye might have heard what happened to him at Banagher, when he commanded the Kilkennys,—ye never heard the story? Well, then, ye shall. Push the sherry along first, though,—old Monsoon there always keeps it lingering beside his left arm.

"Well, when Peter was lieutenant-colonel of the Kilkennys,—who, I may remark, *en passant*, as the French say, were the neediest-looking devils in the whole service,—he never let them alone from morning till night, drilling and pipe-claying and polishing them up. 'Nothing will make soldiers of you,' said Peter, 'but, by the rock of Cashel! I'll keep you as clean as a new musket!' Now, poor Peter himself was not a very warlike figure,—he measured five feet one in his tallest boots; but certainly if Nature denied him length of stature, she compensated for it in another way, by giving him a taste of the longest words in the language. An extra syllable or so in a word was always a strong recommendation; and whenever he could not find one to his mind, he'd take some quaint, outlandish one that more than once led to very awkward results. Well, the regiment was one day drawn up for parade in the town of Banagher, and as M'Manus came down the lines he stopped opposite one of the men whose face, hands, and accoutrements exhibited a most woeful contempt of his orders. The fellow looked more like a turf-stack than a light-company man.

"'Stand out, sir!' cried M'Manus, in a boiling passion. 'Sergeant O'Toole, inspect this individual.' Now, the sergeant was rather a favorite with Mac; for he always pretended to understand his phraseology, and in consequence was pronounced by the colonel a very superior man for his station in life. 'Sergeant,' said he, 'we shall make an exemplary illustration of our system here.'

"'Yes, sir,' said the sergeant, sorely puzzled at the meaning of what he spoke.

"'Bear him to the Shannon, and lave him there.' This he said in a kind of Coriolanus tone, with a toss of his head and a wave of his right arm,—signs, whenever he made them, incontestibly showing that further parley was out of the question, and that he had summed up and charged the jury for good and all.

"'*Lave* him in the river?' said O'Toole, his eyes starting from the sockets, and his whole face working in strong anxiety; 'is it *lave* him in the river yer honor means?'

"'I have spoken,' said the little man, bending an ominous frown upon the sergeant, which, whatever construction he may have put upon his words, there was no mistaking.

"'Well, well, av it's God's will he's drowned, it will not be on my head,' says O'Toole, as he marched the fellow away between two rank and file.

"The parade was nearly over, when Mac happened to see the sergeant coming up all splashed with water and looking quite tired.

"'Have you obeyed my orders?' said he.

"'Yes, yer honor; and tough work we had of it, for he struggled hard.'

"'And where is he now?'

"'Oh, troth, he's there safe. Divil a fear he'll get out.'

"'Where?' said Mac.

"'In the river, yer honor.'

"'What have you done, you scoundrel?'

"'Didn't I do as you bid me?' says he; 'didn't I throw him in and *lave* [leave] him there?'

"And faith so they did; and if he wasn't a good swimmer and got over to Moystown, there's little doubt but he'd have been drowned, and all because Peter McManus could not express himself like a Christian."

In the laughter which followed O'Shaughnessy's story I took the opportunity of making my escape from the party, and succeeded in gaining the street unobserved. Though the note I had just read was not signed, I had no doubt from whom it came; so I hastened at once to my quarters, to make search for the lock of Ned Howard's hair to which the senhora alluded. What was my mortification, however, to discover that no such thing could be found anywhere. I searched all my drawers; I tossed about my papers and letters; I hunted every likely, every unlikely spot I could think of, but in vain,—now cursing my carelessness for having lost it, now swearing most solemnly to myself that I never could have received it. What was to be done? It was already late; my only thought was how to replace it. If I only knew the color, any other lock of hair would, doubtless, do just as well. The chances were, as Howard was young and an Englishman, that his hair was light; light-brown, probably, something like my own. Of course it was; why didn't that thought occur to me before? How stupid I was. So saying, I seized a pair of scissors, and cut a long lock beside my temple; this in a calm moment I might have hesitated about. "Yes," thought I, "she'll never discover the cheat; and besides, I do feel,—I know not exactly why,—rather gratified to think that I shall have left this *souvenir* behind me, even though it call up other recollections than of me." So thinking, I wrapped my cloak about me and hastened towards the Casino.

CHAPTER XLI.

THE ROUTE.

I had scarcely gone a hundred yards from my quarters when a great tramp of horses' feet attracted my attention. I stopped to listen, and soon heard the jingle of dragoon accoutrements, as the noise came near. The night was dark but perfectly still; and before I stood many minutes I heard the tones of a voice which I well knew could belong to but one, and that Fred Power.

"Fred Power!" said I, shouting at the same time at the top of my voice,—"Power!"

"Ah, Charley, is that you? Come along to the adjutant-general's quarters. I'm charged with some important despatches, and can't stop till I've delivered them. Come along, I've glorious news for you!" So saying, he dashed spurs to his horse, and followed by two mounted dragoons, galloped past. Power's few and hurried words had so excited my curiosity that I turned at once to follow him, questioning myself, as I walked along, to what he could possibly allude. He knew of my attachment to Lucy Dashwood,—could he mean anything of her? But what could I expect there; by what flattery could I picture to myself any chance of success in that quarter; and yet, what other news could I care for or value than what bore upon her fate upon whom my own depended? Thus ruminating, I reached the door of the spacious building in which the adjutant-general had taken up his abode, and soon found myself among a crowd of persons whom the rumor of some important event had assembled there, though no one could tell what had occurred. Before many minutes the door opened, and Power came out; bowing hurriedly to a few, and whispering a word or two as he passed down the steps, he seized me by the arm and led me across the street. "Charley," said he, "the curtain's rising; the piece is about to begin; a new commander-in-chief is sent out,—Sir Arthur Wellesley, my boy, the finest fellow in England is to lead us on, and we march to-morrow. There's news for you!" A raw boy, unread, uninformed as I was, I knew but little of his career whose name had even then shed such lustre upon our army; but the buoyant tone of Power as he spoke, the kindling energy of his voice roused me, and I felt every inch a soldier. As I grasped his hand in delightful enthusiasm I lost all memory of my disappointment, and in the beating throb that shook my head; I felt how deeply slept the ardor of military glory that first led me from my home to see a battle-field.

"There goes the news!" said Frederick, pointing as he spoke to a rocket that shot up into the sky, and as it broke into ten thousand stars, illuminated the broad stream where the ships of war lay darkly resting. In another moment the whole air shone with similar fires, while the deep roll of the drum sounded along the silent streets, and the city so lately sunk in sleep became, as if by magic, thronged with crowds of people; the sharp clang of the cavalry trumpet blended with the gay carol of the light-infantry bugle, and the heavy tramp of the march was heard in the distance. All was excitement, all bustle; but in the joyous tone of every voice was spoken the longing anxiety to meet the enemy. The gay, reckless tone of an Irish song would occasionally reach us, as some Connaught Ranger or some 78th man passed, his knapsack on his back; or the low monotonous pibroch of the Highlander, swelling into a war-cry, as some kilted corps drew up their ranks together. We turned to regain our quarters, when at the corner of a street we came suddenly upon a merry party seated around a table before a little inn; a large street lamp, unhung for the occasion, had been placed in the midst of them, and showed us the figures of several soldiers in undress; at the end, and raised a little above his compeers, sat one whom, by the unfair proportion he assumed of the conversation, not less than by the musical intonation of his voice, I soon recognized as my man, Mickey Free.

"I'll be hanged if that's not your fellow there, Charley," said Power, as he came to a dead stop a few yards off. "What an impertinent varlet he is; only to think of him there, presiding among a set of fellows that have fought all the battles in the Peninsular war. At this moment I'll be hanged if he is not going to sing."

Here a tremendous thumping upon the table announced the fact, and after a few preliminary observations from Mike, illustrative of his respect to the service in which he had so often distinguished himself, he began, to the air of the "Young May Moon," a ditty of which I only recollect the following verses:—

"The pickets are fast retreating, boys, The last tattoo is beating, boys, So let every man Finish his can, And drink to our next merry meeting, boys. The colonel so gayly prancing, boys, Has a wonderful trick of advancing, boys, When he sings out so large, 'Fix bayonets and charge!' He sets all the Frenchmen a-dancing, boys. Let Mounseer look ever so big, my boys, Who cares for fighting a fig, my boys? When we play 'Garryowen,' He'd rather go home; For somehow, he's no taste for a jig, my boys."

This admirable lyric seemed to have perfect success, if one were only to judge from the thundering of voices, hands, and drinking vessels which followed; while a venerable, gray-haired sergeant rose to propose Mr. Free's health, and speedy promotion to him.

We stood for several minutes in admiration of the party, when the loud roll of the drums beating to arms awakened us to the thought that our moments were numbered.

"Good-night, Charley!" said Power, as he shook my hand warmly, "good-night! It will be your last night under a curtain for some months to come; make the most of it. Adieu!"

So saying, we parted; he to his quarters, and I to all the confusion of my baggage, which lay in most admired disorder about my room.

CHAPTER XLII.

THE FAREWELL.

The preparations for the march occupied me till near morning; and, indeed, had I been disposed to sleep, the din and clamor of the world without would have totally prevented it. Before daybreak the advanced guard was already in motion, and some squadrons of heavy cavalry had begun their march.

I looked around my now dismantled room as one does usually for the last time ere leaving, and bethought me if I had not forgotten anything. Apparently all was remembered; but stay,—what is this? To be sure, how forgetful I had become! It was the packet I destined for Donna Inez, and which, in the confusion of the night before, I had omitted to bring to the Casino.

I immediately despatched Mike to the commissary with my luggage and orders to ascertain when we were expected to march. He soon returned with the intelligence that our corps was not to move before noon, so that I had yet some hours to spare and make my adieux to the senhora.

I cannot exactly explain the reason, but I certainly did bestow a more than common attention upon my toilet that morning. The senhora was nothing to me. It is true she had, as she lately most candidly informed me, a score of admirers, among whom I was not even reckoned; she was evidently a coquette whose greatest pleasure was to sport and amuse herself with the passions she excited in others. And even if she were not,—if her heart were to be won to-morrow,—what claim, what right, had I to seek it? My affections were already pledged; promised, it is true, to one who gave nothing in return, and who, perhaps, even loved another. Ah, there was the rub; that one confounded suspicion, lurking in the rear, chilled my courage and wounded my spirit.

If there be anything more disheartening to an Irishman, in his little *affaires de coeur*, than another, it is the sense of rivalry. The obstinacy of fathers, the ill-will of mothers, the coldness, the indifference of the lovely object herself,—obstacles though they be,—he has tact, spirit, and perseverance to overcome them. But when a more successful candidate for the fair presents himself; when the eye that remains downcast at *his* suit, lights up with animation at *another's* coming; when the features whose cold and chilling apathy to him have blended in one smile of welcome to another,—it is all up with him; he sees the game lost, and throws his cards upon the table. And yet, why is this? Why is it that he whose birthright it would seem to be sanguine when others despond, to be confident when all else are hopeless,—should find his courage fail him here? The reason is simply—But, in good sooth, I am ashamed to confess it!

Having jogged on so far with my reader, in all the sober seriousness which the matter-of-fact material of these memoirs demands, I fear lest a seeming paradox may cause me to lose my good name for veracity; and that while merely maintaining a national trait of my country, I may appear to be asserting some unheard-of and absurd proposition,—so far have mere vulgar prejudices gone to sap our character as a people.

The reason, then, is this,—for I have gone too far to retreat,—the Irishman is essentially bashful. Well, laugh if you wish, for I conclude that, by this time, you have given way to a most immoderate excess of risibility; but still, when you have perfectly recovered your composure, I beg to repeat,—the Irishman is essentially a bashful man!

Do not for a moment fancy that I would by this imply that in any new or unexpected situation, that from any unforeseen conjuncture of events, the Irishman would feel confused or abashed, more than any other,—far from it. The cold and habitual reserve of the Englishman, the studied caution of the North Tweeder himself, would exhibit far stronger evidences of awkwardness in such circumstances as these. But on the other hand, when measuring his capacity, his means of success, his probabilities of being preferred, with those of the natives of any other country, I back the Irishman against the world for distrust of his own powers, for an under-estimate of his real merits,—in one word, for his bashfulness. But let us return to Donna Inez.

As I rode up to the villa, I found the family assembled at breakfast. Several officers were also present, among whom I was not sorry to recognize my friend Monsoon.

"Ah, Charley!" cried he, as I seated myself beside him, "what a pity all our fun is so soon to have an end! Here's this confounded Soult won't be quiet and peaceable; but he must march upon Oporto, and Heaven knows where besides, just as we were really beginning to enjoy life! I had got such a contract for blankets! And now they've ordered me to join Beresford's corps in the mountains; and you," here he dropped his voice,—"and you were getting on so devilish well in this quarter; upon my life, I think you'd have carried the day. Old Don Emanuel—you know he's a friend of mine—likes you very much. And then, there's Sparks—"

"Ay, Major, what of him? I have not seen him for some days."

"Why, they've been frightening the poor devil out of his life, O'Shaughnessy and a set of them. They tried him by court-martial yesterday, and sentenced him to mount guard with a wooden sword and a shooting jacket, which he did. Old Colbourne, it seems, saw him; and faith, there would be the devil to pay if the route had not come! Some of them would certainly have got a long leave to see their friends."

"Why is not the senhora here, Major? I don't see her at table."

"A cold, a sore throat, a wet-feet affair of last night, I believe. Pass that cold pie down here. Sherry, if you please. You didn't see Power to-day?"

"No: we parted late last night; I have not been to bed."

"Very bad preparation for a march; take some burned brandy in your coffee."

"Then you don't think the senhora will appear?"

"Very unlikely. But stay, you know her room,—the small drawing-room that looks out upon the flower-garden; she usually passes the morning there. Leap the little wooden paling round the corner, and the chances are ten to one you find her."

I saw from the occupied air of Don Antonio that there was little fear of interruption on his part; so taking an early moment to escape unobserved, I rose and left the room. When I sprang over the oak fence, I found myself in a delicious little garden, where roses, grown to a height never seen in our colder climate, formed a deep bower of rich blossom.

The major was right. The senhora was in the room, and in one moment I was beside her.

"Nothing but my fears of not bidding you farewell could palliate my thus intruding, Donna Inez; but as we are ordered away—"

"When? Not so soon, surely?"

"Even so; to-day, this very hour. But you see that even in the hurry of departure, I have not forgotten my trust; this is the packet I promised you."

So saying, I placed the paper with the lock of hair within her hand, and bending downwards, pressed my lips upon her taper fingers. She hurriedly snatched her hand away, and tearing open the enclosure, took out the lock. She looked steadily for a moment at it, then at me, and again at it, and at length, bursting into a fit of laughing, threw herself upon a chair in a very ecstasy of mirth.

"Why, you don't mean to impose this auburn ringlet upon me for one of poor Howard's jetty curls? What downright folly to think of it! And then, with how little taste the deception was practised,—upon your very temples, too! One comfort is, you are utterly spoiled by it."

Here she again relapsed into a fit of laughter, leaving me perfectly puzzled what to think of her, as she resumed:—

"Well, tell me now, am I to reckon this as a pledge of your own allegiance, or am I still to believe it to be Edward Howard's? Speak, and truly."

"Of my own, most certainly," said I, "if it will be accepted."

"Why, after such treachery, perhaps it ought not; but still, as you have already done yourself such injury, and look so very silly, withal—"

"That you are even resolved to give me cause to look more so," added I.

"Exactly," said she, "for here, now, I reinstate you among my true and faithful admirers. Kneel down, Sir Knight—in token of which you will wear this scarf—"

A sudden start which the donna gave at these words brought me to my feet. She was pale as death and trembling.

"What means this?" said I. "What has happened?"

She pointed with her finger towards the garden; but though her lips moved, no voice came forth. I sprang through the open window; I rushed into the copse, the only one which might afford concealment for a figure, but no one was there. After a few minutes' vain endeavor to discover any trace of an intruder, I returned to the chamber. The donna was there still, but how changed; her gayety and animation were gone, her pale cheek and trembling lip bespoke fear and suffering, and her cold hand lay heavily beside her.

"I thought—perhaps it was merely fancy—but I thought I saw Trevyllian beside the window."

"Impossible!" said I. "I have searched every walk and alley. It was nothing but imagination,—believe me, no more. There, be assured; think no more of it."

While I endeavored thus to reassure her, I was very far from feeling perfectly at ease myself; the whole bearing and conduct of this man had inspired me with a growing dislike of him, and I felt already half-convinced that he had established himself as a spy upon my actions.

"Then you really believe I was mistaken?" said the donna, as she placed her hand within mine.

"Of course I do; but speak no more of it. You must not forget how few my moments are here. Already I have heard the tramp of horses without. Ah! there they are. In a moment more I shall be missed; so, once more, fairest Inez—Nay, I beg pardon if I have dared to call you thus; but think, if it be the first it may also be the last time I shall ever speak it."

Her head gently drooped, as I said these words, till it sank upon my shoulder, her long and heavy hair falling upon my neck and across my bosom. I felt her heart almost beat against my side; I muttered some words, I know not what; I felt them like a prayer; I pressed her cold forehead to my lips, rushed from the room, cleared the fence at a spring, and was far upon the road to Lisbon ere I could sufficiently collect my senses to know whither I was going. Of little else was I conscious; my mind was full to bursting; and in the confusion of my excited brain, fiction and reality were so inextricably mingled as to defy every endeavor at discrimination. But little time had I for reflection. As I reached the city, the brigade to which I was attached was already under arms, and Mike impatiently waiting my arrival with the horses.

CHAPTER XXIII.

THE MARCH.

What a strange spectacle did the road to Oliveira present upon the morning of the 7th of May! A hurried or incautious observer might, at first sight, have pronounced the long line of troops which wended their way through the valley as the remains of a broken and routed army, had not the ardent expression and bright eye that beamed on every side assured him that men who looked thus could not be beaten ones. Horse, foot, baggage, artillery, dismounted dragoons, even the pale and scarcely recovered inhabitants of the hospital, might have been seen hurrying on; for the order, "Forward!" had been given at Lisbon, and those whose wounds did not permit their joining, were more pitied for their loss than its cause. More than one officer was seen at the head of his troop with an arm in a sling, or a bandaged forehead; while among the men similar evidences of devotion were not unfrequent. As for me, long years and many reverses have not obliterated, scarcely blunted, the impression that sight made on me. The splendid spectacle of a review had often excited and delighted me, but here there was the glorious reality of war,—the bronzed faces, the worn uniforms, the well-tattered flags, the roll of the heavy guns mingling with the wild pibroch of the Highlander, or scarcely less wild recklessness of the Irish quick-step; while the long line of cavalry, their helmets and accoutrements shining in the morning sun, brought back one's boyish dreams of joust and tournament, and made the heart beat high with chivalrous enthusiasm.

"Yes," said I, half aloud, "this is indeed a realization of what I longed and thirsted for," the clang of the music and the tramp of the cavalry responding to my throbbing pulses as we moved along.

"Close up, there; trot!" cried out a deep and manly voice; and immediately a general officer rode by, followed by an aide-de-camp.

"There goes Cotton," said Power. "You may feel easy in your mind now, Charley; there's some work before us."

"You have not heard our destination?" said I.

"Nothing is known for certain yet. The report goes, that Soult is advancing upon Oporto; and the chances are, Sir Arthur intends to hasten on to its relief. Our fellows are at Ovar, with General Murray."

"I say, Charley, old Monsoon is in a devil of a flurry. He expected to have been peaceably settled down in Lisbon for the next six months, and he has received orders to set out for Beresford's headquarters immediately; and from what I hear, they have no idle time."

"Well, Sparks, how goes it, man? Better fun this than the cook's galley, eh?"

"Why, do you know, these hurried movements put me out confoundedly. I found Lisbon very interesting,—the little I could see of it last night."

"Ah, my dear fellow, think of the lovely Andalusian lasses with their brown transparent skins and liquid eyes. Why, you'd have been over head and ears in love in twenty-four hours more, had we stayed."

"Are they really so pretty?"

"Pretty! downright lovely, man. Why, they have a way of looking at you, over their fans,—just one glance, short and fleeting, but so melting, by Jove—Then their walk,—if it be not profane to call that springing, elastic gesture by such a name,—why, it's regular witchcraft. Sparks, my man, I tremble for you. Do you know, by-the-bye, that same pace of theirs is a devilish hard thing to learn. I never could come it; and yet, somehow, I was formerly rather a crack fellow at a ballet. Old Alberto used to select me for a *pas de zéphyr* among a host; but there's a kind of a hop and a slide and a spring,—in fact you must have been wearing petticoats for eighteen years, and have an Andalusian instep and an india-rubber sole to your foot, or it's no use trying it. How I used to make them laugh at the old San Josef convent, formerly, by my efforts in the cause!"

"Why, how did it ever occur to you to practise it?"

"Many a man's legs have saved his head, Charley, and I put it to mine to do a similar office for me."

"True; but I never heard of a man that performed a *pas seul* before the enemy."

"Not exactly; but still you're not very wide of the mark. If you'll only wait till we reach Pontalegue, I'll tell you the story; not that it's worth the delay, but talking at this brisk pace I don't admire."

"You leave a detachment here, Captain Power," said an aide-de-camp, riding hastily up; "and General Cotton requests you will send a subaltern and two sergeants forward towards Berar to reconnoitre the pass. Franchesca's cavalry are reported in that quarter." So speaking, he dashed spurs to his horse, and was out of sight in an instant.

Power, at the same moment, wheeled to the rear, from which he returned in an instant, accompanied by three well-mounted light dragoons. "Sparks," said he, "now for an occasion of distinguishing yourself. You heard the order, lose no time; and as your horse is an able one, and fresh, lose not a second, but forward."

No sooner was Sparks despatched on what it was evident he felt to be anything but a pleasant duty, than I turned towards Power, and said, with some tinge of disappointment in the tone, "Well, if you really felt there was anything worth doing there, I flattered myself that—"

"Speak out man. That I should have sent you, eh? Is it not so?"

"Yes, you've hit it."

"Well, Charley, my peace is easily made on this head. Why, I selected Sparks simply to spare you one of the most unpleasant duties that can be imposed upon a man; a duty which, let him discharge it to the uttermost, will never be acknowledged, and the slightest failure in which will be remembered for many a day against him, besides the pleasant and very probable prospect of being selected as a bull's eye for a French rifle, or carried off a prisoner; eh, Charley? There's no glory in that, devil a ray of it! Come, come, old fellow, Fred Power's not the man to keep his friend out of the *mêlée*, if only anything can be made by being in it. Poor Sparks, I'd swear, is as little satisfied with the arrangement as yourself, if one knew but all."

"I say, Power," said a tall, dashing-looking man of about five-and-forty, with a Portuguese order on his breast,—"I say, Power, dine with us at the halt."

"With pleasure, if I may bring my young friend here."

"Of course; pray introduce us."

"Major Hixley, Mr. O'Malley,—a 14th man, Hixley."

"Delighted to make your acquaintance, Mr. O'Malley. Knew a famous fellow in Ireland of your name, a certain Godfrey O'Malley, member for some county or other."

"My uncle," said I, blushing deeply, with a pleasurable feeling at even this slight praise of my oldest friend.

"Your uncle! give me your hand. By Jove, his nephew has a right to good treatment at my hands; he saved my life in the year '98. And how is old Godfrey?"

"Quite well, when I left him some months ago; a little gout, now and then."

"To be sure he has, no man deserves it better; but it's a gentlemanlike gout that merely jogs his memory in the morning of the good wine he has drank over night. By-the-bye, what became of a friend of his, a devilish eccentric fellow who held a command in the Austrian service?"

"Oh, Considine, the count?"

"The same."

"As eccentric as ever; I left him on a visit with my uncle. And Boyle,—did you know Sir Harry Boyle?"

"To be sure I did; shall I ever forget him, and his capital blunders, that kept me laughing the whole time I spent in Ireland? I was in the house when he concluded a panegyric upon a friend, by calling him, 'the father to the poor, and uncle to Lord Donoughmore.'"

"He was the only man who could render by a bull what it was impossible to convey more correctly," said Power.

"You've heard of his duel with Dick Toler?"

"Never; let's hear it."

"It was a bull from beginning to end. Boyle took it into his head that Dick was a person with whom he had a serious row in Cork. Dick, on the other hand, mistook Boyle for old Caples, whom he had been pursuing with horse-whipping intentions for some months. They met in Kildare Street Club, and very little colloquy satisfied them that they were right in their conjectures, each party being so eagerly ready to meet the views of the other. It never was a difficult matter to find a friend in Dublin; and to do them justice, Irish seconds, generally speaking, are perfectly free from any imputation upon the score of mere delay. No men have less impertinent curiosity as to the cause of the quarrel; wisely supposing that the principals know their own affairs best, they cautiously abstain from indulging any prying spirit, but proceed to discharge their functions as best they may. Accordingly, Sir Harry and Dick were 'set up,' as the phrase is, at twelve paces, and to use Boyle's own words, for I have heard him relate the story,—

"We blazed away, sir, for three rounds. I put two in his hat and one in his neckcloth; his shots went all through the skirt of my coat.

"'We'll spend the day here,' says Considine, 'at this rate. Couldn't you put them closer?'

"'And give us a little more time in the word,' says I.

"'Exactly,' said Dick.

"Well, they moved us forward two paces, and set to loading the pistols again.

"By this time we were so near that we had full opportunity to scan each other's faces. Well, sir, I stared at him, and he at me.

"'What!' said I.

"'Eh!' said he.

"'How's this?' said I.

"'You're not Billy Caples?' said he.

"'Devil a bit!' said I, 'nor I don't think you are Archy Devine;' and faith, sir, so it appeared, we were fighting away all the morning for nothing; for, somehow, it turned out *it was neither of us!*"

What amused me most in this anecdote was the hearing it at such a time and place. That poor Sir Harry's eccentricities should turn up for discussion on a march in Portugal was singular enough; but after all, life is full of such incongruous accidents. I remember once supping with King Calzoo on the Blue Mountains, in Jamaica. By way of entertaining his guests, some English officers, he ordered one of his suite to sing. We were of course pleased at the opportunity of hearing an Indian war-chant, with a skull and thigh-bone accompaniment; but what was our astonishment to hear the Indian,—a ferocious-looking dog, with an awful scalp-lock, and two streaks of red paint across his chest,—clear his voice well for a few seconds, and then begin, without discomposing a muscle of his gravity, "The Laird of Cockpen!" I need not say that the "Great Raccoon" was a Dumfries man who had quitted Scotland forty years before, and with characteristic prosperity had attained his present rank in a foreign service.

"Halt! halt!" cried a deep-toned, manly voice in the leading column, and the word was repeated from mouth to mouth to the rear.

We dismounted, and picketing our horses beneath the broad-leaved foliage of the cork-trees, stretched ourselves out at full length upon the grass, while our messmen prepared the dinner. Our party at first consisted of Hixley, Power, the adjutant, and myself; but our number was soon increased by three officers of the 6th Foot, about to join their regiment.

"Barring the ladies, God bless them!" said Power, "there are no such picnics as campaigning presents. The charms of scenery are greatly enhanced by their coming unexpectedly on you. Your chance good fortune in the prog has an interest that no ham-and-cold-chicken affair, prepared by your servants beforehand, and got ready with a degree of fuss and worry that converts the whole party into an assembly of cooks, can ever afford; and lastly, the excitement that this same life of ours is never without, gives a zest—"

"There you've hit it," cried Hixley; "it's that same feeling of uncertainty that those who meet now may ever do so again, full as it is of sorrowful reflection, that still teaches us, as we become inured to war, to economize our pleasures, and be happy when we may. Your health, O'Malley, and your uncle Godfrey's too."

"A little more of the pastry."

"What a capital guinea fowl this is!"

"That's some of old Monsoon's particular port."

"Pass it round here. Really this is pleasant."

"My blessing on the man who left that vista yonder! See what a glorious valley stretches out there, undulating in its richness; and look at those dark trees, where just one streak of soft sunlight is kissing their tops, giving them one chaste good-night—"

"Well done, Power!"

"Confound you, you've pulled me short, and I was about becoming downright pastoral. Apropos of kissing, I understand Sir Arthur won't allow the convents to be occupied by troops."

"And apropos of convents," said I, "let's hear your story; you promised it a while ago."

"My dear Charley, it's far too early in the evening for a story. I should rather indulge my poetic fancies here, under the shade of melancholy boughs; and besides, I am not half screwed up yet."

"Come, Adjutant, let's have a song."

"I'll sing you a Portuguese serenade when the next bottle comes in. What capital port! Have you much of it?"

"Only three dozen. We got it late last night; forged an order from the commanding officer and sent it up to old Monsoon,—'for hospital use.' He gave it with a tear in his eye, saying, as the sergeant marched away, 'Only think of such wine for fellows that may be in the next world before morning! It's a downright sin!'"

"I say, Power, there's something going on there."

At this instant the trumpet sounded "boot and saddle," and like one man the whole mass rose up, when the scene, late so tranquil, became one of excited bustle and confusion. An aide-de-camp galloped past towards the river, followed by two orderly sergeants; and the next moment Sparks rode up, his whole equipment giving evidence of a hurried ride, while his cheek was deadly pale and haggard.

Power presented to him a goblet of sherry, which, having emptied at a draught, he drew a long breath, and said, "They are coming,—coming in force!"

"Who are coming?" said Power. "Take time, man, and collect yourself."

"The French! I saw them a devilish deal closer than I liked. They wounded one of the orderlies and took the other prisoner."

"Forward!" said a hoarse voice in the front. "March! trot!" And before we could obtain any further information from Sparks, whose faculties seemed to have received a terrific shock, we were once more in the saddle, and moving at a brisk pace onward.

Sparks had barely time to tell us that a large body of French cavalry occupied the pass of Berar, when he was sent for by General Cotton to finish his report.

"How frightened the fellow is!" said Hixley.

"I don't think the worse of poor Sparks for all that," said Power. "He saw those fellows for the first time, and no bird's-eye view of them either."

"Then we are in for a skirmish, at least," said I.

"It would appear not, from that," said Hixley, pointing to the head of the column, which, leaving the high road upon the left, entered the forest by a deep cleft that opened upon a valley traversed by a broad river.

"That looks very like taking up a position, though," said Power.

"Look,—look down yonder!" cried Hixley, pointing to a dip in the plain beside the river. "Is there not a cavalry picket there?"

"Right, by Jove! I say, Fitzroy," said Power to an aide-de-camp as he passed, "what's going on?"

"Soult has carried Oporto," cried he, "and Franchesca's cavalry have escaped."

"And who are these fellows in the valley?"

"Our own people coming up."

In less than half an hour's brisk trotting we reached the stream, the banks of which were occupied by two cavalry regiments advancing to the main army; and what was my delight to find that one of them was our own corps, the 14th Light Dragoons!

"Hurra!" cried Power, waving his cap as he came up. "How are you, Sedgewick? Baker, my hearty, how goes it? How is Hampton and the colonel?"

In an instant we were surrounded by our brother officers, who all shook me cordially by the hand, and welcomed me to the regiment with most gratifying warmth.

"One of us," said Power, with a knowing look, as he introduced me; and the freemasonry of these few words secured me a hearty greeting.

"Halt! halt! Dismount!" sounded again from front to rear; and in a few minutes we were once more stretched upon the grass, beneath the deep and mellow moonlight, while the bright stream ran placidly beside us, reflecting on its calm surface the varied groups as they lounged or sat around the blazing fires of the bivouac.

CHAPTER XLIV.

THE BIVOUAC.

When I contrasted the gay and lively tone of the conversation which ran on around our bivouac fire, with the dry monotony and prosaic tediousness of my first military dinner at Cork, I felt how much the spirit and adventure of a soldier's life can impart of chivalrous enthusiasm to even the dullest and least susceptible. I saw even many who under common circumstances, would have possessed no interest nor excited any curiosity, but now, connected as they were with the great events occurring around them, absolutely became heroes; and it was with a strange, wild throbbing of excitement I listened to the details of movements and marches, whose objects I knew not, but in which the magical words, Corunna, Vimeira, were mixed up, and gave to the circumstances an interest of the highest character. How proud, too, I felt to be the companion-in-arms of such fellows! Here they sat, the tried and proved soldiers of a hundred fights, treating me as their brother and their equal. Who need wonder if I felt a sense of excited pleasure? Had I needed such a stimulant, that night beneath the cork-trees had been enough to arouse a passion for the army in my heart, and an irrepressible determination to seek for a soldier's glory.

"Fourteenth!" called out a voice from the wood behind; and in a moment after, the aide-de-camp appeared with a mounted orderly.

"Colonel Merivale?" said he, touching his cap to the stalwart, soldier-like figure before him.

The colonel bowed.

"Sir Stapleton Cotton desires me to request that at an early hour to-morrow you will occupy the pass, and cover the march of the troops. It is his wish that all the reinforcements should arrive at Oporto by noon. I need scarcely add that we expect to be engaged with the enemy."

These few words were spoken hurriedly, and again saluting our party, he turned his horse's head and continued his way towards the rear.

"There's news for you, Charley," said Power, slapping me on the shoulder. "Lucy Dashwood or Westminster Abbey!"

"The regiment was never in finer condition, that's certain," said the colonel, "and most eager for a brush with the enemy."

"How your old friend, the count, would have liked this work!" said Hixley. "Gallant fellow he was."

"Come," cried Power, "here's a fresh bowl coming. Let's drink the ladies, wherever they be; we most of us have some soft spot on that score."

"Yes," said the adjutant, singing,—

"*Here's to the maiden of blushing fifteen; Here's to the damsel that's merry; Here's to the flaunting extravagant quean—*"

"And," sang Power, interrupting,—

"*Here's to the 'Widow of Derry.'*"

"Come, come, Fred, no more quizzing on that score. It's the only thing ever gives me a distaste to the service,—the souvenir of that adventure. When I reflect what I might have been, and think what I am; when I contrast a Brussels carpet with wet grass, silk hangings with a canvas tent, Sneyd's claret with ration brandy, and Sir Arthur for a Commander-in-Chief *vice* Boggs, a widow—"

"Stop there!" cried Hixley. "Without disparaging the fair widow, there's nothing beats campaigning, after all. Eh, Fred?"

"And to prove it," said the colonel, "Power will sing us a song."

Power took his pencil from his pocket, and placing the back of a letter across his shako, commenced inditing his lyric, saying, as he did so, "I'm your man in five minutes. Just fill my glass in the mean time."

"That fellow beats Dibdin hollow," whispered the adjutant. "I'll be hanged if he'll not knock you off a song like lightning."

"I understand," said Hixley, "they have some intention at the Horse Guards of having all the general orders set to popular tunes, and sung at every mess in the service. You've heard that, I suppose, Sparks?"

"I confess I had not before."

"It will certainly come very hard upon the subalterns," continued Hixley, with much gravity. "They'll have to brush up their *sol mi fas*. All the solos are to be their part."

"What rhymes with slaughter?" said Power.

"Brandy-and-water," said the adjutant.

"Now, then," said Power, "are you all ready?"

"Ready."

"You must chorus, mind; and mark me, take care you give the hip-hip-hurra well, as that's the whole force of the chant. Take the time from me. Now for it. Air, 'Garryowen,' with spirit, but not too quick.

"Now that we've pledged each eye of blue, And every maiden fair and true, And our green island home,—to you The ocean's wave adorning, Let's give one Hip-hip-hip-hurra! And, drink e'en to the coming day, When, squadron square, We'll all be there, To meet the French in the morning. "May his bright laurels never fade, Who leads our fighting fifth brigade, Those lads so true in heart and blade, And famed for danger scorning. So join me in one Hip-hurra! And drink e'en to the coming day, When, squadron square, We'll all be there, To meet the French in the morning. "And when with years and honors crowned, You sit some homeward hearth around, And hear no more the stirring sound That spoke the trumpet's warning, You'll fill and drink, one Hip-hurra! And pledge the memory of the day, When, squadron square, They all were there, To meet the French in the morning."

"Gloriously done, Fred!" cried Hixley. "If I ever get my deserts in this world, I'll make you Laureate to the Forces, with a hogshead of your own native whiskey for every victory of the army."

"A devilish good chant," said Merivale, "but the air surpasses anything I ever heard,—thoroughly Irish, I take it."

"Irish! upon my conscience, I believe you!" shouted O'Shaughnessy, with an energy of voice and manner that created a hearty laugh on all sides. "It's few people ever mistook it for a Venetian melody. Hand over the punch,—the sherry, I mean. When I was in the Clare militia, we always went in to dinner to 'Tatter Jack Walsh,' a sweet air, and had 'Garryowen' for a quick-step. Ould M'Manus, when he got the regiment, wanted to change: he said, they were damned vulgar tunes, and wanted to have 'Rule Britannia,' or the 'Hundredth Psalm;' but we would not stand it; there would have been a mutiny in the corps."

"The same fellow, wasn't he, that you told the story of, the other evening, in Lisbon?" said I.

"The same. Well, what a character he was! As pompous and conceited a little fellow as ever you met with; and then, he was so bullied by his wife, he always came down to revenge it on the regiment. She was a fine, showy, vulgar woman, with a most cherishing affection for all the good things in this life, except her husband, whom she certainly held in due contempt. 'Ye little crayture,' she'd say to him with a sneer, 'it ill becomes you to drink and sing, and be making a man of yourself. If you were like O'Shaughnessy there, six foot three in his stockings—'Well, well, it looks like boasting; but no matter. Here's her health, anyway."

"I knew you were tender in that quarter," said Power, "I heard it when quartered in Limerick."

"May be you heard, too, how I paid off Mac, when he came down on a visit to that county?"

"Never: let's hear it now."

"Ay, O'Shaughnessy, now's your time; the fire's a good one, the night fine, and liquor plenty."

"I'm *convanient*," said O'Shaughnessy, as depositing his enormous legs on each side of the burning fagots, and placing a bottle between his knees he began his story:—

"It was a cold rainy night in January, in the year '98, I took my place in the Limerick mail, to go down for a few days to the west country. As the waiter of the Hibernian came to the door with a lantern, I just caught a glimpse of the other insides; none of whom were known to me, except Colonel M'Manus, that I met once in a boarding-house in Molesworth Street. I did not, at the time, think him a very agreeable companion; but when morning broke, and we began to pay our respects to each other in the coach, I leaned over, and said, 'I hope you're well, Colonel M'Manus,' just by way of civility like. He didn't hear me at first; so that I said it again, a little louder.

"I wish you saw the look he gave me; he drew himself up to the height of his cotton umbrella, put his chin inside his cravat, pursed up his dry, shrivelled lips, and with a voice he meant to be awful, replied:—

"'You appear to have the advantage of me.'

"'Upon my conscience, you're right,' said I, looking down at myself, and then over at him, at which the other travellers burst out a laughing,—'I think there's few will dispute that point.' When the laugh was over, I resumed,—for I was determined not to let him off so easily. 'Sure I met you at Mrs. Cayle's,' said I; 'and, by the same token, it was a Friday, I remember it well,—may be you didn't pitch into the salt cod? I hope it didn't disagree with you?'

"'I beg to repeat, sir, that you are under a mistake,' said he.

"'May be so, indeed,' said I. 'May be you're not Colonel M'Manus at all; may be you wasn't in a passion for losing seven-and-sixpence at loo with Mrs. Moriarty; may be you didn't break the lamp in the hall with your umbrella, pretending you touched it with your head, and wasn't within three foot of it; may be Counsellor Brady wasn't going to put you in the box of the Foundling Hospital, if you wouldn't behave quietly in the streets—'

"Well, with this the others laughed so heartily, that I could not go on; and the next stage the bold colonel got outside with the guard and never came in till we reached Limerick. I'll never forget his face, as he got down at Swinburne's Hotel. 'Good-by, Colonel,' said I; but he wouldn't take the least notice of my politeness, but with a frown of utter defiance, he turned on his heel and walked away.

"'I haven't done with you yet,' says I; and, faith, I kept my word.

"I hadn't gone ten yards down the street, when I met my old friend Darby O'Grady.

"'Shaugh, my boy,' says he,—he called me that way for shortness,—'dine with me to-day at Mosey's; a green goose and gooseberries; six to a minute.'

"'Who have you?' says I.

"'Tom Keane and the Wallers, a counsellor or two, and one M'Manus, from Dublin.'

"'The colonel?'

"'The same,' said he.

"'I'm there, Darby!' said I; 'but mind, you never saw me before.'

"'What?' said he.

"'You never set eyes on me before; mind that.'

"'I understand,' said Darby, with a wink; and we parted.

"I certainly was never very particular about dressing for dinner, but on this day I spent a considerable time at my toilet; and when I looked in my glass at its completion, was well satisfied that I had done myself justice. A waistcoat of brown rabbit-skin with flaps, a red worsted comforter round my neck, an old gray shooting-jacket with a brown patch on the arm, corduroys, and leather gaiters, with a tremendous oak cudgel in my hand, made me a most presentable figure for a dinner party.

"'Will I do, Darby?' says I, as he came into my room before dinner.

"'If it's for robbing the mail you are,' says he, 'nothing could be better. Your father wouldn't know you!'

"'Would I be the better of a wig?'

"'Leave your hair alone,' said he. 'It's painting the lily to alter it.'

"'Well, God's will be done,' says I, 'so come now.'

"Well, just as the clock struck six I saw the colonel coming out of his room, in a suit of most accurate sable, stockings, and pumps. Down-stairs he went, and I heard the waiter announce him.

"'Now's my time,' thought I, as I followed slowly after.

"When I reached the door I heard several voices within, among which I recognized some ladies. Darby had not told me about them. 'But no matter,' said I; 'it's all as well;' so I gave a gentle tap at the door with my knuckles.

"'Come in,' said Darby.

"I opened the door slowly, and putting in only my head and shoulders took a cautious look round the room.

"'I beg pardon, gentlemen,' said I, 'but I was only looking for one Colonel M'Manus, and as he is not here—'

"'Pray walk in, sir,' said O'Grady, with a polite bow. 'Colonel M'Manus is here. There's no intrusion whatever. I say, Colonel,' said he turning round, 'a gentleman here desires to—'

"'Never mind it now,' said I, as I stepped cautiously into the room, 'he's going to dinner; another time will do just as well.'

"'Pray come in!'

"'I could not think of intruding—'

"'I must protest,' said M'Manus, coloring up, 'that I cannot understand this gentleman's visit.'

"'It is a little affair I have to settle with him,' said I, with a fierce look that I saw produced its effect.

"'Then perhaps you would do me the very great favor to join him at dinner,' said O'Grady. 'Any friend of Colonel M'Manus—'

"'You are really too good,' said I; 'but as an utter stranger—'

"'Never think of that for a moment. My friend's friend, as the adage says.'

"'Upon my conscience, a good saying,' said I, 'but you see there's another difficulty. I've ordered a chop and potatoes up in No. 5.'

"'Let that be no obstacle,' said O'Grady. 'The waiter shall put it in my bill; if you will only do me the pleasure.'

"'You're a trump,' said I. 'What's your name?'

"'O'Grady, at your service.'

"'Any relation of the counsellor?' said I. 'They're all one family, the O'Gradys. I'm Mr. O'Shaughnessy, from Ennis; won't you introduce me to the ladies?'

"While the ceremony of presentation was going on I caught one glance at M'Manus, and had hard work not to roar out laughing. Such an expression of surprise, amazement, indignation, rage, and misery never was mixed up in one face before. Speak he could not; and I saw that, except for myself, he had neither eyes, ears, nor senses for anything around him. Just at this moment dinner was announced, and in we went. I never was in such spirits in my life; the trick upon M'Manus had succeeded perfectly; he believed in his heart that I had never met O'Grady in my life before, and that upon the faith of our friendship, I had received my invitation. As for me, I spared him but little. I kept up a running fire of droll stories, had the ladies in fits of laughing, made everlasting allusions to the colonel; and, in a word, ere the soup had disappeared, except himself, the company was entirely with me.

"'O'Grady,' said I, 'forgive the freedom, but I feel as if we were old acquaintances.'

"'As Colonel M'Manus's friend,' said he, 'you can take no liberty here to which you are not perfectly welcome.'

"'Just what I expected,' said I. 'Mac and I,'—I wish you saw his face when I called him Mac,—'Mac and I were schoolfellows five-and-thirty years ago; though he forgets me, I don't forget him,—to be sure it would be hard for me. I'm just thinking of the day Bishop Oulahan came over to visit the college. Mac was coming in at the door of the refectory as the bishop was going out. "Take off your caubeen, you young scoundrel, and kneel down for his reverence to bless you," said one of the masters, giving his hat a blow at the same moment that sent it flying to the other end of the room, and with it, about twenty ripe pears that Mac had just stolen in the orchard, and had in his hat. I wish you only saw the bishop; and Mac himself, he was a picture. Well, well, you forget it all now, but I remember it as if it was only yesterday. Any champagne, Mr. O'Grady? I'm mighty dry.'

"'Of course,' said Darby. 'Waiter, some champagne here.'

"'Ah, it's himself was the boy for every kind of fun and devilment, quiet and demure as he looks over there. Mac, your health. It's not every day of the week we get champagne.'

"He laid down his knife and fork as I said this; his face and temples grew deep purple; his eyes started as if they would spring from his head; and he put both his hands to his forehead, as if trying to assure himself that it was not some horrid dream.

"'A little slice more of the turkey,' said I, 'and then, O'Grady, I'll try your hock. It's a wine I'm mighty fond of, and so is Mac there. Oh, it's seldom, to tell you the truth, it troubles us. There, fill up the glass; that's it. Here now, Darby,—that's your name, I think,—you'll not think I'm taking a liberty in giving a toast? Here then, I'll give M'Manus's health, with all the honors; though it's early yet, to be sure, but we'll do it again, by-and-by, when the whiskey comes. Here's

M'Manus's good health; and though his wife, they say, does not treat him well, and keeps him down—'

"The roar of laughing that interrupted me here was produced by the expression of poor Mac's face. He had started up from the table, and leaning with both his hands upon it, stared round upon the company like a maniac,—his mouth and eyes wide open, and his hair actually bristling with amazement. Thus he remained for a full minute, gasping like a fish in a landing-net. It seemed a hard struggle for him to believe he was not deranged. At last his eyes fell upon me; he uttered a deep groan, and with a voice tremulous with rage, thundered out,—

"'The scoundrel! I never saw him before.'

"He rushed from the room, and gained the street. Before our roar of laughter was over he had secured post-horses, and was galloping towards Ennis at the top speed of his cattle.

"He exchanged at once into the line; but they say that he caught a glimpse of my name in the army list, and sold out the next morning; be that as it may, we never met since."

I have related O'Shaughnessy's story here, rather from the memory I have of how we all laughed at it at the time, than from any feeling as to its real desert; but when I think of the voice, look, accent, and gesture of the narrator, I can scarcely keep myself from again giving way to laughter.

CHAPTER XLV.
THE DOURO.

Never did the morning break more beautifully than on the 12th of May, 1809. Huge masses of fog-like vapor had succeeded to the starry, cloudless night, but one by one, they moved onwards towards the sea, disclosing as they passed long tracts of lovely country, bathed in a rich golden glow. The broad Douro, with its transparent current, shone out like a bright-colored ribbon, meandering through the deep garment of fairest green; the darkly shadowed mountains which closed the background loomed even larger than they were; while their summits were tipped with the yellow glory of the morning. The air was calm and still, and the very smoke that arose from the peasant's cot labored as it ascended through the perfumed air, and save the ripple of the stream, all was silent as the grave.

The squadron of the 14th, with which I was, had diverged from the road beside the river, and to obtain a shorter path, had entered the skirts of a dark pine wood; our pace was a sharp one; an orderly had been already despatched to hasten our arrival, and we pressed on at a brisk trot. In less than an hour we reached the verge of the wood, and as we rode out upon the plain, what a spectacle met our eyes! Before us, in a narrow valley separated from the river by a low ridge, were picketed three cavalry regiments; their noiseless gestures and perfect stillness bespeaking at once that they were intended for a surprise party. Farther down the stream, and upon the opposite side, rose the massive towers and tall spires of Oporto, displaying from their summits the broad ensign of France; while far as the eye could reach, the broad dark masses of troops might be seen; the intervals between their columns glittering with the bright equipments of their cavalry, whose steel caps and lances were sparkling in the sun-beams. The bivouac fires were still smouldering, and marking where some part of the army had passed the night; for early as it was, it was evident that their position had been changed; and even now, the heavy masses of dark infantry might be seen moving from place to place, while the long line of the road to Vallonga was marked with a vast cloud of dust. The French drum and the light infantry bugle told, from time to time, that orders were passing among the troops; while the glittering uniform of a staff officer, as he galloped from the town, bespoke the note of preparation.

"Dismount! Steady; quietly, my lads," said the colonel, as he alighted upon the grass. "Let the men have their breakfast."

The little amphitheatre we occupied hid us entirely from all observation on the part of the enemy, but equally so excluded us from perceiving their movements. It may readily be supposed then, with what impatience we waited here, while the din and clangor of the French force, as they marched and countermarched so near us, were clearly audible. The orders were, however, strict that none should approach the bank of the river, and we lay anxiously awaiting the moment when this inactivity should cease. More than one orderly had arrived among us, bearing despatches from headquarters; but where our main body was, or what the nature of the orders, no one could guess. As for me, my excitement was at its height, and I could not speak for the very tension of my nerves. The officers stood in little groups of two and three, whispering anxiously together; but all I could collect was, that Soult had already begun his retreat upon Amarante, and that, with the broad stream of the Douro between us, he defied our pursuit.

"Well, Charley," said Power, laying his arm upon my shoulder, "the French have given us the slip this time; they are already in march, and even if we dared force a passage in the face of such an enemy, it seems there is not a boat to be found. I have just seen Hammersley."

"Indeed! Where is he?" said I.

"He's gone back to Villa de Conde; he asked after you most particularly. Don't blush, man; I'd rather back your chance than his, notwithstanding the long letter that Lucy sends him. Poor fellow, he has been badly wounded, but, it seems, declines going back to England."

"Captain Power," said an orderly, touching his cap, "General Murray desires to see you."

Power hastened away, but returned in a few moments.

"I say, Charley, there's something in the wind here. I have just been ordered to try where the stream is fordable. I've mentioned your name to the general, and I think you'll be sent for soon. Good-by."

I buckled on my sword, and looking to my girths, stood watching the groups around me; when suddenly a dragoon pulled his horse short up, and asked a man near me if Mr. O'Malley was there.

"Yes; I am he."

"Orders from General Murray, sir," said the man, and rode off at a canter.

I opened and saw that the despatch was addressed to Sir Arthur Wellesley, with the mere words, "With haste!" on the envelope.

Now, which way to turn I knew not; so springing into the saddle, I galloped to where Colonel Merivale was standing talking to the colonel of a heavy dragoon regiment.

"May I ask, sir, by which road I am to proceed with this despatch?"

"Along the river, sir," said the heavy ———, a large dark-browed man, with a most forbidding look. "You'll soon see the troops; you'd better stir yourself, sir, or Sir Arthur is not very likely to be pleased with you."

Without venturing a reply to what I felt a somewhat unnecessary taunt, I dashed spurs into my horse, and turned towards the river. I had not gained the bank above a minute, when the loud ringing of a rifle struck upon my ear; bang went another, and another. I hurried on, however, at the top of my speed, thinking only of my mission and its pressing haste. As I turned an angle of the stream, the vast column of the British came in sight, and scarcely had my eye rested upon them when my horse staggered forwards, plunged twice with his head nearly to the earth, and then, rearing madly up, fell backwards to the ground. Crushed and bruised as I felt by my fall, I was soon aroused to the necessity of exertion; for as I disengaged myself from the poor beast, I discovered he had been killed by a bullet in the counter; and scarcely had I recovered my legs when a shot struck my shako and grazed my temples. I quickly threw myself to the ground, and creeping on for some yards, reached at last some rising ground, from which I rolled gently downwards into a little declivity, sheltered by the bank from the French fire.

When I arrived at headquarters, I was dreadfully fatigued and heated; but resolving not to rest till I had delivered my despatches, I hastened towards the convent of La Sierra, where I was told the commander-in-chief was.

As I came into the court of the convent, filled with general officers and people of the staff, I was turning to ask how I should proceed, when Hixley caught my eye.

"Well, O'Malley, what brings you here?"

"Despatches from General Murray."

"Indeed; oh, follow me."

He hurried me rapidly through the buzzing crowd, and ascending a large gloomy stair, introduced me into a room, where about a dozen persons in uniform were writing at a long deal table.

"Captain Gordon," said he, addressing one of them, "despatches requiring immediate attention have just been brought by this officer."

Before the sentence was finished the door opened, and a short, slight man, in a gray undress coat, with a white cravat and a cocked hat, entered. The dead silence that ensued was not necessary to assure me that he was one in authority,—the look of command his bold, stern features presented; the sharp, piercing eye, the compressed lip, the impressive expression of the whole face, told plainly that he was one who held equally himself and others in mastery.

"Send General Sherbroke here," said he to an aide-de-camp. "Let the light brigade march into position;" and then turning suddenly to me, "Whose despatches are these?"

"General Murray's, sir."

I needed no more than that look to assure me that this was he of whom I had heard so much, and of whom the world was still to hear so much more.

He opened them quickly, and glancing his eye across the contents, crushed the paper in his hand. Just as he did so, a spot of blood upon the envelope attracted his attention.

"How's this,—are you wounded?"

"No, sir; my horse was killed—"

"Very well, sir; join your brigade. But stay, I shall have orders for you. Well, Waters, what news?"

This question was addressed to an officer in a staff uniform, who entered at the moment, followed by the short and bulky figure of a monk, his shaven crown and large cassock strongly contrasting with the gorgeous glitter of the costumes around him.

"I say, who have we here?"

"The Prior of Amarante, sir," replied Waters, "who has just come over. We have already, by his aid, secured three large barges—"

"Let the artillery take up position in the convent at once," said Sir Arthur, interrupting. "The boats will be brought round to the small creek beneath the orchard. You, sir," turning to me, "will convey to General Murray—but you appear weak. You, Gordon, will desire Murray to effect a crossing at Avintas with the Germans and the 14th. Sherbroke's division will occupy the Villa Nuova. What number of men can that seminary take?"

"From three to four hundred, sir. The padre mentions that all the vigilance of the enemy is limited to the river below the town."

"I perceive it," was the short reply of Sir Arthur, as placing his hands carelessly behind his back, he walked towards the window, and looked out upon the river.

All was still as death in the chamber; not a lip murmured. The feeling of respect for him in whose presence we were standing checked every thought of utterance; while the stupendous gravity of the events before us engrossed every mind and occupied every heart. I was standing near the window; the effect of my fall had stunned me for a time, but I was gradually recovering, and watched with a thrilling heart the scene before me. Great and absorbing as was my interest in what was passing without, it was nothing compared with what I felt as I looked at him upon whom our destiny was then hanging. I had ample time to scan his features and canvass their every lineament. Never before did I look upon such perfect impassibility; the cold, determined expression was crossed by no show of passion or impatience. All was rigid and motionless, and whatever might have been the workings of the spirit within, certainly no external sign betrayed them; and yet what a moment for him must that have been! Before him, separated by a deep and rapid river, lay the conquering legions of France, led on by one second alone to him whose very name had been the *prestige* of victory. Unprovided with every regular means of transport, in the broad glare of day, in open defiance of their serried ranks and thundering artillery, he dared the deed. What must have been his confidence in the soldiers he commanded! What must have been his reliance upon his own genius! As such thoughts rushed through my mind, the door opened and an officer entered hastily, and whispering a few words to Colonel Waters, left the room.

"One boat is already brought up to the crossing-place, and entirely concealed by the wall of the orchard."

"Let the men cross," was the brief reply.

No other word was spoken as, turning from the window, he closed his telescope, and followed by all the others, descended to the courtyard.

This simple order was enough; an officer with a company of the Buffs embarked, and thus began the passage of the Douro.

So engrossed was I in my vigilant observation of our leader, that I would gladly have remained at the convent, when I received an order to join my brigade, to which a detachment of artillery was already proceeding.

As I reached Avintas all was in motion. The cavalry was in readiness beside the river; but as yet no boats had been discovered, and such was the impatience of the men to cross, it was with difficulty they were prevented trying the passage by swimming, when suddenly Power appeared followed by several fishermen. Three or four small skiffs had been found, half sunk in mud, among the rushes, and with such frail assistance we commenced to cross.

"There will be something to write home to Galway soon, Charley, or I'm terribly mistaken," said Fred, as he sprang into the boat beside me. "Was I not a true prophet when I told you 'We'd meet the French in the morning?'"

"They're at it already," said Hixley, as a wreath of blue smoke floated across the stream below us, and the loud boom of a large gun resounded through the air.

Then came a deafening shout, followed by a rattling volley of small arms, gradually swelling into a hot sustained fire, through which the cannon pealed at intervals. Several large meadows lay along the river-side, where our brigade was drawn up as the detachments landed from the boats; and here, although nearly a league distant from the town, we now heard the din and crash of battle, which increased every moment. The cannonade from the Sierra convent, which at first was merely the fire of single guns, now thundered away in one long roll, amidst which the sounds of falling walls and crashing roofs were mingled. It was evident to us, from the continual fire kept up, that the landing had been effected; while the swelling tide of musketry told that fresh troops were momentarily coming up.

In less than twenty minutes our brigade was formed, and we now only waited for two light four-pounders to be landed, when an officer galloped up in haste, and called out,—

"The French are in retreat!" and pointing at the same moment to the Vallonga road, we saw a long line of smoke and dust leading from the town, through which, as we gazed, the colors of the enemy might be seen as they defiled, while the unbroken lines of the wagons and heavy baggage proved that it was no partial movement, but the army itself retreating.

"Fourteenth, threes about! close up! trot!" called out the loud and manly voice of our leader, and the heavy tramp of our squadrons shook the very ground as we advanced towards the road to Vallonga.

As we came on, the scene became one of overwhelming excitement; the masses of the enemy that poured unceasingly from the town could now be distinguished more clearly; and amidst all the crash of gun-carriages and caissons, the voices of the staff officers rose high as they hurried along the retreating battalions. A troop of flying artillery galloped forth at top speed, and wheeling their guns into position with the speed of lightning, prepared, by a flanking fire, to cover the retiring column. The gunners sprang from their seats, the guns were already unlimbered, when Sir George Murray, riding up at our left, called out,—

"Forward! close up! Charge!"

The word was scarcely spoken when the loud cheer answered the welcome sound, and the same instant the long line of shining helmets passed with the speed of a whirlwind; the pace increased at every stride, the ranks grew closer, and like the dread force of some mighty engine we fell upon the foe. I have felt all the glorious enthusiasm of a fox-hunt, when the loud cry of the hounds, answered by the cheer of the joyous huntsman, stirred the very heart within, but never till now did I know how far higher the excitement reaches, when man to man, sabre to sabre, arm to arm, we ride forward to the battle-field. On we went, the loud shout of "Forward!" still ringing in our ears. One broken, irregular discharge from the French guns shook the head of our advancing column, but stayed us not as we galloped madly on.

I remember no more. The din, the smoke, the crash, the cry for quarter, mingled with the shout of victory, the flying enemy, the agonizing shrieks of the wounded,—all are commingled in my mind, but leave no trace of clearness or connection between them; and it was only when the column wheeled to reform behind the advancing squadrons, that I awoke from my trance of maddening excitement, and perceived that we had carried the position and cut off the guns of the enemy.

"Well done, 14th!" said an old gray-headed colonel, as he rode along our line,—"gallantly done, lads!" The blood trickled from a sabre cut on his temple, along his cheek, as he spoke; but he either knew it not or heeded it not.

"There go the Germans!" said Power, pointing to the remainder of our brigade, as they charged furiously upon the French infantry, and rode them, down in masses.

Our guns came up at this time, and a plunging fire was opened upon the thick and retreating ranks of the enemy. The carnage must have been terrific, for the long breaches in their lines showed where the squadrons of the cavalry had passed, or the most destructive tide of the artillery had swept through them. The speed of the flying columns grew momentarily more; the road became blocked up, too, by broken carriages and wounded; and to add to their discomfiture, a damaging fire now opened from the town upon the retreating column, while the brigade of Guards and the 29th pressed hotly on their rear.

The scene was now beyond anything maddening in its interest. From the walls of Oporto the English infantry poured forth in pursuit, while the whole river was covered with boats as they still continued to cross over. The artillery thundered from the Sierra to protect the landing, for it was even still contested in places; and the cavalry, charging in flank, swept the broken ranks and bore down upon the squares.

It was now, when the full tide of victory ran highest in our favor, that we were ordered to retire from the road. Column after column passed before us, unmolested and unassailed, and not even a cannon-shot arrested their steps.

Some unaccountable timidity of our leader directed this movement; and while before our very eyes the gallant infantry were charging the retiring columns, we remained still and inactive.

How little did the sense of praise we had already won repay us for the shame and indignation we experienced at this moment, as with burning check and compressed lip we watched the retreating files. "What can he mean?" "Is there not some mistake?" "Are we never to charge?" were the muttered questions around, as a staff officer galloped up with the order to take ground still farther back, and nearer to the river.

The word was scarcely spoken when a young officer, in the uniform of a general, dashed impetuously up; he held his plumed cap high above his head, as he called out, "14th, follow me! Left face! wheel! charge!"

So, with the word, we were upon them. The French rear-guard was at this moment at the narrowest part of the road, which opened by a bridge upon a large open space; so that, forming with a narrow front and favored by a declivity in the ground, we actually rode them down. Twice the French formed, and twice were they broken. Meanwhile the carnage was dreadful on both sides, our fellows dashing madly forward where the ranks were thickest, the enemy resisting with the stubborn courage of men fighting for their last spot of ground. So impetuous was the charge of our squadrons, that we stopped not till, piercing the dense column of the retreating mass, we reached the open ground beyond. Here we wheeled and prepared once more to meet them, when suddenly some squadrons of cuirassiers debouched from the road, and supported by a field-piece, showed front against us. This was the moment that the remainder of our brigade should have come to our aid, but not a man appeared. However, there was not an instant to be lost; already the plunging fire of the four-pounder had swept through our files, and every moment increased our danger.

"Once more, my lads, forward!" cried out our gallant leader, Sir Charles Stewart, as waving his sabre, he dashed into the thickest of the fray.

So sudden was our charge that we were upon them before they were prepared. And here ensued a terrific struggle; for as the cavalry of the enemy gave way before us, we came upon the close ranks of the infantry at half-pistol distance, who poured a withering volley into us as we approached. But what could arrest the sweeping torrent of our brave fellows, though every moment falling in numbers?

Harvey, our major, lost his arm near the shoulder. Scarcely an officer was not wounded. Power received a deep sabre-cut in the cheek from an aide-de-camp of General Foy, in return for a wound he gave the general; while I, in my endeavor to save General Laborde when unhorsed, was cut down through the helmet, and so stunned that I remembered no more around me. I kept my saddle, it is true, but I lost every sense of consciousness, my first glimmering of reason coming to my aid as I lay upon the river bank and felt my faithful follower Mike bathing my temples with water, as he kept up a running fire of lamentations for my being *murthered* so young.

"Are you better, Mister Charles? Spake to me, alanah! Say that you're not kilt, darling; do now. Oh, wirra! what'll I ever say to the master? and you doing so beautiful! Wouldn't he give the best baste in his stable to be looking at you to-day? There, take a sup; it's only water. Bad luck to them, but it's hard work beatin' them. They 're only gone now. That's right; now you're coming to."

"Where am I, Mike?"

"It's here you are, darling, resting yourself."

"Well, Charley, my poor fellow, you've got sore bones, too," cried Power, as, his face swathed in bandages and covered with blood, he lay down on the grass beside me. "It was a gallant thing while it lasted, but has cost us dearly. Poor Hixley—"

"What of him?" said I, anxiously.

"Poor fellow, he has seen his last battle-field! He fell across me as we came out upon the road. I lifted him up in my arms and bore him along above fifty yards; but he was stone dead. Not a sigh, not a word escaped him; shot through the forehead." As he spoke, his lips trembled, and his voice sank to a mere whisper at the last words: "You remember what he said last night. Poor fellow, he was every inch a soldier."

Such was his epitaph.

I turned my head towards the scene of our late encounter. Some dismounted guns and broken wagons alone marked the spot; while far in the distance, the dust of the retreating columns showed the beaten enemy as they hurried towards the frontiers of Spain.

CHAPTER XLVI.

THE MORNING.

There are few sadder things in life than the day after a battle. The high-beating hope, the bounding spirits, have passed away, and in their stead comes the depressing reaction by which every overwrought excitement is followed. With far different eyes do we look upon the compact ranks and glistening files,—

With helm arrayed,   And lance and blade,   And plume in the gay wind dancing!

and upon the cold and barren heath, whose only memory of the past is the blood-stained turf, a mangled corpse, the broken gun, the shattered wall, the well-trodden earth where columns stood, the cut-up ground where cavalry had charged,—these are the sad relics of all the chivalry of yesterday.

The morning which followed the battle of the Douro was one of the most beautiful I ever remember. There was that kind of freshness and elasticity in the air which certain days possess, and communicate by some magic their properties to ourselves. The thrush was singing gayly out from every grove and wooded dell; the very river had a sound of gladness as it rippled on against its sedgy banks; the foliage, too, sparkled in the fresh dew, as in its robes of holiday, and all looked bright and happy.

We were picketed near the river, upon a gently rising ground, from which the view extended for miles in every direction. Above us, the stream came winding down amidst broad and fertile fields of tall grass and waving corn, backed by deep and mellow woods, which were lost to the view upon the distant hills; below, the river, widening as it went, pursued a straighter course, or turned with bolder curves, till, passing beneath the town, it spread into a large sheet of glassy water as it opened to the sea. The sun was just rising as I looked upon this glorious scene, and already the tall spires of Oporto were tipped with a bright rosy hue, while the massive towers and dark walls threw their lengthened shadows far across the plain.

The fires of the bivouac still burned, but all slept around them. Not a sound was heard save the tramp of a patrol or the short, quick cry of the sentry. I sat lost in meditation, or rather in that state of dreamy thoughtfulness in which the past and present are combined, and the absent are alike before us as are the things we look upon.

One moment I felt as though I were describing to my uncle the battle of the day before, pointing out where we stood, and how we charged; then again I was at home, beside the broad, bleak Shannon, and the brown hills of Scariff. I watched with beating heart the tall Sierra, where our path lay for the future, and then turned my thoughts to him whose name was so soon to be received in England with a nation's pride and gratitude, and panted for a soldier's glory.

As thus I followed every rising fancy, I heard a step approach; it was a figure muffled in a cavalry cloak, which I soon perceived to be Power.

"Charley!" said he, in a half-whisper, "get up and come with me. You are aware of the general order, that while in pursuit of an enemy, all military honors to the dead are forbidden; but we wish to place our poor comrade in the earth before we leave."

I followed down a little path, through a grave of tall beech-trees, that opened upon a little grassy terrace beside the river. A stunted olive-tree stood by itself in the midst, and there I found five of our brother officers standing, wrapped in their wide cloaks. As we pressed each other's hands, not a word was spoken. Each heart was full; and hard features that never quailed before the foe were now shaken with the convulsive spasm of agony or compressed with stern determination to seem calm.

A cavalry helmet and a large blue cloak lay upon the grass. The narrow grave was already dug beside it; and in the deathlike stillness around, the service for the dead was read. The last words were over. We stooped and placed the corpse, wrapped up in the broad mantle, in the earth; we replaced the mould, and stood silently around the spot. The trumpet of our regiment at this moment sounded the call; its clear notes rang sharply through the thin air,—it was the soldier's requiem! and we turned away without speaking, and returned to our quarters.

I had never known poor Hixley till a day or two before; but, somehow, my grief for him was deep and heartfelt. It was not that his frank and manly bearing, his bold and military air, had gained upon me. No; these were indeed qualities to attract and delight me, but he had obtained a stronger and faster hold upon my affections,—he spoke to me of home.

Of all the ties that bind us to the chance acquaintances we meet with in life, what can equal this one? What a claim upon your love has he who can, by some passing word, some fast-flitting thought, bring back the days of your youth! What interest can he not excite by some anecdote of your boyish days, some well-remembered trait of youthful daring, or early enterprise! Many a year of sunshine and of storm have passed above my head; I have not been without my moments of gratified pride and rewarded ambition; but my heart has never responded so fully, so thankfully, so proudly to these, such as they were, as to the simple, touching words of one who knew my early home, and loved its inmates.

"Well, Fitzroy, what news?" inquired I, roused from my musing, as an aide-de-camp galloped up at full speed.

"Tell Merivale to get the regiment under arms at once. Sir Arthur Wellesley will be here in less than half an hour. You may look for the route immediately. Where are the Germans quartered?"

"Lower down; beside that grove of beech-trees, next the river."

Scarcely was my reply spoken, when he dashed spurs into his horse, and was soon out of sight. Meanwhile the plain beneath me presented an animated and splendid spectacle. The different corps were falling into position to the enlivening sounds of their quick-step, the trumpets of the cavalry rang loudly through the valley, and the clatter of sabres and sabretasches joined with the hollow tramp of the horses, as the squadron came up.

I had not a moment to lose; so hastening back to my quarters, I found Mike waiting with my horse.

"Captain Power's before you, sir," said he, "and you'll have to make haste. The regiments are under arms already."

From the little mound where I stood, I could see the long line of cavalry as they deployed into the plain, followed by the horse artillery, which brought up the rear.

"This looks like a march," thought I, as I pressed forward to join my companions.

I had not advanced above a hundred yards through a narrow ravine when the measured tread of infantry fell upon my ears. I pulled up to slacken my pace, just as the head of a column turned round the angle of the road, and came in view. The tall caps of a grenadier company was the first thing I beheld, as they came on without roll of drum and sound of fife. I watched with a soldier's pride the manly bearing and gallant step of the dense mass as they defiled before me. I was struck no less by them than by a certain look of a steady but sombre cast which each man wore.

"What can this mean?" thought I.

My first impression was, that a military execution was about to take place, the next moment solved my doubt; for as the last files of the grenadiers wheeled round, a dense mass behind came in sight, whose unarmed hands, and downcast air, at once bespoke them prisoners-of-war.

What a sad sight it was! There was the old and weather-beaten grenadier, erect in frame and firm in step, his gray mustache scarcely concealing the scowl that curled his lip, side by side with the young and daring conscript, even yet a mere boy; their march was regular, their gaze steadfast,—no look of flinching courage there. On they came, a long unbroken line. They looked not less proudly than their captors around them. As I looked with heavy heart upon them, my attention was attracted to one who marched alone behind the rest. He was a middle-sized but handsome youth of some eighteen years at most; his light helmet and waving plume bespoke him a *chasseur à cheval*, and I could plainly perceive, in his careless half-saucy air, how indignantly he felt the position to which the fate of war had reduced him. He caught my eyes fixed upon him, and for an instant turned upon me a gaze of open and palpable defiance, drawing himself up to his full height, and crossing his arms upon his breast; but probably perceiving in my look more of interest than of triumph, his countenance suddenly changed, a deep blush suffused his cheek, his eye beamed with a softened and kindly expression, and carrying his hand to his helmet, he saluted me, saying, in a voice of singular sweetness,—

"Je vous souhaite un meilleur sort, camarade."

I bowed, and muttering something in return, was about to make some inquiry concerning him, when the loud call of the trumpet rang through the valley, and apprised me that, in my interest for the prisoners, I had forgotten all else, and was probably incurring censure for my absence.

CHAPTER XLVII.

THE REVIEW.

When I joined the group of my brother officers, who stood gayly chatting and laughing together before our lines, I was much surprised—nay almost shocked—to find how little seeming impression had been made upon them, by the sad duty we had performed that morning.

When last we met, each eye was downcast, each heart was full,—sorrow for him we had lost from among us forever, mingling with the awful sense of our own uncertain tenure here, had laid its impress on each brow; but now, scarcely an hour elapsed, and all were cheerful and elated. The last shovelful of earth upon the grave seemed to have buried both the dead and the mourning. And such is war, and such the temperament it forms! Events so strikingly opposite in their character and influences succeed so rapidly one upon another that the mind is kept in one whirl of excitement, and at length accustoms itself to change with every phase of circumstances; and between joy and grief, hope and despondency, enthusiasm and depression, there is neither breadth nor interval,—they follow each other as naturally as morning succeeds to night.

I had not much time for such reflections; scarcely had I saluted the officers about me, when the loud prolonged roll of the drums along the line of infantry in the valley, followed by the sharp clatter of muskets as they were raised to the shoulder, announced the troops were under arms, and the review begun.

"Have you seen the general order this morning, Power?" inquired an old officer beside me.

"No; they say, however, that ours are mentioned."

"Harvey is going on favorably," cried a young cornet, as he galloped up to our party.

"Take ground to the left!" sung out the clear voice of the colonel, as he rode along in front. "Fourteenth, I am happy to inform you that your conduct has met approval in the highest quarter. I have just received the general orders, in which this occurs:—

"'THE TIMELY PASSAGE OF THE DOURO, AND SUBSEQUENT MOVEMENTS UPON THE ENEMY'S FLANK, BY LIEUTENANT-GENERAL SHERBROKE, WITH THE GUARDS AND 29TH REGIMENT, AND THE BRAVERY OF THE TWO SQUADRONS OF THE 14TH LIGHT DRAGOONS, UNDER THE COMMAND OF MAJOR HARVEY, AND LED BY THE HONORABLE BRIGADIER-GENERAL CHARLES STEWART, OBTAINED THE VICTORY'—Mark that, my lads! obtained the victory—'WHICH HAS CONTRIBUTED SO MUCH TO THE HONOR OF THE TROOPS ON THIS DAY.'"

The words were hardly spoken, when a tremendous cheer burst from the whole line at once.

"Steady, Fourteenth! steady, lads!" said the gallant old colonel, as he raised his hand gently; "the staff is approaching."

At the same moment, the white plumes appeared, rising above the brow of the hill. On they came, glittering in all the splendor of aignillettes and orders; all save one. He rode foremost, upon a small, compact, black horse; his dress, a plain gray frock fastened at the waist by a red sash; his cocked hat alone bespoke, in its plume, the general officer. He galloped rapidly on till he came to the centre of the line; then turning short round, he scanned the ranks from end to end with an eagle glance.

"Colonel Merivale, you have made known to your regiment my opinion of them, as expressed in general orders?"

The colonel bowed low in acquiescence.

"Fitzroy, you have got the memorandum, I hope?"

The aide-de-camp here presented to Sir Arthur a slip of paper, which he continued to regard attentively for some minutes.

"Captain Powel,—Power, I mean. Captain Power!"

Power rode out from the line.

"Your very distinguished conduct yesterday has been reported to me. I shall have sincere pleasure in forwarding your name for the vacant majority.

"You have forgotten, Colonel Merivale, to send in the name of the officer who saved General Laborde's life."

"I believe I have mentioned it, Sir Arthur," said the colonel: "Mr. O'Malley."

"True, I beg pardon; so you have—Mr. O'Malley; a very young officer indeed,—ha, an Irishman! The south of Ireland, eh?"

"No, sir, the west."

"Oh, yes! Well, Mr. O'Malley, you are promoted. You have the lieutenancy in your own regiment. By-the-bye, Merivale," here his voice changed into a half-laughing tone, "ere I forget it, pray let me beg of you to look into this honest fellow's claim; he has given me no peace the entire morning."

As he spoke, I turned my eyes in the direction he pointed, and to my utter consternation, beheld my man Mickey Free standing among the staff, the position he occupied, and the presence he stood in, having no more perceptible effect upon his nerves than if he were assisting at an Irish wake; but so completely was I overwhelmed with shame at the moment, that the staff were already far down the lines ere I recovered my self-possession, to which, certainly, I was in some degree recalled by Master Mike's addressing me in a somewhat imploring voice:—

"Arrah, spake for me, Master Charles, alanah; sure they might do something for me now, av it was only to make me a ganger."

Mickey's ideas of promotion, thus insinuatingly put forward, threw the whole party around us into one burst of laughter.

"I have him down there," said he, pointing, as he spoke, to a thick grove of cork-trees at a little distance.

"Who have you got there, Mike?" inquired Power.

"Devil a one o' me knows his name," replied he; "may be it's Bony himself."

"And how do you know he's there still?"

"How do I know, is it? Didn't I tie him last night?"

Curiosity to find out what Mickey could possibly allude to, induced Power and myself to follow him down the slope to the clump of trees I have mentioned. As we came near, the very distinct denunciations that issued from the thicket proved pretty clearly the nature of the affair. It was nothing less than a French officer of cavalry that Mike had unhorsed in the *mêlée*, and wishing, probably, to preserve some testimony of his prowess, had made prisoner, and tied fast to a cork-tree, the preceding evening.

"*Sacrebleu!*" said the poor Frenchman, as we approached, "*ce sont des sauvages!*"

"Av it's making your sowl ye are," said Mike, "you're right; for may be they won't let me keep you alive."

Mike's idea of a tame prisoner threw me into a fit of laughing, while Power asked,—

"And what do you want to do with him, Mickey?"

"The sorra one o' me knows, for he spakes no dacent tongue. Thighum thu," said he, addressing the prisoner, with a poke in the ribs at the same moment. "But sure, Master Charles, he might tache me French."

There was something so irresistibly ludicrous in his tone and look as he said these words, that both Power and myself absolutely roared with laughter. We began, however, to feel not a little ashamed of our position in the business, and explained to the Frenchman that our worthy countryman had but little experience in the usages of war, while we proceeded to unbind him and liberate him from his miserable bondage.

"It's letting him loose, you are, Captain? Master Charles, take care. Be-gorra, av you had as much trouble in catching him as I had, you'd think twice about letting him out. Listen to me, now," here he placed his closed fist within an inch of the poor prisoner's nose,—"listen to me! Av you say peas, by the morreal, I'll not lave a whole bone in your skin."

With some difficulty we persuaded Mike that his conduct, so far from leading to his promotion, might, if known in another quarter, procure him an acquaintance with the provost-marshal; a fact which, it was plain to perceive, gave him but a very poor impression of military gratitude.

"Oh, then, if they were in swarms fornent me, devil receave the prisoner I'll take again!"

So saying, he slowly returned to the regiment; while Power and I, having conducted the Frenchman to the rear, cantered towards the town to learn the news of the day.

The city on that day presented a most singular aspect. The streets, filled with the town's-people and the soldiery, were decorated with flags and garlands; the cafés were crowded with merry groups, and the sounds of music and laughter resounded on all sides. The houses seemed to be quite inadequate to afford accommodation to the numerous guests; and in consequence, bullock cars and forage wagons were converted into temporary hotels, and many a jovial party were collected in both. Military music, church bells, drinking choruses, were all commingled in the din and turmoil; processions in honor of "Our Lady of Succor" were jammed up among bacchanalian orgies, and their very chant half drowned in the cries of the wounded as they passed on to the hospitals. With difficulty we pushed our way through the dense mob, as we turned our steps towards the seminary. We both felt naturally curious to see the place where our first detachment landed, and to examine the opportunities of defence it presented. The building itself was a large and irregular one of an oblong form, surrounded by a high wall of solid masonry, the only entrance being by a heavy iron gate.

At this spot the battle appeared to have raged with violence; one side of the massive gate was torn from its hinges and lay flat upon the ground; the walls were breached in many places; and pieces of torn uniforms, broken bayonets, and bruised shakos attested that the conflict was a close one. The seminary itself was in a falling state; the roof, from which Paget had given his orders, and where he was wounded, had fallen in. The French cannon had fissured the building from top to bottom, and it seemed only awaiting the slightest impulse to crumble into ruin. When we regarded the spot, and examined the narrow doorway which opening upon a flight of a few steps to the river, admitted our first party, we could not help feeling struck anew with the gallantry of that mere handful of brave fellows who thus threw themselves amidst the overwhelming legions of the enemy, and at once, without waiting for a single reinforcement, opened a fire upon their ranks. Bold as the enterprise unquestionably was, we still felt with what consummate judgment it had been planned; a bend of the river concealed entirely the passage of the troops, the guns of the Sierras covered their landing and completely swept one approach to the seminary. The French, being thus obliged to attack by the gate, were compelled to make a considerable *détour* before they reached it, all of which gave time for our divisions to cross; while the brigade of Guards, under General Sherbrooke, profiting by the confusion, passed the river below the town, and took the enemy unexpectedly in the rear.

Brief as was the struggle within the town, it must have been a terrific one. The artillery were firing at musket range; cavalry and infantry were fighting hand to hand in narrow streets, a destructive musketry pouring all the while from windows and house-tops.

At the Amarante gate, where the French defiled, the carnage was also great. Their light artillery unlimbered some guns here to cover the columns as they deployed, but Murray's cavalry having carried these, the flank of the infantry became entirely exposed to the galling fire of small-arms from the seminary, and the far more destructive shower of grape that poured unceasingly from the Sierra.

Our brigade did the rest; and in less than one hour from the landing of the first man, the French were in full retreat upon Vallonga.

"A glorious thing, Charley," said Power, after a pause, "and a proud souvenir for hereafter."

A truth I felt deeply at the time, and one my heart responds to not less fully as I am writing.

CHAPTER XLVIII.

THE QUARREL.

On the evening of the 12th, orders were received for the German brigade and three squadrons of our regiment to pursue the French upon the Terracinthe road by daybreak on the following morning.

I was busily occupied in my preparations for a hurried march when Mike came up to say that an officer desired to speak with me; and the moment after Captain Hammersley appeared. A sudden flush colored his pale and sickly features, as he held out his hand and said,—

"I've come to wish you joy, O'Malley. I just this instant heard of your promotion. I am sincerely glad of it; pray tell me the whole affair."

"That is the very thing I am unable to do. I have some very vague, indistinct remembrance of warding off a sabre-cut from the head of a wounded and unhorsed officer in the *mêlée* of yesterday, but more I know not. In fact, it was my first duty under fire. I've a tolerably clear recollection of all the events of the morning, but the word 'Charge!' once given, I remember very little more. But you, where have you been? How have we not met before?"

"I've exchanged into a heavy dragoon regiment, and am now employed upon the staff."

"You are aware that I have letters for you?"

"Power hinted, I think, something of the kind. I saw him very hurriedly."

These words were spoken with an effort at *nonchalance* that evidently cost him much.

As for me, my agitation was scarcely less, as fumbling for some seconds in my portmanteau, I drew forth the long destined packet. As I placed it in his hands, he grew deadly pale, and a slight spasmodic twitch in his upper lip bespoke some unnatural struggle. He broke the seal suddenly, and as he did so, the morocco case of a miniature fell upon the ground; his eyes ran rapidly across the letter; the livid color of his lips as the blood forced itself to them added to the corpse-like hue of his countenance.

"You, probably, are aware of the contents of this letter, Mr. O'Malley," said he, in an altered voice, whose tones, half in anger, half in suppressed irony, cut to my very heart.

"I am in complete ignorance of them," said I, calmly.

"Indeed, sir!" replied he, with a sarcastic curl of his mouth as he spoke. "Then, perhaps, you will tell me, too, that your very success is a secret to you—"

"I'm really not aware—"

"You think, probably, sir, that the pastime is an amusing one, to interfere where the affections of others are concerned. I've heard of you, sir. Your conduct at Lisbon is known to me; and though Captain Trevyllian may bear—"

"Stop, Captain Hammersley!" said I, with a tremendous effort to be calm,—"stop! You have said enough, quite enough, to convince me of what your object was in seeking me here to-day. You shall not be disappointed. I trust that assurance will save you from any further display of temper."

"I thank you, most humbly I thank you for the quickness of your apprehension; and I shall now take my leave. Good-evening, Mr. O'Malley. I wish you much joy; you have my very fullest congratulations upon *all* your good fortune."

The sneering emphasis the last words were spoken with remained fixed in my mind long after he took his departure; and, indeed, so completely did the whole seem like a dream to me that were it not for the fragments of the miniature that lay upon the ground where he had crushed them with his heel, I could scarcely credit myself that I was awake.

My first impulse was to seek Power, upon whose judgment and discretion I could with confidence rely.

I had not long to wait; for scarcely had I thrown my cloak around me, when he rode up. He had just seen, Hammersley, and learned something of our interview.

"Why, Charley, my dear fellow, what is this? How have you treated poor Hammersley?"

"Treated *him*! Say, rather, how has he treated *me!*"

I here entered into a short but accurate account of our meeting, during which Power listened with great composure; while I could perceive, from the questions he asked, that some very different impression had been previously made upon his mind.

"And this was all that passed?"

"All."

"But what of the business at Lisbon?"

"I don't understand."

"Why, he speaks,—he has heard some foolish account of your having made some ridiculous speech there about your successful rivalry of him in Ireland. Lucy Dashwood, I suppose, is referred to. Some one has been good-natured enough to repeat the thing to him."

"But it never occurred. I never did."

"Are you sure, Charley?"

"I am sure. I know I never did."

"The poor fellow! He has been duped. Come, Charley, you must not take it ill. Poor Hammersley has never recovered a sabre-wound he received some months since upon the head; his intellect is really affected by it. Leave it all to me. Promise not to leave your quarters till I return, and I'll put everything right again."

I gave the required pledge; while Power, springing into the saddle, left me to my own reflections.

My frame of mind as Power left me was by no means an enviable one. A quarrel is rarely a happy incident in a man's life, still less is it so when the difference arises with one we are disposed to like and respect. Such was Hammersley. His manly, straightforward character had won my esteem and regard, and it was with no common scrutiny I taxed my memory to think what could have given rise to the impression he labored under of my having injured him. His chance mention of Trevyllian suggested to me some suspicion that his dislike of me, wherefore arising I knew not, might have its share in the matter; and in this state of doubt and uncertainty I paced impatiently up and down, anxiously watching for Power's return in the hope of at length getting some real insight into the difficulty.

My patience was fast ebbing, Power had been absent above an hour, and no appearance of him could I detect, when suddenly the tramp of a horse came rapidly up the hill. I looked out and saw a rider coming forward at a very fast pace. Before I had time for even a guess as to who it was, he drew up, and I recognized Captain Trevyllian. There was a certain look of easy impertinence and half-smiling satisfaction about his features I had never seen before, as he touched his cap in salute, and said,—

"May I have the honor of a few words' conversation with you?"

I bowed silently, while he dismounted, and passing his bridle beneath his arm, walked on beside me.

"My friend Captain Hammersley has commissioned me to wait upon you about this unpleasant affair—"

"I beg pardon for the interruption, Captain Trevyllian, but as I have yet to learn to what you or your friend alludes, perhaps it may facilitate matters if you will explicitly state your meaning."

He grew crimson on the cheek as I said this, while, with a voice perfectly unmoved, he continued,—

"I am not sufficiently in my friend's confidence to know the whole of the affair in question, nor have I his permission to enter into any of it, he probably presuming, as I certainly did myself, that your sense of honor would have deemed further parley and discussion both unnecessary and unseasonable."

"In fact, then, if I understand, it is expected that I should meet Captain Hammersley for some reason unknown—"

"He certainly desires a meeting with you," was the dry reply.

"And as certainly I shall not give it, before understanding upon what grounds."

"And such I am to report as your answer?" said he, looking at me at the moment with an expression of ill-repressed triumph as he spoke.

There was something in these few words, as well as in the tone in which they were spoken, that sunk deeply in my heart. Was it that by some trick of diplomacy he was endeavoring to compromise my honor and character? Was it possible that my refusal might be construed into any other than the real cause? I was too young, too inexperienced in the world to decide the question for myself, and no time was allowed me to seek another's counsel. What a trying moment was that for me; my temples throbbed, my heart beat almost audibly, and I stood afraid to speak; dreading on the one hand lest my compliance might involve me in an act to embitter my life forever, and fearful on the other, that my refusal might be reported as a trait of cowardice.

He saw, he read my difficulty at a glance, and with a smile of most supercilious expression, repeated coolly his former question. In an instant all thought of Hammersley was forgotten. I remembered no more. I saw him before me, he who had, since my first meeting, continually contrived to pass some inappreciable slight upon me. My eyes flashed, my hands tingled with ill-repressed rage, as I said,—

"With Captain Hammersley I am conscious of no quarrel, nor have I ever shown by any act or look an intention to provoke one. Indeed, such demonstrations are not always successful; there are persons most rigidly scrupulous for a friend's honor, little disposed to guard their own."

"You mistake," said he, interrupting me, as I spoke these words with a look as insulting as I could make it,—"you mistake. I have sworn a solemn oath never to *send* a challenge."

The emphasis upon the word "send," explained fully his meaning, when I said,—

"But you will not decline—"

"Most certainly not," said he, again interrupting, while with sparkling eye and elated look he drew himself up to his full height. "Your friend is—"

"Captain Power; and yours—"

"Sir Harry Beaufort. I may observe that, as the troops are in marching order, the matter had better not be delayed."

"There shall be none on my part."

"Nor mine!" said he, as with a low bow and a look of most ineffable triumph, he sprang into his saddle; then, "*Au revoir*, Mr. O'Malley," said he, gathering up his reins. "Beaufort is on the staff, and quartered at Oporto." So saying, he cantered easily down the slope, and once more I was alone.

CHAPTER XLIX.
THE ROUTE CONTINUED.

I was leisurely examining my pistols,—poor Considine's last present to me on leaving home,—when an orderly sergeant rode up, and delivered into my hands the following order:—

Lieutenant O'Malley will hold himself in immediate readiness to proceed on a particular service. By order of his Excellency the Commander of the Forces. [Signed] *S. GORDON, Military Secretary.*

"What can this mean?" thought I. "It is not possible that any rumor of my intended meeting could have got abroad, and that my present destination could be intended as a punishment?"

I walked hurriedly to the door of the little hut which formed my quarters; below me in the plain, all was activity and preparation, the infantry were drawn up in marching order, baggage wagons, ordnance stores, and artillery seemed all in active preparation, and some cavalry squadrons might be already seen with forage allowances behind the saddle, as if only waiting the order to set out. I strained my eyes to see if Power was coming, but no horseman approached in the direction. I stood, and I hesitated whether I should not rather seek him at once, than continue to wait on in my present uncertainty; but then, what if I should miss him? And I had pledged myself to remain till he returned.

While I deliberated thus with myself, weighing the various chances for and against each plan, I saw two mounted officers coming towards me at a brisk trot. As they came nearer, I recognized one as my colonel, the other was an officer of the staff.

Supposing that their mission had some relation to the order I had so lately received, and which until now I had forgotten, I hastily returned and ordered Mike to my presence.

"How are the horses, Mike?" said I.

"Never better, sir. Badger was wounded slightly by a spent shot in the counter, but he's never the worse this morning, and the black horse is capering like a filly."

"Get ready my pack, feed the cattle, and be prepared to set out at a moment's warning."

"Good advice, O'Malley," said the colonel, as he overheard the last direction to my servant. "I hope the nags are in condition?"

"Why yes, sir, I believe they are."

"All the better; you've a sharp ride before you. Meanwhile let me introduce my friend; Captain Beaumont, Mr. O'Malley. I think we had better be seated."

"These are your instructions, Mr. O'Malley," said Captain Beaumont, unfolding a map as he spoke. "You will proceed from this with half a troop of our regiment by forced marches towards the frontier, passing through the town of Calenco and Guarda and the Estrella pass. On arriving at the headquarters of the Lusitanian Legion, which you will find there, you are to put yourself under the orders of Major Monsoon, commanding that force. Any Portuguese cavalry he may have with him will be attached to yours and under your command; your rank for the time being that of captain. You will, as far as possible, acquaint yourself with the habits and capabilities of the native cavalry, and make such report as you judge necessary thereupon to his Excellency the commander of the forces. I think it only fair to add that you are indebted to my friend Colonel Merivale for the very flattering position thus opened to your skill and enterprise."

"My dear Colonel, let me assure you—"

"Not a word, my boy. I knew the thing would suit you, and I am sure I can count upon your not disappointing my expectations of you. Sir Arthur perfectly remembers your name. He only asked two questions,—

"'Is he well mounted?'

"'Admirably,' was my answer.

"'Can you depend upon his promptitude?'

"'He'll leave in half an hour.' "So you see, O'Malley, I have already pledged myself for you. And now I must say adieu; the regiments are about to take up a more advanced position, so good-by. I hope you'll have a pleasant time of it till we meet again."

"It is now twelve o'clock, Mr. O'Malley," said Beaumont; "we may rely upon your immediate departure. Your written instructions and despatches will be here within a quarter of an hour."

I muttered something,—what, I cannot remember; I bowed my thanks to my worthy colonel, shook his hand warmly, and saw him ride down the hill and disappear in the crowd of soldiery beneath, before I could recall my faculties and think over my situation.

Then all at once did the full difficulty of my position break upon me. If I accepted my present employment I must certainly fail in my engagement to Trevyllian. But I had already pledged myself to its acceptance. What was to be done? No time was left for deliberation. The very minutes I should have spent in preparation were fast passing. Would that Power might appear! Alas, he came not! My state of doubt and uncertainty increased every moment; I saw nothing but ruin before me, even at a moment when fortune promised most fairly for the future, and opened a field of enterprise my heart had so often and so ardently desired. Nothing was left me but to hasten to Colonel Merivale and decline my appointment; to do so was to prejudice my character in his estimation forever, for I dared not allege my reasons, and in all probability my conduct might require my leaving the army.

"Be it so, then," said I, in an accent of despair; "the die is cast."

I ordered my horse round; I wrote a few words to Power to explain my absence should he come while I was away, and leaped into the saddle. As I reached the plain my pace became a gallop, and I pressed my horse with all the impatience my heart was burning with. I dashed along the lines towards Oporto, neither hearing nor seeing aught around me, when suddenly the clank of cavalry accoutrements behind induced me to turn my head, and I perceived an orderly dragoon at full gallop in pursuit. I pulled up till he came alongside.

"Lieutenant O'Malley, sir," said the man, saluting, "these despatches are for you."

I took them hurriedly, and was about to continue my route, when the attitude of the dragoon arrested my attention. He had reined in his horse to the side of the narrow causeway, and holding him still and steadily, sat motionless as a statue. I looked behind and saw the whole staff approaching at a brisk trot. Before I had a moment for thought they were beside me.

"Ah, O'Malley," cried Merivale, "you have your orders; don't wait; his Excellency is coming up."

"Get along, I advise you," said another, "or you'll catch it, as some of us have done this morning."

"All is right, Charley; you can go in safety," said a whispering voice, as Power passed in a sharp canter.

That one sentence was enough; my heart bounded like a deer, my cheek beamed with the glow of delighted pleasure, I closed my spurs upon my gallant gray and dashed across the plain.

When I arrived at my quarters the men were drawn up in waiting, and provided with rations for three days' march; Mike was also prepared for the road, and nothing more remained to delay me.

"Captain Power has been here, sir, and left a note."

159

I took it and thrust it hastily into my sabretasche. I knew from the few words he had spoken that my present step involved me in no ill consequences; so giving the word to wheel into column, I rode to the front and set out upon my march to Alcantara.

CHAPTER L.

THE WATCH-FIRE.

There are few things so inspiriting to a young soldier as the being employed with a separate command; the picket and outpost duty have a charm for him no other portion of his career possesses. The field seems open for individual boldness and heroism; success, if obtained, must redound to his own credit; and what can equal, in its spirit-stirring enthusiasm, that first moment when we become in any way the arbiter of our own fortunes?

Such were my happy thoughts, as with a proud and elated heart I set forth upon my march. The notice the commander-in-chief had bestowed upon me had already done much; it had raised me in my own estimation, and implanted within me a longing desire for further distinction. I thought, too, of those far, far away, who were yet to hear of my successes.

I fancied to myself how they would severally receive the news. My poor uncle, with tearful eye and quivering lip, was before me, as I saw him read the despatch, then wipe his glasses, and read on, till at last, with one long-drawn breath, his manly voice, tremulous with emotion, would break forth: "My boy! my own Charley!" Then I pictured Considine, with port erect and stern features, listening silently; not a syllable, not a motion betraying that he felt interested in my fate, till as if impatient, at length he would break in: "I knew it,—I said so; and yet you thought to make him a lawyer!" And then old Sir Harry, his warm heart glowing with pleasure, and his good-humored face beaming with happiness, how many a blunder he would make in retailing the news, and how many a hearty laugh his version of it would give rise to!

I passed in review before me the old servants, as they lingered in the room to hear the story. Poor old Matthew, the butler, fumbling with his corkscrew to gain a little time; then looking in my uncle's face, half entreatingly, as he asked: "Any news of Master Charles, sir, from the wars?"

While thus my mind wandered back to the scenes and faces of my early home, I feared to ask myself how *she* would feel to whom my heart was now turning. Too deeply did I know how poor my chances were in that quarter to nourish hope, and yet I could not bring myself to abandon it altogether. Hammersley's strange conduct suggested to me that he, at least, could not be *my* rival; while I plainly perceived that he regarded me as *his*. There was a mystery in all this I could not fathom, and I ardently longed for my next meeting with Power, to learn the nature of his interview, and also in what manner the affair had been arranged.

Such were my passing thoughts as I pressed forward. My men, picked no less for themselves than their horses, came rapidly along; and ere evening, we had accomplished twelve leagues of our journey.

The country through which we journeyed, though wild and romantic in its character, was singularly rich and fertile,—cultivation reaching to the very summits of the rugged mountains, and patches of wheat and Indian corn peeping amidst masses of granite rock and tangled brushwood. The vine and the olive grew wild on every side; while the orange and the arbutus, loading the air with perfume, were mingled with prickly pear-trees and variegated hollies. We followed no regular track, but cantered along over hill and valley, through forest and prairie, now in long file through some tall field of waving corn, now in open order upon some level plain,— our Portuguese guide riding a little in advance of us, upon a jet-black mule, carolling merrily some wild Gallician melody as he went.

As the sun was setting, we arrived beside a little stream that flowing along a rocky bed, skirted a vast forest of tall cork-trees. Here we called a halt, and picketing our horses, proceeded to make our arrangements for a bivouac.

Never do I remember a more lovely night. The watch-fires sent up a delicious odor from the perfumed shrubs; while the glassy water reflected on its still surface the starry sky that, unshadowed and unclouded, stretched above us. I wrapped myself in my trooper's mantle, and lay down beneath a tree,—but not to sleep. There was a something so exciting, and withal so tranquillizing, that I had no thought of slumber, but fell into a musing revery. There was a character of adventure in my position that charmed me much. My men were gathered in little groups beside the fires; some sunk in slumber, others sat smoking silently, or chatting, in a low undertone, of some bygone scene of battle or bivouac; here and there were picketed the horses; the heavy panoply and piled carbines flickering in the red glare of the watch-fires, which ever and anon threw a flitting glow upon the stern and swarthy faces of my bold troopers. Upon the trees around, sabres and helmets, holsters and cross-belts, were hung like armorial bearings in some antique hall, the dark foliage spreading its heavy shadow around us. Farther off, upon a little rocky ledge, the erect figure of the sentry, with his short carbine resting in the hollow of his arm, was seen slowly pacing in measured tread, or standing for a moment silently, as he looked upon the fair and tranquil sky,—his thoughts doubtless far, far away, beyond the sea, to some humble home, where,—

"*The hum of the spreading sycamore,   That grew beside his cottage door,*"

was again in his ears, while the merry laugh of his children stirred his bold heart. It was a Salvator-Rosa scene, and brought me back in fancy to the bandit legends I had read in boyhood. By the uncertain light of the wood embers I endeavored to sketch the group that lay before me.

The night wore on. One by one the soldiers stretched themselves to sleep, and all was still. As the hours rolled by a drowsy feeling crept gradually over me. I placed my pistols by my side, and having replenished the fire by some fresh logs, disposed myself comfortably before it.

It was during that half-dreamy state that intervenes between waking and sleep that a rustling sound of the branches behind attracted my attention. The air was too calm to attribute this to the wind, so I listened for some minutes; but sleep, too long deferred, was over-powerful, and my head sank upon my grassy pillow, and I was soon sound asleep. How long I remained thus, I know not; but I awoke suddenly. I fancied some one had shaken me rudely by the shoulder; but yet all was tranquil. My men were sleeping soundly as I saw them last. The fires were becoming low, and a gray streak in the sky, as well as a sharp cold feeling of the air, betokened the approach of day. Once more I heaped some dry branches together, and was again about to stretch myself to rest, when I felt a hand upon my shoulder. I turned quickly round, and by the imperfect light of the fire, saw the figure of a man standing motionless beside me; his head was bare, and his hair fell in long curls upon his shoulders; one hand was pressed upon his bosom, and with the other he motioned me to silence. My first impression was that our party were surprised by some French patrol; but as I looked again, I recognized, to my amazement, that the individual before me was the young French officer I had seen that morning a prisoner beside the Douro.

"How came you here?" said I, in a low voice, to him in French.

"Escaped; one of my own men threw himself between me and the sentry; I swam the Douro, received a musket-ball through my arm, lost my shako, and here I am!"

"You are aware you are again a prisoner?"

"If you desire it, of course I am," said he, in a voice full of feeling that made my very heart creep. "I thought you were a party of Lorge's Dragoons, scouring the country for forage; tracked you the entire day, and have only now come up with you."

The poor fellow, who had neither eaten nor drunk since daybreak, wounded and footsore, had accomplished twelve leagues of a march only once more to fall into the hands of his enemies. His years could scarcely have numbered nineteen; his countenance was singularly prepossessing; and though bleeding and torn, with tattered uniform, and without a covering to his head, there was no mistaking for a moment that he was of gentle blood. Noiselessly and cautiously I made him sit down beside the fire, while I spread before him the sparing remnant of my last night's supper, and shared my solitary bottle of sherry with him.

From the moment he spoke, I never entertained a thought of making him a prisoner; but as I knew not how far I was culpable in permitting, if not actually facilitating, his escape, I resolved to keep the circumstance a secret from my party, and if possible, get him away before daybreak.

No sooner did he learn my intentions regarding him, than in an instant all memory of his past misfortune, all thoughts of his present destitute condition, seemed to have fled; and while I dressed his wound and bound up his shattered arm, he chattered away as unconcernedly about the past and the future as though seated beside the fire of his own bivouac, and surrounded by his own brother officers.

"You took us by surprise the other day," said he. "Our marshal looked for the attack from the mouth of the river; we received information that your ships were expected there. In any case, our retreat was an orderly one, and must have been effected with slight loss."

I smiled at the self-complacency of this reasoning, but did not contradict him.

"Your loss must indeed have been great; your men crossed under the fire of a whole battery."

"Not exactly," said I; "our first party were quietly stationed in Oporto before you knew anything about it."

"*Ah, sacré Dieu!* Treachery!" cried he, striking his forehead with his clinched fist.

"Not so; mere daring,—nothing more. But come, tell me something of your own adventures. How were you taken?"

"Simply thus,—I was sent to the rear with orders to the artillery to cut their traces, and leave the guns; and when coming back, my horse grew tired in the heavy ground, and I was spurring him to the utmost, when one of your heavy dragoons—an officer, too—dashed at me, and actually rode me down, horse and all. I lay for some time bruised by the fall, when an infantry soldier passing by seized me by the collar, and brought me to the rear. No matter, however, here I am now. You will not give me up; and perhaps I may one day live to repay the kindness."

"You have not long joined?"

"It was my first battle; my epaulettes were very smart things yesterday, though they do look a little *passés* to-day. You are advancing, I suppose?"

I smiled without answering this question.

"Ah, I see you don't wish to speak. Never mind, your discretion is thrown away upon me; for if I rejoined my regiment to-morrow, I should have forgotten all you told me,—all but your great kindness." These last words he spoke, bowing slightly his head, and coloring as he said them.

"You are a dragoon, I think?" said I, endeavoring to change the topic.

"I was, two days ago, *chasseur à cheval*, a sous-lieutenant, in the regiment of my father, the General St. Croix."

"The name is familiar to me," I replied, "and I am sincerely happy to be in a position to serve the son of so distinguished an officer."

"The son of so distinguished an officer is most deeply obliged, but wishes with all his heart and soul he had never sought glory under such very excellent auspices. You look surprised, *mon cher*; but let me tell you, my military ardor is considerably abated in the last three days. Hunger, thirst, imprisonment, and this"—lifting his wounded limb as he spoke—"are sharp lessons in so short a campaign, and for one too, whose life hitherto had much more of ease than adventure to boast of. Shall I tell you how I became a soldier?"

"By all means; give me your glass first; and now, with a fresh log to the fire, I'm your man."

"But stay; before I begin, look to this."

The blood was flowing rapidly from his wound, which with some difficulty I succeeded in stanching. He drank off his wine hastily, held out his glass to be refilled, and then began his story.

"You have never seen the Emperor?"

"Never."

"*Sacrebleu!* What a man he is! I'd rather stand under the fire of your grenadiers, than meet his eye. When in a passion, he does not say much, it is true; but what he does, comes with a kind of hissing, rushing sound, while the very fire seems to kindle in his look. I have him before me this instant, and though you will confess that my present condition has nothing very pleasing in it, I should be sorry indeed to change it for the last time I stood in his presence.

"Two months ago I sported the gay light-blue and silver of a page to the Emperor, and certainly, what with balls, *bonbons*, flirtation, gossip, and champagne suppers, led a very gay, reckless, and indolent life of it. Somehow,—I may tell you more accurately at another period, if we ever meet,—I got myself into disgrace, and as a punishment, was ordered to absent myself from the Tuileries, and retire for some weeks to Fontainebleau. Siberia to a Russian would scarcely be a heavier infliction than was this banishment to me. There was no court, no levee, no military parade, no ball, no opera. A small household of the Emperor's chosen servants quietly kept house there. The gloomy walls re-echoed to no music; the dark alleys of the dreary garden seemed the very impersonation of solitude and decay. Nothing broke the dull monotony of the tiresome day, except when occasionally, near sunset, the clash of the guard would be heard turning out, and the clank of presenting arms, followed by the roll of a heavy carriage into the gloomy courtyard. One lamp, shining like a star, in a small chamber on the second floor, would remain till near four, sometimes five o'clock in the morning. The same sounds of the guard and the same dull roll of the carriage would break the stillness of the early morning; and the Emperor—for it was he—would be on his road back to Paris.

"We never saw him,—I say we, for like myself some half-dozen others were also there, expiating their follies by a life of cheerless *ennui*.

"It was upon a calm evening in April, we sat together chatting over the various misdeeds which had consigned us to exile, when some one proposed, by way of passing the time, that we should visit the small flower-garden that was parted off from the rest, and reserved for the Emperor alone. It was already beyond the hour he usually came; besides that, even should he arrive, there was abundant time to get back before he could possibly reach it. The garden we had often seen, but there was something in the fact that our going there was a transgression that so pleased us all that we agreed at once and set forth. For above an hour we loitered about the lonely and deserted walks, where already the Emperor's foot-tracks had worn a marked pathway, when we grew weary and were about to return, just as one of the party suggested, half in ridicule of the sanctity of the spot, that we should have a game of leap-frog ere we left it. The idea pleased us and was at once adopted. Our plan was this,—each person stationed himself in some by-walk or alley, and waited till the other, whose turn it was, came and leaped over him; so that, besides the activity displayed, there was a knowledge of the *locale* necessary; for to any one passed over a forfeit was to be paid. Our game began at once, and certainly I doubt if ever those green alleys and shady groves rang to such hearty laughter. Here would be seen a couple rolling over together on the grass; there some luckless wight counting out his pocket-money to pay his penalty. The hours passed quietly over, and the moon rose, and at last it came to my turn to make the tour of the garden. As I was supposed to know all its intricacies better than the rest, a longer time was given for them to conceal themselves; at length the word was given, and I started.

"Anxious to acquit myself well, I hurried along at top speed, but guess my surprise to discover that nowhere could I find one of my companions. Down one walk I scampered, up another, across a third, but all was still and silent; not a sound, not a breath, could I detect. There was still one part of the garden unexplored; it was a small open space before a little pond which usually contained the gold fish the Emperor was so fond of. Thither I bent my steps, and had not gone far when in the pale moonlight I saw, at length, one of my companions waiting patiently for my coming, his head bent forward and his shoulders rounded. Anxious to repay him for my own disappointment, I crept silently forward on tiptoe till quite near him, when, rushing madly on, I sprang upon his back; just, however, as I rose to leap over, he raised his head, and, staggered by the impulse of my spring, he was thrown forward, and after an ineffectual effort to keep his legs fell flat upon his face in the grass. Bursting with laughter, I fell over him on the ground, and was turning to assist him, when suddenly he sprang upon his feet, and—horror of horrors!—it was Napoleon himself; his usually pale features were purple with rage, but not a word, not a syllable escaped him.

"'*Qui êtes vous?*' said he, at length.

"'St. Croix, Sire,' said I, still kneeling before him, while my very heart leaped into my mouth.

"'St. Croix! *toujours* St. Croix! Come here; approach me,' cried he, in a voice of stifled passion.

"I rose; but before I could take a step forward he sprang at me, and tearing off my epaulettes trampled them beneath his feet, and then he shouted out, rather than spoke, the word '*Allez!*'

"I did not wait for a second intimation, but clearing the paling at a spring, was many a mile from Fontainebleau before daybreak."

CHAPTER LI.

THE MARCH.

Twice the *réveil* sounded; the horses champed impatiently their heavy bits; my men stood waiting for the order to mount, ere I could arouse myself from the deep sleep I had fallen into. The young Frenchman and his story were in my dreams, and when I awoke, his figure, as he lay sleeping beside the wood embers, was the first object I perceived. There he lay, to all seeming as forgetful of his fate as though he still inhabited the gorgeous halls and gilded saloons of the Tuileries; his pale and handsome features wore even a placid smile as, doubtless, some dream of other days flitted across him; his long hair waved in luxuriant curls upon his neck, and his light-brown mustache, slightly curled at the top, gave to his mild and youthful features an air of saucy *fierté* that heightened their effect. A narrow blue ribbon which he wore round his throat gently peeped from his open bosom. I could not resist the curiosity I felt to see what it meant, and drawing it softly forth, I perceived that a small miniature was attached to it. It was beautifully painted, and surrounded with brilliants of some value. One glance showed me,—for I had seen more than one engraving before of her,—that it was the portrait of the Empress Josephine. Poor boy! he doubtless was a favorite at court; indeed, everything in his air and manner bespoke him such. I gently replaced the precious locket and turned from the spot to think over what was best to be done for him. Knowing the vindictive feeling of the Portuguese towards their invaders, I feared to take Pietro, our guide, into my confidence. I accordingly summoned my man Mike to my aid, who, with all his country's readiness, soon found out an expedient. It was to pretend to Pietro that the prisoner was merely an English officer who had made his escape from the French army, in which, against his will, he had been serving for some time.

This plan succeeded perfectly; and when St. Croix, mounted upon one of my led horses, set out upon his march beside me, none was more profuse of his attentions than the dark-brown guide whose hatred of a Frenchman was beyond belief.

By thus giving him safe conduct through Portugal, I knew that when we reached the frontier he could easily manage to come up with some part of Marshal Victor's force, the advanced guard of which lay on the left bank of the Tagus.

To me the companionship was the greatest boon; the gay and buoyant spirit that no reverse of fortune, no untoward event, could subdue, lightened many an hour of the journey; and though at times the gasconading tone of the Frenchman would peep through, there was still such a fund of good-tempered raillery in all he said that it was impossible to feel angry with him. His implicit faith in the Emperor's invincibility also amused me. Of the unbounded confidence of the nation in general, and the army particularly, in Napoleon, I had till then no conception. It was not that in the profound skill and immense resources of the general they trusted, but they actually regarded him as one placed above all the common accidents of fortune, and revered him as something more than human.

"*Il viendra et puis—*" was the continued exclamation of the young Frenchman. Any notion of our successfully resisting the overwhelming might of the Emperor, he would have laughed to scorn, and so I let him go on prophesying our future misfortunes till the time when, driven back upon Lisbon, we should be compelled to evacuate the Peninsula, and under favor of a convention be permitted to return to England. All this was sufficiently ridiculous, coming from a youth of nineteen, wounded, in misery, a prisoner; but further experience of his nation has shown me that St. Croix was not the exception, but the rule. The conviction in the ultimate success of their army, whatever be the merely momentary mishap, is the one present thought of a Frenchman; a victory with them is a conquest; a defeat,—if they are by any chance driven to acknowledge one,—a *fatalité*.

I was too young a man, and still more, too young a soldier, to bear with this absurd affectation of superiority as I ought, and consequently was glad to wander, whenever I could, from the contested point of our national superiority to other topics. St. Croix, although young, had seen much of the world as a page in the splendid court of the Tuileries; the scenes passing before his eyes were calculated to make a strong impression; and by many an anecdote of his former life, he lightened the road as we passed along.

"You promised, by-the-bye, to tell me of your banishment. How did that occur, St. Croix?"

"*Ah, par Dieu!* that was an unfortunate affair for me; then began all my mishaps. But for that, I should never have been sent to Fontainebleau; never have played leap-frog with the Emperor; never have been sent a soldier into Spain. True," said he, laughing, "I should never have had the happiness of your acquaintance. But still, I'd much rather have met you first in the Place des Victoires than in the Estrella Mountains."

"Who knows?" said I; "perhaps your good genius prevailed in all this."

"Perhaps," said he, interrupting me; "that's exactly what the Empress said,—she was my godmother,—'Jules will be a *Maréchal de France yet*.' But certainly, it must be confessed, I have made a bad beginning. However, you wish to hear of my disgrace at court. *Allons donc*. But had we not better wait for a halt?"

"Agreed," said I; "and so let us now press forward."

CHAPTER LII.

THE PAGE.

Under the deep shade of some tall trees, sheltered from the noonday sun, we lay down to rest ourselves and enjoy a most patriarchal dinner,—some dry biscuits, a few bunches of grapes, and a little weak wine, savoring more of the borachio-skin than the vine-juice, were all we boasted; yet they were not ungrateful at such a time and place.

"Whose health did you pledge then?" inquired St. Croix, with a half-malicious smile, as I raised the glass silently to my lips.

I blushed deeply, and looked confused.

"*A ses beux yeux!* whoever she be," said he, gayly tossing off his wine; "and now, if you feel disposed, I'll tell you my story. In good truth, it is not worth relating, but it may serve to set you asleep, at all events.

"I have already told you I was a page. Alas, the impressions you may feel of that functionary, from having seen Cherubino, give but a faint notion of him when pertaining to the household of the Emperor Napoleon.

"The *farfallone amoroso* basked in the soft smiles and sunny looks of the Countess Almaviva; we met but the cold, impassive look of Talleyrand, the piercing and penetrating stare of Savary, or the ambiguous smile, half menace, half mockery, of Monsieur Fouché. While on service, our days were passed in the antechamber, beside the *salle d'audience* of the Emperor, reclining against the closed door, watching attentively for the gentle tinkle of the little bell which summoned us to open for the exit of some haughty diplomate, or the *entrée* of some redoubted general. Thus passed we the weary hours; the illustrious visitors by whom we were surrounded had no novelty, consequently no attraction for us, and the names already historical were but household words with us.

"We often remarked, too, the proud and distant bearing the Emperor assumed towards those of his generals who had been his former companions-in-arms. Whatever familiarity or freedom may have existed in the campaign or in the battle-field, the air of the Tuileries certainly chilled it. I have often heard that the ceremonious observances and rigid etiquette of the old Bourbon court were far preferable to the stern reserve and unbending stiffness of the imperial one.

"The antechamber is but the reflection of the reception-room; and whatever be the whims, the caprices, the littleness of the Great Man, they are speedily assumed by his inferiors, and the dark temper of one casts a lowering shadow on every menial by whom he is surrounded.

"As for us, we were certainly not long in catching somewhat of the spirit of the Emperor; and I doubt much if the impertinence of the waiting-room was not more dreaded and detested than the abrupt speech and searching look of Napoleon himself.

"What a malicious pleasure have I not felt in arresting the step of M. de Talleyrand, as he approached the Emperor's closet! With what easy insolence have I lisped out, 'Pardon, Monsieur, but his Majesty cannot receive you,' or 'Monsieur le Duc, his Majesty has given no orders for your admission.' How amusing it was to watch the baffled look of each, as he retired once more to his place among the crowd, the wily diplomate covering his chagrin with a practised smile, while the stern marshal would blush to his very eyes with indignation! This was the great pleasure our position afforded us, and with a boyish spirit of mischief, we cultivated it to perfection, and became at last the very horror and detestation of all who frequented the levees; and the ambassador whose fearless voice was heard among the councils of kings became soft and conciliating in his approaches to us; and the hardy general who would have charged upon a brigade of artillery was timid as a girl in addressing us a mere question.

"Among the amiable class thus characterized I was most conspicuous, preserving cautiously a tone of civility that left nothing openly to complain of. I assumed an indifference and impartiality of manner that no exigency of affairs, no pressing haste, could discompose or disturb; and my bow of recognition to Soult or Massena was as coolly measured as my monosyllabic answer was accurately conned over.

"Upon ordinary occasions the Emperor at the close of each person's audience rang his little bell for the admission of the next in order as they arrived in the waiting-room; yet when anything important was under consideration, a list was given us in the morning of the names to be presented in rotation, which no casual circumstance was ever suffered to interfere with.

"It is now about four months since, one fine morning, such a list was placed within my hands. His Majesty was just then occupied with an inquiry into the naval force of the kingdom; and as I cast my eyes carelessly over the names, I read little else than Vice-Admiral So-and-so, Commander Such-a-one, and Chef d'Escardron Such-another, and the levee presented accordingly, instead of its usual brilliant array of gorgeous uniform and aiguilletted marshals, the simple blue-and-gold of the naval service.

"The marine was not in high favor with the Emperor; and truly, my reception of these unfrequent visitors was anything but flattering. The early part of the morning was, as usual, occupied by the audience of the Minister of Police, and the Duc de Bassano, who evidently, from the length of time they remained, had matter of importance to communicate. Meanwhile the antechamber filled rapidly, and before noon was actually crowded. It was just at this moment that the folding-door slowly opened, and a figure entered, such as I had never before seen in our brilliant saloon. He was a man of five or six and fifty, short, thickset, and strongly built, with a bronzed and weather-beaten face, and a broad open forehead deeply scarred with a sabre-cut; a shaggy gray mustache curled over and concealed his mouth, while eyebrows of the same color shaded his dark and piercing eyes. His dress was a coarse cut of blue cloth such as the fishermen wear in Bretagne, fastened at the waist by a broad belt of black leather, from which hung a short-bladed cutlass; his loose trousers, of the same material, were turned up at the ankles to show a pair of strong legs coarsely cased in blue stockings and thick-soled shoes. A broad-leaved oil-skin hat was held in one hand, and the other stuck carelessly in his pocket, as he entered. He came in with a careless air, and familiarly saluting one or two officers in the room, he sat himself down near the door, appearing lost in his own reflections.

"'Who can you be, my worthy friend?' was my question to myself as I surveyed this singular apparition. At the same time, casting my eyes down the list, I perceived that several pilots of the coast of Havre, Calais, and Boulogne had been summoned to Paris to give some information upon the soundings and depth of water along the shore.

"'Ha,' thought I, 'I have it. The good man has mistaken his place, and instead of remaining without, has walked boldly forward to the antechamber.'

"There was something so strange and so original in the grim look of the old fellow, as he sat there alone, that I suffered him to remain quietly in his delusion, rather than order him back to the waiting-room without; besides, I perceived that a kind of sensation was created among the others by his appearance there, which amused me greatly.

"As the day wore on, the officers formed into little groups of three or four, chatting together in an undertone,—all save the old pilot. He had taken a huge tobacco-box from his capacious breast-pocket, and inserting an immense piece of the bitter weed in his mouth, began to chew it as leisurely as though he were walking the quarter-deck. The cool*insouciance* of such a proceeding amused me much, and I resolved to draw him out a little. His strong, broad Breton features, his deep voice, his dry, blunt manner, were all in admirable keeping with his exterior.

"'*Par Dieu*, my lad,' said he, after chatting some time, 'had you not better tell the Emperor that I am waiting? It's now past noon, and I must eat something.'

"'Have a little patience,' said I; 'his Majesty is going to invite you to dinner.'

"'Be it so,' said he, gravely; 'provided the hour be an early one, I'm his man.'

"With difficulty did I keep down my laughter as he said this, and continued.

"'So you know the Emperor already, it seems?'

"'Yes, that I do! I remember him when he was no higher than yourself.'

"'How delighted he'll be to find you here! I hope you have brought up some of your family with you, as the Emperor would be so flattered by it?'

"'No, I've left them at home. This place don't suit us over well. We have plenty to do besides spending our time and money among all you fine folks here.'

"'And not a bad life of it, either,' added I, 'fishing for cod and herrings,—stripping a wreck now and then.'

"He stared at me, as I said this, like a tiger on the spring, but spoke not a word.

"'And how many young sea-wolves may you have in your den at home?'

"'Six; and all of them able to carry you with one hand, at arm's length.'

"'I have no doubt. I shall certainly not test their ability. But you yourself,—how do you like the capital?'

"'Not over well; and I'll tell you why—'

"As he said this the door of the audience-chamber opened, and the Emperor appeared. His eyes flashed fire as he looked hurriedly around the room.

"'Who is in waiting here?'"

"'I am, please your Majesty,' said I, bowing deeply, as I started from my seat.

"'And where is the Admiral Truguet? Why was he not admitted?'

"'Not present, your Majesty,' said I, trembling with fear.

"'Hold there, young fellow; not so fast. Here he is.'

"'Ah, Truguet, *mon ami!*' cried the Emperor, placing both hands on the old fellow's shoulders, 'how long have you been in waiting?'

"'Two hours and a half,' said he, producing in evidence a watch like a saucer.

"'What, two hours and a half, and I not know it!'

"'No matter; I am always happy to serve your Majesty. But if that fine fellow had not told me that you were going to ask me to dinner—'

"'He! He said so, did he?' said Napoleon, turning on me a glance like a wild beast. 'Yes, Truguet, so I am; you shall dine with me to-day. And you, sir,' said he, dropping his voice to a whisper, as he came closer towards me,—'and you have dared to speak thus? Call in a guard there. Capitaine, put this person under arrest; he is disgraced. He is no longer page of the palace. Out of my presence! away, sir!'

"The room wheeled round; my legs tottered; my senses reeled; and I saw no more.

"Three weeks' bread and water in St. Pélagie, however, brought me to my recollection; and at last my kind, my more than kind friend, the Empress, obtained my pardon, and sent me to Fontainebleau, till the Emperor should forget all about it. How I contrived again to refresh his memory I have already told you; and certainly you will acknowledge that I have not been fortunate in my interviews with Napoleon."

I am conscious how much St. Croix's story loses in my telling. The simple expressions, the grace of the narrative, were its charm: and these, alas! I can neither translate nor imitate, no more than I can convey the strange mixture of deep feeling and levity, shrewdness and simplicity, that constituted the manner of the narrator.

With many a story of his courtly career he amused me as we trotted along; when, towards nightfall of the third day, a peasant informed us that a body of French cavalry occupied the convent of San Cristoval, about three leagues off. The opportunity of his return to his own army pleased him far less than I expected. He heard, without any show of satisfaction, that the time of his liberation had arrived; and when the moment of leave-taking drew near, he became deeply affected.

"*Eh, bien*, Charles," said he, smiling sadly through his dimmed and tearful eyes. "You've been a kind friend to me. Is the time never to come when I can repay you?"

"Yes, yes; we'll meet again, be assured of it. Meanwhile there is one way you can more than repay anything I have done for you."

"Oh, name it at once!"

"Many a brave fellow of ours is now, and doubtless many more will be, prisoners with your army in this war. Whenever, therefore, your lot brings you in contact with such—"

"They shall be my brothers," said he, springing towards me and throwing his arms round my neck. "Adieu, adieu!" With that he rushed from the spot, and before I could speak again, was mounted upon the peasant's horse and waving his hand to me in farewell.

I looked after him as he rode at a fast gallop down the slope of the green mountain, the noise of the horse's feet echoing along the silent plain. I turned at length to leave the spot, and then perceived for the first time that when taking his farewell of me he had hung around my neck his miniature of the Empress. Poor boy! How sorrowful I felt thus to rob him of what he had held so dear! How gladly would I have overtaken him to restore it! It was the only keepsake he possessed; and knowing that I would not accept it if offered, he took this way of compelling me to keep it.

Through the long hours of the summer's night I thought of him; and when at last I slept, towards morning, my first thought on waking was of the solitary day before me. The miles no longer slipped imperceptibly along; no longer did the noon and night seem fast to follow. Alas, that one should grow old! The very sorrows of our early years have something soft and touching in them. Arising less from deep wrong than slight mischances, the grief they cause comes ever with an alloy of pleasant thoughts, telling of the tender past, and amidst the tears called up, forming some bright rainbow of future hope.

Poor St. Croix had already won greatly upon me, and I felt lonely and desolate when he departed.

CHAPTER LIII.

ALVAS.

Nothing of incident marked our farther progress towards the frontier of Spain, and at length we reached the small town of Alvas. It was past sunset as we arrived, and instead of the usual quiet and repose of a little village, we found the streets crowded with people, on horseback and on foot; mules, bullocks, carts, and wagons blocked up the way, and the oaths of the drivers and the screaming of women and children resounded on all sides.

With what little Spanish I possessed I questioned some of those near me, and learned, in reply, that a dreadful engagement had taken place that day between the advanced guard of the French, under Victor, and the Lusitanian legion; that the Portuguese troops had been beaten and completely routed, losing all their artillery and baggage; that the French were rapidly advancing, and expected hourly to arrive at Alvas, in consequence of which the terror-stricken inhabitants were packing up their possessions and hurrying away.

Here, then, was a point of considerable difficulty for me at once. My instructions had never provided for such a conjuncture, and I was totally unable to determine what was best to be done; both my men and their horses were completely tired by a march of fourteen leagues, and had a pressing need of some rest; on every side of me the preparations for flight were proceeding with all the speed that fear inspires; and to my urgent request for some information as to food and shelter, I could obtain no other reply than muttered menaces of the fate before me if I remained, and exaggerated accounts of French cruelty.

Amidst all this bustle and confusion a tremendous fall of heavy rain set in, which at once determined me, come what might, to house my party, and provide forage for our horses.

As we pushed our way slowly through the encumbered streets, looking on every side for some appearance of a village inn, a tremendous shout rose in our rear, and a rush of the people towards us induced us to suppose that the French were upon us. For some minutes the din and uproar were terrific,—the clatter of horses' feet, the braying of trumpets, the yelling of the mob, all mingling in one frightful concert.

I formed my men in close column, and waited steadily for the attack, resolving, if possible, to charge through the advancing files,—any retreat through the crowded and blocked-up thoroughfares being totally out of the question. The rain was falling in such torrents that nothing could be seen a few yards off, when suddenly a pause of a few seconds occurred, and from the clash of accoutrements, and the hoarse tones of a loud voice, I judged that the body of men before us were forming for attack.

Resolving, therefore, to take them by surprise, I gave the word to charge, and spurring our jaded cattle, onward we dashed. The mob fled right and left from us as we came on; and through the dense mist we could just perceive a body of cavalry before us.

In an instant we were among them; down they went on every side, men and horses rolling pell-mell over each other; not a blow, not a shot striking us as we pressed on. Never did I witness such total consternation; some threw themselves from their horses, and fled towards the houses; others turned and tried to fall back, but the increasing pressure from behind held them, and finally succeeded in blocking us up among them.

It was just at this critical moment that a sudden gleam of light from a window fell upon the disordered mass, and to my astonishment, I need not say to my delight, I perceived that they were Portuguese troops. Before I had well time to halt my party, my convictions were pretty well strengthened by hearing a well-known voice in the rear of the mass call out,—

"Charge, ye devils! charge, will ye? Illustrious Hidalgos! cut them down; *los infidelos, sacrificados los!* Scatter them like chaff!"

One roar of laughter was my only answer to this energetic appeal for my destruction, and the moment after the dry features and pleasant face of old Monsoon beamed on me by the light of a pine-torch he carried in his right hand.

"Are they prisoners? Have they surrendered?" inquired he, riding up. "It is well for them; we'd have made mince-meat of them otherwise; now they shall be well treated, and ransomed if they prefer."

"*Gracios excellenze!*" said I, in a feigned voice.

"Give up your sword," said the major, in an undertone.

"You behaved gallantly, but you fought against invincibles. Lord love them! but they are the most terrified invincibles."

I nearly burst aloud at this.

"It was a close thing which of us ran first," muttered the major, as he turned to give some directions to an aide-de-camp. "Ask them who they are," said he, in Spanish.

By this time I came close alongside of him, and placing my mouth close to his ear, holloed out,—

"Monsoon, old fellow, how goes the King of Spain's sherry?"

"Eh, what! Why, upon my life, and so it is,—Charley, my boy, so it's you, is it? Egad, how good; and we were so near being the death of you! My poor fellow, how came you here?"

A few words of explanation sufficed to inform the major why we were there, and still more to comfort him with the assurance that he had not been charging the general's staff, and the conmander-in-chief himself.

"Upon my life, you gave me a great start; though as long as I thought you were French, it was very well."

"True, Major, but certainly the invincibles were merciful as they were strong."

"They were tired, Charley, nothing more; why, lad, we've been fighting since daybreak,— beat Victor at six o'clock, drove him back behind the Tagus; took a cold dinner, and had at him again in the afternoon. Lord love you! we've immortalized ourselves. But you must never speak of this little business here; it tells devilish ill for the discipline of your fellows, upon my life it does."

This was rather an original turn to give the transaction, but I did not oppose; and thus chatting, we entered the little inn, where, confidence once restored, some semblance of comfort already appeared.

"And so you're come to reinforce us?" said Monsoon; "there was never anything more opportune,—though we surprised ourselves today with valor, I don't think we could persevere."

"Yes, Major, the appointment gave me sincere pleasure; I greatly desired to see a little service under your orders. Shall I present you with my despatches?"

"Not now, Charley,—not now, my lad. Supper is the first thing at this moment; besides, now that you remind me, I must send off a despatch myself, Upon my life, it's a great piece of fortune that you're here; you shall be secretary at war, and write it for me. Here now—how lucky that I thought of it, to be sure! And it was just a mere chance; one has so many things—" Muttering such broken, disjointed sentences, the major opened a large portfolio with writing materials, which he displayed before me as he rubbed his hands with satisfaction, and said, "Write away, lad."

"But, my dear Major, you forget; I was not in the action. You must describe; I can only follow you."

"Begin then thus:—

HEADQUARTERS, ALVAS, JUNE 26. YOUR EXCELLENCY,—Having learned from Don Alphonzo Xaviero da Minto, an officer upon my personal staff—

"Luckily sober at that moment—"

That the advanced guard of the eighth corps of the French army—

"Stay, though, was it the eighth? Upon my life, I'm not quite clear as to that; blot the word a little and go on—"

That the—corps, under Marshal Victor, had commenced a forward movement towards Alcantara, I immediately ordered a flank movement of the light infantry regiment to cover the bridge over the Tagus. After breakfast—

"I'm afraid, Major, that is not precise enough."

"Well—"

About eleven o'clock, the French skirmishers attacked, and drove in our pickets that were posted in front of our position, and following rapidly up with cavalry, they took a few prisoners, and killed old Alphonzo,—he ran like a man, they say, but they caught him in the rear.

"You needn't put that in, if you don't like."

I now directed a charge of the cavalry brigade, under Don Asturias Y'Hajos, that cut them up in fine style. Our artillery, posted on the heights, moving away at their columns like fun. Victor didn't like this, and got into a wood, when we all went to dinner; it was about two o'clock then. After dinner, the Portuguese light corps, under Silva da Onorha, having made an attack upon, the enemy's left, without my orders, got devilish well trounced, and served them right; but coming up to their assistance, with the heavy brigade of guns, and the cavalry, we drove back the French, and took several prisoners, none of whom we put to death.

"Dash that—Sir Arthur likes respect for the usages of war. Lord, how dry I'm getting!"

The French were soon seen to retire their heavy guns, and speedily afterwards retreated. We pursued them for some time, but they showed fight; and as it was getting dark, I drew off my forces, and came here to supper. Your Excellency will perceive, by the enclosed return, that our loss has been considerable. I send this despatch by Don Emanuel Forgales, whose services—

"I back him for mutton hash with onions against the whole regiment—"

—have been of the most distinguished nature, and beg to recommend him to your Excellency's favor. I have the honor, etc.

"Is it finished, Charley? Egad, I'm glad of it, for here comes supper."

The door opened as he spoke, and displayed a tempting tray of smoking viands, flanked by several bottles,—an officer of the major's staff accompanied it, and showed, by his attentions to the etiquette of the table and the proper arrangement of the meal, that his functions in his superior's household were more than military.

We were speedily joined by two others in rich uniform, whose names I now forget, but to whom the major presented me in all form,—introducing me, as well as I could interpret his Spanish, as his most illustrious ally and friend Don Carlos O'Malley.

CHAPTER LIV.

THE SUPPER.

I have often partaken of more luxurious cookery and rarer wines; but never do I remember enjoying a more welcome supper than on this occasion.

Our Portuguese guests left us soon, and the major and myself were once more tête-a-tête beside a cheerful fire; a well-chosen array of bottles guaranteeing that for some time at least no necessity of leave-taking should arise from any deficiency of wine.

"That sherry is very near the thing, Charley; a little, a very little sharp, but the after-taste perfect. And now, my boy, how have you been doing since we parted?"

"Not so badly, Major. I have already got a step in promotion. The affair at the Douro gave me a lieutenancy."

"I wish you joy with all my heart. I'll call you captain always while you're with me. Upon my life I will. Why, man, they style me your Excellency here. Bless your heart, we are great folk among the Portuguese, and no bad service, after all."

"I should think not, Major. You seem to have always made a good thing of it."

"No, Charley; no, my boy. They overlook us greatly in general orders and despatches. Had the brilliant action of to-day been fought by the British—But no matter, they may behave well in England, after all; and when I'm called to the Upper House as Baron Monsoon of the Tagus,—is that better than Lord Alcantara?"

"I prefer the latter."

"Well, then, I'll have it. Lord! what a treaty I'll move for with Portugal, to let us have wine cheap. Wine, you know, as David says, gives us a pleasant countenance; and oil,—I forget what oil does. Pass over the decanter. And how is Sir Arthur, Charley? A fine fellow, but sadly deficient in the knowledge of supplies. Never would have made any character in the commissariat. Bless your heart, he pays for everything here as if he were in Cheapside."

"How absurd, to be sure!"

"Isn't it, though? That was not my way, when I was commissary-general about a year or two ago. To be sure, how I did puzzle them! They tried to audit my accounts, and what do you think I did? I brought them in three thousand pounds in my debt. They never tried on that game any more. 'No, no,' said the Junta, 'Beresford and Monsoon are great men, and must be treated with respect!' Do you think we'd let them search our pockets? But the rogues doubled on us after all; they sent us to the northward,—a poor country—"

"So that, except a little commonplace pillage of the convents and nunneries, you had little or nothing?"

"Exactly so; and then I got a great shock about that time that affected my spirits for a considerable while."

"Indeed, Major, some illness?"

"No, I was quite well; but—Lord, how thirsty it makes me to think of it; my throat is absolutely parched—I was near being hanged!"

"Hanged!"

"Yes. Upon my life it's true,—very horrible, ain't it? It had a great effect upon my nervous system; and they never thought of any little pension to me as a recompense for my sufferings."

"And who was barbarous enough to think of such a thing, Major?"

"Sir Arthur Wellesley himself,—none other, Charley?"

"Oh, it was a mistake, Major, or a joke."

"It was devilish near being a practical one, though. I'll tell you how it occurred. After the battle of Vimeira, the brigade to which I was attached had their headquarters at San Pietro, a large convent where all the church plate for miles around was stored up for safety. A sergeant's guard was accordingly stationed over the refectory, and every precaution taken to prevent pillage, Sir Arthur himself having given particular orders on the subject. Well, somehow,—I never could find out how,—but in leaving the place, all the wagons of our brigade had got some trifling articles of small value scattered, as it might be, among their stores,—gold cups, silver candlesticks, Virgin Marys, ivory crucifixes, saints' eyes set in topazes, and martyrs' toes in silver filagree, and a hundred other similar things.

"One of these confounded bullock-cars broke down just at the angle of the road where the commander-in-chief was standing with his staff to watch the troops defile, and out rolled, among bread rations and salt beef, a whole avalanche of precious relics and church ornaments. Every one stood aghast! Never was there such a misfortune. No one endeavored to repair the mishap, but all looked on in terrified amazement as to what was to follow.

"'Who has the command of this detachment?' shouted out Sir Arthur, in a voice that made more than one of us tremble.

"'Monsoon, your Excellency,—Major Monsoon, of the Portuguese brigade.'

"'The d—d old rogue, I know him!' Upon my life that's what he said. 'Hang him up on the spot,' pointing with his finger as he spoke; 'we shall see if this practice cannot be put a stop to.' And with these words he rode leisurely away, as if he had been merely ordering dinner for a small party.

"When I came up to the place the halberts were fixed, and Gronow, with a company of the Fusiliers, under arms beside them.

"'Devilish sorry for it, Major,' said he; 'It's confoundedly unpleasant; but can't be helped. We've got orders to see you hanged.'

170

"Faith, it was just so he said it, tapping his snuff-box as he spoke, and looking carelessly about him. Now, had it not been for the fixed halberts and the provost-marshal, I'd not have believed him; but one glance at them, and another at the bullock-cart with all the holy images, told me at once what had happened.

"'He only means to frighten me a little? Isn't that all, Gronow?' cried I, in a supplicating voice.

"'Very possibly, Major,' said he; 'but I must execute my orders.'

"'You'll surely not—' Before I could finish, up came Dan Mackinnon, cantering smartly.

"'Going to hang old Monsoon, eh, Gronow? What fun!'

"'Ain't it, though,' said I, half blubbering.

"'Well, if you're a good Catholic, you may have your choice of a saint, for, by Jupiter, there's a strong muster of them here.' This cruel allusion was made in reference to the gold and silver effigies that lay scattered about the highway.

"'Dan,' said I, in a whisper, 'intercede for me. Do, like a good, kind fellow. You have influence with Sir Arthur.'

"'You old sinner,' said he, 'it's useless.'

"'Dan, I'll forgive you the fifteen pounds.'

"'That you owe *me*,' said Dan, laughing.

"'Who'll ever be the father to you I have been? Who'll mix your punch with burned Madeira, when I'm gone?' said I.

"'Well, really, I am sorry for you, Monsoon. I say, Gronow, don't tuck him up for a few minutes; I'll speak for the old villain, and if I succeed, I'll wave my handkerchief.'

"Well, away went Dan at a full gallop. Gronow sat down on a bank, and I fidgeted about in no very enviable frame of mind, the confounded provost-marshal eying me all the while.

"'I can only give you five minutes more, Major,' said Gronow, placing his watch beside him on the grass. I tried to pray a little, and said three or four of Solomon's proverbs, when he again called out: 'There, you see it won't do! Sir Arthur is shaking his head.'

"'What's that waving yonder?'

"'The colors of the 6th Foot. Come, Major, off with your stock.'

"'Where is Dan now; what is he doing?'—for I could see nothing myself.

"'He's riding beside Sir Arthur. They all seem laughing.'

"'God forgive them! what an awful retrospect this will prove to some of them.'

"'Time's up!' said Gronow, jumping up, and replacing his watch in his pocket.

"'Provost-Marshal, be quick now—'

"'Eh! what's that?—there, I see it waving! There's a shout too!'

"''Ay, by Jove! so it is; well, you're saved this time, Major; that's the signal.'

"So saying, Gronow formed his fellows in line and resumed his march quite coolly, leaving me alone on the roadside to meditate over martial law and my pernicious taste for relics.

"Well, Charley, this gave me a great shock, and I think, too, it must have had a great effect upon Sir Arthur himself; but, upon my life, he has wonderful nerves. I met him one day afterwards at dinner in Lisbon; he looked at me very hard for a few seconds: 'Eh, Monsoon! Major Monsoon, I think?'

"'Yes, your Excellency,' said I, briefly; thinking how painful it must be for him to meet me.

"'Thought I had hanged you,—know I intended it,—no matter. A glass of wine with you?'

"Upon my life, that was all; how easily some people can forgive themselves! But Charley, my hearty, we are getting on slowly with the tipple; are they all empty? So they are! Let us make a sortie on the cellar; bring a candle with you, and come along."

We had scarcely proceeded a few steps from the door, when a most vociferous sound of mirth, arising from a neighboring apartment, arrested our progress.

"Are the dons so convivial, Major?" said I, as a hearty burst of laughter broke forth at the moment.

"Upon my life, they surprise me; I begin to fear they have taken some of our wine."

We now perceived that the sounds of merriment came from the kitchen, which opened upon a little courtyard. Into this we crept stealthily, and approaching noiselessly to the window, obtained a peep at the scene within.

Around a blazing fire, over which hung by a chain a massive iron pot, sat a goodly party of some half-dozen people. One group lay in dark shadow; but the others were brilliantly lighted up by the cheerful blaze, and showed us a portly Dominican friar, with a beard down to his waist, a buxom, dark-eyed girl of some eighteen years, and between the two, most comfortably leaning back, with an arm round each, no less a person than my trusty man Mickey Free.

It was evident, from the alternate motion of his head, that his attentions were evenly divided between the church and the fair sex; although, to confess the truth, they seemed much more favorably received by the latter than the former,—a brown earthen flagon appearing to absorb all the worthy monk's thoughts that he could spare from the contemplation of heavenly objects.

"Mary, my darlin',' don't be looking at me that way, through the corner of your eye; I know you're fond of me,—but the girls always was. You think I'm joking, but troth I wouldn't say a lie before the holy man beside me; sure I wouldn't, Father?"

The friar grunted out something in reply, not very unlike, in sound at least, a hearty anathema.

"Ah, then, isn't it yourself has the illigant time of it, Father dear!" said he, tapping him familiarly upon his ample paunch, "and nothing to trouble you; the best of divarsion wherever you go, and whether it's Badahos or Ballykilruddery, it's all one; the women is fond of ye. Father Murphy, the coadjutor in Scariff, was just such another as yourself, and he'd coax the birds off the trees with the tongue of him. Give us a pull at the pipkin before it's all gone, and I'll give you a chant."

With this he seized the jar, and drained it to the bottom; the smack of his lips as he concluded, and the disappointed look of the friar as he peered into the vessel, throwing the others, once more, into a loud burst of laughter.

"And now, your rev'rance, a good chorus is all I'll ask, and you'll not refuse it for the honor of the church."

So saying, he turned a look of most droll expression upon the monk, and began the following ditty, to the air of "Saint Patrick was a Gentleman":—

What an illegant life a friar leads, With a fat round paunch before him! He mutters a prayer and counts his beads, And all the women adore him. It's little he's troubled to work or think, Wherever devotion leads him; A "pater" pays for his dinner and drink, For the Church—good luck to her!—feeds him. From the cow in the field to the pig in the sty, From the maid to the lady in satin, They tremble wherever he turns an eye. He can talk to the Devil in Latin! He's mighty severe to the ugly and ould, And curses like mad when he's near 'em; But one beautiful trait of him I've been tould, The innocent craytures don't fear him. It's little for spirits or ghosts he cares; For 'tis true as the world supposes, With an Ave he'd make them march down-stairs, Av they dared to show their noses. The Devil himself's afraid, 'tis said, And dares not to deride him; For "angels make each night his bed, And then—lie down beside him."

A perfect burst of laughter from Monsoon prevented my hearing how Mike's minstrelsy succeeded within doors; but when I looked again, I found that the friar had decamped, leaving the field open to his rival,—a circumstance, I could plainly perceive, not disliked by either party.

"Come back, Charley, that villain of yours has given me the cramp, standing here on the cold pavement. We'll have a little warm posset,—very small and thin, as they say in Tom Jones,—and then to bed."

Notwithstanding the abstemious intentions of the major, it was daybreak ere we separated, and neither party in a condition for performing upon the tight-rope.

CHAPTER LV.

THE LEGION.

My services while with the Legion were of no very distinguished character, and require no lengthened chronicle. Their great feat of arms, the repulse of an advanced guard of Victor's corps, had taken place the very morning I had joined them, and the ensuing month was passed in soft repose upon their laurels.

For the first few days, indeed, a multiplicity of cares beset the worthy major. There was a despatch to be written to Beresford, another to the Supreme Junta, a letter to Wilson, at that time with the corps of observation to the eastward. There were some wounded to be looked after, a speech to be made to the conquering heroes themselves, and lastly, a few prisoners were taken, whose fate seemed certainly to partake of the most uncertain of war's proverbial chances.

The despatches gave little trouble; with some very slight alterations, the great original, already sent forward to Sir Arthur, served as a basis for the rest. The wounded were forwarded to Alcantara, with a medical staff; to whom Monsoon, at parting, pleasantly hinted that he expected to see all the sick at their duty by an early day, or he would be compelled to report the doctors. The speech, which was intended as a kind of general order, he deferred for some favorable afternoon when he could get up his Portuguese; and lastly, came the prisoners, by far the most difficult of all his cares. As for the few common soldiers taken, they gave him little uneasiness,—

as Sir John has it, they were "mortal men, and food for powder;" but there was a staff-officer among them, aiguilletted and epauletted. The very decorations he wore were no common temptation. Now, the major deliberated a long time with himself, whether the usages of modern war might not admit of the ancient, time-honored practice of ransom. The battle, save in glory, had been singularly unproductive: plunder there was none; the few ammunition-wagons and gun-carriages were worth little or nothing; so that, save the prisoners, nothing remained. It was late in the evening—the mellow hour of the major's meditations—when he ventured to open his heart to me upon the matter.

"I was just thinking, Charley, how very superior they were in olden times to us moderns, in many matters, and nothing more than in their treatment of prisoners. They never took them away from their friends and country; they always ransomed them,—if they had wherewithal to pay their way. So good-natured!—upon my life it was a most excellent custom! They took any little valuables they found about them, and then put them up at auction. Moses and Eleazar, a priest, we are told, took every piece of gold, and their wrought jewels,—meaning their watches, and ear-rings. You needn't laugh, they all wore ear-rings, those fellows did. Now, why shouldn't I profit by their good example? I have taken Agag, the King of the Amalekites,—no, but upon my life, I have got a French major, and I'd let him go for fifty doubloons."

It was not without much laughing, and some eloquence, that I could persuade Monsoon that Sir Arthur's military notions might not accept of even the authority of Moses; and as our headquarters were at no great distance, the danger of such a step as he meditated was too considerable at such a moment.

As for ourselves, no fatiguing drills, no harassing field-days, and no provoking inspections interfered with the easy current of our lives. Foraging parties there were, it was true, and some occasional outpost duty was performed. But the officers for both were selected with a tact that proved the major's appreciation of character; for while the gay, joyous fellow that sung a jovial song and loved his *liquor* was certain of being entertained at headquarters, the less-gifted and less-congenial spirit had the happiness of scouring the country for forage, and presenting himself as a target to a French rifle.

My own endeavors to fulfil my instructions met with but little encouragement or support; and although I labored hard at my task, I must confess that the soil was a most ungrateful one. The cavalry were, it is true, composed mostly of young fellows well-appointed, and in most cases well-mounted; but a more disorderly, careless, undisciplined set of good-humored fellows never formed a corps in the world.

Monsoon's opinions were felt in every branch of the service, from the adjutant to the drumboy,—the same reckless, indolent, plunder-loving spirit prevailed everywhere. And although under fire they showed no lack of gallantry or courage, the moment of danger passed, discipline departed with it, and their only conception of benefiting by a victory consisted in the amount of pillage that resulted from it.

From time to time the rumors of great events reached us. We heard that Soult, having succeeded in re-organizing his beaten army, was, in conjunction with Ney's corps, returning from the north; that the marshals were consolidating their forces in the neighborhood of Talavera; and that King Joseph himself, at the head of a large army, had marched for Madrid.

Menacing as such an aspect of affairs was, it had little disturbed the major's equanimity; and when our advanced posts reported daily the intelligence that the French were in retreat, he cared little with what object of concentrating they retired, provided the interval between us grew gradually wider. His speculations upon the future were singularly prophetic. "You'll see, Charley, what will happen; old Cuesta will pursue them, and get thrashed. The English will come up, and perhaps get thrashed too; but we, God bless us! are only a small force, partially organized and ill to depend on,—we'll go up the mountains till all is over!" Thus did the major's discretion not only extend to the avoidance of danger, but he actually disqualified himself from even making its acquaintance.

Meanwhile our operations consisted in making easy marches to Almarez, halting wherever the commissariat reported a well-stocked cellar or well-furnished hen-roost, taking the primrose path in life, and being, in words of the major, "contented and grateful, even amidst great perils!"

CHAPTER LVI.

THE DEPARTURE.

On the morning of the 10th July a despatch reached us announcing that Sir Arthur Wellesley had taken up his headquarters at Placentia for the purpose of communicating with

Cuesta, then at Casa del Puerto; and ordering me immediately to repair to the Spanish headquarters and await Sir Arthur's arrival, to make my report upon the effective state of our corps. As for me, I was heartily tired of the inaction of my present life, and much as I relished the eccentricities of my friend the major, longed ardently for a different sphere of action.

Not so Monsoon; the prospect of active employment and the thoughts of being left once more alone, for his Portuguese staff afforded him little society, depressed him greatly; and as the hour of my departure drew near, he appeared lower in spirits than I had ever seen him.

"I shall be very lonely without you, Charley," said he, with a sigh, as we sat the last evening together beside our cheerful wood fire. "I have little intercourse with the dons; for my Portuguese is none of the best, and only comes when the evening is far advanced; and besides, the villains, I fear, may remember the sherry affair. Two of my present staff were with me then."

"Is that the story Power so often alluded to, Major; the King of Spain's—"

"There, Charley, hush; be cautious, my boy. I'd rather not speak about that till we get among our own fellows."

"Just as you like, Major; but, do you know, I have a strong curiosity to hear the narrative."

"If I'm not mistaken, there is some one listening at the door,—gently; that's it, eh?"

"No, we are perfectly alone; the night's early; who knows when we shall have as quiet an hour again together? Let me hear it, by all means."

"Well, I don't care; the thing, Heaven knows! is tolerably well known; so if you'll amuse yourself making a devil of the turkey's legs there, I'll tell you the story. It's very short, Charley, and there's no moral; so you're not likely to repeat it."

So saying, the major filled up his glass, drew a little closer to the fire, and began:—

"When the French troops, under Laborde, were marching, upon Alcobaca, in concert with Loison's corps, I was ordered to convey a very valuable present of sherry the Duo d'Albuquerque was making to the Supreme Junta,—no less than ten hogsheads of the best sherry the royal cellars of Madrid had formerly contained.

"It was stored in the San Vincente convent; and the Junta, knowing a little about monkish tastes and the wants of the Church, prudently thought it would be quite as well at Lisbon. I was accordingly ordered, with a sufficient force, to provide for its safe conduct and secure arrival, and set out upon my march one lovely morning in April with my precious convoy.

"I don't know, I never could understand, why temptations are thrown in our way in this life, except for the pleasure of yielding to them. As for me, I'm a stoic when there's nothing to be had; but let me get a scent of a well-kept haunch, the odor of a wine-bin once in my nose, I forget everything except appropriation. That bone smells deliciously, Charley; a little garlic would improve it vastly.

"Our road lay through cross-paths and mountain tracts, for the French were scouring the country on every side, and my fellows, only twenty altogether, trembled at the very name of them; so that our only chance was to avoid falling in with any forage parties. We journeyed along for several days, rarely making more than a few leagues between sunrise and sunset, a scout always in advance to assure us that all was safe. The road was a lonesome one and the way weary, for I had no one to speak to or converse with, so I fell into a kind of musing fit about the old wine in the great brown casks. I thought on its luscious flavor, its rich straw tint, its oily look as it flowed into the glass, the mellow after-taste warming the heart as it went down, and I absolutely thought I could smell it through the wood.

"How I longed to broach one of them, if it were only to see if my dreams about it were correct. 'May be it's brown sherry,' thought I, 'and I am all wrong.' This was a very distressing reflection. I mentioned it to the Portuguese intendant, who travelled with us as a kind of supercargo; but the villain only grinned and said something about the Junta and the galleys for life, so I did not recur to it afterwards. Well, it was upon the third evening of our march that the scout reported that at Merida, about a league distant, he had fallen in with an English cavalry regiment, who were on their march to the northern provinces, and remaining that night in the village. As soon, therefore, as I had made all my arrangements for the night, I took a fresh horse and cantered over to have a look at my countrymen, and hear the news. When I arrived, it was a dark night, but I was not long in finding out our fellows. They were the 11th Light Dragoons, commanded by my old friend Bowes, and with as jolly a mess as any in the service.

"Before half an hour's time I was in the midst of them, hearing all about the campaign, and telling them in return about my convoy, dilating upon the qualities of the wine as if I had been drinking it every day at dinner.

"We had a very mellow night of it; and before four o'clock the senior major and four captains were under the table, and all the subs, in a state unprovided for by the articles of war. So I thought I'd be going, and wishing the sober ones a good-by, set out on my road to join my own party.

174

"I had not gone above a hundred yards when I heard some one running after, and calling out my name.

"'I say, Monsoon; Major, confound you, pull up.'

"'Well, what's the matter? Has any more lush turned up?' inquired I, for we had drank the tap dry when I left.

"'Not a drop, old fellow!' said he; 'but I was thinking of what you've been saying about that sherry.'

"'Well! What then?'

"'Why, I want to know how we could get a taste of it?'

"'You'd better get elected one of the Cortes,' said I, laughing; 'for it doesn't seem likely you'll do so in any other way.'

"'I'm not so sure of that,' said he, smiling. 'What road do you travel to-morrow?'

"'By Cavalhos and Reina.'

"'Whereabouts may you happen to be towards sunset?'

"'I fear we shall be in the mountains,' said I, with a knowing look, 'where ambuscades and surprise parties would be highly dangerous.'

"'And your party consists of—'

"'About twenty Portuguese, all ready to run at the first shot.'

"'I'll do it, Monsoon; I'll be hanged if I don't.'

"'But, Tom,' said I, 'don't make any blunder; only blank cartridge, my boy.'

"'Honor bright!' cried he. 'Your fellows are armed of course?'

"'Never think of that; they may shoot each other in the confusion. But if you only make plenty of noise coming on, they'll never wait for you.'

"'What capital fellows they must be!'

"'Crack troops, Tom; so don't hurt them. And now, good-night.'

"As I cantered off, I began to think over O'Flaherty's idea; and upon my life, I didn't half like it. He was a reckless, devil-may-care fellow; and it was just as likely he would really put his scheme into practice.

"When morning broke, however, we got under way again, and I amused myself all the forenoon in detailing stories of French cruelty; so that before we had marched ten miles, there was not a man among us not ready to run at the slightest sound of attack on any side. As evening was falling we reached Morento, a little mountain pass which follows the course of a small river, and where, in many places, the mule carts had barely space enough to pass between the cliffs and the stream. 'What a place for Tom O'Flaherty and his foragers!' thought I, as we entered the little mountain gorge; but all was silent as the grave,—except the tramp of our party, not a sound was heard. There was something solemn and still in the great brown mountain, rising like vast walls on either side, with a narrow streak of gray sky at top and in the dark, sluggish stream, that seemed to awe us, and no one spoke. The muleteer ceased his merry song, and did not crack or flourish his long whip as before, but chid his beasts in a half-muttered voice, and urged them faster, to reach the village before nightfall.

"Egad, somehow I felt uncommonly uncomfortable; I could not divest my mind of the impression that some disaster was impending, and I wished O'Flaherty and his project in a very warm climate. 'He'll attack us,' thought I, 'where we can't run; fair play forever. But if they are not able to get away, even the militia will fight.' However, the evening crept on, and no sign of his coming appeared on any side; and to my sincere satisfaction, I could see, about half a league distant, the twinkling light of the little village where we were to halt for the night. It was just at this time that a scout I had sent out some few hundred yards in advance came galloping up, almost breathless.

"'The French, Captain; the French are upon us!' said he, with a face like a ghost.

"'Whew! Which way? How many?' said I, not at all sure that he might not be telling the truth.

"'Coming in force!' said the fellow. 'Dragoons! By this road!'

"'Dragoons? By this road?' repeated every man of the party, looking at each other like men sentenced to be hanged.

"Scarcely had they spoken when we heard the distant noise of cavalry advancing at a brisk trot. Lord, what a scene ensued! The soldiers ran hither and thither like frightened sheep; some pulled out crucifixes and began to say their prayers; others fired off their muskets in a panic; the mule-drivers cut their traces, and endeavored to get away by riding; and the intendant took to his heels, screaming out to us, as he went, to fight manfully to the last, and that he'd report us favorably to the Junta.

"Just at this moment the dragoons came in sight; they came galloping up, shouting like madmen. One look was enough for my fellows; they sprang to their legs from their devotions, fired a volley straight at the new moon, and ran like men.

"I was knocked down in the rush. As I regained my legs, Tom O'Flaherty was standing beside me, laughing like mad.

"'Eh, Monsoon! I've kept my word, old fellow! What legs they have! We shall make no prisoners, that's certain. Now, lads, here it is! Put the horses to, here. We shall take but one, Monsoon; so that your gallant defence of the rest will please the Junta. Good-night, good-night! I will drink your health every night these two months.'

"So saying, Tom sprang to his saddle; and in less time than I've been telling it, the whole was over and I sitting by myself in the gray moonlight, meditating on all I saw, and now and then shouting for my Portuguese friends to come back again. They came in time, by twos and threes; and at last the whole party re-assembled, and we set forth again, every man, from the intendant to the drummer, lauding my valor, and saying that Don Monsoon was a match for the Cid."

"And how did the Junta behave?"

"Like trumps, Charley. Made me a Knight of Battalha, and kissed me on both cheeks, having sent twelve dozen of the rescued wine to my quarters, as a small testimony of their esteem. I have laughed very often at it since. But hush, Charley? What's that I hear without there?"

"Oh, it's my fellow Mike. He asked my leave to entertain his friends before parting, and I perceive he is delighting them with a song."

"But what a confounded air it is! Are the words Hebrew?"

"Irish, Major; most classical Irish, too, I'll be bound!"

"Irish! I've heard most tongues, but that certainly surprises me. Call him in, Charley, and let us have the canticle."

In a few minutes more, Mr. Free appeared in a state of very satisfactory elevation, his eyebrows alternately rising and falling, his mouth a little drawn to one side, and a side motion in his knee-joints that might puzzle a physiologist to account for.

"A sweet little song of yours, Mike," said the major; "a very sweet thing indeed. Wet your lips, Mickey."

"Long life to your honor and Master Charles there, too, and them that belongs to both of yez. May a gooseberry skin make a nightcap for the man would harm either of ye."

"Thank you, Mike. And now about that song."

"It's the ouldest tune ever was sung," said Mike, with a hiccough, "barring Adam had a taste for music; but the words—the poethry—is not so ould."

"And how comes that?"

"The poetry, ye see, was put to it by one of my ancesthors,—he was a great inventhor in times past, and made beautiful songs,—and ye'd never guess what it's all about."

"Love, mayhap?" quoth Monsoon.

"Sorra taste of kissing from beginning to end."

"A drinking song?" said I.

"Whiskey is never mentioned."

"Fighting is the only other national pastime. It must be in praise of sudden death?"

"You're out again; but sure you'd never guess it," said Mike. "Well, ye see, here's what it is. It's the praise and glory of ould Ireland in the great days that's gone, when we were all Phenayceans and Armenians, and when we worked all manner of beautiful contrivances in gold and silver,—bracelets and collars and teapots, elegant to look at,—and read Roosian and Latin, and played the harp and the barrel-organ, and eat and drank of the best, for nothing but asking."

"Blessed times, upon my life!" quoth the major; "I wish we had them back again."

"There's more of your mind," said Mike, steadying himself. "My ancestors was great people in them days; and sure it isn't in my present situation I'd be av we had them back again,—sorra bit, faith! It isn't, 'Come here, Mickey, bad luck to you, Mike!' or, 'That blackguard, Mickey Free!' people'd be calling me. But no matter; here's your health again, Major Monsoon—"

"Never mind vain regrets, Mike. Let us hear your song; the major has taken a great fancy to it."

"Ah, then, it's joking you are, Mister Charles," said Mike, affecting an air of most bashful coyness.

"By no means; we want to hear you sing it."

"To be sure we do. Sing it by all means; never be ashamed. King David was very fond of singing,—upon my life he was."

"But you'd never understand a word of it, sir."

"No matter; we know what it's about. That's the way with the Legion; they don't know much English, but they generally guess what I'm at."

This argument seemed to satisfy all Mike's remaining scruples; so placing himself in an attitude of considerable pretension as to grace, he began, with a voice of no very measured compass, an air of which neither by name nor otherwise can I give any conception; my principal amusement being derived from a tol-de-rol chorus of the major, which concluded each verse, and indeed in a lower key accompanied the singer throughout.

Since that I have succeeded in obtaining a free-and-easy translation of the lyric; but in my anxiety to preserve the metre and something of the spirit of the original, I have made several blunders and many anachronisms. Mr. Free, however, pronounces my version a good one, and the world must take his word till some more worthy translator shall have consigned it to immortal verse.

With this apology, therefore, I present Mr. Free's song:

AIR,—Na Guilloch y' Goulen.   Oh, once we were illigint people,   Though we now live in cabins of mud;   And the land that ye see from the steeple   Belonged to us all from the Flood.   My father was then King of Connaught,   My grand-aunt Viceroy of Tralee;   But the Sassenach came, and signs on it, The devil an acre have we.   The least of us then were all earls,   And jewels we wore without name;   We drank punch out of rubies and pearls,—   Mr. Petrie can tell you the same.   But except some turf mould and potatoes,   There's nothing our own we can call;   And the English,—bad luck to them!—hate us, Because we've more fun than them all!   My grand-aunt was niece to Saint Kevin,   That's the reason my name's Mickey Free!   Priest's nieces,—but sure he's in heaven,   And his failins is nothin' to me.   And we still might get on without doctors,   If they'd let the ould Island alone;   And if purple-men, priests, and tithe-proctors   Were crammed down the great gun of Athlone.

As Mike's melody proceeded, the major's thorough bass waxed beautifully less,—now and then, it's true, roused by some momentary strain, it swelled upwards in full chorus, but gradually these passing flights grew rarer, and finally all ceased, save a long, low, droning sound, like the expiring sigh of a wearied bagpipe. His fingers still continued mechanically to beat time upon the table, and still his head nodded sympathetically to the music; his eyelids closed in sleep; and as the last verse concluded, a full-drawn snore announced that Monsoon, if not in the land of dreams, was at least in a happy oblivion of all terrestrial concerns, and caring as little for the woes of green Erin and the altered fortunes of the Free family as any Saxon that ever oppressed them.

There he sat, the finished decanter and empty goblet testifying that his labors had only ceased from the pressure of necessity; but the broken, half-uttered words that fell from his lips evinced that he reposed on the last bottle of the series.

"Oh, thin, he's a fine ould gentleman!" said Mike, after a pause of some minutes, during which he had been contemplating the major with all the critical acumen Chantrey or Canova would have bestowed upon an antique statue,—"a fine ould gentleman, every inch of him; and it's the master would like to have him up at the Castle."

"Quite true, Mike; but let us not forget the road. Look to the cattle, and be ready to start within an hour."

When he left the room for this purpose I endeavored to shake the major into momentary consciousness ere we parted.

"Major, Major," said I, "time is up. I must start."

"Yes, it's all true, your Excellency: they pillaged a little; and if they did change their facings, there was a great temptation. All the red velvet they found in the churches—"

"Good-by, old fellow, good-by!"

"Stand at ease!"

"Can't, unfortunately, yet awhile; so farewell. I'll make a capital report of the Legion to Sir Arthur; shall I add anything particularly from yourself?"

This, and the shake that accompanied it, aroused him. He started up, and looked about him for a few seconds.

"Eh, Charley! You didn't say Sir Arthur was here, did you?"

"No, Major; don't be frightened; he's many a league off. I asked if you had anything to say when I met him?"

"Oh, yes, Charley! Tell him we're capital troops in our own little way in the mountains; would never do in pitched battles,—skirmishing's our forte; and for cutting off stragglers, or sacking a town, back them at any odds."

"Yes, yes, I know all that; you've nothing more?"

"Nothing," said he, once more closing his eyes and crossing his hands before him, while his lips continued to mutter on,—"nothing more, except you may say from me,—he knows me, Sir Arthur does. Tell him to guard himself from intemperance; a fine fellow if he wouldn't drink."

"You horrid old humbug, what nonsense are you muttering there?"

"Yes, yes; Solomon says, 'Who hath red eyes and carbuncles?' they that mix their lush. Pure *Sneyd* never injured any one. Tell him so from me,—it's an old man's advice, and I have drunk some hogsheads of it."

With these words he ceased to speak, while his head, falling gently forward upon his chest, proclaimed him sound asleep.

"Adieu, then, for the last time," said I, slapping him gently on the shoulder. "And now for the road."

CHAPTER LVII.
CUESTA.

The second day of our journey was drawing to a close as we came in view of the Spanish army.

The position they occupied was an undulating plain beside the Teitar River; the country presented no striking feature of picturesque beauty, but the scene before us needed no such aid to make it one of the most interesting kind. From the little mountain path we travelled we beheld beneath a force of thirty thousand men drawn up in battle array, dense columns of infantry alternating with squadrons of horse or dark masses of artillery dotted the wide plain, the bright steel glittering in the rich sunset of a July evening when not a breath of air was stirring; the very banners hung down listlessly, and not a sound broke the solemn stillness of the hour. All was silent. So impressive and so strange was the spectacle of a vast army thus resting mutely under arms, that I reined in my horse, and almost doubted the reality of the scene as I gazed upon it. The dark shadows of the tall mountain were falling across the valley, and a starry sky was already replacing the ruddy glow of sunset as we reached the plain; but still no change took place in the position of the Spanish army.

"Who goes there?" cried a hoarse voice, as we issued from the mountain gorge, and in a moment we found ourselves surrounded by an outpost party. Having explained, as well as I was able, who I was, and for what reason I was there, I proceeded to accompany the officer towards the camp.

On my way thither I learned the reason of the singular display of troops which had been so puzzling to me. From an early hour of that day Sir Arthur Wellesley's arrival had been expected, and old Cuesta had drawn up his men for inspection, and remained thus for several hours patiently awaiting his coming; he himself, overwhelmed with years and infirmity, sitting upon his horse the entire time.

As it was not necessary that I should be presented to the general, my report being for the ear of Sir Arthur himself, I willingly availed myself of the hospitality proffered by a Spanish officer of cavalry; and having provided for the comforts of my tired cattle and taken a hasty supper, issued forth to look at the troops, which, although it was now growing late, were still in the same attitude.

Scarcely had I been half an hour thus occupied, when the stillness of the scene was suddenly interrupted by the loud report of a large gun, immediately followed by a long roll of musketry, while at the same moment the bands of the different regiments struck up, and as if by magic a blaze of red light streamed across the dark ranks. This was effected by pine torches held aloft at intervals, throwing a lurid glare upon the grim and swarthy features of the Spaniards, whose brown uniforms and slouching hats presented a most picturesque effect as the red light fell upon them.

The swell of the thundering cannon grew louder and nearer,—the shouldering of muskets, the clash of sabres, and the hoarse roll of the drum, mingling in one common din. I at once guessed that Sir Arthur had arrived, and as I turned the flank of a battalion I saw the staff approaching. Nothing can be conceived more striking than their advance. In the front rode old Cuesta himself, clad in the costume of a past century, his slashed doublet and trunk hose reminding one of a more chivalrous period, his heavy, unwieldy figure looming from side to side, and threatening at each moment to fall from his saddle. On each side of him walked two figures gorgeously dressed, whose duty appeared to be to sustain the chief in his seat. At his side rode a far different figure. Mounted upon a slight-made, active thorough-bred, whose drawn flanks bespoke a long and weary journey, sat Sir Arthur Wellesley, a plain blue frock and gray trousers being his unpretending costume; but the eagle glance which he threw around on every side, the quick motion of his hand as he pointed hither and thither among the dense battalions, bespoke him every inch a soldier. Behind them came a brilliant staff, glittering in aiguillettes and golden trappings, among whom I recognized some well-remembered faces,—our gallant leader at the Douro, Sir Charles Stewart, among the number.

As they passed the spot where I was standing, the torch of a foot soldier behind me flared suddenly up and threw a strong flash upon the party. Cuesta's horse grew frightened, and plunged so fearfully for a minute that the poor old man could scarcely keep his seat. A smile shot across Sir Arthur's features at the moment, but the next instant he was grave and steadfast as before.

A wretched hovel, thatched and in ruins, formed the headquarters of the Spanish army, and thither the staff now bent their steps,—a supper being provided there for our commander-in-chief and the officers of his suite. Although not of the privileged party, I lingered round the spot for some time, anxiously expecting to find some friend or acquaintance who might tell me the news of our people, and what events had occurred in my absence.

CHAPTER LVIII.
THE LETTER.

The hours passed slowly over, and I at length grew weary of waiting. For some time I had amused myself with observing the slouching gait and unsoldier-like air of the Spaniards as they lounged carelessly about, looking in dress, gesture, and appointment, far move like a guerilla than a regular force. Then again, the strange contrast of the miserable hut with falling chimney and ruined walls, to the glitter of the mounted guard of honor who sat motionless beside it, served to pass the time; but as the night was already far advanced, I turned towards my quarters, hoping that the next morning might gratify my curiosity about my friends.

Beside the tent where I was billeted, I found Mike in waiting, who, the moment he saw me, came hastily forward with a letter in his hand. An officer of Sir Arthur's staff had left it while I was absent, desiring Mike on no account to omit its delivery the first instant he met me. The hand—not a very legible one—was perfectly unknown to me, and the appearance of the billet such as betrayed no over-scrupulous care in the writer.

I trimmed my lamp leisurely, threw a fresh log upon the fire, disposed myself completely at full length beside it, and then proceeded to form acquaintance with my unknown correspondent. I will not attempt any description of the feelings which gradually filled me as I read on; the letter itself will suggest them to those who know my story. It ran thus:—

PLACENTIA, July 8, 1809.   DEAR O'MALLEY,—

Although I'd rather march to Lisbon barefoot   than write three lines, Fred Power insists upon my turning scribe, as he has a notion you'll be up at Cuesta's headquarters about this   time. You're in a nice scrape, devil a lie in it! Here has Fred   been fighting that fellow Trevyllian for you,—all because you would   not have patience and fight him yourself the morning you left the   Douro,—so much for haste! Let it be a lesson to you for life. Poor Fred got the ball in his hip, and the devil a one of the doctors   can find it. But he's getting better any way, and going to Lisbon   for change of air. Meanwhile, since Power's been wounded, Trevyllian's   speaking very hardly of you, and they all say here you must   come back—no matter how—and put matters to rights. Fred has placed the thing in my hands, and I'm thinking we'd better call out   the "heavies" by turns,—for most of them stand by Trevyllian.   Maurice Quill and myself sat up considering it last night; but,   somehow, we don't clearly remember to-day a beautiful plan we hit   upon. However, we'll have at it again this evening. Meanwhile, come over here, and let us be doing something. We hear that old   Monsoon has blown up a town, a bridge, and a big convent. They   must have been hiding the plunder very closely, or he'd never have   been reduced to such extremities. We'll have a brush with the   French soon.   Yours most eagerly,   D. O'SHAUGHNESSY.

My first thought, as I ran my eye over these lines, was to seek for Power's note, written on the morning we parted. I opened it, and to my horror found that it only related to my quarrel with Hammersley. My meeting with Trevyllian had been during Fred's absence, and when he assured me that all was satisfactorily arranged, and a full explanation tendered, that nothing interfered with my departure,—I utterly forgot that he was only aware of one half my troubles, and in the haste and bustle of my departure, had not a moment left me to collect myself and think calmly on the matter. The two letters lay before me, and as I thought over the stain upon my character thus unwittingly incurred; the blast I had thrown upon my reputation; the wound of my poor friend, who exposed himself for my sake,—I grew sick at heart, and the bitter tears of agony burst from my eyes.

That weary night passed slowly over; the blight of all my prospects, when they seemed fairest and brightest, presented itself to me in a hundred shapes; and when, overcome by fatigue and exhaustion, I closed my eyes to sleep, it was only to follow up in my dreams my waking thoughts. Morning came at length; but its bright sunshine and balmy air brought no comfort to me. I absolutely dreaded to meet my brother officers; I felt that in such a position as I stood, no half or partial explanation could suffice to set me right in their estimation; and yet, what opportunity had I for aught else? Irresolute how to act, I sat leaning my head upon my hands, when I heard a footstep approach; I looked up and saw before me no other than my poor friend Sparks, from whom I had been separated so long. Any other adviser at such a moment would, I acknowledge, have been as welcome; for the poor fellow knew but little of the world, and still less of the service. However, one glance convinced me that his heart at least was true; and I shook his outstretched hand with delight. In a few words he informed me that Merivale had secretly commissioned him to come over in the hope of meeting me; that although all the 14th men were persuaded that I was not to blame in what had occurred,—yet that reports so injurious had gone abroad, so many partial and imperfect statements were circulated, that nothing but my return to headquarters would avail, and that I must not lose a moment in having Trevyllian out, with whom all the misrepresentation had originated.

"This, of course," said Sparks, "is to be a secret; Merivale, being our colonel—"

"Of course," said I, "he cannot countenance, much less counsel, such a proceeding; Now, then, for the road."

"Yes; but you cannot leave before making your report. Gordon expects to see you at eleven; he told me so last night."

"I cannot help it; I shall not wait; my mind is made up. My career here matters but little in comparison with this horrid charge. I shall be broke, but I shall be avenged."

"Come, come, O'Malley; you are in our hands now, and you must be guided. You *shall* wait; you shall see Gordon. Half an hour will make your report, and I have relays of horses along the road, and we shall reach Placentia by nightfall."

There was a tone of firmness in this, so unlike anything I ever looked for in the speaker, and withal so much of foresight and precaution, that I could scarcely credit my senses as he spoke. Having at length agreed to his proposal, Sparks left me to think over my return of the Legion, promising that immediately after my interview with the military secretary, we should start together for headquarters.

CHAPTER LXIX.
MAJOR O'SHAUGHNESSY.

"This is Major O'Shaughnessy's quarters, sir," said a sergeant, as he stopped short at the door of a small, low house in the midst of an olive plantation; an Irish wolf-dog—the well-known companion of the major—lay stretched across the entrance, watching with eager and bloodshot eyes the process of cutting up a bullock, which two soldiers in undress jackets were performing within a few yards of the spot.

Stepping cautiously across the savage-looking sentinel, I entered the little hall, and finding no one near, passed into a small room, the door of which lay half open.

A very palpable odor of cigars and brandy proclaimed, even without his presence, that this was O'Shaughnessy's sitting-room; so I sat myself down upon an old-fashioned sofa to wait patiently for his return, which I heard would be immediately after the evening parade. Sparks had become knocked up during our ride, so that for the last three leagues I was alone, and like most men in such circumstances, pressed on only the harder. Completely worn out for want of rest, I had scarcely placed myself on the sofa when I fell sound asleep. When I awoke, all was dark around me, save the faint flickerings of the wood embers on the hearth, and for some moments I could not remember where I was; but by degrees recollection came, and as I thought over my position and its possible consequences, I was again nearly dropping to sleep, when the door suddenly opened, and a heavy step sounded on the floor.

I lay still and spoke not, as a large figure in a cloak approached the fire-place, and stooping down endeavored to light a candle at the fast expiring fire.

I had little difficulty in detecting the major even by the half-light; a muttered execration upon the candle, given with an energy that only an Irishman ever bestows upon slight matters, soon satisfied me on this head.

"May the Devil fly away with the commissary and the chandler to the forces! Ah, you've lit at last!"

With these words he stood up, and his eyes falling on me at the moment, he sprang a yard or two backwards, exclaiming as he did so, "The blessed Virgin be near us, what's this?" a most energetic crossing of himself accompanying his words. My pale and haggard face, thus suddenly presented, having suggested to the worthy major the impression of a supernatural visitor, a hearty burst of laughter, which I could not resist, was my only answer; and the next moment O'Shaughnessy was wrenching my hand in a grasp like a steel vice.

"Upon my conscience, I thought it was your ghost; and if you kept quiet a little longer, I was going to promise you Christian burial, and as many Masses for your soul as my uncle the bishop could say between this and Easter. How are you, my boy? A little thin, and something paler, I think, than when you left us."

Having assured him that fatigue and hunger were in a great measure the cause of my sickly looks, the major proceeded to place before me the *débris* of his day's dinner, with a sufficiency of bottles to satisfy a mess-table, keeping up as he went a running fire of conversation.

"I'm as glad as if the Lord took the senior major, to see you here this night. With the blessing of Providence we'll shoot Trevyllian in the morning, and any more of the heavies that like it. You are an ill-treated man, that's what it is, and Dan O'Shaughnessy says it. Help yourself, my boy; crusty old port in that bottle as ever you touched your lips to. Power's getting all right; it was contract powder, warranted not to kill. Bad luck to the commissaries once more! With such ammunition Sir Arthur does right to trust most to the bayonet. And how is Monsoon, the old rogue?"

"Gloriously, living in the midst of wine and olives."

"No fear of him, the old sinner; but he is a fine fellow, after all. Charley, you are eating nothing, boy."

"To tell you the truth, I'm far more anxious to talk with you at this moment than aught else."

"So you shall: the night's young. Meanwhile, I had better not delay matters. You want to have Trevyllian out,—is not that so?"

"Of course; you are aware how it happened?"

"I know everything. Go on with your supper, and don't mind me; I'll be back in twenty minutes or less."

Without waiting for any reply, he threw his cloak around him, and strode out of the room. Once more I was alone; but already my frame of mind was altered,—the cheering tone of my reckless, gallant countryman had raised my spirits, and I felt animated by his very manner.

An hour elapsed before the major returned; and when he did come, his appearance and gestures bespoke anger and disappointment. He threw himself hurriedly into a seat, and for some minutes never spoke.

"The world's beautifully changed, anyhow, since I began it, O'Malley,—when you thanked a man civilly that asked you to fight him! The Devil take the cowards, say I."

"What has happened? Tell me, I beseech you?"

"He won't fight," said the major, blurting out the words as if they would choke him.

"He'll not fight! And why?"

The major was silent. He seemed confused and embarrassed. He turned from the fire to the table, from the table to the fire, poured out a glass of wine, drank it hastily off, and springing from his chair, paced the room with long, impatient strides.

"My dear O'Shaughnessy, explain, I beg of you. Does he refuse to meet me for any reason—"

"He does," said the major, turning on me a look of deep feeling as he spoke; "and he does it to ruin you, my boy. But as sure as my name is Dan, he'll fail this time. He was sitting with his friend Beaufort when I reached his quarters, and received me with all the ceremonious politeness he well knows how to assume. I told him in a few words the object of my visit; upon which Trevyllian, standing up, referred me to his friend for a reply, and left the room. I thought that all was right, and sat down to discuss, as I believed, preliminaries, when the cool puppy, with his back to the fire, carelessly lisped out, 'It can't be, Major; your friend is too late.'

"'Too late? too late?' said I.

"'Yes, precisely so; not up to time. The affair should have come off some weeks since. We won't meet him now.'

"'This is really your answer?'

"'This is really my answer; and not only so, but the decision of our mess.'

"What I said after this *he* may remember; devil take me if *I* can. But I have a vague recollection of saying something that the aforesaid mess will never petition the Horse Guards to put on their regimental colors; and here I am—"

With these words the major gulped down a full goblet of wine, and once more resumed his walk through the room. I shall not attempt to record the feelings which agitated me during the major's recital. In one rapid glance I saw the aim of my vindictive enemy. My honor, not my life, was the object he sought for; and ten thousand times more than ever did I pant for the opportunity to confront him in a deadly combat.

"Charley," said O'Shaughnessy, at length, placing his hand upon my shoulder, "you must get to bed now. Nothing more can be done to-night in any way. Be assured of one thing, my boy,—I'll not desert you; and if that assurance can give you a sound sleep, you'll not need a lullaby."

CHAPTER LX.
PRELIMINARIES.

I awoke refreshed on the following morning, and came down to breakfast with a lighter heart than I had even hoped for. A secret feeling that all would go well had somehow taken possession of me, and I longed for O'Shaughnessy's coming, trusting that he might be able to confirm my hopes. His servant informed me that the major had been absent since daybreak, and left orders that he was not to be waited for at breakfast.

I was not destined, however, to pass a solitary time in his absence, for every moment brought some new arrival to visit me; and during the morning the colonel and every officer of the regiment not on actual duty came over. I soon learned that the feeling respecting Trevyllian's conduct was one of unmixed condemnation among my own corps, but that a kind of party spirit which had subsisted for some months between the regiment he belonged to and the 14th had given a graver character to the affair, and induced many men to take up his views of the transaction; and although I heard of none who attributed my absence to any dislike to a meeting, yet there were several who conceived that, by my going at the time, I had forfeited all claim to satisfaction at his hands.

"Now that Merivale is gone," said an officer to me as the colonel left the room, "I may confess to you that he sees nothing to blame in your conduct throughout; and even had you been aware of how matters were circumstanced, your duty was too imperative to have preferred your personal consideration to it."

"Does any one know where Conyers is?" said Baker.

"The story goes that Conyers can assist us here. Conyers is at Zaza la Mayor, with the 28th; but what can he do?"

"That I'm not able to tell you; but I know O'Shaughnessy heard something at parade this morning, and has set off in search of him on every side."

"Was Conyers ever out with Trevyllian?"

"Not as a principal, I believe. The report is, however, that he knows more about him than other people, as Tom certainly does of everybody."

"It is rather a new thing for Trevyllian to refuse a meeting. They say, O'Malley, he has heard of your shooting."

"No, no," said another; "he cares very little for any man's pistol. If the story be true, he fires a second or two before his adversary; at least, it was in that way he killed Carysfort."

"Here comes the great O'Shaughnessy!" cried some one at the window; and the next moment the heavy gallop of a horse was heard along the causeway. In an instant we all rushed to the door to receive him.

"It's all right, lads!" cried he, as he came up. "We have him this time!"

"How?" "When?" "Why?" "In what way have you managed?" fell from a dozen voices, as the major elbowed his way through the crowd to the sitting-room.

"In the first place," said O'Shanghnessy, drawing a long breath, "I have promised secrecy as to the steps of this transaction; secondly, if I hadn't, it would puzzle me to break it, for I'll be hanged if I know more than yourselves. Tom Conyers wrote me a few lines for Trevyllian, and Trevyllian pledges himself to meet our friend; and that's all we need know or care for."

"Then you have seen Trevyllian this morning?"

"No; Beaufort met me at the village. But even now it seems this affair is never to come off. Trevyllian has been sent with a forage party towards Lesco. However, that can't be a long absence. But, for Heaven's sake, let me have some breakfast!"

While O'Shaughnessy proceeded to attack the viands before him, the others chatted about in little groups; but all wore the pleased and happy looks of men who had rescued their friend from a menaced danger. As for myself, my heart swelled with gratitude to the kind fellows around me.

"How has Conyers assisted us at this juncture?" was my first question to O'Shaughnessy, when we were once more alone.

"I am not at liberty to speak on that subject, Charley. But be satisfied the reasons for which Trevyllian meets you are fair and honorable."

"I am content."

"The only thing now to be done is to have the meeting as soon as possible."

"We are all agreed upon that point," said I; "and the more so as the matter had better be decided before Sir Arthur's return."

"Quite true. And now, O'Malley, you had better join your people as soon as may be, and it will put a stop to all talking about the matter."

The advice was good, and I lost no time in complying with it; and when I joined the regiment that day at mess, it was with a light heart and a cheerful spirit, for come what might of the affair, of one thing I was certain,—my character was now put above any reach of aspersion, and my reputation beyond attack.

CHAPTER LXI.
ALL RIGHT.

Some days after coming back to headquarters, I was returning from a visit I had been making to a friend at one of the outposts, when an officer whom I knew slightly overtook me and informed me that Major O'Shaughnessy had been to my quarters in search of me, and had sent persons in different directions to find me.

Suspecting the object of the major's haste, I hurried on at once, and as I rode up to the spot, found him in the midst of a group of officers, engaged, to all appearance, in most eager conversation.

"Oh, here he comes!" cried he, as I cantered up. "Come, my boy, doff the blue frock as soon as you can, and turn out in your best-fitting black. Everything has been settled for this evening at seven o'clock, and we have no time to lose."

"I understand you," said I, "and shall not keep you waiting." So saying, I sprang from my saddle and hastened to my quarters. As I entered the room I was followed by O'Shaughnessy, who closed the door after him as he came in, and having turned the key in it, sat down beside the table, and folding his arms, seemed buried in reflection. As I proceeded with my toilet he returned no answers to the numerous questions I put to him, either as to the time of Trevyllian's return, the place of the meeting, or any other part of the transaction. His attention seemed to wander far from all around and about him; and as he muttered indistinctly to himself, the few words I could catch bore not in the remotest degree upon the matter before us.

"I have written a letter or two here, Major," said I, opening my writing-desk. "In case anything happens, you will look to a few things I have mentioned here. Somehow, I could not write to poor Fred Power; but you must tell him from me that his noble conduct towards me was the last thing I spoke of."

"What confounded nonsense you are talking!" said O'Shaughnessy, springing from his seat and crossing the room with tremendous strides, "croaking away there as if the bullet was in your thorax. Hang it, man, bear up!"

"But, Major, my dear friend, what the deuce are you thinking of? The few things I mentioned—"

"The devil! you are not going over it all again, are you?" said he, in a voice of no measured tone.

I now began to feel irritated in turn, and really looked at him for some seconds in considerable amazement. That he should have mistaken, the directions I was giving him and attributed them to any cowardice was too insulting a thought to bear; and yet how otherwise was I to understand the very coarse style of his interruption?

At length my temper got the victory, and with a voice of most measured calmness, I said, "Major O'Shaughnessy, I am grateful, most deeply grateful, for the part you have acted towards me in this difficult business; at the same time, as you now appear to disapprove of my conduct and bearing, when I am most firmly determined to alter nothing, I shall beg to relieve you of the unpleasant office of my friend."

"Heaven grant that you could do so!" said he, interrupting me, while his clasped hands and eager look attested the vehemence of the wish. He paused for a moment, then, springing from his chair, rushed towards me, and threw his arms around me. "No, my boy, I can't do it,—I can't do it. I have tried to bully myself into insensibility for this evening's work,—I have endeavored to be rude to you, that you might insult me, and steel my heart against what might happen; but it won't do, Charley, it won't do."

With these words the big tears rolled down his stern cheeks, and his voice became thick with emotion.

"But for me, all this need not have happened. I know it; I feel it. I hurried on this meeting; your character stood fair and unblemished without that,—at least they tell me so now; and I still have to assure you—"

"Come, my dear, kind friend, don't give way in this fashion. You have stood manfully by me through every step of the road; don't desert me on the threshold of—"

"The grave, O'Malley?"

"I don't think so, Major; but see, half-past six! Look to these pistols for me. Are they likely to object to hair-triggers?"

A knocking at the door turned off our attention, and the next moment Baker's voice was heard.

"O'Malley, you'll be close run for time; the meeting-place is full three miles from this."

I seized the key and opened the door. At the same instant, O'Shaughnessy rose and turned towards the window, holding one of the pistols in his hand.

"Look at that, Baker,—what a sweet tool it is!" said he, in a voice that actually made me start. Not a trace of his late excitement remained; his usually dry, half-humorous manner had returned, and his droll features were as full of their own easy, devil-may-care fun as ever.

"Here comes the drag," said Baker. "We can drive nearly all the way, unless you prefer riding."

"Of course not. Keep your hand steady, Charley, and if you don't bring him down with that saw-handle, you're not your uncle's nephew."

With these words we mounted into the tax-cart, and set off for the meeting-place.

CHAPTER LXII.

THE DUEL.

A small and narrow ravine between the two furze-covered dells led to the open space where the meeting had been arranged for. As we reached this, therefore, we were obliged to descend from the drag, and proceed the remainder of the way afoot. We had not gone many yards when a step was heard approaching, and the next moment Beaufort appeared. His usually easy and *dégagé* air was certainly tinged with somewhat of constraint; and though his soft voice and half smile were as perfect as ever, a slightly flurried expression about the lip, and a quick and nervous motion of his eyebrow, bespoke a heart not completely at ease. He lifted his foraging cap most ceremoniously to salute us as we came up, and casting an anxious look to see if any others were following, stood quite still.

"I think it right to mention, Major O'Shaughnessy," said he, in a voice of most dulcet sweetness, "that I am the only friend of Captain Trevyllian on the ground; and though I have not the slightest objection to Captain Baker being present, I hope you will see the propriety of limiting the witnesses to the three persons now here."

"Upon my conscience, as far as I am concerned, or my friend either, we are perfectly indifferent if we fight before three or three thousand. In Ireland we rather like a crowd."

"Of course, then, as you see no objection to my proposition, I may count upon your co-operation in the event of any intrusion,—I mean, that while we, upon our sides, will not permit any of our friends to come forward, you will equally exert yourself with yours."

"Here we are, Baker and myself, neither more nor less. We expect no one, and want no one; so that I humbly conceive all the preliminaries you are talking of will never be required."

Beaufort tried to smile, and bit his lips, while a small red spot upon his cheek spoke that some deeper feeling of irritation than the mere careless manner of the major could account for, still rankled in his bosom. We now walked on without speaking, except when occasionally some passing observation of Beaufort upon the fineness of the evening, or the rugged nature of the road, broke the silence. As we emerged from the little mountain pass into the open meadow land, the tall and soldier-like figure of Trevyllian was the first object that presented itself. He was standing beside a little stone cross that stood above a holy well, and seemed occupied in deciphering the inscription. He turned at the noise of our approach, and calmly waited our coming. His eye glanced quickly from the features of O'Shaughnessy to those of Baker; but seeming rapidly reassured as he walked forward, his face at once recovered its usual severity and its cold, impassive look of sternness.

"All right!" said Beaufort, in a whisper the tones of which I overheard, as he drew near to his friend. Trevyllian smiled in return, but did not speak. During the few moments which passed in conversation between the seconds, I turned from the spot with Baker, and had scarcely time to address a question to him, when O'Shaughnessy called out, "Hollo, Baker!—come here a moment!" The three seemed now in eager discussion for some minutes, when Baker walked towards Trevyllian, and saying something, appeared to wait for his reply. This being obtained, he joined the others, and the moment afterwards came to where I was standing. "You are to toss for first shot, O'Malley. O'Shaughnessy has made that proposition, and the others agree that with two crack marksmen, it is perhaps the fairest way. I suppose you have no objection?"

"Of course, I shall make none. Whatever O'Shaughnessy decides for me I am ready to abide by."

"Well, then, as to the distance?" said Beaufort, loud enough to be heard by me where I was standing. O'Shaughnessy's reply I could not catch, but it was evident, from the tone of both parties, that some difference existed on the point.

"Captain Baker shall decide between us," said Beaufort, at length, and they all walked away to some distance. During all the while I could perceive that Trevyllian's uneasiness and impatience seemed extreme; he looked from the speakers to the little mountain pass, and strained his eyes in every direction. It was clear that he dreaded some interruption. At last, unable any longer to control his feelings, he called out, "Beaufort, I say, what the devil are we waiting for now?"

"Nothing at present," said Beaufort, as he came forward with a dollar in his hand. "Come, Major O'Shaughnessy, you shall call for your friend."

He pitched the piece of money as he spoke high into the air, and watched it as it fell on the soft grass beneath.

"Head! for a thousand," cried O'Shaughnessy, running over and stooping down; "and head it is!"

"You've won the first shot," whispered Baker; "for Heaven's sake be cool!"

Beaufort grew deadly pale as he bent over the crownpiece, and seemed scarcely to have courage to look his friend in the face. Not so Trevyllian; he pulled off his gloves without the slightest semblance of emotion, buttoned up his well-fitting black frock to the throat, and throwing a rapid glance around, seemed only eager to begin the combat.

"Fifteen paces, and the words, 'One, two!'"

"Exactly. My cane shall mark the spot."

"Devilish long paces you make them," said O'Shaughnessy, who did not seem to approve of the distance. "They have some confounded advantage in this, depend upon it," said the major, in a whisper to Baker.

"Are you ready?" inquired Beaufort.

"Ready,—quite ready!"

"Take your ground, then!"

As Trevyllian moved forward to his place, he muttered something to his friend. I did not hear the first part, but the latter words which met me were ominous enough: "For as I intend to shoot him, 'tis just as well as it is."

Whether this was meant to be overheard and intimidate me I knew not; but its effect proved directly opposite. My firm resolution to hit my antagonist was now confirmed, and no compunctious visitings unnerved my arm. As we took our places some little delay again took place, the flint of my pistol having fallen; and thus we remained full ten or twelve seconds steadily regarding each other. At length O'Shaughnessy came forward, and putting my weapon in my hand, whispered low, "Remember, you have but one chance."

"You are both ready?" cried Beaufort.

"Ready!"

"Then: One, two—"

The last word was lost in the report of my pistol, which went off at the instant. For a second the flash and smoke obstructed my view; but the moment after I saw Trevyllian stretched upon the ground, with his friend kneeling beside him. My first impulse was to rush over, for now all feeling of enmity was buried in most heartfelt anxiety for his fate; but as I was stepping forward, O'Shaughnessy called out, "Stand fast, boy, he's only wounded!" and the same moment he rose slowly from the ground, with the assistance of his friend, and looked with the same wild gaze around him. Such a look! I shall never forget it; there was that intense expression of searching anxiety, as if he sought to trace the outlines of some visionary spirit as it receded before him. Quickly reassured, as it seemed, by the glance he threw on all sides, his countenance lighted up, not with pleasure, but with a fiendish expression of revengeful triumph, which even his voice evinced as he called out: "It's my turn now."

I felt the words in their full force, as I stood silently awaiting my death wound. The pause was a long one. Twice did he interrupt his friend, as he was about to give the word, by an expression of suffering, pressing his hand upon his side, and seeming to writhe with torture; and yet this was mere counterfeit.

O'Shaughnessy was now coming forward to interfere and prevent these interruptions, when Trevyllian called out in a firm tone, "I'm ready!" At the words, "One, two!" the pistol slowly rose; his dark eye measured me coolly, steadily; his lip curled; and just as I felt that my last moment of life had arrived, a heavy sound of a horse galloping along the rocky causeway seemed to take off his attention. His frame trembled, his hand shook, and jerking upwards his weapon, the ball passed high above my head.

"You bear me witness I fired in the air," said Trevyllian, while the large drops of perspiration rolled from his forehead, and his features worked as if in a fit.

"You saw it, sir; and you, Beaufort, my friend, you also. Speak! Why will you not speak?"

"Be calm, Trevyllian; be calm, for Heaven's sake! What's the matter with you?"

"The affair is then ended," said Baker, "and most happily so. You are, I hope, not dangerously wounded."

As he spoke, Trevyllian's features grew deadly livid; his half-open mouth quivered slightly, his eyes became fixed, and his arm dropped heavily beside him, and with a low moan he fell fainting to the ground.

As we bent over him I now perceived that another person had joined our party; he was a short, determined-looking man of about forty, with black eyes and aquiline features. Before I had time to guess who it might be, I heard O'Shaughnessy address him as Colonel Conyers.

"He is dying!" said Beaufort, still stooping over his friend, whose cold hand he grasped within his own. "Poor, poor fellow!"

"He fired in the air," said Baker, as he spoke in reply to a question from Conyers.

What he answered I heard not, but Baker rejoined,—

"Yes, I am certain of it. We all saw it."

"Had you not better examine his wounds?" said Conyers, in a tone of sarcastic irony I could almost have struck him for. "Is your friend not hit? Perhaps he is bleeding?"

"Yes," said O'Shaughnessy, "let us look to the poor fellow now." So saying, with Beaufort's aid he unbuttoned his frock and succeeded in opening his waistcoat. There was no trace of blood anywhere, and the idea of internal hemorrhage at once occurred to us, when Conyers, stooping down, pushed me aside, saying at the same time,—

"Your fears for his safety need not distress you much,—look here!" As he spoke he tore open his shirt, and disclosed to our almost doubting senses a vest of chain-mail armor fitting close next the skin and completely pistol-proof.

I cannot describe the effect this sight produced upon us. Beaufort sprang to his feet with a bound as he screamed out, rather than spoke, "No man believes me to have been aware—"

"No, no, Beaufort, your reputation is very far removed from such a stain," said Conyers.

O'Shaughnessy was perfectly speechless. He looked from one to the other, as though some unexplained mystery still remained, and only seemed restored to any sense of consciousness as Baker said, "I can feel no pulse at his wrist,—his heart, too, does not beat."

Conyers placed his hand upon his bosom, then felt along his throat, lifted up an arm, and letting it fall heavily upon the ground, he muttered, "He is dead!"

It was true. No wound had pierced him,—the pistol bullet was found within his clothes. Some tremendous conflict of the spirit within had snapped the cords of life, and the strong man had perished in his agony.

CHAPTER LXIII.

NEWS FROM GALWAY.

I have but a vague and most imperfect recollection of the events which followed this dreadful scene; for some days my faculties seemed stunned and paralyzed, and my thoughts clung to the minute detail of the ground,—the persons about, the mountain path, and most of all the half-stifled cry that spoke the broken heart,—with a tenacity that verged upon madness.

A court-martial was appointed to inquire into the affair; and although I have been since told that my deportment was calm, and my answers were firm and collected, yet I remember nothing of the proceedings.

The inquiry, through a feeling of delicacy for the friends of him who was no more, was made as brief and as private as possible. Beaufort proved the facts which exonerated me from any imputation in the matter; and upon the same day the court delivered the decision: "That Lieutenant O'Malley was not guilty of the charges preferred against him, and that he should be released from arrest, and join his regiment."

Nothing could be more kind and considerate than the conduct of my brother officers,—a hundred little plans and devices for making me forget the late unhappy event were suggested and practised,—and I look back to that melancholy period, marked as it was by the saddest circumstance of my life, as one in which I received more of truly friendly companionship than even my palmiest days of prosperity boasted.

While, therefore, I deeply felt the good part my friends were performing towards me, I was still totally unsuited to join in the happy current of their daily pleasures and amusements. The gay and unreflecting character of O'Shaughnessy, the careless merriment of my brother officers, jarred upon my nerves, and rendered me irritable and excited; and I sought in lonely rides and unfrequented walks, the peace of spirit that calm reflection and a firm purpose for the future rarely fail to lead to.

There is in deep sorrow a touch of the prophetic. It is at seasons when the heart is bowed down with grief, and the spirit wasted with suffering, that the veil which conceals the future seems to be removed, and a glance, short and fleeting as the lightning flash, is permitted us into the gloomy valley before us.

Misfortunes, too, come not singly,—the seared heart is not suffered to heal from one affliction ere another succeeds it; and this anticipation of the coming evil is, perhaps, one of the most poignant features of grief,—the ever-watchful apprehension, the ever-rising question, "What next?" is a torture that never sleeps.

This was the frame of my mind for several days after I returned to my duty,—a morbid sense of some threatened danger being my last thought at night and my first on awakening. I had not heard from home since my arrival in the Peninsula; a thousand vague fancies haunted me now that some brooding misfortune awaited me. My poor uncle never left my thoughts. Was he well; was he happy? Was he, as he ever used to be, surrounded by the friends he loved,—the old familiar faces around the hospitable hearth his kindliness had hallowed in my memory as something sacred? Oh, could I but see his manly smile, or hear his voice! Could I but feel his hand upon my head, as he was wont to press it, while words of comfort fell from his lips, and sunk into my heart!

Such were my thoughts one morning as I sauntered, unaccompanied, from my quarters. I had not gone far, when my attention was aroused by the noise of a mule-cart, whose jingling bells and clattering timbers announced its approach by the road I was walking. Another turn of the way brought it into view; and I saw from the gay costume of the driver, as well as a small orange flag which decorated the conveyance, that it was the mail-cart with letters from Lisbon.

Full as my mind was with thoughts of home, I turned hastily back, and retraced my steps towards the camp. When I reached the adjutant-general's quarters, I found a considerable number of officers assembled; the report that the post had come was a rumor of interest to all, and accordingly, every moment brought fresh arrivals, pouring in from all sides, and eagerly inquiring, "If the bags had been opened?" The scene of riot, confusion, and excitement, when that event did take place, exceeded all belief, each man reading his letter half aloud, as if his private affairs and domestic concerns must interest his neighbors, amidst a volley of exclamations of surprise, pleasure, or occasional anger, as the intelligence severally suggested,—the disappointed expectants cursing their idle correspondents, bemoaning their fate about remittances that never arrived, or drafts never honored; while here and there some public benefactor, with an outspread "Times" or "Chronicle," was retailing the narrative of our own exploits in the Peninsula or the more novel changes in the world of politics since we left England. A cross-fire of news and London gossip ringing on every side made up a perfect Babel most difficult to form an idea of. The jargon partook of every accent and intonation the empire boasts of; and from the sharp precision of the North Tweeder to the broad doric of Kerry, every portion, almost every county, of Great Britain had its representative. Here was a Scotch paymaster, in a lugubrious tone, detailing to his friend the apparently not over-welcome news that Mistress M'Elwain had just been safely delivered of twins, which, with their mother, were doing as well as possible. Here an eager Irishman, turning over the pages rather than reading his letter, while he exclaimed to his friend,—

"Oh, the devil a rap she's sent me. The old story about runaway tenants and distress notices,—sorrow else tenants seem to do in Ireland than run away every half-year."

A little apart some sentimental-looking cockney was devouring a very crossed epistle which he pressed to his lips whenever any one looked at him; while a host of others satisfied themselves by reading in a kind of buzzing undertone, every now and then interrupting themselves with some broken exclamation as commentary,—such as, "Of course she will!" "Never knew him better!" "That's the girl for my money!" "Fifty per cent, the devil!" and so on. At last I was beginning to weary of the scene, and finding that there appeared to be nothing for me, was turning to leave the place, when I saw a group of two or three endeavoring to spell out the address of a letter.

"That's an Irish post-mark, I'll swear," said one; "but who can make anything of the name? It's devilish like Otaheite, isn't it?"

"I wish my tailor wrote as illegibly," said another; "I'd keep up a most animated correspondence with him."

"Here, O'Shaughnessy, you know something of savage life,—spell us this word here."

"Show it here. What nonsense, it's as plain as the nose on my face: 'Master Charles O'Malley, in foreign parts!'"

A roar of laughter followed this announcement, which, at any other time, perhaps, I should have joined in, but which now grated sadly on my ruffled feelings.

"Here, Charley, this is for you," said the major; and added in a whisper,—"and upon my conscience, between ourselves, your friend, whoever he is, has a strong action against his writing-master,—devil such a fist ever I looked at!"

One glance satisfied me as to my correspondent. It was from Father Rush, my old tutor. I hurried eagerly from the spot, and regaining my quarters, locked the door, and with a beating heart broke the seal and began, as well as I was able, to decipher his letter. The hand was cramped and stiffened with age, and the bold, upright letters were gnarled and twisted like a rustic fence, and demanded great patience and much time in unravelling. It ran thus:—

*THE PRIORY, Lady-day, 1809. MY DEAR MASTER CHARLES,—Your uncle's feet are so big and so uneasy that he can't write, and I am obliged to take up the pen myself, to tell you how we are doing here since you left us. And, first of all, the master lost the lawsuit in Dublin, all for the want of a Galway jury,—but they don't go up to town for strong reasons they had; and the Curranolick property is gone to Ned M'Manus, and may the devil do him good with it! Peggy Maher left this on Tuesday; she was complaining of a weakness; she's gone to consult the doctors. I'm sorry for poor Peggy. Owen M'Neil beat the Slatterys out of Portunma on Saturday, and Jem, they say, is fractured. I trust it's true, for he never was good, root nor branch, and we've strong reasons to suspect him for drawing the river with a net at night. Sir Harry Boyle sprained his wrist, breaking open his bed-room, that he locked when he was inside. The count and the master were laughing all the evening at him. Matters are going very hard in the country,—the people paying their rents regularly, and not caring half as much as they used about the real gentry and the old families. We kept your birthday at the Castle in great style,—had the militia band from the town, and all the tenants. Mr. James Daly danced with your old friend Mary Green, and sang a beautiful song, and was going to raise the devil, had I interfered; he burned down half the blue drawing-room the last night with his tricks,—not that your uncle cares, God preserve him to us! it's little anything like that would fret him. The count quarrelled with a young gentleman in the course of the evening, but found out he was only an attorney from Dublin, so he didn't shoot him; but he was ducked in the pond by the people, and your uncle says he hopes they have a true copy of him at home, as they'll never know the original. Peter died soon after you went away, but Tim hunts the dogs just as well. They had a beautiful run last Wednesday, and the Lord [2] sent for him and gave him a five-pound note; but he says he'd rather see yourself back again than twice as much. They killed near the big turnip-field, and all went down to see where you leaped Badger over the sunk fence,—they call it "Hammersley's Nose" ever since. Bodkin was at Ballinasloe the last fair, limping about with a stick; he's twice as quiet as he used to be, and never beat any one since that morning. Nellie Guire, at the cross-roads, wants to send you four pair of stockings she knitted for you, and I have a keg of potteen of Barney's own making this two months, not knowing how to send it. May be Sir Arthur himself would like a taste,—he's an Irishman himself, and one we're proud of, too! The Maynooth chaps are flying all about the country, and making us all uncomfortable,—God's will be done, but we used to think ourselves good enough! Your foster-sister, Kitty Doolan, had a fine boy; it's to be called after you, and your uncle's to give a christening. He bids me tell you to draw on him when you want money, and that there's £400 ready for you now somewhere in Dublin,—I forget the name, and as he's asleep, I don't like asking him. There was a droll devil down here in the summer that knew you well,—a Mr. Webber. The master treated him like the Lord Lieutenant, had dinner parties for him, and gave him Oliver Cromwell to ride over to Meelish. He is expected again for the cock-shooting, for the master likes him greatly. I'm done at last, for my paper is finished and the candle just out; so with every good wish and every good thought, remember your own old friend,—
PETER RUSH. P.S. It's Smart and Sykes, Fleet Street, has the money. Father O'Shaughnessey, of Ennis, bids me ask if you ever met his nephew. If you do, make him sing "Larry M'Hale." I hear it's a treat. How is Mickey Free going on? There are three decent young women in the parish he promised to marry, and I suppose he's pursuing the same game with the Portuguese. But he was never remarkable for minding his duties. Tell him I am keeping my eye on him. P. R.*

[Footnote:2 To excuse Father Rush for any apparent impiety, I must add that, by "the Lord," he means "Lord Clanricarde."]

Here concluded this long epistle; and though there were many parts I could not help smiling at, yet upon the whole I felt sad and dispirited. What I had long foreseen and anticipated was gradually accomplishing,—the wreck of an old and honored house, the fall of a name once the watch-word for all that was benevolent and hospitable in the land. The termination of the lawsuit I knew must have been a heavy blow to my poor uncle, who, every consideration of money apart, felt in a legal combat all the enthusiasm and excitement of a personal conflict. With him there was less a question of to whom the broad acres reverted, so much as whether that "scoundrel Tom Basset, the attorney at Athlone, should triumph over us;" or "M'Manus live in the house as master where his father had officiated as butler." It was at this his Irish pride took offence; and straitened circumstances and narrowed fortunes bore little upon him in comparison with this feeling.

I could see, too, that with breaking fortunes, bad health was making heavy inroads upon him; and while, with the reckless desperation of ruin, he still kept open house, I could picture to myself his cheerful eye and handsome smile but ill concealing the slow but certain march of a broken heart.

My position was doubly painful: for any advice, had I been calculated to give it, would have seemed an act of indelicate interference from one who was to benefit by his own counsel; and although I had been reared and educated as my uncle's heir, I had no title nor pretension to succeed him other than his kind feelings respecting me. I could, therefore, only look on in silence, and watch the painful progress of our downfall without power to arrest it.

These were sad thoughts, and came when my heart was already bowed down with its affliction. That my poor uncle might be spared the misery which sooner or later seemed inevitable, was now my only wish; that he might go down to the grave without the embittering feelings which a ruined fortune and a fallen house bring home to the heart, was all my prayer. Let him but close his eyes in the old wainscoted bed-room, beneath the old roof where his fathers and grand-fathers have done so for centuries. Let the faithful followers he has known since his childhood stand round his bed; while his fast-failing sight recognizes each old and well-remembered object, and the same bell which rang its farewell to the spirit of his ancestors toll for him, the last of his race. And as for me, there was the wide world before me, and a narrow resting-place would suffice for a soldier's sepulchre.

As the mail-cart was returning the next day to Lisbon, I immediately sat down and replied to the worthy Father's letter, speaking as encouragingly as I could of my own prospects. I dwelt much upon what was nearest my heart, and begged of the good priest to watch over my uncle's health, to cheer his spirits and support his courage; and that I trusted the day was not far distant when I should be once more among them, with many a story of fray and battle-field to enliven their firesides. Pressing him to write frequently to me, I closed my hurried letter; and having despatched it, sat sorrowfully down to muse over my fortunes.

CHAPTER LXIV.
AN ADVENTURE WITH SIR ARTHUR.

The events of the last few days had impressed me with a weight of years. The awful circumstances of that evening lay heavily at my heart; and though guiltless of Trevyllian's blood, the reproach that conscience ever carries when one has been involved in a death-scene never left my thoughts.

For some time previously I had been depressed and dis-spirited, and the awful shock I had sustained broke my nerve and unmanned me greatly.

There are times when our sorrows tinge all the colorings of our thoughts, and one pervading hue of melancholy spreads like a pall upon what we have of fairest and brightest on earth. So was it now: I had lost hope and ambition; a sad feeling that my career was destined to misfortune and mishap gained hourly upon me; and all the bright aspirations of a soldier's glory, all my enthusiasm for the pomp and circumstance of glorious war, fell coldly upon my heart, and I looked upon the chivalry of a soldier's life as the empty pageant of a dream.

In this sad frame of mind, I avoided all intercourse with my brother officers; their gay and joyous spirits only jarred upon my brooding thoughts, and feigning illness, I kept almost entirely to my quarters.

The inactivity of our present life weighed also heavily upon me. The stirring events of a campaign—the march, the bivouac, the picket—call forth a certain physical exertion that never fails to react upon the torpid mind.

Forgetting all around me, I thought of home; I thought of those whose hearts I felt were now turning towards me, and considered within myself how I could have exchanged the home, the days of peaceful happiness there, for the life of misery and disappointment I now endured.

A brooding melancholy gained daily more and more upon me. A wish, to return to Ireland, a vague and indistinct feeling that my career was not destined for aught of great and good crept upon me, and I longed to sink into oblivion, forgotten and forgot.

I record this painful feeling here, while it is still a painful memory, as one of the dark shadows that cross the bright sky of our happiest days.

Happy, indeed, are they, as we look back to them and remember the times we have pronounced ourselves "the most miserable of mankind." This, somehow, is a confession we never make later on in life, when real troubles and true afflictions assail us. Whether we call in more philosophy to our aid, or that our senses become less acute and discerning, I'm sure I know not.

As for me, I confess by far the greater portion of my sorrows seemed to come in that budding period of existence when life is ever fairest and most captivating. Not, perhaps, that the fact was really so, but the spoiled and humored child, whose caprices were a law, felt heavily the threatening difficulties of his first voyage; while as he continued to sail over the ocean of life, he braved the storm and the squall, and felt only gratitude for the favoring breeze that wafted him upon his course.

What an admirable remedy for misanthropy is the being placed in a subordinate condition in life! Had I, at the period that I write, been Sir Arthur Wellesley; had I even been Marshal Beresford,—to all certainty I'd have played the very devil with his Majesty's forces; I'd have brought my rascals to where they'd have been well-peppered, that's certain.

But as, luckily for the sake of humanity in general and the well-being of the service in particular, I was merely Lieutenant O'Malley, 14th Light Dragoons, the case was very different. With what heavy censure did I condemn the commander of the forces in my own mind for his want of daring and enterprise! Whole nights did I pass in endeavoring to account for his inactivity and lethargy. Why he did not *seriatim* fall upon Soult, Ney, and Victor, annihilate the French forces, and sack Madrid, I looked upon as little less than a riddle; and yet there he waited, drilling, exercising, and foraging, as if he were at Hounslow. Now most fortunately here again I was not Sir Arthur.

Something in this frame of mind, I was taking one evening a solitary ride some miles from the camp. Without noticing the circumstance, I had entered a little mountain tract, when, the ground being broken and uneven, I dismounted and proceeded a-foot, with the bridle within my arm. I had not gone far when the clatter of a horse's hoofs came rapidly towards me, and though there was something startling in the pace over such a piece of road, I never lifted my eyes as the horseman came up, but continued my slow progress onwards, my head sunk upon my bosom.

"Hallo, sir!" cried a sharp voice, whose tones seemed, somehow, not heard for the first time. I looked up, saw a slight figure closely buttoned up in a blue horseman's cloak, the collar of which almost entirely hid his features; he wore a plain, cocked hat without a feather, and was mounted upon a sharp, wiry-looking hack.

"Hallo, sir! What regiment do you belong to?"

As I had nothing of the soldier about me, save a blue foraging cap, to denote my corps, the tone of the demand was little calculated to elicit a very polished reply; but preferring, as most impertinent, to make no answer, I passed on without speaking.

"Did you hear, sir?" cried the same voice, in a still louder key. "What's your regiment?"

I now turned round, resolved to question the other in turn; when, to my inexpressible shame and confusion, he had lowered the collar of his cloak, and I saw the features of Sir Arthur Wellesley.

"Fourteenth Light Dragoons, sir," said I, blushing as I spoke.

"Have you not read the general order, sir? Why have you left the camp?"

Now, I had not read a general order nor even heard one for above a fortnight. So I stammered out some bungling answer.

"To your quarters, sir, and report yourself under arrest. What's your name?"

"Lieutenant O'Malley, sir."

"Well, sir, your passion for rambling shall be indulged. You shall be sent to the rear with despatches; and as the army is in advance, probably the lesson may be serviceable." So saying, he pressed spurs to his horse, and was out of sight in a moment.

CHAPTER LXV.

TALAVERA.

Having been despatched to the rear with orders for General Crawfurd, I did not reach Talavera till the morning of the 28th. Two days' hard fighting had left the contending armies still face to face, and without any decided advantage on either side.

When I arrived upon the battle-field, the combat of the morning was over. It was then ten o'clock, and the troops were at breakfast, if the few ounces of wheat sparingly dealt out among them could be dignified by that name. All was, however, life and animation on every side; the merry laugh, the passing jest, the careless look, bespoke the free and daring character of the soldiery, as they sat in groups upon the grass; and except when a fatigue party passed by, bearing some wounded comrade to the rear, no touch of seriousness rested upon their hardy features. The morning was indeed a glorious one; a sky of unclouded blue stretched above a landscape unsurpassed in loveliness. Far to the right rolled on in placid stream the broad Tagus, bathing in its eddies the very walls of Talavera, the ground from which, to our position, gently undulated across a plain of most fertile richness and terminated on our extreme left in a bold height, protected in front by a ravine, and flanked by a deep and rugged valley.

The Spaniards occupied the right of the line, connecting with our troops at a rising ground, upon which a strong redoubt had been hastily thrown up. The fourth division and the Guards were stationed here, next to whom came Cameron's brigade and the Germans, Mackenzie and Hill holding the extreme left of all, which might be called the key of our position. In the valley beneath the latter were picketed three cavalry regiments, among which I was not long in detecting my gallant friends of the Twenty-third.

As I rode rapidly past, saluting some old familiar face at each moment, I could not help feeling struck at the evidence of the desperate battle that so lately had raged there. The whole surface of the hill was one mass of dead and dying, the bearskin of the French grenadier lying side by side with the tartan of the Highlander. Deep furrows in the soil showed the track of the furious cannonade, and the terrible evidences of a bayonet charge were written in the mangled corpses around.

The fight had been maintained without any intermission from daybreak till near nine o'clock that morning, and the slaughter on both sides was dreadful. The mounds of fresh earth on every side told of the soldier's sepulchre; and the unceasing tramp of the pioneers struck sadly upon the ear, as the groans of the wounded blended with the funeral sounds around them.

In front were drawn up the dark legions of France,—massive columns of infantry, with dense bodies of artillery alternating along the line. They, too, occupied a gently rising ground, the valley between the two armies being crossed half way by a little rivulet; and here, during the sultry heat of the morning, the troops on both sides met and mingled to quench their thirst ere the trumpet again called them to the slaughter.

In a small ravine near the centre of our line were drawn up Cotton's brigade, of whom the Fusiliers formed a part. Directly in front of this were Campbell's brigade, to the left of which, upon a gentle slope, the staff were now assembled. Thither, accordingly, I bent my steps, and as I came up the little scarp, found myself among the generals of division, hastily summoned by Sir Arthur to deliberate upon a forward movement. The council lasted scarcely a quarter of an hour, and when I presented myself to deliver my report, all the dispositions for the battle had been decided upon, and the commander of the forces, seated upon the grass at his breakfast, looked by far the most unconcerned and uninterested man I had seen that morning.

He turned his head rapidly as I came up, and before the aide-de-camp could announce me, called out:—

"Well, sir, what news of the reinforcements?"

"They cannot reach Talavera before to-morrow, sir."

"Then, before that, we shall not want them. That will do, sir."

So saying, he resumed his breakfast, and I retired, more than ever struck with the surprising coolness of the man upon whom no disappointment seemed to have the slightest influence.

I had scarcely rejoined my regiment, and was giving an account to my brother officers of my journey, when an aide-de-camp came galloping at full speed down the line, and communicating with the several commanding officers as he passed.

What might be the nature of the orders we could not guess at; for no word to fall in followed, and yet it was evident something of importance was at hand. Upon the hill where the staff were assembled no unusual bustle appeared; and we could see the bay cob of Sir Arthur still being led up and down by the groom, with a dragoon's mantle thrown over him. The soldiers, overcome by the heat and fatigue of the morning, lay stretched around upon the grass, and everything bespoke a period of rest and refreshment.

"We are going to advance, depend upon it!" said a young officer beside me; "the repulse of this morning has been a smart lesson to the French, and Sir Arthur won't leave them without impressing it upon them."

"Hark, what's that?" cried Baker; "listen!"

As he spoke, a strain of most delicious music came wafted across the plain. It was from the band of a French regiment, and mellowed by the distance, it seemed in the calm stillness of the morning air like something less of earth than heaven. As we listened, the notes swelled upwards yet fuller; and one by one the different bands seemed to join, till at last the whole air seemed full of the rich flood of melody.

We could now perceive the stragglers were rapidly falling back, while high above all other sounds the clanging notes of the trumpet were heard along the line. The hoarse drum now beat to arms; and soon after a brilliant staff rode slowly from between two dense bodies of infantry, and advancing some distance into the plain, seemed to reconnoitre us. A cloud of Polish cavalry, distinguished by their long lances and floating banners, loitered in their rear.

We had not time for further observation, when the drums on our side beat to arms, and the hoarse cry, "Fall in,—fall in there, lads!" resounded along the line.

It was now one o'clock, and before half an hour the troops had resumed the position of the morning, and stood silent and anxious spectators of the scene before them.

Upon the table-land to the rear of the French position, we could descry the gorgeous tent of King Joseph, around which a large and splendidly-accoutred staff were seen standing. Here, too, the bustle and excitement seemed considerable, for to this point the dark masses of the infantry seemed converging from the extreme right; and here we could perceive the royal guards and the reserve now forming in column of attack.

From the crest of the hill down to the very valley, the dark, dense ranks extended, the flanks protected by a powerful artillery and deep masses of heavy cavalry. It was evident that the attack was not to commence on our side, and the greatest and most intense anxiety pervaded us as to what part of our line was first to be assailed.

Meanwhile Sir Arthur Wellesley, who from the height had been patiently observing the field of battle, despatched an aide-de-camp at full gallop towards Campbell's brigade, posted directly in advance of us. As he passed swiftly along, he called out, "You're in for it, Fourteenth; you'll have to open the ball to-day."

Scarcely were the words spoken, when a signal gun from the French boomed heavily through the still air. The last echo was growing fainter, and the heavy smoke breaking into mist, when the most deafening thunder ever my ears heard came pealing around us; eighty pieces of artillery had opened upon us, sending a very tempest of balls upon our line, while midst the smoke and dust we could see the light troops advancing at a run, followed by the broad and massive columns in all the terror and majesty of war.

"What a splendid attack! How gallantly they come on!" cried an old veteran officer beside me, forgetting all rivalry in his noble admiration of our enemy.

The intervening space was soon passed, and the tirailleurs falling back as the columns came on, the towering masses bore down upon Campbell's division with a loud cry of defiance. Silently and steadily the English infantry awaited the attack, and returning the fire with one withering volley, were ordered to charge. Scarcely were the bayonets lowered, when the head of the advancing column broke and fled, while Mackenzie's brigade, overlapping the flank, pushed boldly forward, and a scene of frightful carnage followed; for a moment a hand-to-hand combat was sustained, but the unbroken files and impregnable bayonets of the English conquered, and the French fled, leaving six guns behind them.

The gallant enemy were troops of tried and proved courage, and scarcely had they retreated when they again formed; but just as they prepared to come forward, a tremendous shower of grape opened upon them from our batteries, while a cloud of Spanish horse assailed them in flank and nearly cut them in pieces.

While this was passing on the right, a tremendous attack menaced the hill upon which our left was posted. Two powerful columns of French infantry, supported by some regiments of light cavalry, came steadily forward to the attack; Anson's brigade were ordered to charge.

Away they went at top speed, but had not gone above a hundred yards when they were suddenly arrested by a deep chasm; here the German hussars pulled short up, but the Twenty-third dashing impetuously forward; a scene of terrific carnage ensued, men and horses rolling indiscriminately together under a withering fire from the French squares. Even here, however, British valor quailed not, for Major Francis Ponsonby, forming all who came up, rode boldly upon a brigade of French chasseurs in the rear. Victor, who from the first had watched the movement, at once despatched a lancer regiment against them, and then these brave fellows were absolutely cut to atoms, the few who escaped having passed through the French columns and reached Bassecour's Spanish division on the far right.

During this time the hill was again assailed, and even more desperately than before; while Victor himself led on the fourth corps to an attack upon our right and centre.

The Guards waited without flinching the impetuous rush of the advancing columns, and when at length within a short distance, dashed forward with the bayonet, driving everything before them. The French fell back upon their sustaining masses, and rallying in an instant, again came forward, supported by a tremendous fire from their batteries. The Guards drew back, and the German Legion, suddenly thrown into confusion, began to retire in disorder. This was the most critical moment of the day, for although successful upon the extreme right and left of our line, our centre was absolutely broken. Just at this moment Gordon rode up to our brigade; his face was pale, and his look flurried and excited.

"The Forty-eighth are coming; here they are,—support them, Fourteenth."

These few words were all he spoke; and the next moment the measured tread of a column was heard behind us. On they came like one man, their compact and dense formation looking like some massive wall; wheeling by companies, they suffered the Guards and Germans to retire behind them, and then, reforming into line, they rushed forward with the bayonet. Our artillery opened with a deafening thunder behind them, and then we were ordered to charge.

We came on at a trot; the Guards, who have now recovered their formation, cheered us as we proceeded. The smoke of the cannonade obscured everything until we had advanced some distance, but just as we emerged beyond the line of the gallant Forty-eighth, the splendid panorama of the battle-field broke suddenly upon us.

"Charge, forward!" cried the hoarse voice of our colonel; and we were upon them. The French infantry, already broken by the withering musketry of our people, gave way before us, and unable to form a square, retired fighting but in confusion, and with tremendous loss, to their position. One glorious cheer, from left to right of our line, proclaimed the victory, while a deafening discharge of artillery from the French replied to this defiance, and the battle was over. Had the Spanish army been capable of a forward movement, our successes at this moment would have been, much more considerable; but they did not dare to change their position, and the repulse of our enemy was destined to be all our glory. The French, however, suffered much more severely than we did; and retiring during the night, fell back behind the Alberche, leaving us the victory and the battle-field.

CHAPTER LXVI.

NIGHT AFTER TALAVERA.

The night which followed the battle was a sad one. Through the darkness, and under a fast-falling rain, the hours were spent in searching for our wounded comrades amidst the heap of slain upon the field; and tho glimmering of the lanterns, as they flickered far and near across the wide plain, bespoke the track of the fatigue parties in their mournful round; while the groans of the wounded rose amidst the silence with an accent of heart-rending anguish; so true was it, as our great commander said, "There is nothing more sad than a victory, except a defeat."

Around our bivouac fires, the feeling of sorrowful depression was also evident. We had gained a great victory, it was true: we had beaten the far-famed legions of France upon a ground of their own choosing, led by the most celebrated of their marshals and under the eyes of the Emperor's own brother; but still we felt all the hazardous daring of our position, and had no confidence whatever in the courage or discipline of our allies; and we saw that in the very *mêlée* of the battle the efforts of the enemy were directed almost exclusively against our line, so confidently did they undervalue the efforts of the Spanish troops. Morning broke at length, and scarcely was the heavy mist clearing away before the red sunlight, when the sounds of fife and drum were heard from a distant part of the field. The notes swelled or sank as the breeze rose or fell, and many a conjecture was hazarded as to their meaning, for no object was well visible for more than a few hundred yards off; gradually, however, they grew nearer and nearer, and at length, as the air cleared, and the hazy vapor evaporated, the bright scarlet uniform of a British regiment was seen advancing at a quick-step.

As they came nearer, the well-known march of the gallant 43d was recognized by some of our people, and immediately the rumor fled like lightning: "It is Crawfurd's brigade!" and so it was; the noble fellow had marched his division the unparalleled distance of sixty English miles in twenty-seven hours. Over a burning sandy soil, exposed to a raging sun, without rations, almost without water, these gallant troops pressed on in the unwearied hope of sharing the glory of the battle-field. One tremendous cheer welcomed the head of the column as they marched past, and continued till the last file had deployed before us.

As these splendid regiments moved by we could not help feeling what signal service they might have rendered us but a few hours before. Their soldier-like bearing, their high and effective state of discipline, their well-known reputation, were in every mouth; and I scarcely think that any corps who stood the brunt of the mighty battle were the subject of more encomium than the brave fellows who had just joined us.

The mournful duties of the night were soon forgotten in the gay and buoyant sounds on every side. Congratulations, shaking of hands, kind inquiries, went round; and as we looked to the hilly ground where so lately were drawn up in battle array the dark columns of our enemy, and where not one sentinel now remained, the proud feeling of our victory came home to our hearts with the ever-thrilling thought, "What will they say at home?"

I was standing amidst a group of my brother officers, when I received an order from the colonel to ride down to Talavera for the return of our wounded, as the arrival of the commander-in-chief was momentarily looked for. I threw myself upon my horse, and setting out at a brisk pace, soon reached the gates.

On entering the town, I was obliged to dismount and proceed on foot. The streets were completely filled with people, treading their way among wagons, forage carts, and sick-litters. Here was a booth filled with all imaginable wares for sale; there was a temporary gin-shop established beneath a broken baggage-wagon; here might be seen a merry party throwing dice for a turkey or a kid; there, a wounded man, with bloodless cheek and tottering step, inquiring the road to the hospital. The accents of agony mingled with the drunken chorus, and the sharp crack of the provost-marshal's whip was heard above the boisterous revelling of the debauchee. All was confusion, bustle, and excitement. The staff officer, with his flowing plume and glittering epaulettes, wended his way on foot, amidst the din and bustle, unnoticed and uncared for; while the little drummer amused an admiring audience of simple country-folk by some wondrous tale of the great victory.

My passage through this dense mass was necessarily a slow one. No one made way for another; discipline for the time was at an end, and with it all respect for rank or position. It was what nothing of mere vicissitude in the fortune of war can equal,—the wild orgies of an army the day after a battle.

On turning the corner of a narrow street, my attention was attracted by a crowd which, gathered round a small fountain, seemed, as well as I could perceive, to witness some proceeding with a more than ordinary interest. Exclamations in Portuguese, expressive of surprise and admiration, were mingled with English oaths and Irish ejaculations, while high above all rose other sounds,—the cries of some one in pain and suffering; forcing my way through the dense group, I at length reached the interior of the crowd when, to my astonishment, I perceived a short, fat, punchy-looking man, stripped of his coat and waist-coat, and with his shirt-sleeves rolled up to his shoulder, busily employed in operating upon a wounded soldier. Amputation knives, tourniquets, bandages, and all other imaginable instruments for giving or alleviating torture were strewed about him, and from the arrangement and preparation, it was clear that he had pitched upon this spot as an hospital for his patients. While he continued to perform his functions with a singular speed and dexterity, he never for a moment ceased 'a running fire of small talk, now addressed to the patient in particular, now to the crowd at large, sometimes a soliloquy to himself, and not unfrequently, abstractedly, upon things in general. These little specimens of oratory, delivered in such a place at such a time, and, not least of all, in the richest imaginable Cork accent, were sufficient to arrest my steps, and I stopped for some time to observe him.

The patient, who was a large, powerfully-built fellow, had been wounded in both legs by the explosion of a shell, but yet not so severely as to require amputation.

"Does that plaze you, then?" said the doctor, as he applied some powerful caustic to a wounded vessel; "there's no satisfying the like of you. Quite warm and comfortable ye'll be this morning after that. I saw the same shell coming, and I called out to Maurice Blake, 'By your leave, Maurice, let that fellow pass, he's in a hurry!' and faith, I said to myself, 'there's more where you came from,—you're not an only child, and I never liked the family.' What are ye grinning for, ye brown thieves?" This was addressed to the Portuguese. "There, now, keep the limb quiet and easy. Upon my conscience, if that shell fell into ould Lundy Foot's shop this morning, there'd be plenty of sneezing in Sacksville Street. Who's next?" said he, looking round with an expression that seemed to threaten that if no wounded man was ready he was quite prepared to carve out a patient for himself. Not exactly relishing the invitation in the searching that accompanied it, I backed my way through the crowd, and continued my path towards the hospital.

Here the scene which presented itself was shocking beyond belief,—frightful and ghastly wounds from shells and cannon-shot were seen on all sides, every imaginable species of suffering that man is capable of was presented to view; while amidst the dead and dying, operations the most painful were proceeding with a haste and bustle that plainly showed how many more waited their turn for similar offices. The stairs were blocked up with fresh arrivals of wounded men, and even upon the corridors and landing-places the sick were strewn on all sides.

I hurried to that part of the building where my own people were, and soon learned that our loss was confined to about fourteen wounded; five of them were officers. But fortunately, we lost not a man of our gallant fellows, and Talavera brought us no mourning for a comrade to damp the exultation we felt in our victory.

CHAPTER LXVII.

THE OUTPOST.

During the three days which succeeded the battle, all things remained as they were before. The enemy had gradually withdrawn all his forces, and our most advanced pickets never came in sight of a French detachment. Still, although we had gained a great victory, our situation was anything but flattering. The most strenuous exertions of the commissariat were barely sufficient to provision the troops; and we had even already but too much experience of how little trust or reliance could be reposed in the most lavish promises of our allies. It was true, our spirits failed us not; but it was rather from an implicit and never-failing confidence in the resources of our great leader, than that any among us could see his way through the dense cloud of difficulty and danger that seemed to envelop us on every side.

To add to the pressing emergency of our position, we learned on the evening of the 31st that Soult was advancing from the north, and at the head of fourteen thousand chosen troops in full march upon Placentia; thus threatening our rear, at the very moment too, when any further advance was evidently impossible.

On the morning of the 1st of August, I was ordered, with a small party, to push forward in the direction of the Alberche, upon the left bank of which it was reported that the French were again concentrating their forces, and if possible, to obtain information of their future movements. Meanwhile the army was about to fall back upon Oropesa, there to await Soult's advance, and if necessary, to give him battle; Cuesta engaging with his Spaniards to secure Talavera, with its stores and hospitals, against any present movement from Victor.

After a hearty breakfast, and a kind "Good-by!" from my brother officers, I set out. My road along the Tagus, for several miles of the way, was a narrow path scarped from the rocky ledge of the river, shaded by rich olive plantations that throw a friendly shade over us during the noonday heat.

We travelled along silently, sparing our cattle from time to time, but endeavoring ere nightfall to reach Torrijos, in which village we had heard several French soldiers were in hospital. Our information leading us to believe them very inadequately guarded, we hoped to make some prisoners, from whom the information we sought could in all likelihood be obtained. More than once during the day our road was crossed by parties similar to our own, sent forward to reconnoitre; and towards evening a party of the 23d Light Dragoons, returning towards Talavera, informed us that the French had retired from Torrijos, which was now occupied by an English detachment under my old friend O'Shaughnessy.

I need not say with what pleasure I heard this piece of news, and eagerly pressed forward, preferring the warm shelter and hospitable board the major was certain of possessing, to the cold blast and dripping grass of a bivouac. Night, however, fell fast; darkness, without an intervening twilight, set in, and we lost our way. A bleak table-land with here and there a stunted, leafless tree was all that we could discern by the pale light of a new moon. An apparently interminable heath uncrossed by path or foot-track was before us, and our jaded cattle seemed to feel the dreary uncertainty of the prospect as sensitively as ourselves,—stumbling and over-reaching at every step.

Cursing my ill-luck for such a misadventure, and once more picturing to my mind the bright blazing hearth and smoking supper I had hoped to partake of, I called a halt, and prepared to pass the night. My decision was hastened by finding myself suddenly in a little grove of pine-trees whose shelter was not to be despised; besides that, our bivouac fires were now sure of being supplied.

It was fortunate the night was fine, though dark. In a calm, still atmosphere, when not a leaf moved nor a branch stirred, we picketed our tired horses, and shaking out their forage, heaped up in the midst a blazing fire of the fir-tree. Our humble supper was produced, and even with the still lingering revery of the major and his happier destiny, I began to feel comfortable.

My troopers, who probably had not been flattering their imaginations with such *gourmand* reflections and views, sat happily around their cheerful blaze, chatting over the great battle they had so lately witnessed, and mingling their stories of some comrade's prowess with sorrows for the dead and proud hopes for the future. In the midst, upon his knees beside the flame, was Mike, disputing, detailing, guessing, and occasionally inventing,—all his arguments only tending to one view of the late victory: "That it was the Lord's mercy the most of the 48th was Irish, or we wouldn't be sitting there now!"

Despite Mr. Free's conversational gifts, however, his audience one by one dropped off in sleep, leaving him sole monarch of the watch-fire, and—what he thought more of—a small brass kettle nearly full of brandy-and-water. This latter, I perceived, he produced when all was tranquil, and seemed, as he cast a furtive glance around, to assure himself that he was the only company present.

Lying some yards off, I watched him for about an hour, as he sat rubbing his hands before the blaze, or lifting the little vessel to his lips; his droll features ever and anon seeming acted upon by some passing dream of former devilment, as he smiled and muttered some sentences in an under-voice. Sleep at length overpowered me; but my last waking thoughts were haunted with a singular ditty by which Mike accompanied himself as he kept burnishing the buttons of my jacket before the fire, now and then interrupting the melody by a recourse to the copper.

"Well, well; you're clean enough now, and sure it's little good brightening you up, when you'll be as bad to-morrow. Like his father's son, devil a lie in it! Nothing would serve him but his best blue jacket to fight in, as if the French was particular what they killed us in. Pleasant trade, upon my conscience! Well, never mind. That's beautiful *sperets*, anyhow. Your health, Mickey Free; it's yourself that stands to me.

"It's little for glory I care; Sure ambition is only a fable; I'd as soon be myself as Lord Mayor, With lashings of drink on the table. I like to lie down in the sun   And drame, when my faytures is scorchin' That when I'm too ould for more fun, Why, I'll marry a wife with a fortune. "And in winter, with bacon and eggs, And a place, at the turf-fire basking, Sip my punch as I roasted my legs, Oh, the devil a more I'd be asking! For I haven't a janius for work,— It was never the gift of the Bradies,— But I'd make a most illigant Turk, For I'm fond of tobacco and ladies."

This confounded *refrain* kept ringing through my dream, and "tobacco and ladies" mingled with my thoughts of storm and battle-field long after their very gifted author had composed himself to slumber.

Sleep, and sound sleep, came at length, and many hours elapsed ere I awoke. When I did so, my fire was reduced to its last embers. Mike, like the others, had sunk in slumber, and midst the gray dawn that precedes the morning, I could just perceive the dark shadows of my troopers as they lay in groups around.

The fatigues of the previous day had so completely overcome me, that it was with difficulty I could arouse myself so far as to heap fresh logs upon the fire. This I did with my eyes half closed, and in that listless, dreamy state which seems the twilight of sleep.

I managed so much, however, and was returning to my couch beneath a tree, when suddenly an object presented itself to my eyes that absolutely rooted me to the spot. At about twenty or thirty yards distant, where but the moment before the long line of horizon terminated the view, there now stood a huge figure of some ten or twelve feet in height,—two heads, which surmounted this colossal personage, moved alternately from side to side, while several arms waved loosely to and fro in the most strange and uncouth manner. My first impression was that a dream had conjured up this distorted image; but when I had assured myself by repeated pinchings and shakings that I was really awake, still it remained there. I was never much given to believe in ghosts; but even had I been so, this strange apparition must have puzzled me as much as ever, for it could not have been the representative of anything I ever heard of before.

A vague suspicion that some French trickery was concerned, induced me to challenge it in French; so, without advancing a step, I halloed out, "*Qui va là?*"

My voice aroused a sleeping soldier, who, springing up beside me, had his carbine at the cock; while, equally thunderstruck with myself, he gazed at the monster.

"*Qui va là?*" shouted I again, and no answer was returned, when suddenly the huge object wheeled rapidly around, and without waiting for any further parley, made for the thicket.

The tramp of a horse's feet now assured me as to the nature of at least part of the spectacle, when click went the trigger behind me, and the trooper's ball rushed whistling through the brushwood. In a moment the whole party were up and stirring.

"This way, lads!" cried I, as drawing my sabre, I dashed into the pine wood.

For a few moments all was dark as midnight; but as we proceeded farther, we came out upon a little open space which commanded the plain beneath for a great extent.

"There it goes!" said one of the men, pointing to a narrow, beaten path, in which the tall figure moved at a slow and stately pace, while still the same wild gestures of heads and limbs continued.

"Don't fire, men! don't fire!" I cried, "but follow me," as I set forward as hard as I could.

As we neared it, the frantic gesticulations grew more and more remarkable, while some stray words, which we half caught, sounded like English in our ears. We were now within pistol-shot distance, when suddenly the horse—for that much at least we were assured of—stumbled and fell forward, precipitating the remainder of the object headlong into the road.

In a second we were upon the spot, when the first sounds which greeted me were the following, uttered in an accent by no means new to me:—

"Oh, blessed Virgin! Wasn't it yourself that threw me in the mud, or my nose was done for? Shaugh, Shaugh, my boy, since we are taken, tip them the blarney, and say we're generals of division!"

I need not say with what a burst of laughter I received this very original declaration.

"I ought to know that laugh," cried a voice I at once knew to be my friend O'Shaughnessy's. "Are you Charles O'Malley, by any chance in life?"

"The same, Major, and delighted to meet you; though, faith, we were near giving you a rather warm reception. What, in the Devil's name, did you represent, just now?"

"Ask Maurice, there, bad luck to him. I wish the Devil had him when he persuaded me into it."

"Introduce me to your friend," replied the other, rubbing his shins as he spoke. "Mr. O'Mealey,"—so he called me,—"I think. Happy to meet you; my mother was a Ryan of Killdooley, married to a first cousin of your father's before she took Mr. Quill, my respected progenitor. I'm Dr. Quill of the 48th, more commonly called Maurice Quill. Tear and ages! how sore my back is! It was all the fault of the baste, Mr. O'Mealey. We set out in search of you this morning, to bring you back with us to Torrijos, but we fell in with a very pleasant funeral at Barcaventer, and joined them. They invited us, I may say, to spend the day; and a very jovial day it was. I was the chief mourner, and carried a very big candle through the village, in consideration of as fine a meat-pie, and as much lush as my grief permitted me to indulge in afterwards. But, my dear sir, when it was all finished, we found ourselves nine miles from our quarters; and as neither of us were in a very befitting condition for pedestrian exercise, we stole one of the leaders out of the hearse,—velvet, plumes, and all,—and set off home.

"When we came upon your party we were not over clear whether you were English, Portuguese, or French, and that was the reason I called out to you, 'God save all here!' in Irish. Your polite answer was a shot, which struck the old horse in the knee, and although we wheeled about in double-quick, we never could get him out of his professional habits on the road. He had a strong notion he was engaged in another funeral,—as he was very likely to be,—and the devil a bit faster than a dead march could we get him to, with all our thrashing. Orderly time for men in a hurry, with a whole platoon blazing away behind them! But long life to the cavalry, they never hit anything!"

While he continued to run on in this manner, we reached our watch-fire, when what was my surprise to discover, in my newly-made acquaintance, the worthy doctor I had seen a day or two before operating at the fountain at Talavera.

"Well, Mr. O'Mealey," said he, as he seated himself before the blaze, "What is the state of the larder? Anything savory,—anything drink-inspiring to be had?"

"I fear, Doctor, my fare is of the very humblest; still—"

"What are the fluids, Charley?" cried the major; "the cruel performance I have been enacting on that cursed beast has left me in a fever."

"This was a pigeon-pie, formerly," said Dr. Quill, investigating the ruined walls of a pasty; "and,—but come, here's a duck; and if my nose deceive me not, a very tolerable ham. Peter—Larry—Patsy—What's the name of your familiar there?"

"Mickey—Mickey Tree."

"Mickey Free, then; come here, avick! Devise a little drink, my son,—none of the weakest—no lemon—-hot! You understand, hot! That chap has an eye for punch; there's no mistaking an Irish fellow, Nature has endowed them richly,—fine features and a beautiful absorbent system! That's the gift! Just look at him, blowing up the fire,—isn't he a picture? Well, O'Mealey, I was fretting that we hadn't you up at Torrijos; we were enjoying life very respectably,—we established a little system of small tithes upon fowl, sheep, pigs' heads, and wine skins that throve remarkably for the time. Here's the lush! Put it down there, Mickey, in the middle; that's right. Your health, Shaugh. O'Mealey, here's a troop to you; and in the mean time I'll give you a chant:—

'Come, ye jovial souls, don't over the bowl be sleeping, Nor let the grog go round like a cripple creeping; If your care comes, up, in the liquor sink it, Pass along the lush, I'm the boy can drink it. Isn't that so, Mrs. Mary Callaghan? Isn't that so, Mrs. Mary Callaghan?'

"Shaugh, my hearty, this begins to feel comfortable."

"Your man, O'Mealey, has a most judicious notion of punch for a small party; and though one has prejudices about a table, chairs, and that sort of thing, take my word for it, it's better than fighting the French, any day."

"Well, Charley, it certainly did look quite awkward enough the other day towards three o'clock, when the Legion fell back before that French column, and broke the Guards behind them."

"Yes, you're quite right; but I think every one felt that the confusion was but momentary,—the gallant Forty-eighth was up in an instant."

"Faith, I can answer for their alacrity!" said the doctor "I was making my way to the rear with all convenient despatch, when an aide-de-camp called out,—

"'Cavalry coming! Take care, Forty-eighth!'

"'Left face, wheel! Fall in there, fall in there!' I heard on every side, and soon found myself standing in a square, with Sir Arthur himself and Hill and the rest of them all around me.

"'Steady, men! Steady, now!' said Hill, as he rode around the ranks, while we saw an awful column of cuirassiers forming on the rising ground to our left.

"'Here they come!' said Sir Arthur, as the French came powdering along, making the very earth tremble beneath them.

"My first thought was, 'The devils are mad, and they'll ride down into us, before they know they're kilt!' And sure enough, smash into our first rank they pitched, sabring and cutting all before them; when at last the word 'Fire!' was given, and the whole head of the column broke like a shell, and rolled horse over man on the earth.

"'Very well done! very well, indeed!' said Sir Arthur, turning as coolly round to me as if he was asking for more gravy.

"'Mighty well done!' said I, in reply; and resolving not to be outdone in coolness, I pulled out my snuff-box and offered him a pinch, saying, 'The real thing, Sir Arthur; our own countryman,—blackguard.'

"He gave a little grim kind of a smile, took a pinch, and then called out,—

"'Let Sherbroke advance!' while turning again towards me, he said, 'Where are your people, Colonel?'

"'Colonel!' thought I; 'is it possible he's going to promote me?' But before I could answer, he was talking to another. Meanwhile Hill came up, and looking at me steadily, burst out with,—

"'Why the devil are you here, sir? Why ain't you at the rear?'

"'Upon my conscience,' said I, 'that's the very thing I'm puzzling myself about this minute! But if you think it's pride in me, you're greatly mistaken, for I'd rather the greatest scoundrel in Dublin was kicking me down Sackville Street, than be here now!'

"You'd think it was fun I was making, if you heard how they all laughed, Hill and Cameron and the others louder than any.

"'Who is he?' said Sir Arthur, quickly.

"'Dr. Quill, surgeon of the Thirty-third, where I exchanged, to be near my brother, sir, in the Thirty-fourth.'

"'A doctor,—a surgeon! That fellow a surgeon! Damn him, I took him for Colonel Grosvenor! I say, Gordon, these medical officers must be docked of their fine feathers, there's no knowing them from the staff,—look to that in the next general order.'

"And sure enough they left us bare and naked the next morning; and if the French sharpshooters pick us down now, devil mend them for wasting powder, for if they look in the orderly books, they'll find their mistake."

"Ah, Maurice, Maurice!" said Shaugh, with a sigh, "you'll never improve,—you'll never improve!"

"Why the devil would I?" said he. "Ain't I at the top of my profession—full surgeon— with nothing to expect, nothing to hope for? Oh, if I had only remained in the light company, what wouldn't I be now?"

"Then you were not always a doctor?" said I.

"Upon my conscience, I wasn't," said he. "When Shaugh knew me first, I was the Adonis of the Roscommon militia, with more heiresses in my list than any man in the regiment; but Shaugh and myself were always unlucky."

"Poor Mrs. Rogers!" said the major, pathetically, drinking off his glass and heaving a profound sigh.

"Ah, the darling!" said the doctor. "If it wasn't for a jug of punch that lay on the hall table, our fortune in life would be very different."

"True for you, Maurice!" quoth O'Shaughnessy.

"I should like much to hear that story," said I, pushing the jug briskly round.

"He'll tell it you," said O'Shaughnessy, lighting his cigar, and leaning pensively back against a tree,—"he'll tell it you."

"I will, with pleasure," said Maurice. "Let Mr. Free, meantime, amuse himself with the punch-bowl, and I'll relate it."

END OF VOLUME I.